KNIGHT OF THE BLAZING SUN

THE BEAST WAS large enough to attack a mounted man without difficulty and as Goetz's horse shied away, the brute roared out a challenge in its own barbarous tongue.

'Come on then!' Goetz shouted back. He kneed his mount and the warhorse reared, lashing out. The orc howled as a knife-edged hoof plucked one of its bat-like ears from its head. It drove one massive shoulder into the horse's belly, toppling it onto its side. Goetz rolled from the saddle as his horse fell, losing hold of his shield. He retained his sword however and managed to block a blow that would have taken his head from his shoulders.

The orc loomed over him, its teeth bared in a grin. The edge of the axe inched downwards towards Goetz's face.

More Warhammer from the Black Library

A WARHAMMER NOVEL

KNIGHT OF THE BLAZING SUN

Josh Reynolds

BLACK LIBRARY

For Sylvie.

A BLACK LIBRARY PUBLICATION

First published in Great Britain in 2012 by
Black Library,
Games Workshop Ltd.,
Willow Road, Nottingham,
NG7 2WS, UK.

10 9 8 7 6 5 4 3 2 1

Cover illustration by Clint Langley.

A CIP record for this book is available from the British Library.

UK ISBN: 978 1 84970 140 2
US ISBN: 978 1 84970 141 9

See the Black Library on the internet at
www.blacklibrary.com

Find out more about Games Workshop
and the world of Warhammer at
www.games-workshop.com

Printed and bound in the UK by CPI Group (UK) Ltd, Croydon, CR0 4YY

This is a dark age, a bloody age, an age of daemons
and of sorcery. It is an age of battle and death, and of the
world's ending. Amidst all of the fire, flame and fury
it is a time, too, of mighty heroes, of bold deeds
and great courage.

At the heart of the Old World sprawls the Empire, the
largest and most powerful of the human realms. Known for
its engineers, sorcerers, traders and soldiers, it is
a land of great mountains, mighty rivers, dark forests
and vast cities. And from his throne in Altdorf reigns
the Emperor Karl Franz, sacred descendant of the
founder of these lands, Sigmar, and wielder
of his magical warhammer.

But these are far from civilised times. Across the
length and breadth of the Old World, from the knightly
palaces of Bretonnia to ice-bound Kislev in the far north,
come rumblings of war. In the towering Worlds Edge
Mountains, the orc tribes are gathering for another assault.
Bandits and renegades harry the wild southern lands of
the Border Princes. There are rumours of rat-things, the
skaven, emerging from the sewers and swamps across the
land. And from the northern wildernesses there is the
ever-present threat of Chaos, of daemons and beastmen
corrupted by the foul powers of the Dark Gods.
As the time of battle draws ever nearer,
the Empire needs heroes
like never before.

1

THE ORCS CAME down out of the Worlds Edge Mountains into Ostermark like a green tide, sweeping villages and towns before them in a cascade of flame and pillage. But the men of the Mark stood firm and met the orcs with pike, shot and sword. Soldiers in purple and yellow livery crashed against barbaric green-skinned savages, matching Imperial steel and age-old strategy against inhuman muscle and brute cunning. Men and orcs screamed and died as the frozen ground turned to mud and the sun swung high in the sky.

Elsewhere, horses pawed the frost-covered earth in nervous anticipation. Their breath escaped in bursts of steam which drifted haphazardly through the close-set scrub trees that surrounded them and their riders. Hector Goetz reached down and stroked his mount's muscular neck. The warhorse whinnied eagerly. 'Easy Kaspar,' he said. 'Easy. Miles to go yet.' Goetz was a tall man, and he wore the gilded armour of a knight of the

Order of the Blazing Sun easily, if not entirely comfortably. He glanced down the row of similarly armoured riders that spread out to either side of him and wished he felt more confident in his chances of surviving the coming engagement.

'Just give him a thump, boy,' someone said. Goetz twisted in his saddle, meeting the cheerful gaze of his hochmeister. Tancred Berlich was a big, bluff man with a grey-streaked beard and a wide grin. Red cheeks and a splotchy nose completed the image of a man more concerned with food and drink than fighting and death. He had commanded the Kappelburg Komturie for as long as Goetz could remember. 'Horses are like soldiers… a thump or three is good for morale.'

Goetz chuckled as Berlich gave a booming laugh. His smile faded as Berlich's opposite number from the Bechafen Komturie glared at them through the open visor of his ornate helmet.

'I know that proper military discipline is difficult for you, Tancred, but I would like to remind you that *this is an ambush*!' the man hissed through gritted teeth. Of an age with his fellow Hochmeister, Alfonse Wiscard looked older. His face was a hatchet made of wrinkles and his eyes were like chips of ice. Those cool orbs swivelled to Goetz a moment later. 'Control your hochmeister, brother, or the orcs will be on us far sooner than we anticipate,' he said.

'Leave the boy alone, Wiscard,' Berlich said before Goetz could reply. 'He's got more experience than all of the puppies you brought along combined. Don't you boy?'

'I… have seen my share,' Goetz said, looking straight ahead. 'More than most perhaps.'

'The Talabeclander insults us!' one of Wiscard's men said.

'Quiet,' Wiscard snapped. His face was twisted into as sour an expression as Goetz had ever seen. He felt impressed despite himself. 'Quiet, all of you. We are here to fight orcs, not rehash old grudges.' The provinces of Talabecland and Ostermark had been at each other's throats for decades, for one reason or another. While the only loyalties the members of the Order were supposed to hold were to Myrmidia, the Order itself and the Emperor, in that order, occasionally the old traditional disagreements crept in.

'Besides, the boy's not *really* a Talabeclander; he's from Solland!' Berlich said, pounding Goetz on the shoulder.

'Solland hasn't existed for a long time. Longer than my lifetime,' Goetz protested.

'Modesty. I think he's the heir,' Berlich whispered loudly to Wiscard. 'Old Helborg owes the boy a sword, or my name isn't Tanty!'

'Sudenland is gone, hochmeister. As is its elector,' Goetz said patiently. 'Sudenland' was how his mother had insisted on referring to the dead province, now long since absorbed by Wissenland. It was a peculiarity of the old families, and one Goetz had never been able to shake. 'And your name is Tancred. I have never heard anyone refer to you as "Tanty".'

'See? See? Only royalty talks down its nose like that! Boy'll be Emperor if he survives,' Berlich laughed.

Goetz craned his neck as a young pistolier rode up. Both horse and rider were clearly exhausted. The pistolier had sweat dripping down his youthful features, cutting tracks in the grime that otherwise covered his face. 'Milords,' he wheezed. 'The Lord Elector Hertwig requests that you see to the flank!'

'Ha! Finally!' Berlich growled, slamming a fist into his thigh.

Goetz watched the young man lead his horse away, both of them covered in sweat and reeking of a hard ride and exhaustion. It hadn't been so long ago that he himself had ridden among the ranks of the pistolkorps. They had taught him the art of riding and of the usefulness of black powder. Thinking of that last one, he wondered what he wouldn't give for a brace of pistols now. Even just one would mean one less orc to face up close. Unfortunately, while Myrmidia was a goddess of battlefield innovation, her followers were forced to follow the law of the land. Gunpowder was far too rare and unstable to be given to a force prone to reckless headlong charges into the maw of the enemy army.

Goetz sighed. He'd earned his spurs as a pistolier, against orcs then as well. Of course, the raiders he and his compatriots had put to flight then had been as nothing compared to the horde that now crawled across his field of vision, from horizon to horizon. He was suddenly quite thankful for the heavy plate he wore, with all of its dwarf-forged strength between him and the crude axes of the green-skinned savages he was even now readying himself to face. He'd seen what an orc could do to an unarmoured man – and an armoured one, come to that – and the more layers between him and that gruesome fate was well worth the inevitable sweat and chafing. Not to mention the smell.

Still, a pistol would have been nice.

'Don't look so glum, boy,' Berlich said, jostling him out of his reverie. 'Cheer up! We'll be charging any minute now!' The hochmeister grinned eagerly, and bounced slightly in his saddle like an excited urchin. 'Blood and thunder, we'll turn them into so much paste!'

Goetz turned back around, peering through the protective embrace of the thicket where they were waiting. While most of the orc army was already engaged in the swirling melee beyond, some canny boss had managed to restrain his impetuous followers. That was impressive, and slightly frightening. Orcs usually had all the restraint of a rabid hound. When one proved capable of thinking beyond putting its axe through the nearest skull, it meant trouble for anyone unlucky enough to be caught in its path. Right at that moment, the unlucky ones looked to be the eastern flank of elector Hertwig's battered force, as a stomping, snorting, squealing flood of orcish Boar Riders hurtled towards the purple-and-gold lines. Goetz tightened his grip on his reins and took hold of his lance, jerking it up from where he'd stabbed it into the ground.

'Thunder and lightning, that's how it'll be!' Berlich said, lifting his own lance. Goetz took a deep breath and set his shield. He caught Wiscard's eye, and the hochmeister nodded briskly.

'We go where we are needed,' Wiscard said, intoning the first part of the Order's creed.

'We do what must be done,' Goetz replied along with all the rest.

'And Myrmidia have mercy on those green buggers because I'll have none!' Berlich roared, standing up in his saddle. 'Let's have at them! Hyah!' Then, with a slow rumble that built to a thunderous crescendo, the Order of the Blazing Sun rode to war. They brushed aside the thicket with the force of their passage and the Order's specially-bred warhorses bugled bloodthirsty cries as they launched forwards.

Seconds later, wood met flesh with a thunderous roar, and the ground trembled at the point of impact. Lances cracked and splintered as they tore through the orc lines, shoving bodies back atop bodies and creating eddies in the green tide. Goetz's teeth rattled inside his helmet as his lance was reduced to a jagged stump of brightly painted wood. He tossed it aside and drew his sword, wheeling his horse around even as the broken weapon struck the ground. Goetz lashed out as a green shape crashed against him in the press of combat.

The orc's mouth gaped wide, its foul breath spilling out from between a gate of yellowed tusks as the sword passed between its bulbous head and its sloped shoulders. The head, still mouthing now-silent curses, tumbled forward, striking Goetz's shield and springing away into the depths of the melee.

The body, its neck-stump spurting blood, was carried in the opposite direction by the snorting, kicking boar its legs were still clamped around. Goetz hauled on his horse's reins, forcing the trained destrier to sidestep the grunting beast. The horse bucked and kicked at the fleeing pig and then swung around at Goetz's signal, lunging towards the next opponent with a savage whinny.

Goetz's sword chopped down left and right until his arm began to ache from the strain. The orcs kept coming, treading on the bodies of their dead or dying fellows in their excitement as they fought to get to grips with the men who had crashed into their flank.

It had been a bold move, and a necessary one, but

Goetz wasn't so sure that it had been a *smart* one. Fifty men, even fifty fully-armoured knights of the Order of the Blazing Sun, could not stand against the full weight of an orc horde, no matter how righteous their cause or how strong their sword-arms. Now, with their task accomplished, they found themselves surrounded by an army of angry berserkers as the rest of the elector's forces attempted to reach them. It was not a position that Goetz enjoyed being in.

A crude spear crashed against his thigh and skittered off his armour, leaving a trail of sparks in its wake. Goetz swung his horse around and iron-shod hooves snapped out, pulping a malformed green skull with deadly efficiency. He brought his shield up instinctively as a swift movement caught his eye. Arrows sprouted from the already battered face of the shield and Goetz chopped his sword down, slicing through the hafts as he whispered a quiet prayer to Myrmidia.

'Hear me, Lady of Battle; keep me from harm and kill my enemy, if you please,' he said as he took a moment to catch his breath. He looked around. The battle had devolved into a chaotic melee, with ranks and order forgotten in the heat of battle. A volley of handguns barked nearby; men screamed and died, their cries barely audible above the cacophony of the orcish battle-cries. He caught sight of Hertwig's standard, waving above the battle.

'Ware!' someone yelled. Another knight, his armour flecked with gore, gestured wildly and Goetz twisted in his saddle, catching a gnaw-toothed axe on the edge of his sword. His arm went numb from the force of the blow and he was forced to bring his shield around to catch a second blow.

The shield crumpled inward as the axe crashed against it. The orc who wielded it was as large a monster as Goetz had ever seen. It had a dull, dark hue to its thick hide and heavy armour decorating its muscular limbs. The beast was large enough to attack a mounted man without difficulty and as Goetz's horse shied away, the brute roared out a challenge in its own barbarous tongue.

'Come on then!' Goetz shouted back. He kneed his mount and the warhorse reared, lashing out. The orc howled as a knife-edged hoof plucked one of its bat-like ears from its head. It drove one massive shoulder into the horse's belly, toppling it onto its side. Goetz rolled from the saddle as his horse fell, losing hold of his shield. He retained his sword however and managed to block a blow that would have taken his head from his shoulders.

The orc loomed over him, its teeth bared in a grin. The edge of the axe inched downwards towards Goetz's face, despite the interposed sword blade. Muscles screaming, he drove a fist into the orc's jaw, surprising it as well as numbing his hand in the process. It had been like punching a sack of granite.

The beast stepped aside, more from shock than pain, but the hesitation was enough. Goetz swung around, chopping his sword into the orc's side. It roared and backhanded him, denting his helm and sending it flying. He fell onto his back, skull ringing.

Bellowing in agony, the orc jerked at the sword, trying to pull it free. It gave up after a moment and, bloody froth decorating its jaws, swung its axe up for a killing blow despite the presence of Goetz's sword still buried hilt-deep in its side. Before the blow could land a lance point burst through the orc's throat. It dropped its axe and grabbed at the jagged mass of wood, bending double and nearly yanking its wielder from his saddle.

'Are you just going to sit there all day, brother, or are you going to help me?' the knight cried out as Goetz looked up at him. Goetz's reply was to throw himself towards the hilt of his sword. The orc arched its back, gagging as it tried to remove the obstruction in its throat. Even now, nearly chopped in two and with a lance through the neck it was still fighting... and still more than capable of killing.

Goetz caught the hilt with his palms and shoulder and thrust forward with all of his weight. The orc's roar turned shrill as the sword resumed its path through the beast's midsection. Goetz stumbled as dark blood sprayed him. The orc fell in two directions, fists and heels thumping the ground spasmodically.

Rising, Goetz caught his horse's bridle. 'Easy, Kaspar, easy,' he murmured, knuckling the horse at the base of its jaw as it nuzzled him. He hauled himself awkwardly up into the saddle. Muscles aching, he turned to his rescuer.

'My thanks, brother,' he said, jerking on his mount's reins and turning it. The other man raised his visor and snorted. Goetz recognised the fine-boned features as those of the man who had taken offence at Berlich's comments earlier. Velk, he thought the man was called.

'Save your thanks, Talabeclander,' Velk said. 'If I'd known it was one of you lot, I might have let the brute finish you off.'

Goetz spat out a mouthful of dust and shook his head. 'I see the hospitality of the Mark is as generous as ever.'

Velk glared at him and opened his mouth to reply when a sharp voice interrupted. 'Brothers! Cease this nonsense. There are still orcs to kill.' Goetz turned and saw Wiscard, riding towards them, a blood-stained warhammer dangling loosely from his hand. Three other knights trailed after him, including Berlich, who looked as cheerful as ever despite the blood matting his beard.

As Wiscard drew close, he motioned with the hammer and said, 'Look!' Goetz followed the gesture and saw a crude standard rising above a cloud of dust. The tattered remnants of a number of banners, some from regiments native to the Empire, others from Bretonnia and one or two from places that Goetz didn't recognise, hung from the crossbeam of the standard, flapping amidst an assortment of skulls and gewgaws. As they watched, the elector's standard, gleaming gold and purple, hurtled towards the other.

'Must be their warlord,' Berlich said, setting his horse into motion with a swift kick. 'Having fun, Brother Goetz?' he said, grinning at the younger knight.

'More than is decent, hochmeister,' Goetz said. The knights began to trot forward as a solid wedge, resting their horses for a moment. Even the strongest animal could only do so much carrying the weight of a fully armoured knight.

Berlich laughed and slapped Goetz a ringing blow on the shoulder. He looked at Wiscard. 'Didn't I tell you the boy had spirit?'

'As a matter of fact, no,' Wiscard said. 'Then, I rarely pay attention to your blathering, Tancred.'

'Blathering?' Berlich said with a guffaw. 'Do I blather, Brother Goetz?'

'Incessantly, Hochmeister Berlich,' Goetz said, recognising the game. Berlich liked to pretend he was nothing more than a common soldier, despite having more titles than fingers. The Kappelburg Komturie was a place of little truck with authority or discipline.

Berlich clutched his chest. 'Cut to the quick! And by a fellow knight… the ignominy of it all.'

'From what I know of Talabeclanders, you should have expected as much,' Velk interjected. 'Traitorous pack of killers, the lot of you.'

Berlich ignored him. 'What say we introduce ourselves to yon beastie, Wiscard you old stick?' he said, gesturing with his sword to the warlord's standard.

'My thoughts exactly,' Wiscard said. He slapped his visor down and the other knights did the same. 'Velk, Goetz, form up on me.'

As one, they charged. They crashed into the orcs from behind, bowling several over. Goetz leaned over his horse's neck, chopping down on those orcs not quick enough to get out of the way. Surprised, several of the creatures ran, and those that didn't fell soon enough.

One of the creatures, however, spun and chopped down on Velk's horse with a vicious looking doublebladed axe. The horse fell squealing and rolled over its rider, leaving him in the dust. Goetz yanked hard on the reins and sent his own horse leaping between the downed knight and his would-be slayer. 'Haro Talabecland!' he roared, shouting the battle-cry of his home province. 'Up, Talabheim!'

The orc yowled as Goetz's sword took its hands off at the wrists. His second blow cracked its skull. Velk was on his feet by then, his face tight with pain. One arm hung at an awkward angle, and he grudgingly nodded at Goetz. A moment later, his eyes widened as a massive shape loomed up out of the dust.

A stone-headed maul crashed against the armoured head of Goetz's horse, killing the animal instantly and throwing Goetz to the ground for a second time. He skidded across the rocky ground, narrowly avoiding being trampled by the other combatants. His eyes widened as he looked up at what had to be the leader of the orc horde.

The creature was far larger than the dark-skinned brute from earlier, and its skin gleamed like polished obsidian. A horned, crimson-crested helmet rode on its square head and made it look even taller as it spread its ape-like arms and bellowed. The motion and the sound caused the oddments of plate and mail that it wore to clatter loudly. With a start, Goetz realised that the beast had its standard strapped to its back, as well as a basket full of smaller, vicious looking creatures, all clad in black cloaks and hoods and armed with crude bows. Goblins, he realised, as he rolled out of the way of a spatter of arrows.

'Myrmidia's oath,' Velk said, stumbling back. 'It's huge!'

'That just means it's easier to hit!' Berlich roared, swooping past them towards the warlord. Whooping, the hochmeister swung his sword overhand, shearing off one of the horns on the orc's helmet. The monster howled in outrage and spun much more quickly than Goetz thought possible for a creature that size.

Berlich grunted as the stone maul rose up and rang down on his shield, shattering both it and the arm it had been strapped to. Goetz watched in horror as Berlich's horse sank to its knees from the force of the impact and a second blow swept the knight from his saddle and sent him sailing. Berlich landed with a sickening thump several dozen yards away and did not move.

'No!' Goetz surged to his feet and brought his sword down on the side of the orc warlord's head, cutting a divot out of its helmet and its face. The maul swung out at him and he leapt back, ignoring the weight of his armour and the growing ache in his limbs.

'The Mark! The Mark!' Velk shouted, sounding his own province's battle-cry and stumbling towards the creature from the other side. His sword struck sparks off the orc's mail, but did little else. An almost casual jab of a titanic elbow sent him tumbling.

The orc made to finish Velk off and Goetz hacked through the haft of its weapon, more through luck than intention. He swung again, slicing links from the brute's rusty suit of mail. The creature's spade-sized hands crashed against his shoulders and he was hoisted into the air. As it opened its mouth, he realised that in absence of its weapon it intended to bite his head off.

'Myrmidia make me lucky rather than stupid,' he hissed as he kicked out, driving a foot into its teeth. The blow shattered several tusks. Squirming, Goetz freed his sword-arm and stabbed clumsily at the orc's face. Most of the blows landed on its helmet, but one found a yellow eye, popping it like a blister. Yellow pus erupted from the creature's socket and it shrieked and dropped Goetz.

'Ha!' Gripping his sword with both hands, he rammed it into the creature's belly and cut upwards. The orc's shriek grew louder as Goetz dug the blade in, trying to pierce its heart. Great fists crashed down on him, snapping off a pauldron and cracking his shoulder.

Goetz ignored the pain and forced the blade in deeper, until, at last, the brute's cries faded and it went limp. He staggered back as it fell, its remaining eye glazed over and its jaws wide. One hand clawed momentarily at the earth but then splayed flat.

Somewhere a cheer went up. Goetz turned, exhausted, and raised his sword over his head. A moment later a sharp pain flared through him and he grunted. He stumbled forward, reaching towards his back.

A thin shaft had sprouted from a gap in his armour. A second shaft, and then a third and a fourth thudded home. A burning sensation erupted from the points of impact and slithered through him. He wobbled around, body going numb. His sword slid from nerveless fingers and he sank to his knees. He saw the goblins clamber out of the crumpled basket on the warlord's back. He clawed awkwardly for his sword.

Evil green faces glared at him in malicious glee as several dark shapes darted forward, crude blades drawn. As the goblins closed in, chuckling and slinking, Goetz collapsed, his world melting into fire.

ATHALHOLD LOOKED AT the man in bemused silence. The common room of the coaching house had fallen silent, and every eye was on the disparate duo at the bar. Athalhold wore light mail and jerkin bearing the emblem of the Order of the Blazing Sun, and was far larger than the man who'd accosted him. One hand rested on the pommel of his sword and he smiled slightly.

'Repeat that, if you please,' he said. He had only arrived in the free-city of Marienburg a few hours earlier, and while he knew of the city's reputation, he hadn't expected to be confronted with the evidence of it quite so quickly.

'I said, we don't want your kind here,' the man said, smoothing his moustaches with the side of one hand. He bared his teeth at the knight. He was slender and dark-skinned, with a dancer's grace to his movements. In contrast to the knight, he was clad in fine silks and tights; in other words, every inch the stereotypical Marienburg fop.

'My kind?'

'Knights. Arrogant, jumped-up, foreign bully boys.' The man turned to the common room and swept his hands out. 'We don't need their kind here, do we? Marienburg is a free-city, isn't it?'

'The Order of the Blazing Sun goes where it is needed,' Athalhold said, paraphrasing part of the Order's creed. 'Even to free-cities.'

The glove struck him lightly across the face. It was such an unexpected gesture that Athalhold could only blink in surprise. 'You are challenged,' the fop said. 'Outside is the traditional venue. If you accept the challenge, that is.'

'Have I offended you in some way?' Athalhold said.

'No. Do you accept the challenge or not?'

Athalhold looked around, then back at the man before him. 'Why do you want to fight me?'

'I don't, particularly.'

Athalhold grunted. He had been a member of the Order for close to two decades, and a member of the Middenheim aristocracy since birth, and had been witness to and participated in many challenges. Granted, most had taken place on the field of battle, but every so often some young puppy fresh from the upper reaches of the nobility decided to test their spurs. This man, however, was neither a soldier nor an aristocrat. Athalhold took in the scars on the man's long fingers and those that decorated his cheeks. And despite his fancy clothing, the hilt of the rapier on his hip was well worn and shiny from use.

A professional then, Athalhold decided. Likely looking to improve his reputation by duelling a knight of the Empire. In other words, a waste of time. He decided to fall back on his usual response to such things. 'Go away, little man. There's no sport for you here today.' Athalhold turned away.

The hiss of a sword leaving its sheath alerted him a moment before the tip of the blade would have pinked his hand where it sat on the bar. Athalhold jerked his hand away and turned. The blade slid lightly across his cheek. Instinctively he slapped a palm to his cheek. His fingers came away wet.

The rapier tip waggled in front of his eyes like the head of a cobra, then dipped backwards over the fop's shoulder. 'Just because you refuse doesn't mean I don't get to kill you,' he said with a sneer.

Athalhold rubbed a thumb across his cheek and looked at it. Then his eyes flickered up to the duellist. 'Do you know who I am? Who I represent?'

'Of course. I challenged you didn't I?' the duellist said. 'Now, are you going to fight, or are you going to just stand there while I slice bits off you?'

Athalhold frowned. A second later, his sword sprang from its sheath and cut the air just beneath the duellist's nose. The latter danced backwards, upending a table in his haste to get clear. His rapier twirled forward, curling around the knight's blade and scratching against his jerkin. The two men broke apart and began to circle one another.

The knight was impressed despite himself. The duellist was fast and skilled, for a hired blade. More so than many professional soldiers. But Athalhold had been tested on fields of combat more dangerous than any Marienburg back-alley. He lunged suddenly, trapping his opponent's rapier with the flat of his blade and grabbing for the man's wrist. If he could disarm him–

A wooden club connected with his shoulder, momentarily numbing the attached arm. Athalhold turned and sliced through the club as it came down a second time. The burly thug who held it jerked back in surprise. Athalhold's eyes narrowed as he saw several more men advancing from out of the crowd. They carried daggers and clubs.

He looked at the duellist. 'Is this your idea of a duel?' he said.

The duellist shrugged. 'Marienburg rules,' he said, and then lunged. Athalhold swatted the blow aside and backed towards the door. While he was confident of his ability to handle the newcomers, he needed room to do it.

He backed out into the courtyard, blade extended. The men followed. Four of them, in all. The duellist leaned against the door frame, watching calmly. 'Be gentle lads. We wouldn't want people to start questioning our hospitality,' he said.

A club snapped out towards Athalhold's chest and he removed the wielder's fingers before turning and

smashing his blade down on a second tough's col-
larbone. The other two men hesitated, and Athalhold
dispatched the closest with a quick sweep, taking his
leg off at the knee. The last man made a desperate leap
but only succeeded in spitting himself on the knight's
blade.

Using his boot heel to shove the twitching body
off his sword, Athalhold turned to confront the duellist, fully expecting to find the man gone. Instead, the
rapier point dug for Athalhold's face, then whipped
across his forehead, releasing a curtain of red into the
knight's face.

Momentarily blinded, Athalhold reacted on instinct,
swinging wildly. The duellist was forced to jerk back
out of reach. Athalhold scraped the blood from his face
and rammed an elbow into the other man's chin. His
opponent staggered and the knight swatted him on the
side of the head with the flat of his sword, knocking
him to the ground.

The knight stomped down on the duellist's wrist
a moment later, trapping his sword-hand. Then he
placed the tip of his own weapon against the hollow
of the downed man's throat and said, 'Now, tell me
what this was about.'

'I should have thought it was obvious,' the duellist
grunted, his eyes on Athalhold's sword. 'Someone has
a bone to pick with you.'

'Who?'

'How should I know? Who have you annoyed?'

'You don't even know who you're working for?'
Athalhold said in amazement.

'I know who paid me,' the man said. 'You'd be surprised at how rarely that's the same thing.'

'Enlighten me.'

'Do I look like a priest?'

Athalhold didn't reply. He grunted and stepped back. 'Get out of here. You failed.'

'Maybe.' The duellist rose smoothly, then, like quicksilver, he was moving, a thin-bladed knife in one hand. It scraped across Athalhold's side as he turned and his sword flashed out, separating the duellist's head from his shoulders. There was a surprised expression on the latter's face as his head bounced away.

Athalhold touched his side, relieved to feel no pain. The knife hadn't done much more than slice through his jerkin. He straightened and his ears caught a faint hiss of air. He turned and his face moved through a variety of expressions before settling on puzzlement. The expression deepened as he reached up hesitantly to touch the point of the crossbow bolt that had suddenly sprouted from his throat. Athalhold blinked and gurgled, swaying. Then he sank to his knees and slumped forward, head bowed, his blood pooling in the spaces between the stones of the courtyard.

The crossbowman hidden on the roof of the coaching house nodded in satisfaction. He had hoped that the bravos would have accomplished things without his intervention, but the thing was done regardless, more the pity.

He pulled his cloak tighter about himself and glanced at the scraggly looking crow perched nearby. It cocked its head and one beady black eye fixed on him. 'It's done,' he murmured, stroking the puckered brand that covered the inside of his wrist. 'He's dead.' Then, 'Was it really necessary?'

The crow croaked and he flinched. A moment later

it flapped scabrous wings and took to the air, leaving him alone with his regrets.

IN THE DARKNESS, daemons shrieked. The old man ignored them with a courage born of experience. His spirit flew on wings of ice, high above the rocks and raging waters of the Sea of Claws. The air was thick with the ghosts of others who had made this trip and failed to return, sailor and shaman alike. The old man ignored them as well.

Ulfar Asgrimdalr had faced both ghosts and dae-mons in his time as his tribe's *gudja* and neither held any fear for him these days, though both had left scars on both his body and his soul. He had left the warmth of his body, his hall and his hearth this night for one reason only and that reason was directly below him.

It was an old duty, one held by his predecessor and his predecessor's predecessor, for as long as the sea had been wet and the ice, cold. Nevertheless, Ulfar did not regard it as one of the more pleasant responsibilities he was tasked with. It had claimed too many lives for that. Too many souls.

The island bled a sour chill into the spirit-world. It was encircled by a dome of frozen ghosts, all scream-ing silently and eternally bound to the rock by skeins of Dark Magic. The old man passed over the curve of the dome and tried to spy upon what went on within, but all he could see was the same black pressure that always boiled there. A sense of relief flooded him.

The daemon was still bound, still trapped. Hopefully it would remain so for as long as he lived. Let some other gudja deal with it. A younger man. Stronger. At one time, it would have been Ulfar's own blood who would be tasked with the job, but now… no, best not to think of such things. Bad memories brought real pain in the between-lands.

Satisfied, Ulfar banked and turned back towards home. A moment later a scream of agony escaped him as claws of smoke and ash tore through his wings. He tumbled through the air as his attacker harried him. He twisted, trying to return the favour, and a familiar face shoved through the filthy cloud and grinned at him. 'Too slow, Asgrimdalr,' the face hissed at him as smoky tendrils pierced his limbs. 'Too old.'

'You–' Ulfar began. The face changed, becoming an avian nightmare. A beak studded with crooked fangs bit down and Ulfar screamed again. Though neither he nor his attacker were physical, the pain was real enough. Ulfar beat withered fists against the beak, and the face dissolved into smoke. Laughter filled his head and the darkness within the dome of spirits pulsed in time.

It couldn't be! Not here! Not now!

'Hexensnacht comes, old wolf,' the thing hissed. 'The bonds you and your foul kin placed on her weaken! She will be free to devour you all!'

Ulfar tore away from the foul smoke, hurling himself towards the clean air. Suddenly, ethereal fingers tore at his wounds, digging for the raw matter of his spirit. He flung the spectres that tried to swarm over him aside with desperate strength. To a strong man, ghosts were an inconvenience. To a weakened one, they were dangerous. But then, his opponent had known that.

A screaming phantom clutched at him, icy teeth snapping. Ulfar slapped it aside and raced for safety with every ghost in the Sea of Claws hurtling after him.

If they caught him – no! He pushed the thought aside and concentrated on the path ahead. He skidded over the savage waves, his spirit shape transforming from bird to seal as he ducked beneath the water and shot towards the shore.

Instantly, he realised that he'd made a mistake as something foul and dark barrelled after him, teeth like spears crashing together. It was one of the many daemon-things that lived on the border between the Sea of Claws and the Sea of Chaos. Subsisting on the spirits of drowned men, they hunted in both worlds. If he could make it to the shore, the rune markers he had laid would protect him.

He dodged this way and that as the daemon-thing pursued him and as he drew within the protective circle of his magics, the entity gave a terrible howl and whipped away, back into the depths. His seal-shape sprang from the water even as it unravelled into diaphanous strands and sought his physical frame.

His eyes sprang open a moment later and he gasped, lurching upright out of his furs. Instinctively he clutched at himself, feeling for wounds that weren't there. Blunt fingers skidded over the protective sigils carved into his flesh and the tattoos etched where the sigils left off. He was a skinny man, all leather and sinew, with skin baked brown by the northern sun. Heart thudding in his sunken chest, he reached for his staff.

'Father?' a woman said as she ducked through the hide curtain in the doorway. She was a tall woman, young and muscular. She wore a battered hauberk under her furs and carried a naked sword in one hand. 'Father?' she said again, warily.

Ulfar coughed and gestured. She grabbed a ladle out

of a nearby bucket of melting ice and extended it cautiously. Ulfar grabbed it and greedily sucked the chill slush into his mouth. Smacking his lips, he looked at her and nodded brusquely. 'It is me, Dalla. You may sheathe your blade.'

Dalla let out a sigh and sat beside him, her sword planted point down into the floor between her feet. 'When you screamed, I thought–'

Ulfar waved a hand, cutting her off. It was a depressingly common occurrence for a shaman to leave his body and for something else to return in his place. 'I am fine, I said. Where is the *godi*?' he snapped, grabbing his staff and using it to pull himself to his feet.

Dalla blinked. 'He's in council–'

'Come then. I must speak with him. Now.'

'Father, you can't simply interrupt him!' Dalla said, grabbing one of his stick-like arms.

'Am I not the gudja? I can interrupt whomsoever I please!' Ulfar snarled, ripping his arm free. 'Especially when I tell him what I have learned.' Slinging a wolf-skin cloak around his hunched shoulders he hobbled out into the night. Dalla followed him.

'What is it? What have you seen?'

'The end of everything, daughter. Nothing less than that,' Ulfar said.

CONRAD BALK, HOCHMEISTER of the Svunum Komturie and knight of the Order of the Blazing Sun, shivered as the chill of the sea wrapped around him. He clutched his axe more tightly and kept his eyes on the horizon. It was not meet to watch the goddess's representative when she was about her business. Nor was it particularly conducive to a restful night's sleep.

The first time he had seen the twitching, spasming ordeal of a trance, he had been horrified. But age and familiarity had brought the reassurance that the priestess could not – would not – harm herself. Still, it always raised his hackles.

Swallowing his nervousness, he draped his fingers over the head of his axe and leaned forward, peering out of the mouth of the cavern. The mist that clung to the surface of the Sea of Claws was as thick as stone, but Balk knew where the southern coast of Norsca was. In his head, a map unfolded and he saw the scars of memory. He saw the place where his predecessor Hochmeister Greisen had died, the place Greisen's own predecessor, Kluger, had fallen; in both cases, the Norscans were to blame.

In his darker moments, Balk supposed that they would be responsible for his own death as well. He took a breath and pushed the thought aside. Death was unavoidable. Better to think about what could be accomplished before that moment, whenever it came.

Better to think about what could yet be built.

A crow swooped into the cavern and hopped onto a rock near Balk. It cocked its head and croaked. Balk nodded and stepped aside. The crow flew past him and a few moments later he heard the priestess stand.

'Well, Lady Myrma?' he said, not turning. He knew what he would see… a young woman, lithe and limber, shrouded in a feathered cloak with her face covered in tribal tattoos. As she moved into the light, the tattoos briefly seemed to writhe into a different pattern, though he knew that was impossible. Lady Myrma, the latest in a long line of priestesses and the third by that name known to the men of his Order.

'Dead,' she said, her youthful timbre touched with an inhuman resonance.

Balk closed his eyes and said a quick prayer. Then he said, 'How?'

'Does it matter?'

'Yes. Did he die well?' Balk said intently.

'As well as can be expected,' the priestess said, pulling the edges of her cloak more tightly about her. She tapped two fingers against her temple. 'He felt nothing.'

Balk sighed and kissed the flat of his axe. 'Good.'

'Do not indulge in guilt, Master Balk. It is a useless thing and self-indulgent.' She looked at him and stroked the crow that sat on her shoulder. 'Besides, it will be forgotten soon enough. The Enemy is at our gate.'

'The–' Balk's eyes widened. 'You felt something? Learned something?'

'Felt, tasted and chased,' Myrma purred, licking her fingers. She frowned. 'Unfortunately, I did not catch him. He is cunning and cruel, that one.'

'A shame,' Balk said. He looked out at the sea and gestured with his axe. 'Well, he will be waiting on us, I suppose. Whoever he is.' He pulled the axe back and let it rest on his shoulder. 'They all will. Goddess pity them…'

'For we will not,' Myrma said, laying a hand on his arm. 'Norsca will be burned clean in the fires of her wrath, Master Balk. It will be your hand that sets those fires alight come the Witching Night.'

Balk hesitated. 'I still dislike that aspect of it. As nights go, that's not an auspicious one…'

'Is it not? A night where the winds of magic roar and where the gods themselves can step onto the skin of the world?' Myrma said. 'What other night could it be?'

Balk grunted and made his way towards the roughly hewn stone steps that led upwards to the komturie. The woman watched him go, her dark eyes considering. Then, as if coming to a decision, she shook her head.

'No. He is not the one, is he?'

She cocked her head, as if listening to the roar of the surf as it thundered against the rock. Beneath her feet, the bedrock of the island trembled slightly. 'No, you are right as ever, Mistress,' she said, stroking the crow. It croaked in pleasure and flapped its wings. Myrma looked at it and smiled.

'But the one is coming, eh?' Her smile split, revealing cruelly filed teeth in a carnivorous grin. 'Yes. He is coming.'

2

Goetz dreamed of fire. Not a cleansing fire, but a sickly one. A witch-fire, that flickered and curled between dark trees. In the fire, something danced and howled and called his name.

He tried to ignore it, to concentrate on something else, but there was nothing. Just the darkness, the fire and the voice. It slithered into his skull and caressed his thoughts the way a miser fondled coins. Pain spiked through him and he screamed himself awake.

Sweat coated his trembling form as the priestess of Shallya dabbed at his face with a wet cloth. 'Rest easy, sir knight,' she said. 'Rest easy. The battle is done.'

'I... what... where...?' Goetz mumbled. He was burning up. His skin felt as if it were inundated with spiders riding the curve of his bones. He hunched up on the cot, his arms wrapped around his middle. 'What happened? What happened to me?'

'You were poisoned,' the priestess said, running the cloth across his brow. 'Rest.'

Goetz slapped her hand away as a flare of pain speared through his back. Bending forwards, he clawed at the bandages on his back, ripping them away in a haze of agony. Twisting, he looked and then immediately wished he hadn't.

The coiling wounds were leaking dark pus and the flesh around them was turning the colour of rotten meat. As he watched, something black moved beneath the pus and dead flesh. Another lash of pain rippled through him and he squirmed on the cot.

'What is it?' he hissed.

'Poison,' the priestess said, her voice rougher than it had been previously. Rougher and more menacing. Goetz looked at her and bit back a scream.

Bird-like talons dug into his cheeks. He was shoved back. A scream of pain escaped him as the priestess – the thing that had been the priestess – ripped him from his cot and thrust him into the air. Feathers the colour of a diseased rainbow graced the impossibly thin wrist that turned him this way and that as the thing examined him.

'Poisoned,' it croaked. 'You were poisoned.'

'N… no,' Goetz said, grabbing at the thing's face. He ripped away handfuls of feathers in a frenzy, revealing not the priestess's face but that of – who?

'You were poisoned,' the woman said, her strong face radiating a terrible peace. Goetz let the greasy feathers drift from his unresponsive hands.

He awoke with a start. Truly awoke this time, by the pain in his limbs and the ache in his middle. He staggered upright and lurched towards a chamberpot.

When he'd finished, he staggered back to the bed, collapsing even as the door opened and a jolly red face peered into the chamber.

'The dream again, yes?' the owner of the face said.

'Pasqual?' Goetz said. 'What are you–'

'The hochmeister wishes to see you, young Goetz,' the other man said softly, in a liquid accent. Pasqual Caliveri was a transplant from one of the Tilean city-states, just which one no one was sure, and like Goetz, he was a knight of the Order. He wore a plain brown robe, the sigil of the Blazing Sun dangling from his neck.

The Knights of the Blazing Sun, unlike the other knightly orders that made the Empire their home, welcomed members from foreign climes. They were an inclusive brotherhood and Pasqual was only one of many. Within this komturie there were accents from Bretonnia, Tilea and Estalia as well as from Kislev and Middenheim. The only commonality was the quality of the blood. The Order of the Blazing Sun, like the other major knightly orders sanctioned within the borders of the Empire, chose their members almost exclusively from the loftier tiers of society.

Goetz's family, while noble in theory, were hardly high on the scale of the aristocracy, having originally come from Solland. He'd never been much further than the Mark himself. His father, Armin Goetz, had donated land and money to the Order to secure his son's place as a novice. It was a decision Goetz was determined he not regret.

'It was the dream, yes?' Pasqual said, reaching out a hand. Goetz batted it away.

'I don't know what you're talking about.' Goetz

swung his legs off the cot. He rubbed his face again, and groaned. The freshly-healed wounds in his back pulled tight beneath the bandages as he stretched, and he winced. 'The hochmeister wants to see me?'

'I said so, yes?'

'Yes.' Goetz stood and rubbed his side. Pasqual looked at his back and clucked in concern. The Tilean was a worse mother-hen than any priestess of Shallya.

'They are still bothering you, yes?'

'No.' Goetz grunted as a soft pain flared up again and made him a liar. He rubbed the bandages and felt the small, twisting marks there. The goblin arrows had been crude, barbed things and cutting had been necessary for their removal. Gently, he probed their edges and felt for something that the doctors assured him wasn't there.

Goetz knew what he felt, however. It was there, eating through him like a particularly slow acid. There had been a fungus smeared on the arrows that had entered his flesh through the joins in his armour. Some cave-brewed poison that had entered his bloodstream in minutes and burned through his mind for days afterwards, leaving him a raving wreck. There were still splinters of those arrows imbedded in him he knew, no matter what they said. How else could the dreams be explained? 'No. I'm fine.'

'Hrmph.' Pasqual frowned, his red face disapproving. 'Ten minutes, young Goetz, yes? In the library.'

'Ten minutes.'

Pasqual swept out of the room, and Goetz rose to splash some water on his face. The reflection in the basin was that of a young man, tall and broad in all the right places with the pale, fair features of the aristocracy.

His hair was shorn close to the scalp beneath his helmet, as was proper for one of his Order, and his wrists and shoulders were thick with muscle.

He genuflected to the altar to Myrmidia in the corner, making the sign of the twin-tailed comet. His eyes slid towards his armour. Next to that sat his sheathed sword. While he had been raised in the Sigmarite tradition, Myrmidia was the patron of the Order of the Blazing Sun, and had been since its founding.

The story itself was an odd one. Half anecdote and half miracle, with the undignified humour that characterised much about the Order itself. They had quite literally been created by accident. During the wars in Araby, when the Sultan's armies had invaded Estalia, a number of knights from both the Empire and Bretonnia had gone south under the Crusader's Hammer. Not many, but enough. In Magritta, a band of knights had found themselves pushed back into the grand temple of the war-goddess Myrmidia, hemmed in by the swords of the Black Scimitar Guard, and near death.

Then, like a literal bolt from the blue, the great statue of Myrmidia had toppled and buried their attackers, killing most of them and putting the rest to flight. At the time, the surviving knights had claimed it as a miracle, and pledged themselves then and there to following the path the goddess in her mercy had cleared for them.

Goetz, being something of a practical sort, doubted the event had occurred in exactly that fashion. Faith was all well and good, but a toppling statue was usually the work of shoddy construction, rather than divine intervention. 'No offence,' he said quickly, making a bow to the altar. The small bust of the goddess seemed to smile up at him and he was reminded of the face in his dream for just a moment.

He blinked and began to dress as quickly as possible. It wouldn't do to keep the hochmeister waiting. He felt better after he buckled his armour on. It was a skin of burnished metal between the world and him, though whether he was wearing it to keep something out or something in, he couldn't say. The feeling had been with him since he could recall… uncomfortable in his own skin, that was how his father had described him. Goetz thought it was less about comfort and more about satisfaction. He was dissatisfied with his lot in life, though he couldn't say why.

The corridor outside his room was empty, but then that was no surprise. There was training to be done, and most of the komturie were likely engaged in helping with the harrying of the remainder of the orc army back up into the mountains. That was the sort of thing that he was just as happy to avoid.

'And what would old Berlich say about that, hmm?' he muttered to himself. Nothing, a traitorous part of his mind whispered, because he's resting in the crypts below this structure even as we speak. Unconsciously, his fists clenched. The old hochmeister had died from the wounds he'd suffered at the hands of the orc warlord, and when the rest of the Kappelburg knights had returned to Talabecland earlier in the week, they'd left his body to lie in state until arrangements could be made. But Goetz had come close to death many times in his short career, and it didn't frighten him.

'But it should mean something, shouldn't it?' he said out loud. He stopped and looked up at the colourful tapestry that occupied the wall of the corridor.

It showed the events of the infamous (at least among members of the Order) Conference of Brass, where the sultan-sorcerer Jaffar made his dark compact with the powers of Chaos. As with all art commissioned or created by members of the Order, the known facts were stuck to with almost religious rigidity. Jaffar, rather than being daemonised, was depicted as the handsome, if rather ordinary, man he had reportedly been. Clad in colourful silks and armour wrought of the black iron favoured by the daemon-worshippers of the wastes, Jaffar stood in the centre of a ruined arena and raised his hands in awe at the sight of the daemonic throng that watched him from the stands.

Whether he had, in fact, summoned daemons to his banner was a matter of some conjecture among Imperial scholars, Goetz knew. Even the historians of the Order of the Blazing Sun weren't entirely positive that Jaffar hadn't been, in the end, simply an excellent strategist and politician.

After all, he had welded together a coalition of desert tribes and minor caliphates without any help, daemonic or otherwise. He'd turned his own small kingdom into a vigorous empire within a few short years. That's when the trouble had started. Heading north, Jaffar's army had crashed into Estalia like a thunderbolt and subsequently provoked the Crusades.

Goetz moved on. The next tapestry showed the issuing of the Edict of Magritta by the Grand Theogonist of the time, Helmut Karr. The Edict had sent a number of nascent templar-orders scurrying off to the south to join their opposite numbers from Tilea, Bretonnia and Sartosa in driving the Arabyans from Estalia. Which they had done in the end, despite suffering one alarming defeat after another on the way.

Goetz stopped in front of the next tapestry and genuflected, as was the tradition. It was a highly stylised depiction of Myrmidia's Blessing – the day the goddess had turned the tide of battle in favour of a few weary knights.

Those same knights had been looked on with suspicion after they returned, bearing with them their new goddess. For most Imperial citizens, whether they were poor or noble, a Southern goddess was no sort of deity. More than one knight had been lashed to a post and sent to Myrmidia's citadel on wings of smoke and flame by overzealous witch hunters and priests.

In 1470, the Order had gone to war with the Church of Ulric, and knights wearing wolf-pelts had clashed with knights clad in burnished metal in the streets of Middenheim. Political pressure had put a stop to the feud in the end, but even today there was no komturie in the City of the White Wolf. Not that Goetz had heard anyone complaining. He'd been to Middenheim once, on one of his father's trips. It hadn't been pleasant.

'A long and storied tradition,' he said quietly, and it was. The only problem was that Goetz did not believe in either stories or traditions. In one blazing moment, he'd had all claim to such illusions stripped from him. They hadn't, as yet, come back. In a way, he hoped they never would. His wounds from the goblin arrows had only reinforced his belief in the essential meaninglessness of the whole business.

He turned. The library doors sat at the end of the corridor. Wiscard was waiting. He went to the doors.

The library was a grand example of its kind.

Rough-hewn shelves of books and parchments from the world over occupied much of the space in the room. Between these shelves were smooth nooks where busts of past Grand Masters and heroes of the Order glared out at Goetz as he passed them.

Wiscard sat at a heavy table in the centre of the room. Like Pasqual, he wore a rough robe over a suit of ceremonial chainmail. He was just finishing a letter when Goetz stopped before his desk.

'You requested my presence, Hochmeister Wiscard?' Goetz said, after several moments of silence. Wiscard looked up after carefully scattering drying-sand on the letter. He blew the sand off and smiled.

'Brother Goetz. Up and walking, I see. Praise Myrmidia.' He folded the letter and tapped it on his desk. 'Do you know what this is, brother?'

'A letter?'

Wiscard looked at him, frowning slightly. 'Yes. Quite. A letter which recounts your actions in battle against the orcs here recently, as well as the wounds you suffered which have kept you here in Bechafen since that time, and away from your duties in Talabheim. Your new hochmeister, by the way, is most eager for you to return to those duties as soon as possible.'

Goetz flinched, wondering who the new hochmeister would be.

'Granted, he will be disappointed in that regard,' another voice said. Goetz turned, surprised. A tall figure, one he hadn't noticed before, turned from the bookshelves and fixed him with keen eyes. Goetz automatically sank to one knee, his head bowed.

'Grand Master,' he said.

* * *

DALLA HAD BEEN born on a battlefield; or, more properly, a scene of slaughter. Her first blurry infant-memories had been of fire and blood. She could still smell the stink of that day deep in her nostrils. It tainted everything she had experienced since, though she felt no grudge. Indeed, she was proud. She had proven her strength from the cradle, and none could deny it.

She moved through her exercises, loosening up her limbs and thoughts. Snow crunched beneath her bare feet as she spun and twisted, bringing the sword up, around and down in an ever-more complex series of movements.

The Pattern of Steel was as much a religious rite as it was an exercise in swordplay. The Great Planner valued intricacy in all things, or so her father said. What Dalla knew from the gods would fill a helmet, and a small one at that. Still, as she thrust and chopped at imaginary foes, she kept to the Pattern, as Ulfar had taught her.

It was good, he said, to honour the gods in all things so that you avoided the risk of dishonouring them in some things. Thus, she indulged in pleasure to honour the Lover, and consecrated the blood she shed to the Blood-Wolf and left a bowl of meat to rot for the Crow-Father. In return, they left her alone. To Dalla's way of thinking, that was the best possible outcome.

She stamped forwards, crunching snow beneath her toes, and let the sword sing out. The edge bit into the wooden pole and she ripped it free and whirled, chopping the top of the pole off. 'Faaah,' she breathed out, crouching, every muscle tensed.

Behind her, something crunched across the snow.

She turned and her blade stopped inches from her father's throat. Ulfar smiled and pushed the sword away with his knuckles. 'You are getting better,' he said, eyeing the pole.

Dalla said nothing. She leaned on the pommel of her sword, sweat rolling down her face and beneath her hauberk. Besides a loincloth it was all she wore, the cold being no more bother to her than it was to her father.

'You do your brother's sword proud,' he said.

'Would that he were carrying it now,' she said, snatching up a handful of snow and rubbing it over her face.

Ulfar frowned. 'That is not what I meant girl. Your mother carried that sword before him. They still sing songs about her, in the high crags. As they'll sing of you.' He took her chin in his palm and smiled. 'A shieldmaiden makes for better sagas than an old gudja any day.'

'Hardly a maiden,' Dalla said with a snort. Ulfar chuckled and shook his head.

'Too much to hope for, I suppose.'

'Too much to ask,' Dalla said, baring her teeth. Like many in the tribe, she had filed them to shark-like points. Ulfar knew too well that she had used them more than once. 'What do the spirit-winds say old man?'

'They say we are drawing close to interesting times. A child of the Great Planner spins webs within webs, and we are all caught in the threads.'

'Child...?' Dalla blinked. 'Svunum?'

'Your mind is as quick as your sword, daughter,' Ulfar said. 'It stirs. On the Witching Night it will awake, unless we stop it.'

'It always stirs, since the *einsark* arrived.'

'This is different. It is stronger. It has eaten souls aplenty in these past years and now it grows hungrier still. For vengeance, among other things.' He smiled crookedly. 'Though they deal in treachery, they cannot abide betrayal.'

'Then they are more like men than most would care to admit,' Dalla said, raising her sword and making a slow thrust. 'The godi is looking for you.'

'Is he?'

'He is quite angry.'

'I cannot imagine why,' Ulfar said.

Dalla looked at him. 'Try harder. You summoned a council of chieftains, old man. *Against* his wishes. You'll be lucky he doesn't feed you to that troll he keeps in the stables.'

'I do not have to be lucky. I am right. And he knows it.'

'He is worse than an old woman,' Dalla said. Ulfar looked at her and she flushed. 'He is!'

'Eyri Goldfinger is many things,' Ulfar said. 'A woman is not one of them.'

'Well, at least your eyes haven't yet succumbed to age. I wish I could say the same about your brain, old man,' a rough voice interjected. Eyri Goldfinger was as broad as Dalla was lithe, and as squat as she was tall. Someone had once joked that Eyri's father had been a dwarf, but only once. If there had been truth to the joke, however, no one would have been surprised. Dark, small and built like an overturned cauldron, he stumped forward, his thumbs hooked into his belt, and faced down the woman he'd once tried to claim as his wife and her father. 'Calling an *alvthing*? Without my say-so? Are you mad?'

Ulfar shrugged. 'Desperate perhaps. But not mad.'

'One and the same I'd say!' Eyri spat. 'Calling a council of chieftains is the prerogative of the chieftains, not some wizened old–'

'Careful,' Dalla said mildly, the blade of her sword drifting towards Eyri's throat. He swatted the blade aside with the two remaining fingers and thumb on his left hand. Dalla had taken the others for what Eyri had, when deep in his cups, often referred to as her dowry.

'I'm *godar*. People should be careful around me. Not vice-versa!' he snapped. 'Now you've roused the Skaelingers and the Bjornlings and the Sarls – a dozen chieftains are on their way here now! Here! Now!' His voice rose an octave as he flushed crimson. 'Do you have any idea what that means?'

'Yes. They will bring men. Men we will need come the Witching Night,' Ulfar said calmly.

'Men I will have to feed! Men I will have to watch lest they filch my steading out from under me!' Eyri snarled, gesticulating. 'You may just as well have stabbed me in the gut old man. Mermedus take you, you old fool.' Eyri slumped, his round shoulders dipping. He shook his head and blew out a frustrated breath. 'Why?' he said, looking at Ulfar.

'I told you why,' Ulfar said. 'You did not listen.'

'Listen? To what? Ghost stories?'

'A warning.' Ulfar's eyes narrowed. 'She stirs.'

'She? She who?'

Ulfar said nothing. Helplessly, Eyri spun to look at Dalla. 'Tell him he's mad!'

'He's not.' It was her turn to shrug. 'You know that as well as I do.'

Eyri groaned and ran calloused hands through his

braided hair. 'Of course I do! But I can't – this steading is small! Small!'

'It's about to get bigger. And noisier,' Dalla said.

Eyri shot a glare at her. 'We'll be needing to bolster the stocks.' He pointed at Dalla. 'That means you too.'

'Me?'

'I need a scout. And the Southerners don't pay as much attention to pretty lasses as they should.' He flashed a grin. 'I want a fat merchantman before the other godar arrive. Mead, ale and the like. Those Southern wines that taste of fruit or oak. You'll mark me a ship.'

Dalla laughed suddenly. 'Why didn't you say? It has been too long since I've gone *avyking*. Where?'

'Marienburg,' Eyri said.

BENEATH THE ISLAND, a ceremony was taking place. It was as old as time itself, or insofar as could be recalled. The attendants wore feathered cloaks and masks of seal-hide. They chanted softly as the initiates saw to the culling of the herd-beasts. Saw-toothed stone knives flashed through worm-pale rubbery hide and the great bulks moaned, floundered and bled out in the tidal pools.

They had been men once, the herd-beasts. Now they were flabby things, more fungus than seal and more seal than man. They made dull groans as their watery blood spilled across the rocks. Passive and dull-witted, they neither fled nor resisted, their tiny minds filled with her grace and their eyes blinded by her ever-shifting radiance. Yet one more gift she had given to Myrma and her people.

Myrma watched the slaughter of the mutants with

only partial interest. She had seen the same ceremony performed so many times before, over so many long years that it had lost the ability to elicit all but the dimmest of emotions in her. Idly she looked down at her body. Nude and youthful, it held no more fascination for her than a set of borrowed clothing. The only thing that concerned her was how long it would last. There were already streaks of grey in her hair and wrinkles beneath her eyes. How long before she must find another skin?

She was not vain; youth held no more joy than age held horror. But if she were to serve her mistress ably and well, she must maintain her vigour. She plucked at the skin, feeling the looseness, and looked up, gauging the nude bodies of the initiates. They were daughters of her line, for the most part, five and six generations removed, their blood freshened with that of slaves and captives. One of them would serve her as her skin in time.

A slab of white meat was brought to her and she bit into the pink muscle. She chewed thoughtfully, letting the blood soothe the torn runnels in her throat. She waved the attendants aside. 'Feed the rest to her children and empty the blood into a pool,' she said, indicating the upper reaches of the cavern ceiling where dim, almost wraith-like leathery shapes humped and quarrelled. She looked up, trying to differentiate between them for a moment, but it was a vain effort. They were not really here in any sense. Only partially, if that. Gripping the world's rim with ghostly talons, held in this place by the will of their mistress and by the regular blood sacrifices Myrma and her folk offered them. Hungry ghosts that howled silently in their mother's womb.

In truth, that was what it was. She looked around, letting the mingled smells of blood and salt invade her nostrils. A rocky womb, in which her people would be reborn. As she herself was reborn again and again, reinvigorated by the sacrifice of her debased kin. Though it was early days yet, she lived by the idiom of 'waste not, want not'. The initiates emptied the bodies of the herd-beasts into a stone trough, letting their brackish blood fill it. Stepping lightly, Myrma stepped into the lukewarm pool and sank down, letting the oily bloody coat her flesh. She hissed in pleasure as she felt abused muscles and cramped tendons heal and grow strong. It kept the borrowed skins she wore flexible and pliant. Cupping her hands, she scooped up the blood and drank it down in messy gulps. It tingled, bitter with the stuff of Chaos which had made the beasts what they were.

The same stuff had kept her young and had made her people strong. It had made them fierce and terrifying to the brute Norsii, upon whom they had preyed like wolves. It would make them strong again, when the time came.

As the blood filled her, so too did the voice of her mistress. The cavern shuddered gently, the rocks enfolding her with gentle strength. The island was no rock, but a protean thing, able to shift and change as needed. At one time, before the arrival of their allies, it had drifted across the sea, carrying them out of danger or into battle.

It had ever been thus. A goddess's favour for those who still followed her.

Then had come, the conclave and the great reaping. Longships, daubed in blood and protective sigils, had made landfall. As the Norsii had met her folk blade-to-blade at the behest of their warlords, the *gudjii* had pitted their magics against hers. Chaos winds had howled across the rocks, bursting men like over-ripe fruit and burning the very stones and in the end, at the behest of jealous kin, her lady had been bound in place. Trapped twice over by ungrateful powers.

Now island and goddess had both set down mighty roots and things grew in the depths. Black seed-pods nestled in the nooks and crannies of the cavern, growing ripe with the fruit of her workings. Myrma's eyes sought the pods and she let her gaze slide across the hairy sacks that would ripen and burst on the Witching Night. They were not meant for her folk. A brief moment of bitterness spiked through her exultation. No, those were for the Lady's newest followers... then, waste not, want not. She smiled crookedly and sank down to her cheeks in the blood.

Hadn't *that* been a surprise when it came? She could still remember the day – the brief moment of terror – as the armoured shapes of the Knights of the Blazing Sun stepped onto the island's rocky shore. They had brought strange engines with them, and their weapons were mightier still than any her people had taken in their long-ago raids. Her people had never recovered from that last great battle with the Northern dogs, and they had been able to muster only a feeble resistance to the newcomers.

She ran bloody fingers through her hair, forcing down the familiar pulse of anger that always came when she thought of that day. Their power had been broken for all time that day. Their remaining temples burned, their herd-beasts driven into the deepest depths and their people enslaved. Oh, not that they knew they were enslaving them, these knights, but she had recognised it for what it was. After all, did not the Great Schemer bind his servants tight in bonds of thought and counter-thought? So what difference then, between one sort of binding and another?

They had sought to change their thoughts, who they were. They had sought to make of her folk something much like the herd-beasts… dull, witless and helpless. She bared her teeth. But that was not to be, no. No, the changers had succumbed to changes themselves, though not the physical kind. They had been perfect. In time, she had realised why her Lady had brought them, had let them burn and pillage… they were strong. Stronger even than the Norsii. With them as the spear-point, her people could finish the Task.

She felt a thrill of excitement. After so long, it was all coming to an end. Her Lady would be free to rejoin the Great Game and take her place once more in the All-Pattern with her brothers and her father, the Changer and Shaper.

For her part, she would see the old wolf spitted and cured like ham. 'Ulfar,' she hissed, almost lovingly. It was a beautiful thought, and one she cherished above all others. She closed her eyes and stretched her newly reinvigorated limbs. 'Oh my Lady. Oh mighty S'Vanashi, daughter of the Great Mutator, Queen of Crows,' she murmured. 'Enfold me in your web that I might better further your design.' And slay my enemy, she thought.

All at once, as if in response, from their perches on the surrounding stalagmites the crows set up a croaking rhythm. In its harsh melody, Myrma could hear the voice of her mistress. Calling for her. Welcoming her.

'I am coming, my Lady. I am coming.' She rose from the blood, eager and dripping, and allowed the initiates to help her up. As they wrapped her in her cloak, she opened her thoughts and breathed in the harsh gases of the cavern, letting the Lady's breath fill her fully. The cavern warped and shattered like a mirror, scattering shards of reality across the expanse of the space between moments. A smell filled her nostrils, like a rookery but somehow harsher. She heard the clatter of iron feathers in the darkness and smiled in welcome as the Queen of Crows enfolded her in her mighty wings.

3

OTTO BERENGAR, THE Grand Master of the Order of the Blazing Sun, was an older man, older than Wiscard, but strongly built. He was tall and broad like Goetz himself, but with the beaky face of a Reiklander. Berengar was said to be a scholarly man, though he'd been in the forefront of every battle the Order had directly participated in.

He was by turns informal and infuriating, and many a member of the Order had been reduced to stammering confusion by the old man's sudden line of questioning at an inappropriate time. While the other knightly orders of the Empire were content to create warriors, the Grand Master of the Blazing Sun wanted something more. As such, he was less than popular among his peers, but a figure of awe to those he led.

'Grand Master,' Goetz said, on one knee.

'Oh do get up,' Berengar said irritably, snapping his fingers. 'Five heartbeats of honour is five heartbeats

53

of thought lost. Up. Up!' Goetz rose as rapidly as his armour would allow. 'Full armour, young Goetz? Am I so frightening?' Berengar went on, motioning for Goetz to rise.

'Sir, I–' Goetz began. The Grand Master waved a hand heavy with thin scars.

'Hector Goetz. Goetz is a Solland name, I believe? Yes. Your family fled that province when the Ironclaw put it to the torch. Minor aristocrats, I believe they were. In any event, your father sells grain now. You had a brother who was promised to the Order, but who instead chose a different path. Your father sent you in his place.'

Goetz nodded dumbly, fighting to restrain the instinctive grimace that mention of his brother always brought to his face. Berengar stroked his beard. 'You are a replacement knight, Brother Goetz. But a very effective one, I am told. Thus, you will be playing replacement again.'

'Milord?'

'Never mind. Describe the flag of the Reikland, boy.'

'The–?' Goetz cleared his throat. 'An eagle rampant, Grand Master.'

'Correct. But not just any eagle… it is specifically Myrmidia's eagle. Did you know this?' Berengar said, twitching a finger like a schoolmaster.

'No, Grand Master.'

'What was the symbol of the Sudenland?' Berengar continued rapidly.

'A… ah… a blazing sun, Grand Master.' Goetz frowned. 'Also a sign of Myrmidia.'

Berengar smiled. 'Well done, boy. We'll make a scholar of you yet.' The smile grew thin. 'Some say the crown of Solland was taken by the Ironclaw and twisted to fit his barbaric brow. Others say that that crown was merely the electoral circlet, and that the true crown was hidden away. It was said to be shaped like a sun as well, and that it was divided into twelve parts and those parts were given to twelve retainers... the Myrmidons.'

'I wasn't aware that there was a crown of Sudenla–Solland,' Goetz said.

'No. Why would you be?' Berengar's smile filled out. 'Goetz – Gohtz, in the original dialect – was the family name of one of those retainers. In a way, I suppose, your family has served the goddess since time immemorial. Interesting, eh?'

'Yes,' Goetz said noncommittally. Berengar chuckled.

'No interest in history, brother? Well, we'll fix that. What do you see, young Goetz?' the Grand Master asked, rapping his knuckles against the great map spread across the far wall of the library.

'A map,' Goetz said. He peered more closely and saw a number of pins stabbed into the material of the map at odd points. Suddenly, he recalled seeing a similar map in the library of his own komturie. 'Those markers... they indicate our komturies, don't they?'

'Very good,' Berengar said as he nodded in a manner disturbingly similar to that of one of Goetz's old tutors. 'These pins are an illustration of our current strength. They are an indication of our resources and our presence.'

'You make it sound like a military campaign,' Wiscard grumbled. The Grand Master grinned like a naughty child and nodded.

'Exactly; it is a campaign, in fact. A very long, much

extended, campaign.' He turned to look at the map
and the grin faded. 'A campaign we are not winning…'
He trailed off.

'Sir?' Goetz said.

'Pins on a map, young Goetz… that is all we are. Pins
on a map,' Berengar said, shaking himself. He rapped
the map again. 'Now, what does all of this tell you?'

Goetz, who had never truly paid attention to the
map before, took a guess. 'Our Order has spread far.'

'Our Order has spread faster and further than any
other in the Empire, though we do not brag of that
fact. Fancy a guess as to why?'

Goetz opened his mouth to reply but the Grand Master interrupted him. 'It is because we are not bound by
tradition. We are not servants to dogma or slaves to the
chains of thought that bind our brother-orders.' Berengar held up two fingers. 'Our creed is but two-fold…
We go where we are needed, and…'

'We do what must be done,' Goetz finished the creed
instinctively.

'Excellent. 2478 as per the Imperial Calendar, young
Goetz. Describe it to me.'

'Sir?' Goetz said.

'The year,' the Grand Master said. He gestured.
'Come, come. You know your history better than most,
young Goetz. Or so I'm assured. And it is among your
duties to know, after all.' He fixed Goetz with a star-
tlingly blue stare. 'After all, if you do not know where it
is that you come from, how can you ever know where
to go?'

'Go?' Goetz said.

'Here. Take this,' Berengar said, tossing a book to
Goetz. Behind him, the hochmeister hissed. The Grand

Master chuckled. 'Oh do relax, Wiscard. Books can be replaced far more easily than the men who write them.'

Goetz looked at the book. 'Marienburg?'

'I thought you might want to brush up on the customs before you go. I know many young aristocrats take the Grand Tour of the lands outside the Empire, or which were formerly part of the Empire, but…' The Grand Master trailed off.

'I wasn't one of them,' Goetz said. Berengar sniffed.

'No?'

'No. I was learning about grain prices, milord. And bridges.'

'Bridges?' The Grand Master looked taken aback.

'I wanted to build them. Sir.' Goetz swallowed.

'Hmph. So, you've never been to Marienburg.'

'No, sir,' Goetz said.

'A shame. Do you know the customs then, at least? The dialect?'

'Somewhat. I had well-travelled tutors.' Goetz flipped through the book.

'Always beneficial. There are some who say that isolation is our only protection from foreign corruption. I, personally, believe that a little foreign corruption is somewhat inoculating against the more fatal kind. Svunum.'

'Svunum?' Goetz felt like a fool, mindlessly repeating the Grand Master's words, but the old man's mind was like quicksilver, dancing from one thought to the next with seemingly little connection between them.

'An island. Our island, actually. In the Sea of Claws. A gift, in 2478, from a grateful merchant-prince. One of a council made up of the leading families of Marienburg.' Berengar grunted. 'Fifty-odd years ago, we were given the rock in payment for spilled blood. There have been three hochmeisters in that time, with the third being one Conrad Balk, a Talabheimer of some note. Have you read *Siegecraft in the Time of the Three Emperors*?'

'We're talking about *that* Balk?' Goetz said.

'Yes. Precocious boy. Very keen on the intricacies of campaign organisation. Would have made a brilliant general, I'm told.' Berengar snapped his fingers again. 'But, back to Svunum. The year 2478, boy. Show me you have a brain.'

'The Pirate Wars,' Goetz said, slightly stung as things clicked into place. 'The year the last of the Westerland enclaves were burned out.'

'There we go. Sometimes I despair of the younger generation,' the Grand Master said. 'Svunum is a rock. On that rock, we built a komturie. In time, it became something a bit more. It was given to us with the charter to defend against further naval incursions from the north. Nowadays, our brothers in Svunum mostly hunt Westerland pirates and Norscan raiders.'

'There's a difference?' Goetz said, before he could stop himself. The Grand Master chuckled, and Goetz flushed.

'Depending on who you're speaking to, but yes. For our purposes, not so much.' The Grand Master tapped the book with a finger. 'We receive yearly reports. How much income they've taken in bounties, how many knights they have and such.'

'You want me to go to Svunum,' Goetz said.

The Grand Master gave him an irritated glance. 'I thought that was obvious, yes.'

'May I ask why?'

'I'm getting to that. The impatience of youth,' Berengar sighed. 'We haven't received a report from Svunum in three years. Four years ago, the brothers of our komturie in Marienburg moved to Svunum, to help bolster the defences during one of those interminable seaborne invasions from the North Lands. They tend to inflame the coasts.'

'And we've sent no one to check on them?' Goetz said.

'We have been busy, young Goetz. The recent overland Northern incursions have kept our meagre resources otherwise occupied.' Goetz frowned at the rebuke, but the Grand Master went on. 'I did send a messenger, however. Brother Athalhold, a knight of this very house.'

'And?' Goetz said.

'He died,' Wiscard grated. 'Killed in a back-alley brawl, according to witnesses.'

'How?' Goetz said automatically.

'Shot in the back.'

Goetz's hand instinctively brushed against his back. If either man saw the gesture, they gave no indication. 'Who shot him? Why?' he said, after a moment.

The Grand Master frowned. 'We don't know. You will rectify that, however.'

'Me?' Goetz said.

'You.' Berengar leaned forward. 'You acquitted yourself well I understand. In the recent set-to.'

'Not as well as I could have,' Goetz said, swallowing as the memory of his earlier dream washed across his mind's eye.

'And in the Drakwald,' Berengar said.

Goetz froze. A sudden bloom of memory paralysed

him for a moment. A witch-fire flickering between dark trees and the cavorting shadows of beasts. He smelt blood and heard the whispered promises of something that had crawled up out of the dark between worlds. The pain of the goblin-wounds flared madly and a muscle in his jaw bobbed as he clenched his teeth. 'Most of the men I led into the forest died.'

'Men die. You survived. Therefore, you accrue the collective glory,' the Grand Master said bluntly. 'Your guilt does you credit, though it is unnecessary.' His hand fell on Goetz's shoulder. The young knight could feel the weight of the Grand Master's hand even through his armour. 'It is also a cancer.'

Wiscard cleared his throat. 'Brother Pasqual tells me that you have done little but sleep since recovering from your wounds. You have not gone out, not requested leave to return to your komturie or requested a transfer to an ongoing military assignment.'

'I–' Goetz began. The Grand Master silenced him with a gesture.

'Wiscard has allowed it, because you are young. Because you are among the youngest of our Order to win your spurs and because you had, perhaps, earned a rest. You have fought hard and continuously since you took your oath. It shakes a man, to face the darkness that often. But it can only be allowed to shake him for so long.'

Goetz said nothing. Berengar searched his face and then, as if he'd found what he was looking for, turned away. 'You will leave in the morning for Marienburg. There's a river ferry heading that way. You will be on it. Warrants of travel have been obtained. You will visit the temple of Myrmidia in Marienburg and pay your respects prior to boarding whatever ship's berth you can acquire. I gather our brothers on Svunum have been lax in that area as well. Or so the abbot says.'

'And then?' Goetz said. The Grand Master turned.

'Then you will see what there is to see and report back to me. I want to know why we've had no contact with our brothers. Does our Order still hold Svunum?' His eyes held Goetz's own. 'And I want to know what happened to Brother Athalhold.'

'As you say, Grand Master.' Goetz banged his fist against his breastplate and bowed his head. The Grand Master waved the gesture away, his face irritated.

'Just come back alive, young Goetz. We've lost two whole houses, not to mention an experienced knight. I'll not lose a single man more.'

Goetz nodded and turned. He felt the Grand Master's eyes on him the entire way. He closed the library doors behind him and leaned back against them, trembling slightly. He banged his fist against his side, and winced.

Was it a test? It felt that way. He knew that men could be wounded in more ways than the physical, and that his wound was perhaps one of those. Perhaps the Grand Master knew it as well. Perhaps–

He shook his head, and pushed away from the door. It didn't matter. Marienburg then. That far from the forests, maybe his dreams would fade.

'You may as well share your opinion, Wiscard. I know you're dying to,' Berengar said as he listened to the fading boot-steps.

'I? You must have me confused with someone else. I would never think to countermand the Grand Master.'

Wiscard bent over his papers, his mouth set. Berengar sighed and looked up at the ceiling, and then turned.

'Tell me what you think.' It wasn't a command. Not really. Berengar did not command so much as manoeuvre.

Wiscard grunted and looked up. 'He is ill. There's a shadow over his soul.'

'Very poetic.'

'Truth, not poetry. I have read the reports of the incident in the Drakwald. He exceeded his authority, was almost killed and faced a – a thing of Chaos,' Wiscard said.

'And defeated it,' Berengar said. 'Not many can claim that sort of victory.'

'Did he really defeat it, or did he simply survive?' Wiscard countered. 'Berlich was good at playing the fool, but he knew enough to keep the boy busy in minor skirmishes and with unimportant assignments. Until we could see–'

'See what?' Berengar interjected. 'See whether he has been – what? – tainted perhaps? Marked by the Ruinous Powers in some way? Are we Sigmarites now, to see devilry and corruption in every shadow?' He gave a snort of disgust. 'Are we followers of Ulric, to condemn one of our own for having the bad luck to meet and survive an encounter with the enemies of mankind instead of dying bravely and uselessly?'

'I merely meant that we do not know how he has been affected. Brother Pasqual says that he hasn't been sleeping.'

'Sleep is a useless vice,' Berengar said, chopping the air with a hand. 'I don't sleep. Are you implying that it's a problem?'

'Be that as it may,' Wiscard said, avoiding the question, 'He has been having nightmares.'

'Then he needs something to keep him busy. Travel is the best cure for brooding.' Berengar tapped a spot on the map. 'Speaking of brooding... your brother-hochmeister. Balk. Your opinions?'

'I told you what I thought before you sent Athalhold,' Wiscard said, resisting the urge to add *to his death*. From the look the Grand Master gave him, Wiscard knew that though it had been unspoken, Berengar had heard it all the same.

'Has your opinion changed?' he said.

'Balk – the Balk I knew – was over-eager. Over-zealous as well,' Wiscard said carefully. 'In many ways, the opposite of Brother Goetz. Full of faith and fury.'

'And Brother Goetz is full of... what?' Berengar said, looking back to the map. His finger traced the path Goetz was to take, stopping on the marker for Marienburg. 'Sense, I hope. Dedication and faith I have in abundance. I need a man who can think. No, not just can, *will*.'

'The question is: will he think the *right* thoughts?' Wiscard said. Berengar didn't answer. He glared at the map, as if willing it to assume sentience and speak.

He had been Grand Master for twenty years; politicking had become second nature to him. The Order had been a small thing when he had taken the reins, and under his watch it had flourished. Not just in terms of martial glory, but in other, more important ways. The Order's funds had gone into public works and into the coffers of academics and engineers and artists. As a young knight, Berengar had carried materials with which to teach children the art of writing in his saddlebag and he had never wanted for students. Civilisation was more than just weapons and grand strategies. Without those other things, it was not worth the having.

He knew his fellow Grand Masters would not agree with him. They saw the world in terms of war and survival. For them, the Empire lurched drunkenly on the edge of a precipice, and one wrong step could send it reeling into the maw of Chaos. But Berengar knew the truth – Chaos was already here. It lurked in every flagellant's mad eyes and in every witch hunter's heart. It gnawed at the roots of civilisation, reducing men to beasts. Reducing them to savages, who thought of nothing more than the next conquest, the next enemy.

The Great Enemy could not be defeated with sword and pike, however. Only with knowledge. Myrmidia was the Goddess of Knowledge, even as she was the Mistress of War.

'He wanted to build bridges, Wiscard,' he said after a moment.

'What?' Wiscard said, looking up.

Berengar shook his head and looked at the other man. 'What did you want to be, old friend? Did you dream of bridges?'

Wiscard grimaced. 'Poetry,' he said flatly.

Berengar raised an eyebrow. 'Were you any good?'

'I was horrible at it, frankly.'

'Ah. Well then, best for all concerned that you found your true calling, eh?' Berengar said, smiling.

4

'HE'S A FINE horse, sir,' the stable hand said, running the curry-comb over the stallion's flanks. He was a young boy, pledged to the Order fairly recently, if Goetz was any judge. 'Good chest on him.'

'I can see that,' Goetz said, scrubbing the horse's neck. He'd been given a new mount, since his old one had died during the battle with the orcs. 'You've taken good care of him,' he said. The boy beamed. Goetz had worked in the stables himself, his first few months after joining the Order. It was an often thankless job, and a bit of recognition was worth its weight in honours or ribbons. The horse whickered softly and he extended a slice of apple. The horse lipped it and crunched contentedly.

'I will ride a horse like this some day,' the boy said, bolder now that Goetz had complimented him.

'Will you?' Goetz said.

'I will be a knight,' the boy said, bending to check the horse's hooves.

'When I was your age I wanted to build bridges,' Goetz said, feeding the horse another slice of apple.

The boy looked up at him incredulously. 'Bridges?'

'Bridges. Big ones. Small ones too. The world needs more bridges, I think.' Goetz smiled as the boy stared at him as if he were insane. 'Don't you think so?'

Someone cleared their throat, saving the boy from having to answer. Goetz turned. 'Brother Velk,' he said, nodding to the other knight.

'Brother Goetz.' Velk gestured to the stablehand. 'Get out.' The boy looked at Goetz, who nodded, and then scampered out, edging carefully past Velk.

'Hector, I–' Velk began and then stopped.

Goetz smiled as Velk's face moved through a variety of ever more torturous expressions, before finally showing pity. 'We go where we are needed, brother. We do what must be done.'

'You're just making this harder,' Velk snapped. Velk had avoided him in the weeks since the battle, though whether from an Osterman's natural distaste for those from Talabecland or for some other reason, Goetz couldn't say. Nor, in truth, did he particularly care.

'Sorry. Carry on making faces, by all means,' Goetz said, turning back to the horse. The animal, for its part, nudged his hand, sniffing for another bit of apple.

'I knew Athalhold,' Velk said, finally. 'He was a good man. A fine knight, despite being far too practical.' He stared down at his feet for a moment, then looked up. 'If someone killed him…'

'I'll be careful,' Goetz said.

'Athalhold was careful,' Velk said sharply. 'You have to be more than that.'

'Why the sudden concern?'

Velk made a face. 'A Velk always pays his debts, regardless of the recipient. You saved me, and it cost you. So now I'm telling you to be careful.'

'Consider the debt paid, then,' Goetz said, pushing away from the horse and facing the other knight. Velk frowned.

'The debt's clearance is mine to judge, not yours,' he said. With a final glare, he spun and stalked away across the courtyard. Goetz watched him go in bemusement, then turned back to the horse.

'Bridges are fine things,' he said, patting it on the nose. 'They're never as confusing as the people who walk across them.' The horse merely snorted in reply. Goetz sighed and left the stable.

For all his posturing, Velk had made an important point, and one Goetz would have to be blind not to recognise. Someone had killed Athalhold, that much the Grand Master had seemed certain of. The question was who? And why?

He shook his head and stopped to watch the novices beginning their afternoon training. Wearing padded armour and wielding wooden practice weapons, the boys went at each other with commendable fierceness as an elderly knight barked orders.

He wondered if he had ever been that fierce. 'Probably not,' he said out loud. The old knight glanced at him, hand half-raised in greeting, eyebrow quirked. Goetz waved at him.

As he continued to watch, a number of squires trooped out of the dormitories, their packs slung across their backs. They were young men, all on the cusp of adulthood and only a few years younger than himself. One by one, they climbed into the back of a wagon that sat near the side-gate of the komturie as a grizzled rider watched them from the back of his horse. The man wore the ornate cuirass and plumed helmet of an outrider, and the fat scar that decorated his face from brow to chin attested to a life of hard service. A brace of heavy pistols was holstered within easy reach on his saddle, and his hands rested on the wide barrel of the repeater handgun that lay across his lap.

He caught Goetz watching and raised a finger to the brim of his helmet. Goetz returned the gesture and continued on. He remembered the day he'd climbed into a similar wagon, watched over by another outrider. Perhaps even the same man, though he didn't think so.

Life as a pistolier was exciting, though the squires looked more nervous than eager. Goetz wondered if he'd looked the same, on his day of leaving. Probably so, and possibly worse. Mostly, they would be used as couriers, carrying messages from one place to another, or as road wardens, patrolling the Imperial highways. They would learn the ways of the horseman, as well as how to fight in a group.

It was also a chance for those who had neither the desire nor the ability to become fully-fledged templars of the Order to find a worthy calling. A chance to avoid the shame of being dismissed from the komturie and the Order for failing to live up to the demands placed upon them. Glancing again at the outrider, Goetz wondered whether that wouldn't have been the better choice where he himself was concerned.

He closed his eyes, imagining the look on his father's face. Wouldn't that have been a sight? Goetz smiled and shook his head. He didn't hold his father particularly accountable, or bear him any real grudge. The old man was a tree stump, rooted in place by ideas, desires and determinations that had little consideration for the same in others.

Their family was an old one, and it had old ideas and traditions. Every generation had provided a son to the Order and Myrmidia. It had apparently been a tradition among the Old Families. Twelve Sons of Sudenland, every twelve years. Myrmidia's Due, his father had called it, the Myrmidons. Even now, though Solland was long gone and the Families with it, the sons still went, and the Due was still owed and the Myrmidons were still needed. Or so his father had said. As far as Goetz knew, he was the only Myrmidon in the Order.

In the end, he could have simply said 'no'. But he hadn't, and now he was here, following the edicts of a goddess he didn't particularly believe in and the tenets of a philosophy that only broadly appealed to his sense of progress. He sighed and thumped the door frame. Across the courtyard, the wagon rolled out through the portcullis. Goetz watched it for a few moments more, and then went inside.

He left that evening without fanfare, his armour gleaming with a fresh coat of polish. Unlike the other knightly orders, the Knights of the Blazing Sun disdained the use of tabards, instead wearing plain jerkins embroidered with the Order's sigil beneath the heavy plate. It was a utilitarian garment, being more akin to what a hedge-knight or a mercenary might wear than the garment of one of the leading orders of the Empire.

Goetz, for his part, found the plainness of the thing comforting. At the end of the day, knights were soldiers.

Better armed and equipped than other soldiers, true, but soldiers nonetheless. Flash was all well and good when you were on parade, but was uncomfortable the rest of the time.

He patted the bundle of armour strapped to his saddle affectionately. Still, it was nice to have the option, should the need arise. He carried neither lance nor spear, instead relying on a small, triangular shield tethered to his saddle pommel, and the sword belted at his waist.

Lances had never been his forte, though he admitted they had their uses. Tools were tools, and sometimes you needed a certain tool for a given task. He preferred swords however. Especially this sword.

A snarling lion's head carved from ivory adorned the pommel, and the hilt was wrapped in pale leather. His father had bought it from a trader, who'd sworn up and down that the sword was elven made, though Goetz doubted it. He'd seen elven swords and they were light, needle-shaped things. This sword was a chunky thing, broad and long.

His father had gifted it to him when he'd won his spurs. A congratulatory gift Goetz had known was intended for his brother, despite his father's pre-emptive protestations to the contrary.

So many of his father's hopes and plans had relied on Stefan. Come to that, so had most of Goetz's. He smiled ruefully. It was Stefan who was to join the Order, Stefan who was to bring glory to the Goetz name, to make his father's business associates forget that the Goetz family had come penniless from a forgotten province and been reduced to tradesmen.

Stefan, Stefan, Stefan. Stefan would have done it

all. Little Hector would have been free to do – what? Anything he wanted. Instead, Stefan had flung himself from one insane venture to the next, obsessing over trivia and sour bits of history, determined to make his own name, to restore the family honour, until finally he'd been swallowed up by it. He'd stolen away in the dead of night, a number of precious heirlooms in his possession, never to be seen again. Oh, there had been no token of death, no sprawled body or eyewitness account, but Goetz knew he was dead. What else could he be? Why else would he not have contacted his family or returned home?

What had the Grand Master called him? A replacement knight. Goetz frowned. There was no shame in it, he knew.

But then, neither was there especially any honour.

He kicked his horse into motion and set off at a gallop. The ferry would be leaving at sunrise, and Goetz was to be on it.

'You know what to do then?' Eyri said for the fifteenth time since they had left the coast of Norsca behind them. Dalla scraped a lock of salt-encrusted hair out of her face and gave him a hard look. He raised his maimed hand in a placatory manner and grinned. 'I'm just checking.'

'I have done this before, Goldfinger,' she said, hopping up onto the rail. The longship crested the waves as its crew plied the oars. There was a wind out, but it was low and they were in dangerous waters. She looked down into the open hold where the slaves and crew alike swung the oars to the rhythmic beat of a drum. Occasionally a whip would snake out and leave a red mark across someone's shoulder or back, encouraging them to move faster. Warriors paced the decks, geared for war, their eyes on the horizon.

Eyri followed her gaze and grimaced. 'We're running close to that blasted island.'

'Too close?' Dalla said. 'How close is too close?'

'We're not in their waters, if that's what you mean.'

'How can you tell?'

'Because we're not being peppered with arrows and rocks from those damnable galleys of theirs,' he said. 'Even if they do spot us, I still have those letters of mark from the old hochmeister...' He caught her expression. 'What?'

'They are our enemies,' she said.

'No, they are *your* enemies. Yours and the old man's. They are merely irritants to me,' he said. He hooked his thumbs in his belt and shook his head. 'Things were fine under the others. I paid my tolls and they let my ships be. But this new one – Balk – he's mad. Madder than any Kurgan.'

'Paid my toll,' Dalla mimicked, pitching her voice teeth-shiveringly high. Eyri glared at her and she laughed. 'You really are a woman, aren't you? What man of Miklgardr has ever paid a toll to sail the seas? Are you a lackloin? Is that why you've dressed this ship up like a hog-wallow?' She gestured to the thin planks and panels that had been loosely nailed to the hull in order to hide the distinctive lines of the longship. It wouldn't hold up under close scrutiny, but at a distance it would appear to be any other merchant vessel as opposed to a sleek raider. 'Deception is the way of the coward.'

'Careful girl,' Eyri said. 'This is my ship and I can have you pitched overboard easily enough.'

'Who here would dare?' Dalla said, glaring at the nearest warriors. To a man they shied back or looked away. She snorted in satisfaction and slapped the hilt of her sword.

Eyri shook his head in disgust. His eyes rolled upwards. 'This is what I get for having you around, isn't it? The gods are mockers.'

'Ware! Sails! Ware!' A young boy dropped from the mast onto the deck, his overlarge hauberk rattling. 'Black sails, my chief!'

Eyri spun to the rail with a curse. Dalla twisted, peering towards the horizon. Black sails with a golden sun emblazoned in their centre sped towards them, and the whine of cornets and horns set her teeth on edge. Her hand found her sword-hilt, but Eyri grabbed her wrist. 'No,' he said. 'I'll not endanger this trip because you can't hold your sword.' He turned. 'Run up the flags we took from those ships last time out! Stow the oars and let the sails pull!' he bellowed. 'At a distance they might confuse us for something harmless.'

'And if they don't?' Dalla said.

Eyri grunted and patted the hatchet stuffed through his broad leather belt. 'Then we see who the gods really favour, Dalla Ulfarsdottir.'

'There's the man I almost didn't maim,' she said, smiling.

'Almost?' Eyri eyed his maimed hand.

Dalla shrugged. 'For a few moments. I was feeling sentimental, so I was.'

'Sentimental,' Eyri muttered.

'I could have killed you.'

Eyri chuckled. 'Aye, so you could have.' He turned his attention back to the approaching ships. If they could just keep the wind… He frowned and thumped his knuckles on the rail. Old Greisen had been all right, as far as Southerners went. A practical man, that one. He knew who the threats were, and he knew that a bit of piracy was inevitable. Eyri was by no means the worst captain on the Sea of Claws, and he traded more than he stole. Trade was a much more sensible undertaking than staggering through the surf with a torch in one hand and a screaming wench over his shoulder. Not that he hadn't done that in his younger days, but there was no real profit in it, not in the long term.

The world moved on, no matter how much you might want to turn it back. He bared his teeth in a humourless grin. Among the other godar, he was a bit of a black sheep. They called him a merchant and thought it was an insult. Yet they bought the good steel weapons he sold and the materials to waterproof their longships and hovels.

None of it would have been possible without the help of the einsark – the iron-skins. 'Knights' the Southerners called them. Old Greisen had funded him in building his steading, had set him up. After all, why fight a man when you can buy him? Eyri had no qualms about being bought, as long as the buyer could meet his price.

Staying bought, on the other hand… now that was a trick he'd never mastered. But Greisen had deserved it. Thought he'd had himself a tame Norscan, rather than an ally. Eyri hadn't done the deed himself, but he'd arranged it, and if the einsark ever found out… He grunted and shook himself. They'd become more savage since Greisen had died. More like – well, more like Norscans.

There were new stories on the ice these days: stories of black-sailed galleys rowing up the rivers and of burned and empty villages. Of men and women chained and herded into the galleys at the point of einsark swords. He watched the sails draw closer and wondered if that doom awaited him in his future. He gripped his hatchet, but found it less than comforting.

Wouldn't it be a funny thing, if he had set this path by setting the trap that killed Greisen? Greisen had had many faults, but he was a predictable sort. Balk wasn't. Eyes like black ice and a brain to match, all cold angles and cunning schemes. He'd have made a good Norscan, would Balk. Except that he seemed to detest them with a personal loathing that Eyri found frightening. Not that he would admit to such in public.

In truth, if the old man hadn't called the alvthing, Eyri likely would have, though not on the basis of old stories about daemon-islands and witches. There were more than enough of those in Norsca, and they held no fear for him.

But, an armed enemy, crouching on his doorstep like a snow-bear... that was a real danger. Balk hated him, he knew that. Maybe because he suspected that Eyri had got Greisen killed, or maybe just because he hated Norscans.

As he watched the black-sailed galleys skim across the waters and prayed that they wouldn't draw any closer, he wondered idly whether that hatred might not be deserved.

5

BEASTS DANCED BENEATH the dark pines of the Drakwald, pawing the soil around a crackling witch-fire and braying out abominable hymns. Mingled amongst the brute forms of the beasts were the smaller shapes of men and women. All were nude, save for unpleasant sigils daubed onto their flesh by means of primitive dyes and paints.

The shriek of crude pipes slithered beneath the trees, their rhythms carrying the gathered throng into berserk ecstasy as the dance sped up. The flames curled higher, turning an unhealthy hue, casting a weird light over the proceedings as man and beast engaged in unholy practices.

As vile as it was, however, Hector Goetz couldn't look away from the foul spectacle, no matter how much he might wish to. Crouching deep in the trees above the madness, Goetz ran his fingers across the double-tailed comet embossed on his breastplate. Then he touched the blazing sun engraved at the base of the blade laying flat across his knees.

It had only been three weeks since he'd won his spurs in a test of strength. This hunt was to be his first duty upon becoming a full knight of the Order of the Blazing Sun and he was only just now feeling the full weight of that responsibility. The men hiding around him in the forest were all that remained of his first command.

'Sir knight?'

Goetz started at the harsh whisper, nearly jumping out of his skin. He turned slightly. 'Are they in position?' he asked the scruffy looking woodsman who had crept up behind him. The man was dressed in animal skins and rough leathers and he stank of an ointment meant to keep his scent hidden. He clutched a bow in one scarred hand.

'Every mother's son, sir knight,' he said, displaying rotten teeth in a fierce grin. 'Just waiting on your signal.'

Goetz licked his lips and looked back at the fire. It seemed to play tricks on his eyes, showing him first this many gathered around it, then fewer. He tasted bile in the back of his throat.

'Sir?' the woodsman said, eyes narrowed. The young knight looked back at him, then nodded jerkily.

'Kill them. All of them.'

The woodsman growled and rose to his feet, scraping the head of an arrow across the bark of a nearby tree. The specially-treated arrow burst into flame and he fired it straight up. With a shout, Goetz kicked aside the blind and rose to his feet as the assembled militia let loose with a withering rain of arrows from the darkness of the trees.

The battle was a confused mess of darting shapes and screaming voices. Goetz blundered towards the fire, sweeping his sword out with instinctive skill. He lopped off an offending sword-hand and kicked something with too many limbs away. Then something struck him across the back, nearly knocking him into the fire and slapping the air from his lungs.

Flat on his belly, Goetz tried to pull air in. He coughed as a raw, animal scent invaded the confines of his helmet. His eyes opened, and he looked up into a face out of nightmare. The beastman was an ugly thing, all muscle, fang and claw. Piecemeal armoured plates strung together with twine and less savoury things clung to its bulky frame, less protection than decoration. Horns like those of a stag curled up from its flat skull and back in on themselves. Dark eyes glared balefully at him from beneath heavy brows, and snaggle teeth snapped together in a bovine mouth, its foul breath misting in the cold air as it grunted querulously.

Using his sword as a crutch, Goetz levered himself to his knees and stifled a groan. His body felt like a bag of broken sticks. He shook his head, trying to clear it. He could hear the gentle rumble of the river nearby, somewhere past the crooked, close-set pines of the forest.

The beastman pawed the ground and snorted. Some of them, it was said, could speak. This one showed no such inclination. It lunged clumsily, swinging its crude axe towards Goetz.

Still on one knee, Goetz guided the blow aside with a twist of his wrist and countered with his own weak thrust. The beastman stumbled back with an annoyed bleat as his sword sliced a patch of rusty mail from its cuirass. It was larger than the others, larger than Goetz himself by more inches than he cared to consider. Its axe was so much hammered scrap, but no less dangerous for that.

It was strong too. Muscles like smooth stones moved under its porous, hairy hide as it swung the axe-blade up again and brought it down towards Goetz's head. He caught the blow on his sword and grunted at the weight. Equal parts adrenaline and terror helped him surge to his feet, shoving the creature back. Weapons locked, they strained against one another. Goetz blinked as the weird runes scratched into the creature's axe-blade seemed to squirm beneath his gaze. Its smell, like a slaughterhouse on a hot day, bit into his sinuses and made it hard to breathe. Goetz kicked out, catching the creature's knee. It howled and staggered, and they broke apart.

Steady on his feet now, Goetz stepped back, raising his sword. The beastman clutched its weapon in both hands and gave a throaty snarl. Teeth bared, it bulled towards him.

Despite his guard, the edge of the axe skidded across Goetz's breastplate, dislodging the ornaments of his Order and the ribbons of purity he wore in order to announce his status as a novice of the Order of the Blazing Sun. Sparks flew as Northern iron met Imperial steel, and Goetz found himself momentarily off balance.

The beastman was quick to capitalise. It crashed against him, clawed hand scrabbling at his helm, trying to shove his head back to expose his throat even as it flailed at him awkwardly with its axe.

Smashing the hilt of his sword against its skull, Goetz thrust his forearm against its throat and forced the snapping jaws away from him. They fell, locked together, and rolled across the ground, struggling.

Goetz lost hold of his sword, but managed to snatch the dagger from his belt. He drove it into the beast-man's side, angling the blade up aiming for the heart, his old fencing teacher's admonitions ringing in his mind. The beastman squealed in pain and clawed at him. He closed his eyes and forced the blade in deeper, ignoring the crunch of bone and the hot wet foulness that gushed suddenly over his gauntlet. The creature's struggles grew weaker and weaker until they stopped completely. It expired with a whimper, its limbs flopping down with a relieving finality.

Breathing heavily, Goetz pushed the dead weight off himself and stared up at the stars dancing between the talon-like branches of the pines. The sky seemed to spin, and for a moment, just a moment, he thought he could make out a face, looking down at him. A woman's face, he thought, before he dismissed the idea as ridiculous.

Grimacing, he climbed to his feet. Dead men lay all around, their bodies mixed among those of the creatures they had been hunting. In the flickering witch-light, it was almost impossible to distinguish them from one another. His eyes were pulled towards the fire and what it contained.

Staggering, he moved towards it, and it seemed to curl and quiver at his approach. The stink of the weird flames grew heavier, almost solid. He caught a glimpse of bones scattered around it, and in the light of the fire he though he saw something floating within. Something that turned in its bloated womb to look at him with eyes like open wounds.

Deep in the woods, something had been born. Something horrible and beautiful. A whisper of sound caressed his ears, and a lovely voice spoke to him, making promises and predictions. A sweet smell, like sugar on ice, tickled his nose and he hesitated.

What had he been doing? What–

Behind him, something growled. Fear shot through him. He stooped for his sword, and froze as he realised that it wasn't where it had fallen.

Goetz whirled even as the beastman, bloody froth decorating its black lips, drove his own sword up through him, lifting him off his feet. Goetz screamed in pain and shock. Blood filled his mouth as the creature released the sword and he fell onto his side.

Goetz looked up, his vision already blurring. 'This – this isn't how it happened,' he said, clutching weakly at the hilt of the sword. 'Not how it happened–' The beastman loomed over him, an indistinct shadow, somehow no longer bovine but... avian? It reached down, claws caressing his face.

'Poisoned,' it snarled in a woman's voice. 'Poisoned.'

Hector Goetz woke up, covered in sweat, his heart thundering in his chest. He sat up and dug the heels of his palms into his eyes, trying to ignore the fear that gripped him. Swallowing, he looked down at his chest in something approaching panic. Other than sweat, it was barren of liquid. No blood, no wound, only bandages. He wasn't in the Drakwald. He was on a boat.

It was hard to say which was worse.

He had been given a corner of the crew's berth for his own, including a hammock that had seen better days. He'd left his horse at the ferry junction, where it would be sent back to the komturie, hopefully. He hadn't trusted the look of the crossing-master, but there was little enough he could do about it. As he brooded, a dark hand rose and thin, strong fingers tugged at the hair on his chest. 'Bad dream?' the young woman said sleepily.

'Ah – yes,' Goetz said, removing her hand and holding it. 'Hello, Francesca. I didn't realise you'd still be here,' he said lamely. Francesca sat up, dislodging the thin blanket that had covered her. She blinked and a slow smile spread across her face. She was pretty, with olive skin and eyes the colour of dark ale. Curly dark hair spilled across her bare shoulders and other, more interesting portions of her anatomy.

'Of course I'm still here,' she said teasingly. 'Why would I leave when we were having so much fun? I didn't think knights could get bad dreams, eh?' she continued slyly, reaching up to stroke his head. 'Maybe if I kiss it, it will make it better, hmm?'

'And maybe if you don't get back to your cabin before your father finds you missing, I'll wind up having to swim to Marienburg,' Goetz said. He swung his legs over the edge of the hammock and hung his head. It hadn't been a good one, as ideas went, but he found it hard to resist an interesting face. The gaff-hook scar that coiled across Francesca's cheek and the knife trails on her sides had been like a book he simply had to read.

'He wouldn't throw you off the boat,' she said, pouting slightly.

'He would if he knew what we had been doing since Altdorf,' Goetz said. 'Besides, I need to practise.' He stood, pulled on his trousers and hefted his sword, falling into the Stance of Seven Thrusts. Slowly he worked out the kinks, thrusting against imaginary enemies in the confined space. Francesca watched him for a moment, then, realising that he wasn't coming back to the hammock, she sniffed loudly and dressed. Goetz, already lost in the pattern of swordplay, didn't hear her pad out.

Mind blank, he moved from the Seven Thrusts into the Eagle's Beak and then on into the Hohenstaffen Gambit, easily compensating for the pitch and yaw of the deck beneath his feet. From the Gambit he moved easily into the Liptz Cross and let the hilt of his sword roll in his palm as he sank into a Crogan Hook with an Altdorf Curve. Behind him, something scraped against the wood of the deck.

He spun on his heel, sweeping the edge of the blade out and pulling it short at the last moment as the cabin boy stared at him in horrified fascination. Goetz twisted his wrist and turned the edge to the flat, lightly swatting the side of the boy's head. 'Don't sneak up on armed men, Wilhelm, or you might find yourself short a head.'

'I–' Eyes still on the sword, Wilhelm stammered unintelligibly. Goetz pulled the sword back and let it rest on his bare shoulder.

'Take a breath,' Goetz said, smiling.

'Th... the captain requests your pre... presence on deck, sir knight!' Wilhelm yelped.

Goetz repressed a flinch. This was likely going to be awkward. He forced a smile and nodded. 'I'll be up in a moment, Wilhelm. I just need to dress,' he said. The boy nodded jerkily and scampered up the stairs. 'In retrospect, it was probably a mistake to sleep with the captain's daughter,' Goetz said to himself. He looked at the hammock and chuckled. 'Fun though.'

The look of incredulity on Francesca's face when he'd responded to her flirtations had been priceless in and of itself. While some knightly orders practised the monastic discipline of celibacy, Myrmidia's followers had never been among them. Goetz dressed quickly, arming himself as well. He doubted he was in for more than a bit of play-acting, but it never hurt to be prepared. He paused as he ran his thumb over the engraved sun on his sword blade. He felt a twinge in his side and shook the feeling off.

The deck was awash with activity when he got up there. The crew – hardened rivermen all – ran back and forth, most carrying weapons. Francesca was armed, wearing a short blade belted to her narrow waist and carrying an ugly-looking knife in her hand. She blew him a kiss and he turned away. The captain was at the tiller and he waved Goetz over. 'We're passing through the fringes of the Drakwald now,' he said. 'Where the forest thins into the Cursed Marshes.' Captain Stiglitz was a big man, running to fat. A patchy blond beard clung tenaciously to his jowls and his thinning hair was swept back from his pink pate. Still, the hands that held the tiller looked strong enough to crack stones and the well-cared for handgun that rested near his foot looked deadly enough.

'The Drakwald,' Goetz said hollowly. His good mood had evaporated and he looked at the trees that clung to the shore to either side of them. Stiglitz eyed him.

'Been here before then?'

'Yes. Not this far north, but… yes.' Goetz shook himself. He nudged the handgun resting against the rail. 'Expecting trouble?'

'It's the Drakwald. What do you think?' Stiglitz said, his eyes on the river bank. 'But… attacks have been increasing, they say.' He met Goetz's eyes and nodded. 'Oh aye, the Fen-Guard have been having running battles with bands of mutants and beastmen in the Marshes, or so the gallows-patterers scream. Something has stirred them up, that's for sure.'

'Something is always stirring them up,' Goetz said. He felt a chill pass through him as he caught sight of something white flitting between the trees. Leaning over the rail, he squinted against the glare of the setting sun, trying to make it out. When he did, he bit back a startled curse.

The woman was tall, taller than any woman had a right to be. She held a long spear in one hand and carried a battered circular shield on the other. On her head was an archaic helmet and her eyes flashed like exploding stars as she met Goetz's gaze and held it the way a child might hold a struggling moth. Recognition flooded him, and with it a terror that he had not felt since childhood. Her mouth opened as in greeting, or perhaps in warning, and she stabbed her spear at the sky. The blade caught the light and Goetz ducked his head, blinking spots out of his eyes.

It was only because of that, that he avoided the swoop of the scimitar that would have removed his head from his shoulders. Jerking back with an oath, Goetz narrowly dodged the bite of the blade as it hissed through the air. The cyclopean monster that clutched it hissed in frustration and swung itself up onto the boat with one jerk of a thickly muscled arm. The colour of river mud, with a head shaped like a bird's skull save for the single burning orb that occupied the centre of its face, it was a huge brute and simian-broad, with a reptilian tail that jerked and thumped dangerously.

Someone rang the alarm bell as other creatures, beastmen and more human-looking mutants, scrambled aboard, dripping wet. They had been waiting in the water, Goetz realised, and had climbed aboard as silently as cats. If he hadn't seen the woman, they might not have realised until it was too late. Looking past the brute that stomped towards him on splayed feet, he saw that the woman – whoever she was – had vanished as if she'd never been. Then he had no more time to think about it as the rusty scimitar swiped out again and he was duelling for his life.

The creature shrieked, exposing needle-like fangs, and brought its blade down on his with bone-crushing force. Its inhuman muscles bunched and Goetz, off balance, sank to his knees and bent backwards. It hunched over him, grunting in triumph. Goetz let himself fall back and swept his leg up, catching it in the junction of its own bandy limbs. It shrilled in agony and stumbled sideways. Goetz rolled to his feet and slashed out, carving a red trench through its brown flesh and piecemeal armour. Agonised, its knobbly tail thudded into the deck inches from him, spattering him with splinters. Goetz chopped the bulging tip of the limb off and the mutant crashed into him, carrying him back against the rail hard enough to cause his armour to creak and for bolts of pain to shoot up and down his spine.

Spade-sized hands made a go at throttling him and Goetz slugged the mutant, breaking teeth. 'Get off me, filth!' he snarled, hitting it again. It shrieked into his face and, desperate, Goetz stabbed hooked fingers into its single bulging eye. The eye burst and the mutant

howled. It released him and staggered back, groping at
its wounded face.

With his sword-arm unpinned, Goetz let his blade
drift out and the mutant toppled, its cries cut short. He
turned, scanning the deck. He caught sight of Francesca gutting a scrawny creature that was more sheep
than ape with an almost gentle brush of her blade.
Another crewman wielded a boar-spear with experienced precision as he impaled a croaking frog-thing
with more eyes than fingers. In other places, the fight
wasn't going so well... something that had a wrinkled
child's face clubbed down a sailor with hairy arms and
bawled out hymns in a grunting tongue. Two goat-
headed beastmen tore another hapless man in half and
brayed out in victory as his insides spilled across the
deck. Everywhere, crewmen strained against mutants
across a blood-slick deck and Goetz knew that it could
go either way. He spotted Captain Stiglitz trying to
hold off an axe-wielding beastman with his smoking
handgun and moved to help.

As Goetz approached, the beastman, a vulture-
headed monster, shoved Stiglitz down and spun,
axe ready. Goetz raised his sword, only to hesitate
as the beastman's bestial eyes widened comically. It
squawked and stumbled back, waving its axe. Goetz
took a step forward and it turned and hopped towards
the rail, throwing itself overboard.

'What?' Goetz said, turning to the others. All eyes,
human and mutant alike, were on him now. Slowly, as
if compelled, the latter disengaged and retreated to the
rails with low moans and snarls. Goetz advanced on
them, but before he could reach the creatures they too
fled, heaving themselves into the river with desperate

abandon. Goetz stared after them in shock as the crew set up a cheer. Still befuddled, he didn't even resist when Francesca threw aside her own bloody blade and leapt into his arms, kissing him full on the lips in front of her scowling father.

Why had they run from him? Could it have been simply because he killed their chieftain or champion, assuming that was what the fiend had been? He glanced back at the mutant's body where it lay sprawled near the rail. A crow was perched on its deflated skull, one black eye cocked it Goetz's direction. It croaked and took wing a moment later, flying towards Marienburg.

THE LONGSHIP DRIFTED into the harbour, watched by the keen gazes of the Marienburg Sea-Watch. Men in green livery, wearing breastplates emblazoned with the face of the sea-god Manann, stalked the docks in a professional manner, clutching halberds and crossbows. Boats full of watchmen and bureaucrats met the longship on its way to the shore and Eyri greeted the latter with an easy grin and wide arms.

'My friends! My friends! Welcome aboard!'

As he enfolded the lead official in a bone-breaking hug, Dalla stealthily slipped over the side into the water, the oilskins she was wearing wrapped around her limbs keeping out the cold of the water. It was a practice of the Marienburg Merchants' Association to count the number of Norscans in every crew and count them again as they weighed anchor. More than one seaborne invasion had come as a result of spies left behind by cagey captains. While Dalla couldn't fault them their caution, she could – and did – curse them for it all the same as the cold of the water seeped through the oilskins and tugged at her limbs. Snow she could handle, and ice, but the water was all around her. Inescapable and all-consuming.

They had lost sight of the einsark ships as they drifted into Marienburg waters. Eyri had been confident that it had simply been a patrol, seeing what they were about. Dalla wasn't so sure. If her father was correct, something was going on. Pushing the thought aside, she concentrated on swimming.

Dragging her sword and a waterproof pouch behind her with the belt of the sheath clenched between her teeth, she swam with short, easy strokes. She avoided the orange patches of water where the light of the torches and lanterns fell, keeping instead to the sides of the other vessels anchored in the docklands. Propelling herself along off the keel of a fishing trawler, she shot into the shadows beneath the docks. She coasted through the forest of wooden posts and flotsam that had been swept into the tangle.

Beneath the docks it was another world. A city of shattered wreckage and forgotten vessels. Some were still whole, moored in secret spots, waiting for owners who would never return. Marienburg was a city of spies and assassins and neither was a profession that inclined to longevity. She took a moment to scan her surroundings. There was more than wreckage beneath Marienburg's docks... mutants and worse things prowled the shallows. More than once on one of Eyri's trips she had had to fight with things with too many limbs or none at all beneath these docks.

Pulling herself up onto the upright prow of a half-sunken rowboat, she perched and stripped the wet oilskins off her arms and legs and tossed them aside.

Hanging her sword across her chest, she opened the waterproof pouch and dressed swiftly. Above her, boots thudded across the wood of the dock. She froze and looked up, watching the drizzle of torchlight as it passed over the gaps between the boards.

There were more guards about than was entirely normal. Holding her sword tight against her so it wouldn't get caught, she jumped lightly from the prow to a broken spar, then from the spar to a dangling sheet of fraying fishing net. Even as she landed, a pinkish tentacle speared out of the water and wrapped itself around her leg. With barely enough time to grunt in surprise, she was yanked backwards and into the water, her elbow connecting painfully with a floating crate on the way down.

She bounced along the bottom for a moment, teeth gritted against the urge to suck in a breath. Breathing in the foul slop-waters of Marienburg would be just as fatal as falling to the lamprey teeth of the scavenger that had snagged her. It was shaped like a pink anemone, all teeth and lazily moving limbs. Something that had likely been caught in the nets of a fisherman who had drifted too close to the Sea of Chaos and got free in Marienburg waters. Pink tendrils shot towards her. She snatched her sword free of its sheath and cut through the lot. Foul-tasting blood spurted into the water, creating a cloud around her. She shoved off from the silt and pinned the squirming creature to a post with her sword. With a fire in her lungs from lack of oxygen, she grabbed the hilt in both hands and twisted savagely. She heard a sound like bells, and wondered if it was the creature squealing. Ripping her sword free, she watched it tumble down into the mud, tentacles trailing after it limply. Then, with a flash of her legs, she propelled herself to the surface.

Snagging the fishing net, she hauled herself up out of the water. Climbing to the top, she looked back down. Behind her, a fin rose from the water, navigating the bobbing detritus with ease. Clinging to the net, she watched it pass. When it had gone, she scampered up the net and pressed her palms against the rough board above. Gripping her sheathed sword, she smacked the pommel against the edge of the board. The rusty nails popped loose with a groan. She paused, waiting. Then, reaching up, she moved the board aside and shimmied up through the gap.

Crouching on the dock, she replaced the board and looked around again. The bobbing lanterns of the guards were at some distance. She rose to her feet and, leaving a trail of water behind her, padded away from the docks.

6

THE RIVER TALABEC was a wild thing, all raging currents and cascading eddies. The river-ferry moved through a combination of current and muscle-power, propelled along by twelve-foot poles of polished wood. It was said that the river had killed more men than any invasion from the North. Regardless or not whether that was true, Goetz was glad to see the back of it.

Marienburg sat on the mouth of the river, where it entered the sea. A *freistadt*, it was a city independent of the Empire and it rulers, yet still in some ways a part of it. Resting on the Northern coast, Marienburg was one of the largest trading centres in the Old World. Ships from every corner of every civilised land made port here, and the narrow streets were full of languages that could be heard nowhere else and the canals were full of barges bulging with trade-goods of every description.

As Goetz paced the deck impatiently, the river-ferry joined others of its kind in a slow queue through the river-bar. The bar was composed of two square towers connected by an iron portcullis that could be lowered into the river in order to block traffic.

Goetz grimaced as he caught sight of the gibbets dangling just above the river. Bodies huddled in each, though whether they were living or dead he couldn't say. Each cage bore a crude placard stating the prisoner's crime… 'PIRACY' was the most prevalent, though one simply said 'LUST'. Crows flew back and forth between the cages, causing them to rattle and shudder. Goetz cast his eyes downward, where skiffs carrying watchmen in the liveries of the various merchant-counsellors who ruled Marienburg checked cargo manifests and passenger rolls with the bored detachment of men who hadn't seen nearly enough action in their careers.

Goetz leaned against the rail, his bundle and pack by his feet. The trip downriver had taken several days thanks to the damage the ferry had taken, as well as the need to avoid any more attacks, and Goetz hadn't slept well for the duration. In his dreams, beastmen cavorted with orcs, strange fungi burst from his pores and his skin felt slick and greasy at times. The terrified bird-face of the beastman mingled with that of its one-eyed leader, both of them staring at him in horror as the fungi spread into iron feathers that flared and cut him to pieces from the inside out. Consequently he was in a sour mood. With his shield strapped to his back, his sword on his hip and the emblem of the Order prominently displayed across his chest, he was hoping for as little trouble as possible from the River-Watch. Armed men attracted undue attention in most cities, and a knight of the Empire wasn't likely to be welcomed with open arms in Marienburg, considering the associations.

If he were being honest, there weren't many places they were welcomed. Not unless there was fighting to be done. Goetz smiled sourly and tapped his fingers on the rail. For all that he was dedicated to the Order, and understood its importance, Goetz knew that not all of his fellow knights shared his disposition. Too many of them had been bred for battle and command, rather than common sense. The other knightly orders all too often simply reinforced that straightforward view.

Honour was what you made of it, not a thing in and of itself. It could neither be broken, nor insulted, lacking as it did either a personality or a physical form. That was his view anyway. Even among his own Order, he knew that it wasn't likely to be a popular one.

'We go where we are needed,' he murmured. 'We do what must be done.'

'What?' Francesca said.

Goetz turned. 'Nothing. You look lovely,' he said automatically. Francesca snorted and rubbed the scar on her cheek.

'Liar. Father says we'll be at dock soon enough.'

'Does he – ah–?' Goetz made a helpless gesture.

Francesca chuckled throatily. 'If he didn't, he wouldn't be much of a captain, eh? Yes.' She shot a glance at her father and frowned. 'And if he knows what's good for him, he'll hold his tongue.' She looked back at Goetz and patted his wrist. 'I just wanted to wish you good luck. Maybe I'll see you on the journey back to Ostermark, eh?' Feeling slightly flustered, Goetz watched her as she moved away, her rear twitching like a cat's.

Clearing his throat, he turned back to the rail. As a second son, he hadn't given much thought to either

women or marriage, at least not in serious terms. It
was a given that he'd be married off to one well-bred
daughter of Talabheim or another. Now, as with so
many things, with Stefan gone and his pledge to the
Order, there was no telling what would be expected of
him. As long as he was in the field, he could avoid it.

For that reason, as much as any other, he hadn't
wanted to return to his komturie after his near miss
with the goblins. It would have meant avoiding his
father's well-intentioned bluster and his step-mother's
subtle dealings to see him married off to someone with
a better bloodline to raise their family a rank or two in
the Game.

He sniffed. The 'Game'… in Talabheim, that meant
the game of politics. Like the other great cities of the
Empire, Talabheim was a hotbed of political warfare.
Claimants to thrones, positions and provinces pushed
and pulled against one another with a viciousness that
rats would envy. It hurt his head even thinking about
it.

As the ferry neared the guard post, he straightened.
Watchmen clambered aboard the ferry, their ber-
ibboned halberds making the entire process more
awkward than it had to be. Goetz settled for watching the traffic. The river was a hodgepodge of tightly
clustered craft. He watched as a flotilla of merchant
rafts pressed tight up against the iron-bound hull of
a dwarfen paddle boat and slid around it, their crews
jeering at the cursing dwarfs.

Turning from the scene, he caught a bulldog-faced
watchman with a halberd cradled in the crook of his
arm watching him with narrow-eyed speculation. The
man turned away as Goetz's eyes met his own and

conferred with a compatriot. The back of Goetz's neck prickled and the ache in his back flared up, just enough to remind him it was there. A harsh croak caught his attention a moment later and he looked up.

A number of crows had alighted on the prow rail of the ferry. The one that had made the noise sat a little way away from its fellows and was a scraggly example of its kind, with sickly grey skin showing beneath ragged feathers. Goetz felt a thrill of revulsion as it hopped down onto the deck and moved towards him, head cocked. It croaked again and his fingers instinctively sought his sword. He wondered if it was the same one he'd seen perched on the mutant's body days earlier.

'I have neither bread nor seed, Brother Crow,' Goetz said. The crow eyed him for an uncomfortable moment and then took wing in a shower of mangy feathers. One drifted across Goetz's arm and he cringed unconsciously, swatting it away. When he looked up, the watchmen had disembarked when their search was over. The ferry was moving on. A sense of relief flooded him, though he knew there had been little enough reason to be concerned.

Perhaps it was simply Velk's warning coming back to haunt him. What the Grand Master had told him had made him nervous enough, but Velk had only added to his worries. Goetz kept his eyes averted as the ferry passed beneath the dangling cages and didn't look up again until the vessel docked. Somewhere in this city was an assassin… a killer with a thirst for knightly blood. The question was – how exactly did one go about the process of hunting an assassin?

Goetz had no training for such things. He was no watchman or road warden to be investigating a crime.

He didn't know the first place to start. Disembarking, he caught sight of his earlier observer standing away from the crush of the crowd that milled about on the wharf. The watchman was speaking to someone and apparently gesturing at Goetz, or at least in his general direction.

'And that's not suspicious in the least,' Goetz murmured. The sound of shattering glass caught his attention. The tavern sat just across the street and on the corner. It was three stories tall and a monument to the eccentricities of Marienburg's architects. A man was propelled out onto the street by a boot to the rear as Goetz came to a halt.

Dressed finely, if a few years out of fashion, he was spindly, but handsome. He rolled across the filth of the street and scrambled upright, features white, jaw slack. The man who followed him out was dressed in dark clothing, weighed down by a plethora of implements of violence. In contrast to the deadly devices, however, was the lute he clutched in one hand.

'Hercule Portos, you are challenged. Also, your playing is horrible,' the man clutching the lute said. He swung the lute against the doorpost, wrecking the instrument. Tossing the remains aside, he drew his rapier and pointed the tip at the man in the street. 'Draw your sword, sir.'

'I... I... I have no sword,' Portos said, climbing to his feet, hands spread. 'I am no warrior! I merely sing of them!'

'You do that badly as well. How did you become so popular?' the swordsman said. 'On your feet. Someone will lend you a blade, I'm certain.' He glanced around. 'Anyone?'

No one moved. Goetz was suddenly aware that the narrow street was packed. Gulls wheeled overhead, crying loudly. Duelling, while not common where he was from, still happened and Goetz's father had joked that it was a way of pruning the dead branches of certain family trees. In Marienburg, however, it was practically a profession.

This however was more along the lines of an assassination. The swordsman's demeanour didn't suggest an excess of passion. It was clinical, even professional. Goetz was less squeamish than he had been before that night in the forest, but even so, the thought rankled. A duel was the result of passion; of honour stolen, or wrongs done. It wasn't done in the street, the way a man might kill a dog.

'A blade, damn it!' the swordsman barked.

'Let his patron give him a blade!' someone in the back of the crowd shouted.

'No, I think we'll let you do it,' the swordsman snarled, gesturing with his sword. 'Push that bastard forwards or I'll gut the first three rows!' He swiped the air with his rapier and it made an evil hiss.

Goetz, almost hypnotised to this point, found his hand clenched around his own hilt. He stepped forward, drawing his own blade. The swordsman looked at him with narrow eyes.

'He can use mine,' Goetz said. He flipped his long sword around and proffered it hilt-first to the still-kneeling Portos. The swordsman shook his head.

'No. He wouldn't even know how to lift it.'

He slashed out without turning, the tip of his sword slicing through a nearby rough's sword-belt. As it fell, he caught it with the flat of his own blade and sent it spinning across the street towards Portos.

'That's a better fit, I think.' He looked at the rough, who pressed back into the crowd, palms extended. He looked back at Goetz and saluted him crisply. 'Thank you anyway, sir knight.'

Goetz said nothing, merely nodded and turned on his heel. As he waded through the crowd, he heard the rasp of steel on leather. The crowd took in a deep breath. Goetz didn't stop.

Belatedly, he realised that he'd lost sight of the watchman and whoever he'd been talking to. He began to make his way towards where he'd last seen the duo when something jabbed his neck, eliciting a yelp of pain. Goetz spun, one hand slapping to the hilt of his sword. The crow, startled, took wing and flapped away, croaking. Goetz felt his neck and his fingers came away dappled with blood.

DALLA CURSED AND pressed herself back against the door frame, turning her face away from the street as the city watch patrol tromped past. Hard-eyed men in brass armour with turquoise and amethyst livery, kept their hands tight on the hafts of their halberds. Something was going on. She had been to Marienburg a few times, and never before had she seen this many patrols in the streets. These were heading somewhere in particular.

As they passed, she pushed away from the door and continued on her way. She wore a plain robe with a hood, but beneath its concealing folds there was her hauberk, much patched and cut down to fit her properly. She had her sword as well, a battered thing of crude manufacture. She would need a new one, if what her father believed was true.

If, if, if. She watched the legs of the market crowds shuffle past, and watched thieves eel among them and the alley cats filching fish from the stalls. If her father was right, all of this would soon be done. It was not a pleasant thought. She did not like the city, nor its inhabitants, but to think of *that* befalling them – she restrained a shudder.

She had once skirted the coast of the Chaos Wastes on a raid and seen what happened to lands that fell under the sway of such things. While her folk might worship the Great Powers, at their most rampant they could be terrible. The thing that her father's father's father had sealed within the stone of Svunum was as rampant as any of them.

It was an old story, handed down through the generations of the tribes whose gudjas had supposedly been involved. Five men of power had gone to the Island That Walked and forced it to remain in one place, and scattered the ruined tribe who lived on it like fleas. Later still, her father had led a raid onto that cursed shore and pruned the tribe back yet again, in retaliation for the raid that had taken the lives of her mother and brothers. Yet still they lingered; still they were dangerous. Such was the way of things. Fire and sword could only do so much.

In its stone cage, the daemon stirred and the land groaned in sympathy. She could see the marks of the Great Planner's followers scratched into lintel posts and in the brick of the walls, marking those houses safe for worship. To one who knew what to look for, this city was teeming with the human lice who battened on the power of such beings. No wonder the guard patrols had been increased.

There were stories back home, as well as brought by merchants and escaped slaves, of the Kurgan stirring in their blasted fastness, and lone prophets spouting nonsense. When one daemon stirred, they all did, it seemed. One tug on the Pattern, and all of the threads felt it. She bared her teeth, eliciting a yelp from a nosey matron who scurried away. That was her father's business… hers was merely to find prey for Eyri in preparation for the alvthing – the council of chieftains her father had called.

She had only seen one other alvthing in her lifetime, just prior to the raid her father had led to Svunum. A gathering of the mightiest chieftains of Southern Norsca, and their best jarls and thanes with them. A mighty conclave of heroes. She snorted. Robbers and bandits, more like. But they had done well enough, harrying the beasts who had killed her mother and brother.

Dalla slapped the sword on her hip. Perhaps, soon enough, she would get to do the same.

7

TEMPLES CLUSTERED TOGETHER like scabs on a doomsayer. One of his father's more cherished sayings, but Goetz agreed despite that. Even in Talabheim, the temple district was a crowded one. Sigmarite chapels brushed shared stonework with the altars of Ulric and Taal. Here, in Marienburg, there were even more options for the religiously inclined. Shrines to Manann dotted even the most isolated of cul-de-sacs, and brass plates wrought in the shape of the god's face, foamy beard and all, hung everywhere.

The largest temple, and the most gaudy by far, was that of Handrich. The patron of merchants occupied a rarefied position in the city's celestial hierarchy, being beloved of the upper classes. Overly ornate and gilded to the point of being extremely dangerous on sunny days, his temple acted as a gathering spot for traders of all types and it occupied the centre of the district with the stolid arrogance of a fortress.

In comparison, the temple of Myrmidia was a slight thing. Unassuming, even, for all its size. Goetz made for the doors, noting with a moment of trepidation that a number of crows lined the archway. Glittering black eyes watched him, and he stopped in the middle of the street, suddenly struck by a flash of agony. It had been building for the last hour. A deep, savage pain, echoing outward from the place, and he knew with a sure certainty that its cause was not, as he had thought – as you hoped, part of him whispered – goblin poisons.

No, it was something worse.

He stepped back from the temple and leaned in what he hoped was a casual manner against a doorway. Eyes closed, he took several deep breaths, wishing he could breathe the pain away. It wasn't in his head, not entirely. He took his hand away from the old wound and examined it, half-expecting to see blood.

'Unclean!'

Goetz jerked his head up, startled. The yell had come from the lips of a ragged-robed flagellant who stood on a busted plinth nearby. He was wrapped in rusty chains and his bearded aesthete's face was bulging with barely contained fervour. The man rattled the cowbells attached to his chains and shrieked again. 'Unclean! Worshippers of heathen idols!'

Snarling, he speared the growing crowd with a dagger-gaze. 'Repent! Repent of your bilious ways! The only path to redemption is through Sigmar! Only Sigmar can save you from the talons of daemons, from the maws of dragons and the tusks of orcs!' He shook a fist shrouded in a rust-splotched metal gauntlet for emphasis. 'Doom rides to night-winds!

The Queen of Crows stirs in her eyrie and the Children of Abomination flock to banners of flyblown meat! Unclean!' he roared, pointing a metal finger at Goetz. 'Follower of a false god!'

Goetz frowned and opened his mouth to reply when a stone spanged off his armour. Surprised, he stepped back. The crowd had turned ugly, seemingly in the space of a few moments. Above, the crows had taken flight. They croaked and rasped, making noises that were disturbingly close to laughter.

'Foreign devil!' the flagellant continued, bent over, his neck muscles bulging with the force of his screaming. 'Lapdog of wicked gods! Only Sigmar can save you! Only Sigmar! Sigmar!'

Goetz backed away as the crowd murmured and heaved, growing agitated. They had somehow got between him and the sanctuary of the temple doors. His hand dipped for his sword, but he resisted the urge. Drawing a weapon now would only provoke the crowd, and he couldn't take the chance that they'd rush him. So, instead, he began to back away down the street.

The flagellant continued to howl imprecations. A street-rough dove at Goetz. Goetz caught him across the jaw and sent him reeling back into the crowd. Somewhere in the mass of humanity, a fight broke out. Then another, and another. Mobs were fragile things. Goetz stepped into a side-street as the crowd forgot about him and focused on the half-dozen brawls going on within its own ranks. From somewhere, he heard the thin trill of one of the brass whistles the city watch used to clear the streets. He hurried down the street, not wanting to be caught in a riot. He'd witnessed the

Pudding-Tax Riots in Altdorf as a boy, and it wasn't a memory he cherished.

The street opened onto a narrow passage and a curving stone walkway that scalloped over a canal. Barges laden with goods going to one of the dozen market squares in the city passed beneath it, the bargemen singing lurid songs to accompany the thud of their poles. Goetz paused at the apex of the bridge, looking back towards the temple district. The pain in his back had receded as he'd left the temple behind and that fact caused a chill of despair to prod gently at him.

What did it mean? Why now? He had gone almost two years since he'd faced that thing in the Drakwald. Almost two years since he'd plunged into a storm of witchfire and put the unclean thing growing in a sour patch on the earth to the sword. It had been the making of him, his first duty as a full knight, and almost his last.

He had led an ad hoc assemblage of militia-men and foresters into the Drakwald on the trail of what he had thought, at the time, was a band of everyday bandits. Instead, he had found himself on the hunt for a herd of beastmen and mutants. Not to mention that half of his men had turned out to be cultists, their true loyalties to the nightmare thing that the beastmen's raids were responsible for keeping fed.

In the end, he had killed it, though not before it had invaded his mind and touched his spirit in some indefinable and horrible way. He repressed an instinctive shudder. The wounds from where it had touched him had festered for weeks. He had been too in shock at first to realise it, but it had left its mark on him sure enough.

Now the dreams had begun again. Old nightmares rising through the sludge of forced forgetfulness. Maybe it was simply the hallucinogens in the goblin arrows, or perhaps it was simply an egg that had at last begun to hatch. Either way, it wasn't just pain growing in him. He smiled grimly... wouldn't it be amusing if that flagellant had been right, and he was unclean?

'No,' he said aloud, shaking himself. 'Not in the least.'

Still, the thought lingered. He had been a born sceptic, unsure of anything that he could not touch and shape with his own two hands. Killing in the name of a distant, divine being had never sat well in his stomach. Killing for any reason, really. He was no milksop or pacifist; violence was second nature to him by now. But it was an automatic thing, an instinct as opposed to a calling. An instinct he tried to deny at most opportunities. Though sometimes...

He felt eyes on him and looked up. Down the canal, a distant shape seemed to float across another footbridge. Pale and marble-hued, the woman turned to look at him, her blazing tresses spilling from beneath an archaic helmet. 'What?' he said, half to himself. She raised a hand and the sun seemed to flare. He blinked spots out of his eyes.

He felt a tug at his belt and looked down to find a gap-toothed urchin attempting to filch his dirk. The boy froze as Goetz spotted him and then gave a frenzied yank and fell back, clutching the dagger in his hands. Goetz cursed as the boy took off as fast as his skinny legs could take him. He followed as fast as he could. He'd been so preoccupied, he hadn't noticed the cutpurse. Though why the boy would want a dagger, Goetz couldn't fathom.

The chase led him away from the temple district and through a crowded market forum. Goetz followed the boy into a cul-de-sac, leaving a trail of cursing merchants and customers behind him. The youth skidded to a stop and spun, chest heaving. He couldn't have been more than six years of age, and his eyes were wide with terror. Goetz felt a pang of guilt for having been the cause of it. 'Easy,' he said, keeping his hands away from his sword. 'Easy. Give it back, and we'll say no more about it.'

'Well, you won't, at any rate,' a voice said.

The gate to the cul-de-sac slammed shut and the boy dropped the dagger and eeled past Goetz, vanishing into a gap in one wall. Goetz turned as a bevy of armed men stepped out of the shadows. They were a motley lot, with the look of hardened mercenaries. One was quite obviously a Kislevite judging by his moustaches and top knot, while another had the lean, feral look of a Tilean dock-tough. There were five in all, and they were armed to the teeth. Snatching up his dagger, Goetz straightened and let his palm fall to his sword. 'Gentlemen.'

'Gentlemen,' the Tilean repeated mockingly. His dark eyes took in Goetz's cuirass and harness and he grinned, displaying a mouthful of golden teeth. 'Those will fetch a pretty penny. Oleg was right, the fat fool.' With a start, Goetz realised that they were likely referring to the watchman who'd been paying undue attention to him earlier.

'What is this about?' Goetz said, as they spread out around him, slowly.

'Call it a tax,' said one, a pinch-faced thug dressed in stained leathers.

'A tax?' Goetz said, playing for time. There was no way out. It looked as if he were going to have to fight.

'On foreigners,' a second said, tapping his cheek with an iron-banded cudgel.

'If you fight, it will only be worse for you,' another rumbled, stroking the plaits of his beard. He wore a battered breastplate, the Imperial eagle painted on it having faded to an anaemic-looking buzzard, and had the brawny look of a Nordlander. 'I would prefer not to fight a knight of the Empire.'

'Then leave, you cod-eating brute,' the Tilean snapped, tightening his grip on the halberd he carried. 'More money for the rest of us!'

'Stop talking and take him!' the Kislevite barked, drawing twin hatchets from the silk sash around his waist. He lunged with a wild yell, chopping down even as Goetz drew his sword. Goetz slid back and whipped his sword out and around, slicing through the man's belly. As the Kislevite stumbled past, dying, Goetz moved towards the others with the sure, smooth steps of a trained fighter.

'You want a fight? Fine. Have at it!' he said, gliding towards them as violence surged up in him, washing away all questions and doubts. His sword drew sparks as it slid along the length of the pinch-faced thug's blade. Goetz beat the man's weapon down and slashed upwards, opening his thin face to the bone. As he stumbled back, clutching at his face, Goetz shouldered him into the one with the cudgel. The two went down in a tangle and Goetz drove his boot into the second man's temple. Bone cracked as his head bounced off the cobbles.

'*Fastarda!*' the Tilean hissed as he came in low, the

wicked point of the halberd gleaming as it skidded off Goetz's breastplate. Goetz turned and slugged him and then spun to meet the big man with the plaits in his beard. The Nordlander's sword met Goetz's with a steely hiss and the two men strained against one another for a moment.

'Now's your chance to give up, if you don't want to fight,' Goetz grunted. The big man didn't reply. They stamped in a circle, moving back and forth. They broke apart and then slammed together again. Goetz set his feet and shoved, causing the big man to stumble. The latter screamed as, a moment later, a crossbow bolt sprouted from his back!

The big man sank to his knees, pawing weakly at the shaft of the bolt that had killed him. Goetz, in shock, looked up. On top of the cul-de-sac gate, a robed figure hastily reloaded a crossbow. Goetz reacted swiftly and charged forward, scooping up the Tilean's discarded halberd as he went.

Without stopping, he hurled the weapon at the crossbowman. Awkward as the halberd was, it didn't come anywhere close to its target. Nonetheless, the crossbowman gave up on his weapon and leapt down from his perch. Goetz hit the flimsy gate at a run, smashing it off its hinges even as the cloaked figure fled into the crowded street.

Thoughts of what had happened to his predecessor flashed through Goetz's head as he shoved through the crowd and he wondered if this might be the same man that had done for Athalhold. After all, how many renegade crossbowmen were there in Marienburg? Bloodied sword in hand, he followed the man through the winding streets, intent on finding out.

People scrambled out of his way and a hue and cry went up as he forced his way into the crowd choking the runnels of the street-market. The crossbowman fled on, tipping over a cart full of overripe produce as he passed. Goetz trod through it unheeding, every iota of his attention fixed on the fleeing man's back.

Unfortunately, the man was faster than he was. Much faster, and he had a head start. Growling in frustration, Goetz stopped and snatched a melon from a stand. It squished unpleasantly in his hand.

'Here now, you need to pay for that–' the fruit-monger began, stepping out from behind his counter threateningly. Goetz ignored him. He wound his arm back and then let it snap forward. The melon flew like a stone erupting from a catapult.

It caught the fleeing man in the back of the head and sent him tumbling head over heels into the gutter. Groaning, the would-be assassin began to crawl away. Goetz stalked towards him and used the tip of his sword to flick the melon out of the way as he went. 'I'm not in the habit of giving assassins second chances,' Goetz said, lifting his sword point and tapping the crossbowman's rear. The man continued to crawl. The knight stomped a foot down on his concealing robe, momentarily trapping him.

'Now my fine friend, you'll–' He paused as he heard the snap of wings and glanced up as a shadow fell across him. The crow's talons scraped the cheek-guards of his helmet and Goetz stumbled back with a curse. Mangy wings battered his face and head and a hideous croaking assailed his ears. He flailed, trying to drive the bird away.

When the crow flapped away, Goetz dropped his

arms to find that the crossbowman had scrambled to his feet and made off. Cursing, Goetz started after him, but a burly form interposed itself. The fruit-monger glared up at him. 'You owe me a pretty karl, my friend,' he grunted, rubbing his finger and thumb together beneath Goetz's nose.

'What?'

'That melon came all the way from Magritta, friend. Two karls.'

'Two – it was half-rotten!' Goetz protested.

'It had character! Three karls!'

'I'm not paying three anything for a half-rotten melon I bounced off someone's head!' Goetz resisted the urge to shove the man aside and stepped back, sheathing his sword.

'Just like one of you Imperial louts. Cheating an honest merchant of a day's wage,' the fruit-monger said, glowering at Goetz. He looked around at the gathering crowd. 'You all heard him! He refused to pay!'

A grim mutter swept the crowd, and Goetz tensed, suddenly realising that he was at the centre of a situation spinning rapidly out of hand. His first instinct was to draw his sword again, but he knew that if he did that, someone would die. Several someones, and considering the ever-expanding size of the crowd, he was likely to be one of those someones. So, just as before, he firmly drew his hand away from his sword-hilt.

'I said I wasn't paying three karls,' Goetz said, laying on his best sneer. His tutors had been good for some things. 'Not for something that couldn't even stun a man for longer than a few seconds.'

'Fruit's for eating, not throwing,' the fruit-monger said.

'Same principle,' Goetz snapped. 'If it squishes on the head, it would have squished in my mouth, right?' He looked around, nodding. Unwittingly, several others did so as well. 'One, and I don't report you to the grocers' guild.' Goetz didn't even know if Marienburg had a grocers' guild, but from the look on the fruit-monger's face, they did and he had scored a telling point.

'That's highway robbery!' the man blustered, but without very much heat.

'We're not on a highway, and I'm not robbing you. One karl,' Goetz said, digging into his purse. He held up a gold coin and tossed it to the fruit-monger. The man caught it and bit it, then glared at Goetz.

'Fine. I still don't see why you had to go and waste a perfectly good melon.'

'It'll feed the rats, won't it?' Goetz said, already moving through the dispersing crowd. Slowly, he released the breath he'd been holding and looked around. His quarry was well and truly gone. Above, a crow – perhaps even the same one – eyed him from a window sill. Goetz stopped and watched it for a moment, until it took wing and flew away. He shuddered and turned his steps back towards the temple district.

THE CAVERN FADED as Myrma took a deep breath and let the strands of volcanic smoke enter her. Inside her head, the skeins of destiny unwound and extended into the silent cacophony of the Pattern of Fate. Worlds upon worlds, each more different than the last, bled into one another like a vast field of soap bubbles and darting bird-like shapes dove in an out of the bubbles, popping a few on the way.

She shivered instinctively as one of the bird-shapes headed for her, only to bank at the last second and plunge into a newborn world. The Lords of Change, some men called them. To her, they were the Sons of the Master Planner and each one carried within its shape a fragment of the Great Mutator's mighty design. Each world, each scheme and skein, birthed new additions to the Pattern, expanding the field of bubbles past the limits of her puny vision. As always, it left her reeling and frightened by its sheer complexity.

Something massive swam through the sea of too-vibrant colours towards her, great iron wings cutting silently through the pink and turquoise clouds. An avian shadow, smelling of lightning and sugar. A voice like the tolling of a dozen bells echoed wordlessly around the priestess. It was a question, though it was shaped like a wave.

'Yes,' she answered, raising her staff. 'He yet survives! He moves on, wrapping himself in our snares ever more tightly!'

Another rumble and the Queen of Crows enfolded her in a barrier of feathers, protecting her from the sight of the Pattern Unchecked. Comforted, Myrma writhed in pleasure as the tips of the feathers wrought changes in her form. Though never were they changes for changes sake. That set the Maiden of Colours apart from her kin, or so she whispered to Myrma. Change for change's sake was not true change but merely indecision, and there was nothing Old Father Fate despised more than indecision. Without decision, there could be no movement, no future.

Talons scraped along the edges of her spirit, teasing out hidden secrets. It was the toll for this communion:

deep desires and forgotten fantasies, memories of lost loves and never-helds. She was always surprised by what her Lady dredged up from the depths of her past to gobble down like a sweetmeat.

'He is the one, then,' she said as the Lady held her. 'The one who will set the Great Game in motion?' A coloured mist of assent swept around her, teasing her ear drums with its delicate harmonies. She clutched her staff to herself and bent her head back, inhaling the beautiful vapour. Images of possibilities trampled down her thoughts… a city dedicated to the worship of the Pattern, with every man engaged in the contemplation of its skeins; a land purged of competing indulgences, where only one banner swayed in the cosmic wind; a land protected by black-armoured sorcerer-soldiers who worshipped at the feet of a Great and Terrible Queen of Air and Darkness, and who schemed eternally against one another. For such was the desire of any who served the Great Mutator… he who fed upon eternal change and alteration fed too upon the schemes of those positioned to cause change.

But not for the Queen of Crows the petty schemes of barbarians or the shallow ambition of pampered aristocrats. No, like a gourmand, she desired only the tastiest, most ambitious, most convoluted patterns for her feast. Minds turned towards eternal alternates, where every decision cascaded into a billion-billion possibilities.

The Great Game. Tzeentch's Game. The only game that mattered.

8

GOETZ HAD DECIDED to go to the watch in the end. By the time a patrol responded to the site of the ambush, the bodies had been picked clean by street-dwelling scavengers. The watchmen were singularly unhelpful, but then Goetz hadn't expected them to be. Murder in Marienburg was a commonplace occurrence and street-duels even more so.

'Crossbow is a common enough tool. Cheap manufacture,' said the watch-sergeant in charge of the small group of men who'd responded to the fight. 'By which I mean Imperial,' he added, giving Goetz a careful look.

'I'm from Talabheim,' Goetz said automatically. 'I wouldn't know.'

'Hnh.' The sergeant played with his ribbon of rank and looked down at the bodies. His men were 'scouring the streets for the assassin', which Goetz knew meant that they were standing off to the side somewhere inconspicuously, asking mild questions and carefully keeping their eyes vacant. If you wanted a long career, asking pointed questions wasn't the best way to go about it in Marienburg. 'You sure you didn't know any of them?'

'If I had, would I have killed them?' The sergeant looked at him and Goetz shook his head. 'Never mind. No, I didn't know them. Do you have a guard working for you by the name of Oleg?' Goetz said. If the 'Oleg' who had hired his attackers was also behind the cross-bowman, then he might be one step closer to finding Athalhold's killer.

'Why do you ask?'

'I heard the name,' Goetz said.

'Where?'

'Does it matter?'

'If you're asking about my men, yes. Yes it matters,' the sergeant replied pugnaciously.

Goetz held up his hands in surrender. 'Forget about it, sergeant. It was of no importance, I expect.'

'Then why are you bothering my men with it, sir knight?' the sergeant began. His eyes widened slightly as he took in something over Goetz's shoulder. Goetz turned as the sound of hoof-beats filled the air. The horse was a slender Arabyan, with silk bows in its mane and an evil glint in its eye. Its rider was a stout man, resembling for all the world an overfed bird of paradise. Colourful livery and expensively enamelled armour competed with an over-large hat with an indecently sized feather for attention.

'I am Lieutenant Ulfgo, sir knight. I have come to escort you to the prince,' the peacock said.

'Which prince?' Goetz said. 'Marienburg has a surplus, I'm given to understand.' The sergeant stifled a chuckle.

'The only one who matters,' Ulfgo said, his chubby features displaying not a twitch at the jibe. 'My Lord Aloysious Ambrosius, Lord Justicar of Marienburg and Master of the Fens.'

'Very impressive,' Goetz said. 'Why does he wish to see me?'

'You will have to ask him, sir knight.' Ulfgo inclined his head towards a second horse behind his, which impatiently scraped a hoof on the cobbles. 'You know how to ride, I trust?'

Goetz didn't bother to reply. Instead he swung into the saddle smoothly and jerked the reins, turning the horse around. He gestured. 'Lead the way, lieutenant, by all means.'

The ride was a swift one, taking them to the nearest canal, where a resplendent gondola awaited them. The prow had been carved into the shape of a bird's head and it had a canopy that was both garish and sublime. Armed men, wearing the livery of the Marsh-Watch, stood to attention both alongside the canal and on the gondola itself, clutching the wicked tridents that were their weapon of choice. Breastplates engraved with Manann's scowling visage and bronze full-face helms completed the image of deadly competence. From what Goetz knew of the Marsh-Watch, it was a reputation they deserved. They were as hardened a fighting force as any in the Empire, for all that their masters rarely employed them beyond the boundaries of the Cursed Marshes.

A seneschal, clad in fur and silk, stepped out from under the canopy and beckoned to Goetz with fingers dripping with jewellery. 'This way, if you please sir knight,' the man said in a high-pitched voice. Goetz dismounted and strode towards the gondola. As he made to board, one of the watchmen extended his trident and said, gruffly, 'No weapons.'

Goetz nodded. 'Then no discussion,' he said genially. He turned back towards the horse, his hand on the hilt of his sword. Two more watchmen stepped between him and his mount, their tridents not quite aimed at him. Goetz stopped and cocked his head. 'I've already killed five men today. Two more won't weigh any more heavily on my conscience,' he said, without menace. It never failed to surprise him how much truth was in him when he said such things. He felt a dim sadness at the prospect, but no worry. No fear.

Ulfgo leaned forward across his saddle horn, his stiff features turning a slightly darker shade. 'Remove your sword, sir knight. It is not your right to refuse an audience with the Lord Justicar.'

'The last time I looked, I wasn't a citizen of Marienburg. Therefore, I am hardly bound by its peculiarities,' Goetz said. 'But, since it's a mercantile sort of place, I'll haggle – my sword stays, but I'll happily peace-bind it, if you wish.'

Ulfgo made to draw his own weapon, and the watchmen levelled their tridents. Goetz sighed and shrugged. 'I tried,' he said, drawing his own sword.

'Not very hard, I must say. Enough, gentlemen. Enough.' There was a sharp clap immediately following these words and the watchmen backed off. 'I'm sure that the good knight means me no harm.' Goetz turned unhurriedly. The seneschal had backed away and a rangy man of indeterminate age had replaced him. He was clad not in silk, but in leather, with polished armour and a trident insignia emblazoned on his hauberk. One eye was covered with a large green eye-patch with a similar insignia and his hard mouth quirked in a flat smile. 'I am Aloysious Ambrosius, sir knight. I would be obliged if you would speak to me.'

'All you had to do was ask,' Goetz said, sheathing his sword.

'I thought I was asking. Thank you for correcting me.' Ambrosius eyed him as he stepped onto the gondola. 'Would you have really fought? No. Never mind. You would have, of course.'

'Of course,' Goetz said.

'Knights are all the same in that regard,' Ambrosius said, grinning slightly. 'At least in my experience.'

'What you know of proper knightly behaviour wouldn't fill a tankard, Ambrosius,' a voice said from within the canopy. As Ambrosius gestured for Goetz to step under it, a short shape stood, armour creaking. The man within wore armour the colour of kelp, its surface intricately engraved with aquatic motifs. Beneath it, he wore robes of a turquoise hue, which did little to hide the overall impression of a barrel that had grown legs. The scarred face glared frightfully at Goetz, and the hand that was extended in greeting was no hand at all, but instead a miniature trident, affixed to the stump of the man's wrist by a steel bracer.

'Sir Hector Goetz, of the Order of the Blazing Sun, if I might introduce you to the honourable Grand Master of the Knights of Manann, Dietrich Ogg,' Ambrosius said.

'Grand Master,' Goetz said, inclining his head in a shallow bow. The templars devoted to Manann were a strange lot, half political animal, half military organisation, they were centred in Marienburg and had been since they had been created by an edict of the merchant-princes. Religion had little to do with their day-to-day function, or so Goetz had heard. But then, that could be said of more than one knightly order, his own included.

'You Myrmidians are far too casual for my tastes,' Ogg grunted. 'I get more respect from the blasted Reiksguard!'

'That's a lie,' Ambrosius said helpfully. He sat down on a cushioned bench and draped his arms over the gondola rail as his men pushed the gondola off into the flow of the canal. 'The Reiksguard, being loyal Imperial citizens, rarely acknowledge our existence, let alone pay a visit to an order of templars that the Imperial Grand Master of the Knightly Orders doesn't recognise.' He sniffed. 'But by all means, continue to grouse.'

'I will, thank you,' Ogg said, stumping back to his bench and sitting with a clatter. He cast a baleful eye at Goetz. 'It's ours, you know.'

'He means Svunum,' Ambrosius supplied. 'Please take a seat, sir knight. We have much to discuss.'

'Do we?' Goetz said, sitting on the bench Ambrosius had indicated. He glanced out at the canal. Marienburg looked almost beautiful from this angle. Serene, even.

'Oh yes,' Ambrosius said, leaning forward. He shoved a finger beneath his eye-patch and scratched furiously. 'It wouldn't do to have two members of your prestigious Order lying dead in our fair streets, now would it?'

Goetz froze. Ambrosius chuckled. 'Oh yes, I took note of that. I know an assassination when I see one you might say, sir knight,' he said, tapping his patch.

Ogg sniggered and rubbed his trident.

'We both do,' the Grand Master said, still chuckling.

'Who killed him?' Goetz said quietly.

'You'd know better than us. I'm given to understand you almost caught him,' Ambrosius said, scratching at his socket again. The gesture made Goetz's skin crawl.

'Almost being the operative word. I never saw his face.'

'A shame.' Ambrosius sighed and leaned back. He looked at Ogg. 'That would have simplified things immensely.'

'Our lot is not a simple one, Lord Justicar,' Ogg said, his tone mocking. He looked at Goetz. 'Why did Berengar really send you?' he demanded.

'To re-establish contact with our brothers on Svunum,' Goetz said carefully. Something was going on here. He could almost taste it, like the charge in the air just before a lightning storm.

'And to investigate this murder?'

Goetz said nothing. Ogg snorted and jabbed the air with his trident. 'I knew it! He's too damn clever by half!' He looked at Goetz and smiled a shark's smile. 'I know bait when I smell it. How many of you blazing bastards are in the city? Is it Knock you're reporting to? I never trusted him! Abbot my soggy–'

'As you can see, paranoia is a disease and my friend has caught it,' Ambrosius interjected. 'I doubt Dietrich here would have even allowed you off the boat. If your Grand Master hadn't offered to sell your Marienburg Komturie to us–'

'What?' Goetz said, slightly appalled. Berengar hadn't mentioned that.

'Oh, you didn't know?' Ambrosius said. 'Our

esteemed paladins share the temple of Manann with the priests. We would, however, like to expand their holdings, you might say. And since your people all left and have yet to return… well.' He shrugged. 'You could see how it was an arrangement that interested us.'

'Yes,' Goetz said. He frowned, puzzled. 'Us?'

'Well… me,' Ambrosius said, smiling broadly. 'Do you know what I was before I was Lord Justicar?' He chuckled. 'A mercenary. And before that, I was a member of the most esteemed Order of the Gryphon, in Altdorf.'

'They cashiered him,' Ogg said. 'Stripped him of his lands and titles,' he continued, taking an almost perverse pleasure in recounting Ambrosius's disgrace. Goetz was slightly taken aback.

'Why?' he said, before he could stop himself.

'A woman,' Ambrosius said off-handedly.

'A man,' Ogg corrected. 'Specifically, a nephew. The Grand Master's nephew. I know, because we were picking the bodies of Altdorf swords-for-hire out of the canals for weeks after you arrived. That alone would have garnered you a commission, mind…'

'And my point was that we must not be beholden to foreign bodies or past ties,' Ambrosius said firmly. 'The Order of the Blazing Sun bears no loyalty to Marienburg. Grand Master Ogg happens to agree with me. He also agrees that Svunum can – and should – belong to the Order of Manann.'

Goetz forced himself to relax. 'Why are you telling me this?'

'I merely want you to understand your position,' Ambrosius said. 'Like as not Berengar sent you here as bait to draw out an assassin. An assassin he thinks has some connection to your Order, if I judge his mind right, the crooked devil. Or at the very least, a grudge.'

'And if so?' Goetz said, keeping his face neutral.

'And so we'd like you to succeed, thank you very much,' Ogg snapped. 'The quicker we find out who killed your man, the quicker you can get to the important bit – getting that lot of brass-plated squatters off my island!'

'I am merely to re-establish contact,' Goetz said. 'You'll have to take the rest of it up with the Grand Master.'

'Oh we will,' Ambrosius said. The gondola bumped against a mooring post. 'You, however, must be sure not to die in the meantime. I have no doubts that Berengar would lead your Order to war in our streets if he thought it was necessary. And two knights dead might convince him of that necessity. Then what, eh? Our streets full of bronze-armoured crusaders, which is the exact opposite of what we want. We're here, by the by.'

Goetz turned and saw that the ride had taken them back to the temple district. Watchmen patrolled the streets and there was no sign of the mob from before, nor of the flagellant who had roused them to action. 'Was this little talk just to warn me to be careful?' Goetz said, stepping onto the jetty.

'In a way,' Ambrosius said. 'More, I wanted to see what kind of man Berengar had sent.'

'And?'

'You certainly are a man of some type or other. I haven't decided which type yet,' the Lord Justicar said, gesturing to his men. The gondola drifted away from the jetty. 'I'm glad we had this talk.'

Goetz watched them go, hoping the puzzlement

he felt wasn't showing on his face. There was more to things than what the Grand Master had told him, it seemed. He was no stranger to schemes, political or otherwise, but he felt as if he had wandered into some-one else's story. Shaking his head, he moved towards the temple and stepped through the doors.

A moment later a gong sounded as the great brass-bound doors closed behind him. Strange Southern spices burned in the braziers that lined the entryway, eradicating the stink of the city beyond and putting Goetz in mind of somewhere warmer. Ceremonial bronze-tipped spear-butts thudded into the stone floor with rhythmic force.

Goetz did not look at either of the ceremonial guards, clad in their archaic armour and crimson robes. Over the robes they wore burnished breastplates with sculpted gleaming muscles. The full-face helmets they wore were engraved with prayers to Myrmidia, and crimson-dyed horsehair crests added inches to their height. 'Who comes?' one said.

'A seeker,' Goetz replied, looking straight ahead, his helmet beneath his arm, his palm resting on the pom-mel of his sword.

'What do you seek?' the second guard said.

'The path forward,' Goetz intoned, bowing his head.

'A seeker comes! Illuminate his path!' the first guard cried, slapping his spear blade against the long oval shield decorating his other arm. As the echoes of metal on metal faded, the ornate lanterns lining the walls flared to life, one after the other. Goetz blinked, trying to clear the sudden burst of light from his eyes.

'Impressive,' he said.

'I'm glad you think so. It was for your benefit,' a man

said, shuffling down the corridor to meet him. He was broad shouldered and, Goetz suspected, bow-legged beneath his rough, homespun robes. 'We get so few official visitors that we felt a proper display was called for,' he went on, throwing back his hood to reveal a narrow face. 'You're late, by the way. I am Abbot Knock. Be welcome and may enlightenment be yours,' the man said, bowing his tonsured head. When he looked up, he was grinning. 'Now that that bit of business is out of the way... how is my old friend Berengar?'

'You know the Grand Master?' Goetz said, slightly taken aback.

'Of course! A man should know his cousin, even if he is an Imperial lickspittle.' Knock smiled, as if to show it had been a joke. Goetz blinked, suddenly aware of the resemblance between the two men. 'I trust he's well?' Knock went on as Goetz fell in step with him and they started down the corridor.

'I'm not privy to his thoughts, but he seemed healthy enough,' Goetz said hesitantly.

'For an old man, you mean?' Knock said, chuckling. 'Don't fool yourself, sir knight. Berengar will outlive us both, I have no doubt.' He looked at Goetz. 'You are... Goetz, yes?'

'Hector Goetz, Master Abbot,' Goetz said.

'Solland name that. "Gohtz" or "Steadfast" in the old tongue of the Merogen. Old name. There was a Gohtz at Hergig, you know, when Gorthor the Beastlord of foul memory tried to sack Hochland. He was a Myrmidon – one of the twelve retainers of the electoral household. He was a knight of the Order as well.'

'Yes,' Goetz said. 'He died, as I recall.'

'All men die. You're a bit young to be a knight, I

should think.' Knock smiled before Goetz could reply. 'No matter. All men look young to me.' Goetz made to protest, but Knock shushed him. 'Never mind boy. We have other things to discuss.' He looked Goetz up and down, his eyes lingering on the symbol of the Order engraved on his cuirass. 'Namely, the death of one of our brothers.'

'Athalhold,' Goetz said.

'Yes. He was to meet with me. Instead I had to go and claim his body from the brethren at the temple of Morr.'

'You almost had to do the same for me,' Goetz said.

'What?' Knock's eyes widened.

'I was attacked not far from here.' Goetz slapped his sword. 'I almost got the same surprise Athalhold did, in fact.'

Knock hesitated. 'Did you see him? Catch him?'

'Almost.' It was Goetz's turn to hesitate. 'I wasn't fast enough.'

'Hmph.' Knock led him through the temple. Its influences were plain, mimicking the circular temples of Tilea and Estalia. Smooth columns held up the roof, and the floor was tiled with oven-hardened ceramic that Goetz feared would crack with every step he took.

'I'm not even certain it was the same attacker,' Goetz said hesitantly.

'How could you be? No, the crossbow is a common enough killer's tool in Marienburg.' Knock gestured sharply. 'Still, while I have faith in many things, coincidence is not one of them.'

'The Lord Justicar seems to share your suspicions.'

'Ambrosius?' Knock said, pausing and looking at Goetz. 'You've met him?'

'Just now,' Goetz said. 'He learned of my attack and wanted to speak to me.'

'I'll bet he did. As cunning a snake as ever slithered, that one,' Knock said, running his fingers over his pate thoughtfully. 'If he's involved, there's definitely more to things than I first suspected.' He looked at Goetz. 'And more to Athalhold's death than misadventure.'

'But why would someone try to kill me? Or any knight of our Order?'

'I don't know. We could always try asking her,' Knock said, leading Goetz into the rotunda. Goetz stopped short, his breath catching in his throat.

The statue of Myrmidia rose up through the centre of the temple, bathed in a shaft of sunlight descending from the open roof. It was small, as such statues went, but then, so was the temple, and the statue loomed in the limited space available. Goetz examined her with a boldness born of familiarity. Clad in ancient armour, one hand on a spear, the other on a shield, she was both beautiful and terrible in the way that all goddesses were. Mounted on a winged horse, she was the personification of victory.

Yet there was something else to her; something inexplicable. She looked down on Goetz with marble eyes, her expression as blank as the stone she was carved from. Briefly, he was reminded of the face that had stared down at him from the night sky in his dream and then, with a twinge of foreboding, the pale shape he'd seen on the river. Could that have been her? Was Myrmidia watching over him, even in his nightmares?

'She is beautiful, isn't she?' Knock said softly.

Goetz tore his eyes from the statue. 'All goddesses are.'

'But she is different,' Knock said, spreading his hands. 'She is ours, and we are hers and thus her beauty affects us in ways we cannot fathom.'

'You make her sound like a lover,' Goetz protested.

'Not quite that poetic, perhaps.' Knock shrugged. 'Then again, maybe so. Who can say?'

Uncomfortable, Goetz turned away from the statue. 'You have a room prepared for me, I believe?'

'That we do,' Knock said. 'I'll show you to it.'

'An abbot showing around a simple knight?' Goetz said. 'People will talk.'

'This is Marienburg, lad. People are always talking. Incessantly, as a matter of fact. Can't get them to shut up. Besides, you're the first of your Order we've played host to in many a year.'

'What of the brethren of the Marienburg Komturie?' Goetz asked. 'Surely you had some contact with them? Before they left, I mean.'

'Not enough,' Knock said. He sighed. 'They were a small group, and cliquish. And when they left…' He paused.

'Yes?' Goetz encouraged.

'When they left, we were the last to know,' Knock said plainly. 'Otherwise, I would have organised the brethren here for war. We might be priests, but we are quite capable of fighting. Indeed, I fear most of the younger initiates look forward to it.' Knock peered at Goetz as they moved out of the rotunda. 'You seem as if you've seen your share of it yourself.'

'More than I cared to,' Goetz said, idly knuckling the small of his back.

'Sensible,' Knock said, clasping his hands behind his back. 'Never look for a fight, lad. Inevitably, one will come to you.' Knock shook his head. 'More is the pity.'

'The Grand Master has a different take on the matter,' Goetz said diffidently. Knock snorted.

'Of course he does! That's why he is who he is and why I am who I am.' He smiled again. 'Still, there is room enough for both of us, here beneath the sun.' He gestured upwards to the ceiling. Goetz glanced up, noting for the first time how a series of suns had been carved into the stone there.

Goetz traced the sun on his cuirass and nodded. 'Would that its light had protected Athalhold as well.'

THE CROW CIRCLED the temple roof, careful not to draw too close. There were only a few weak points in the spiritual armour of the place, and it would not do to land elsewhere. It had followed its prey through the twisty canal-streets of Marienburg throughout the day, watching him as he went looking for answers.

The crow knew all about answers; and questions and rhymes and schemes and other things. It knew more than a crow ought, because it was not alone in its skull. Another looked through its eyes and that other grunted impatiently as she inhaled the deep gasses of the island. Myrma squatted over the natural vent and let the gasses inundate her sinuses. She was nude, save for the crude tattoos which curled across her pale flesh like a lover's caresses.

'Well?' Balk demanded. He stood out of reach of the gasses, holding the edge of his cloak up over his nose.

'He's in the city,' she said hoarsely.

'The assassins–'

'Failed,' she said curtly. 'He is faster than the other. Younger. More alert.'

'Then use more men! Use your magic! I want him dead! If Berengar figures out what we're up to...' He trailed off and frowned. 'If it were up to the Grand Master, this island – everything we have built – would be forgotten like so much refuse. I cannot allow that to happen. I won't!'

It was less a justification than a rationalisation. In his own mind, Balk saw the knight's presence for what it almost certainly was. The Grand Master was no fool. He had allowed Greisen to build up the island's strength, but only so he could sell it to the damn merchant-princes! Fury filled Balk and the haft of his axe creaked as his grip tightened.

Myrma's eyes flickered to the axe. It was an old weapon, crafted for a chieftain of her acquaintance, back long ago before they'd been driven from their ancestral lands by the upstart Sigmar. Before he'd welded the Svanii to his own Unberogen, and scattered to the wilderness any who opposed him. The axe had not served its owner well then, when Sigmar's hammer had fallen on his skull.

Balk knew nothing of this, of course. For him, it was merely a weapon – a gift given by a grateful, if primitive people. In truth, it was one more link in a chain binding him to her Mistress's designs. Funnily enough, or perhaps not, it was his own ancestor who had first wielded that axe. One of the first chieftains of old Sudenland, or Solland, as it became known.

'Kill him,' Balk said again. 'But I want no connection to us!'

'As you wish,' the priestess said, smiling slyly. 'As you wish.' She let her mind strike out again, and she touched the brain of the thing shaped like a crow, angling it towards the sill of one cell window in particular. Its talons itched as it landed, and it eyed the scene within with avian derision. The man was a tool – a pawn, not even of the level of Balk or the others. But useful nonetheless.

There were many such in the city – tools tailor-made for Old Father Fate. Men who schemed and plotted and worshipped the Nine Unfolding Paths, venerating the Great Mutator even as they were cast aside when their usefulness dimmed. This one was not one of them, but much like them in many ways. A true believer, with a fanatic's determination.

'He is here!' Brother Oleg, initiate of the Myrmidian temple, hissed as he crouched before the shrine to the goddess that adorned one corner of his cell. 'Here! In this temple!' He paused, head cocked as if listening. 'No, I – they failed.' Then, a moment later, 'I failed.' He cast a guilty glance at the crossbow he had hastily shoved beneath his cot upon returning. He had not expected him to be so fast. The other one hadn't been that fast, had he?

He wrung his hands together until they knotted painfully. The ivory-faced statuette stared blankly at him. He'd hoped the men he'd hired would do the deed, but, just as in the case of the other, they had failed. What had he been thinking? Mere mercenaries, hardened or not, against a knight of the Order? Madness.

No. Optimism. A hope he would not have to sully his own hands with the blood of a holy brother. 'Why,' he said plaintively, half-stretching his hand towards the statue. 'Why must it be this way? This cannot be right. It cannot–'

Pain flared in his arm and he snatched his hand back,

cradling it to his chest. Hissing in agony, he glared at the claw-like brand on the inside of his wrist. The mark of loyalty burned as badly as it had the day he had received it. As badly as the day the others had left the city for Svunum.

A croak startled him and he whipped around. Perched on the sill of the slender window of his cell, the crow cocked its pointed skull and fixed him with a dark gaze. A feeling of contentment flooded through him, causing the pain to fade. The crow squawked again. The Estalians said that Myrmidia might wage war with eagles, but that she spoke through crows, the cleverest of the clever birds. *And more readily found on battlefields*, a voice whispered in his head. He shook it aside. 'I understand,' Oleg breathed. 'But… here?'

The crow fluttered past him and perched on the statuette. It dipped its head, and Oleg stood, his hands clenching and unclenching nervously. 'Yes. Yes, I'll do it, if it can be done. And then? Then will you–'

But the bird took off before he could finish, leaving the same way it had entered. Leaving Oleg alone again. While it was terrifying to be in its – her – presence, it was somehow more frightening in her absence. Fear was a new thing for Oleg. He had had no fear of anything as a young man, but now that he was older, it gnawed at him. Fear of dying, fear of being found out by that treacherous abbot. His fingers curled, making fists.

Knock was of a kind with that fool, Berengar. That was what she had said. They were men who mouthed the Duties and paid lip-service to the goddess, but who were, in truth, merely politicians; pigs scrambling for temporal scraps.

He looked down at the mark on his wrist again. It was shaped vaguely like a feather. Like the feathers of her messengers. He stroked the brand and prepared his mind for what was to come.

There were those he could contact. Men of faith, though it was a darker faith than his own. The goddess had many weapons, and some were more horrid than others. He shuddered again. 'Goddess forgive me. We do what must be done.'

9

NIGHT FELL ON Marienburg, and though he was tried, Goetz found himself for once unable to sleep. The air smelt of foreign spices and rotten fish as the moon rose. It was a heady scent, and Goetz found it annoyingly pervasive. It had taken up residence in his clothes and in his hair and didn't look to be leaving anytime soon. His joints ached with the exertions of the day, and his head was full of questions. He lay on the rough cot that had been provided for him, and tried to puzzle it all out – his meeting with the Lord Justicar, the assassins, all of it.

Sweat rolled across the smooth planes of his face and neck, carving a trail down beneath the sackcloth shirt he wore. It was humid in the little cell, thanks to the marshes Marienburg sat on, and the only relief was from the sea breeze issuing through the window. He pressed his forearms to the stone and bowed his head, closing his eyes as he listened to the sounds of the city beyond.

The marks on his neck and face where the bird had attacked him were healing already though they ached almost as badly as the scars on his back. He'd learned that it wasn't unusual for the crows to do so, though he had to wonder about the timing. Something was going on, that much was obvious. Goetz was neither a witch hunter nor a spy, but he could smell a conspiracy easily enough. The question was how big was it? And what was its purpose?

Thinking dark thoughts, he went to the basin in the corner, where he splashed water on his face and chest. Water dripping down his face, he looked around. The cell was barren save for a lithograph of Myrmidia, which gazed down on him from over the basin. 'I don't suppose you'd like to illuminate me?' he said. The picture didn't answer. He didn't know whether to be grateful or not. As Goetz scraped his skin dry with his wadded-up shirt, someone knocked on the door.

'Enter,' he said, sliding into his shirt. The heavy wooden door of the cell swung inwards and admitted a young novice. Pale and stocky like most Marienburgers, the young man glanced curiously at the sword and armour in the corner before meeting Goetz's inquiring gaze.

'You asked to be woken after the final bell, brother-knight.'

'Yes, thank you, Brother Jerome,' Goetz said. Without waiting for a reply, he began to dress. The young man watched him for a while, eyeing Goetz's sword with something that might have been envy. Goetz ignored him until he slipped out. The brothers of the Myrmidian temple meant well, he was sure, but they grated on his nerves. There was nothing worse than a building full of would-be warriors with no real war to fight.

There were battles aplenty within the confusing jangle of Marienburg's almost organic streets, of course. Every minor princeling with a grudge was on the warpath six months out of a given year, looking to increase his portfolio or his influence. That discounted the so-called blood claimants to the long-vacant Barony of Westerland. Every two or three years, some minor cousin of the third sister's descendant would find foreign backing and take to the streets, looking to seat his thin-blooded rear on the throne.

In the end, it never amounted to anything. Regardless, the Myrmidians, as servants of the war-goddess, went to battle eagerly. As much so as the priests of Ulric, at any rate. But it was unsatisfying on a spiritual level to kill the same people over and over again. Half the younger novices prayed daily for another invasion from the north, and one that would reach their walls.

It all smacked of asking for trouble, from Goetz's perspective. Not a very knightly thing to think, but then, Goetz had never really wanted to be a knight. Architecture had been his passion as a boy. The shaping of stone and wood into something greater than either. He looked around the room again, noting the obvious dwarfish influence to the curve of the ceiling, and sighed. Nowadays, his studies tended more towards the construction of trebuchet and fortifications than simple habitation or decoration. Architecture was so much simpler than people. Stone held few secrets, plotted no schemes.

'I wanted to build bridges,' he said softly, meeting Myrmidia's gaze. 'But you wouldn't understand that, would you?' He scooped up his sword and drew it a few inches from its utilitarian sheath, examining the twin-tailed comet that had been stamped on the base of the blade just before he'd left Talabheim the first time. The sword had seen him through a number of battles. Steel never let down flesh. Invariably, it was the other way around. Slamming the sword back into its sheath, he buckled the belt around his waist and snatched up his helmet.

A few minutes later, after a last, long genuflection to the lithograph, Goetz made his way through the halls of the temple. Robed priests passed him, murmuring softly among themselves. They nodded to him, more out of respect to the sigils displayed prominently on his breastplate than any familiarity.

The rotunda of the temple of Myrmidia was a quiet place. Old weapons and battered, now useless, suits of armour decorated the curved walls. The latter rested in specially prepared niches, were they were cared for by the lay brothers who scoured them and anointed them in oils. The weapons and arms belonged to men who had died for civilisation in all its forms, martyrs to progress. Martyrs to the cause of order.

It gave Goetz a chill to see those cracked and empty shells with their deep brown stains and gaping rents. Not all belonged to men of the Order, some simply to adherents of the faith. There a Tilean hauberk, there an Estalian bowl helmet, and there, a mangled gauntlet, boiled in the gut acids of some breed of troll. Goetz touched his own breastplate, with its delicately engraved sun in the centre, and wondered whether or not it would ever decorate a niche like these.

His eyes were drawn to a dented helmet, its feathered crest shaved to a few pitiful quills that dipped depressingly. The date on the niche marked it as having belonged to a knight who'd fallen in battle with the Westerland pirates. In the Pirate Wars, when the merchant fleets of Marienburg had sought to eliminate the pestiferous enclaves that had, at that time, dotted the coasts of what had been Westerland and Nordland like rat-nests, the knights of the Order had supported them, sending armsmen and brother-knights alike.

Despite being mostly waged at sea, there had been land battles as well, as the Marienburgers had sought to take the pirate-towns that clustered in the marshes and wastes from their owners and put them to the torch. The Knights of the Blazing Sun had been at the forefront, there, as the only knightly order of the Empire to become involved in what was considered at the time to be the ever-independent city-state's problem and no one else's.

Standing in the temple proper, eyes closed, Goetz could almost hear the howls of the pirates as the knights thundered forwards on horseback, and the ground seemed to tremble beneath his feet. It must have seemed that the End Times had come for those doomed, sinful wretches. They had only their scurrilous captains to look to for command. But the knights had the goddess.

Goetz knelt at the feet of the statue, his sword flat across his knees. He had waited until the temple was empty to make his prayers, wanting the privacy. Eyes closed, he tried to clear his mind. Hands clasped about the blade, he brought the crosspiece to his lips and whispered a short prayer. Myrmidia, as ever, didn't bother to answer. Likely she had more important things to do. He sighed and stood.

'It is an honour to have you here, you know.'

Goetz turned. The priest was clothed as simply as the rest of his brethren, but his broad shoulders and scarred hands spoke of another life, one outside of the confines of the temple. 'It is rare that one of the men who brought her to us sets foot within these walls these days,' the priest continued.

'I had heard that they all left some time ago,' Goetz said. 'Gone to Svunum, I'm told, Brother…?'

'Oleg. Yes. Like others I could mention,' the priest said. He frowned. 'She is more than just a war-goddess, you know,' he said, gesturing to the statue. 'She is also the Patroness of Civilisation. That was what the Tileans call her. The Queen of Muses and the Mother of Invention.'

'Yes,' Goetz said, looking at the statue again. Why did the priest's name sound familiar? Where had he heard it before? Before he could puzzle it out, the shadows drifting across the marble face of Myrmidia seemed to alter it, and Goetz looked away, uncomfortable with the illusory expression he had seen there. 'Unfortunately, we of the Order are more often called upon for duties of war, rather than peace.'

'Both bring about the same thing, do they not, brother?' Oleg said, looking at Goetz intently. 'Order.' He made a fist. 'The goddess brings order.'

'I just wish that it didn't have to come at the point of a sword,' Goetz said, patting the hilt of his own. 'Still, if wishes were horses, every man would be a knight, eh brother?'

Oleg turned back to the statue of the goddess. 'Yes. I wanted to be one myself.'

'But?'

'A distinct lack of noble blood, I'm afraid,' Oleg said, smiling sadly.

Goetz shifted uncomfortably. 'I'm sorry.'

'It's hardly your fault, sir knight. More that of my parents, I should think.' Oleg chuckled.

'There are orders that do not require noble birth, brother,' Goetz said gently. Oleg snorted.

'Yes. But none who serve our goddess, eh?' He scratched at his wrist and gazed adoringly at the statue. 'She speaks to me, you know.'

'She speaks to all of us.'

'No!' Oleg said, his voice suddenly filled with heat. 'Not like me!'

'Brother–' Goetz blinked as realisation set in. Oleg! He recalled then why that name sounded familiar. But it couldn't be, could it?

'I'm sorry, sir knight. But it is the Second Duty… we do what must be done!' Oleg cried, drawing a knife from within his robe. Before Goetz could draw his sword, Oleg hurled himself upon him and they crashed to the floor, struggling.

'I didn't want to kill him!' Oleg hissed, straining to plunge the dagger into Goetz's throat. 'But she commanded it! And she must be obeyed!'

'Who?' Goetz snarled.

'Her! Myrmidia must be obeyed!' Oleg howled. Goetz drove a fist into the man's jaw, sending him sprawling. Even as he got to his feet, a shout set him spinning. Men clad in iridescent robes and brass, bird-shaped masks, lunged out of the darkness. Nine of them in all, they seemed to dance towards him with disturbing eagerness. He met the first one, his heavy blade sweeping aside the man's rapier and crashing through his screeching mask.

A sabre slashed across his arm, freeing mail links. Goetz backhanded the wielder, sending him flying and desperately parried a jabbing trident. 'Myrmidia!' he roared, hoping to wake the temple. 'Myrmidia!' He stamped on the trident and, as it dipped, cracked an elbow into its bearer's head, knocking him to the side. Goetz chopped down on the man's exposed neck, separating his head from his shoulders.

The sabre scraped against his cuirass and Goetz caught the blade with his arm, forcing it flat against his side. Turning, he ripped it from the man's hands and hacked at him, carving a canyon through his sternum. Shoving the twitching body away with his boot, he turned, countering another blow. The remaining six attackers swooped towards him en masse like a flock of birds, and they uttered weird, shrill cries as they came. Goetz fell back until he found himself pressed against Myrmidia's shield. 'Myrmidia!' he shouted again.

'Manann!' came a response and one of the remaining assassins slumped as a trident punctured his heart. Dietrich Ogg yanked his deadly prosthesis free and grinned savagely. 'Hello again, boy,' he said. Behind him, Aloysious Ambrosius parried a sword thrust and spitted his opponent with a thrust of his own, and the men of the Marsh-Watch moved forward with tridents ready. Somewhere above, an alarm bell was ringing, and the Myrmidians were spilling into the rotunda, clutching their weapons. Abbot Knock led them, a broad-bladed axe clutched in his hands.

'What in Myrmidia's name is going on here?' he roared.

'Ask Brother Oleg,' Goetz snarled. 'Where is he?'

'Brother–?' Knock paled. He turned one of the other priests. 'Find Oleg! And someone check on the seneschals!'

'Too late for them, I'm afraid,' Ambrosius said, cleaning his sword on a dead assassin's robe. 'These killed them as they entered. I am sorry, abbot,' he continued, nodding politely to Knock.

'How did you two come to be here?' Goetz said, glaring at them.

'We followed these, as a matter of fact,' Ogg said. He gestured with his trident. 'A thank you wouldn't be out of order.'

'My thanks, Grand Master,' Goetz said, after a moment. He shook his head and tried to catch his breath. 'I meant no disrespect.'

'None taken,' Ogg grunted. 'Sons of the Crow,' he said, kicking a body.

'What?' Goetz said.

'That's who they are,' Ambrosius said, sinking to his haunches and yanking a sleeve back from a limp arm. A feather-shaped brand stood out against the pale flesh. 'The Sons of the Crow. Or the Feathered Children, as they're called in Altdorf.' He stood and scratched at his eye-patch. 'They're worshippers of the Ruinous Powers. Cultists.'

'And why are they in my temple?' Knock said, staring at the bodies.

'One of your men opened the doors,' Ogg said bluntly.

'Oleg,' Goetz said, rubbing his back. He felt slightly sick as he contemplated it. 'Oleg let them in. He said that he was doing what had to be done.'

'Killing you,' Knock said slowly.

'Killing Athalhold as well,' Goetz said. 'He admitted it, as he was trying to do the same to me.' He looked up at the statue and tried to discern some sense from the pristine features that gazed blindly down at him. 'He said Myrmidia had commanded him.'

'There are cultists everywhere. At every level of our society,' Ambrosius continued. 'I'm satisfied that these were responsible for the death of your brother, and the attempts on you.'

'Because it's expedient to do so,' Goetz said dully. He looked at Ambrosius. 'You allowed them to enter. You want this whole affair swept away.'

'Yes,' Ambrosius said, meeting his gaze. 'We'll continue to look for this... Oleg, but like as not he was a secret cultist. I know these ones, they like schemes and deceits. Their plot was likely a simple one; get the Order at our throat and watch the fun.'

'You don't believe that for a moment, do you?' Goetz said.

'No. No, I think they were just as much pawns as the men you killed in that cul-de-sac, sacrificed to hide another move in someone's game.' He tapped his eye-patch. 'Regardless of the reason, it doesn't take two eyes to see that someone doesn't want you getting to Svunum.'

'Which is why it's in our best interests to see that you do,' Ogg put in. 'Beyond the obvious reasons of course.'

Goetz leaned back against the statue, a number of things falling into place. 'Athalhold... he wasn't sent to investigate anything. He was sent to deliver the order to abandon Svunum,' he said slowly. 'You think that's why he was killed.'

Ambrosius tapped the side of his nose. 'Berengar was right. You are a thinker.'

'He wanted the assassin almost as badly as we do. Killing knights can't be allowed. It gives the common man ideas,' Ogg said, jabbing at Goetz with his trident.

'Be fair. They already have ideas. But it shows them it can be done.' Ambrosius knocked his knuckles against his hip. 'Athalhold – was that his name? – was here to make your brethren leave. Only someone killed him before he got to do that. Initially, we suspected a private concern was the cause, but recent – ah – incidents...'

'Chaos,' Ogg said gruffly, rubbing his trident again. 'The fen-beasts are getting riled up. And we've got trouble in the walls as well. Strange things have been seen... not to mention these scum, painting the walls with corpse-daub and stealing beggars for midnight rites.'

'The Norscans are quiet,' Ambrosius said. 'And that's never good. Something is building, out there beyond the horizon. Interesting that it should do so now, eh?' he said, fixing Goetz with his good eye. 'Since the last sea-herd of Norscans bent on pillage crashed into our harbours, every member of your Order here has been penned up on that hunk of rock. We see their ships at a distance. Merchants trade with them. But they have abandoned the city... and perhaps more.'

'More?'

'Gunpowder. Iron. Stone. Wood. The makings of an army, a fleet. Any number of things.' Ambrosius ticked his fingers as he spoke. 'What are they building out there? Out of our waters, but close enough to – what?' He looked hard at Goetz. 'Some say it's an Imperial plot to re-take the city... a crusade for these uncertain times. We'd be quite the feather in Karl Franz's cap, eh?'

'We don't serve the Emperor,' Goetz said.

'Only when it suits you,' Ambrosius countered. 'Others say the knights are intent on invading Norsca. Laughable, but if they do, who shall bear the North-men's rage when such an attempt inevitably fails? Marienburg.' He smiled sadly. 'I think it's somewhere inbetween those two, myself. I think that whoever is in charge out there has now decided to declare his inde-pendence from any law save his own. And I think your brother's death, and the attempts on you, is nothing but collateral damage in an attempt to ensure that no one found out about it before they – whoever they are – were ready.'

'You can't think that they had anything to do with Athalhold's murder!' Goetz said. 'Surely Oleg was act-ing alone, or on behalf of this cult!'

'They wouldn't be the first men to turn pirate,' Ogg said. 'Or the last.'

'They aren't men. They are knights. Servants of Myr-midia,' Goetz said flatly.

'So was Oleg,' Ambrosius said quietly. Goetz sank down. There was nothing to say. 'It's a moot point any-way,' the Lord Justicar went on. 'We'll be setting sail for Svunum soon. I've got agreement from the Council, as well as the Naval Guild and the fleet-lords.'

'You intend to take it by force,' Goetz said, his mouth suddenly very dry.

'We intend to evict your brethren by any means nec-essary.' Ambrosius scrubbed beneath his eye-patch. 'I'll give you a week, barring travel time, to convince them to leave peacefully. After that... well.' He shrugged apologetically. 'Hexensnacht. An inauspicious day, what with the connotations of witchcraft, but appropriate enough, I suppose if you read into such things.'

'This isn't right,' Goetz said, looking at his hands. He looked up at the ceiling, where the painted face of Myrmidia seemed to frown down at him. 'We won that island through sweat and blood.'

'And we'll take it the same way,' Ogg said firmly, scraping the tines of his trident across his breastplate.

'A week,' Ambrosius said. He nodded to Knock. 'Abbot. We'll see ourselves out. My men will remove the bodies to the temple of Morr so that these festering carcasses do not foul your temple any longer.'

Knock watched them go, his wrinkled hands curling into fists. Shaking his head, he turned back to Goetz. 'I hope Berengar knows what he's doing.'

'How can they do this?' Goetz said. He looked at the abbot. 'How can the Grand Master just give away something our brethren died for?'

'Because he is Grand Master, Hector. It is his prerogative. And in this case, a wise one.' Knock held up a hand to forestall Goetz's protest. 'We – you – are fighting a war, boy. Not a skirmish, or a battle, but a war. A war against forces which we cannot hope to defeat. But we can forestall them, until such time as they can, and will, be defeated. Berengar knows this. He knows that not every piece on the board is valuable, and that value changes based on the board and on the players. Svunum is a rock, but it is also a stepping stone. An anchor. Worth more than every man on it, and worth nothing at all. Do you see?'

'I–' Goetz began. 'No. No, I don't see it. I can't see the world that way.'

'We're playing dice with the gods themselves, boy,' Knock said, putting a hand on his shoulder. 'Pray we win this throw and all the ones that follow.'

10

GOETZ LOOKED UP at the bearded face of Manann that glowered down at him from a spot over the archway to the immense double doors that led inside. The doors were open, indicating that the temple was open for business. The smell of fish was even stronger in the morning than it was in the evening, though the heat was less oppressive. Marienburg woke early and the clamour of the harbour rolled over this section of the city like a blanket.

He was tired, but hadn't been able to sleep. Oleg had not been found, and nothing in his cell had seemed out of place. Goetz fingered the amulet Knock had given him before he had departed. It was a simple thing, shaped like a spear-point and engraved with the Litany of Battle. *No Plan Survives Contact With The Enemy.* 'That's why he's called the enemy,' he said, finishing the Litany as he rubbed the ancient Tilean script. True enough, he supposed. His own plans seemed to have been co-opted by those belonging to others.

Why hadn't the Grand Master simply told him? Because he knew you'd protest. Maybe because Wiscard didn't know. Maybe no one knows except him… answers came quickly, though none seemed to fit the question perfectly. There could be many reasons that the Grand Master no longer wanted Svunum counted among the komturies of the Order; and just as many reasons for those there to want to keep it. But would they kill to do so? Kill a member of their own Order?

Consciously, Goetz knew that men killed for many reasons and if blood-relation didn't stay their hand, then why would shared allegiance? But it rankled nonetheless. 'If it's true,' he murmured, shaking the thoughts away. Perhaps Ambrosius's assertion was correct… perhaps the cult had undertaken the assassinations in order to sow confusion and chaos. Perhaps it was as simple as that. They could have waylaid messengers and stolen missives as well, especially if they had a man inside the temple of Myrmidia.

Maybe that was why Berengar wanted to dispense with the place. It was too much trouble, and too far from the Order's centre of power. It had outlived its usefulness, and the Brothers could better serve elsewhere. Still, to ask – no, to demand that they leave… Goetz sighed and clamped down on such thoughts. They served no purpose save to stall him from his duty.

Goetz stepped inside the temple, his boot heels loud on the polished pearl tiles that covered the floor. Fishing nets hung from the ceilings and he carefully brushed them aside as he made his way into the temple. Voices crashed over him like a wave as he stepped into the main rotunda. Tables carved from the bones of leviathans were scattered across the floor and, around each, men and women gathered, all talking at once. Some were merchants, others were seamen, and all were engaged in negotiations. Priests in sea-green robes threaded through the knots of argument, holding aloft smoking incense that smelt faintly of rotting seaweed.

'Brother Goetz?'

Goetz turned and looked into a face the colour of coral. A man's face, wrought from metal. A moment later a green-enamelled gauntlet raised the visor and a bearded face grinned at him. He was big and broad, with a broken nose and scars on his lips and cheeks. He was also fully-armoured from head to foot in the most intricately engraved suit of plate-mail that Goetz had ever seen. Goetz hesitated, then extended his hand and the man clasped his forearm.

'Erkhart Dubnitz,' the man said, still grinning. 'A humble sword-brother of the Order of Manann. I was asked to meet you and – ah – guide you through things.'

'Ogg,' Goetz said. 'He sent you to shepherd me?'

'The Grand Master is a – ah – a man who worries easily,' Dubnitz said. He pulled off his helmet, revealing a shorn scalp covered in scars.

'He's paranoid, you mean.'

'That too.' Dubnitz gestured to the crowd. 'Though, in fairness, it can be a bit confusing, if you're not used to it.'

'Yes,' Goetz said, looking around. 'You allow merchants in your temple?'

'Not my temple. His,' Dubnitz said, indicating the statue of Manann that loomed over the gathering.

Manann crouched on scaly legs, balancing his weight on a trident.

'Impressive,' Goetz said.

'Not quite as nice to look at as your goddess, but we're partial to him, yes.' Dubnitz chuckled. Goetz bristled slightly, but forced a chuckle. 'This is your first time in our fair freistadt I understand?'

'Yes,' Goetz said. 'I was born in Talabheim, but this…'

'It's a cesspit, right enough,' Dubnitz said, nodding. 'But it's ours.'

'I didn't mean to imply–'

'Didn't say you did, didn't say you did!' Dubnitz swatted Goetz on the shoulder. 'Calm, brother. With a knight of Manann to guide you, you'll find your way safely to shore.'

'I place myself in your capable hands,' Goetz said, smiling despite himself.

'That's the spirit,' Dubnitz said. 'Now, I've made some preliminary introductions with a captain of my acquaintance – he's a Hochlander, but we shouldn't hold that against him.' He laughed and swatted Goetz again. For a brief, painful moment Goetz was reminded of Berlich. Dubnitz was a similar sort – loud and boisterous, with an easy manner. He led Goetz through the crowd, most of whom got out of the way quick enough. Dubnitz didn't appear to be one to slow his stride just because someone was in the way.

'I thought we might get a bite to eat first, however,' Dubnitz went on, clapping his hands to his belly. 'Bargaining on an empty stomach is the surest way to get the worst end of the deal.'

He led Goetz through the crowd, towards a long

galley lined with tables groaning beneath the bounty of the seas. Great platters heaped with boiled seaweed and fish squeezed inbetween immense, intricately carved wooden bowls of chowder and stew. Goetz found his eyes drawn towards a roasting spit where a full-grown shark was rotated slowly by a priest in a sea-green robe.

'This is...' He trailed off, at a loss for words. Dubnitz nodded happily and began piling a plate high.

'Manann's bounty, brother. Eat and enjoy!'

'Is this all fresh?'

'Every day. Pickled cod?' Dubnitz said, extending the bobbing morsel to Goetz. When the latter shook his head, the big knight dropped the slimy chunk into his mouth and chewed with relish. 'I do so love pickled cod. Manann's gift to humanity.'

'Some might disagree with you there,' Goetz said, staring queasily at the other man's plate. 'Me among them.'

'Bah. You have the palate of a bumpkin,' Dubnitz said, slapping one paw on the closest table and causing it to tremble. 'A bumpkin!'

'I heard you the first time,' Goetz said. 'I prefer my food hoofed and horned rather than be-finned, is all.'

'Try some octopus. It's like a cow,' Dubnitz said, his mouth full.

'How exactly?'

'It has legs.' Dubnitz caught his look and shrugged. 'Fine. But if your growling belly interrupts our negotiations, don't blame me.'

'Your Order is a strange one, friend,' Goetz said as they moved to a table to sit. 'You open your temple to merchants, you put out a feast...'

'All in Manann's name,' Dubnitz said, plucking tiny fish bones out of his mouth. 'Besides, we have to fund our activities somehow.' He cast a mock baleful look at Goetz. 'It used to be that we hunted pirates.'

'Oh,' Goetz said, leaning back in his seat. 'Was our Order that effective then?'

'By all rights, Svunum should have been ours,' Dubnitz said, cracking open a crab shell. 'It's been a bone of contention for several generations now. Or so I'm told. I don't pay much attention to politics, I'm afraid,' he continued, unconvincingly.

'Really?'

'Fine. I do, but in this city it's a survival trait. Crab claw?'

'No thank you,' Goetz said, pushing the proffered claw away. 'And how did the men of my Order feel about that?'

'As far as I know, they barely acknowledged it. We're a small – if prosperous – order. The Merchant Council though, they had a few issues.' Dubnitz shook the crab claw. 'Imperial ties, they said. Spies for the Empire, they bellowed,' he said theatrically. 'Quietly, of course.'

'Of course,' Goetz said, leaning forward. 'Our Order bears no great loyalty to the Empire though.'

'No?' Dubnitz sucked the meat out of the claw and tossed the shell onto his plate. 'I suppose the Merchant Council didn't see it that way. And my Order certainly didn't.'

'Is that why they're planning to invade then?' Goetz said, fighting to keep the bitterness out of his voice.

'Ah. Yes, well,' Dubnitz looked embarrassed. 'That is a bit awkward. But that's why we're here, eh?' He gestured at the temple. 'To get you out there so that the awkwardness is limited to bad feelings as opposed to grievous bodily harm?'

'Yes,' Goetz said. Still frowning, he watched as an urchin in a frayed blue uniform scurried up to Dubnitz. The big man bent low and listened as the boy whispered into his ear. He stood and motioned for the boy to sit.

'Be a good lad and finish my plate for me.' He looked at Goetz. 'It looks like the Hochlander is here, brother. Would you care to speak to him?' The urchin stared at the heaped food in evident greed and Goetz chuckled.

'I suppose so. Lead on, brother.'

The Hochlander's name was Feldmeyer and he was waiting for them at a table covered in squid-like carvings. 'Captain Feldmeyer,' he snapped as Dubnitz introduced them. Feldmeyer was a screw-eyed man clad in naval motley, with scars on his face and hands. 'I didn't know I'd be playing host to one of his sort,' he continued, jerking a calloused thumb at Goetz.

'One of my sort?' Goetz said.

Feldmeyer held up a hand. 'No offence, sir knight.' He looked at Dubnitz. 'I have enough trouble with those on Svunum. I'm not taking one on my ship.'

'What sort of trouble?' Goetz said, leaning forward and thrusting his face towards Feldmeyer. 'Speak up man. What sort of trouble?'

Feldmeyer hesitated and then looked at Dubnitz who knocked his knuckles on the top of his helmet. 'Honesty is always the best policy, captain,' Dubnitz said.

'Trouble is all,' Feldmeyer said, sitting back with a frown.

'Is the Order's hospitality not to your liking?' Goetz said, trying for humour.

'Svunum isn't to my liking,' Feldmeyer said, yanking on his beard. 'Nothing that close to the Sea of Chaos ever did a man any good. You'd do well to remember that, Sir Knight.'

'Thank you for your concern, captain, but I'm quite certain I can handle myself,' Goetz said. 'I won't be staying long in any event.'

'You're young to be wearing that ribbon,' Feldmeyer said, gesturing to the ribbon of rank attached to Goetz's breastplate by a hardened seal of wax. The seal had been chipped in the fight in the cul-de-sac, but it still held firm.

'And you're old to be a boat captain,' Goetz said.

Feldmeyer blinked. 'It's a ship.'

'There's a difference?' Goetz said innocently. Dubnitz stifled a chuckle and Feldmeyer yanked on his beard again.

'Enough, Feldmeyer, you old pirate,' Dubnitz said, slapping a palm on the table. 'I named a price earlier. Is it still fair?'

'I suppose.' Feldmeyer made a face. 'But only because we're already going that way!' he said, making a sharp gesture. 'And I want Manann's blessings.'

'Do I look like a priest?' Dubnitz said, rising. He waved a hand at one of the green-robed men and summoned him over. Feldmeyer looked at Goetz.

'We catch the tide at sunrise, sir knight. If you're not there, we won't be coming back to get you,' he said.

'Have no fear, captain. I won't be late,' Goetz said.

'That's what I'm afraid of,' Feldmeyer mumbled. Goetz stood and joined Dubnitz, who stood waiting for him a little ways away.

'I want to thank you for going to the trouble...' Goetz began.

Dubnitz made a rude noise. 'It's not me, as I said. Besides, we sword-brothers need to stick together, aye?'

'Stand together or hang separately, you mean?' Goetz said, smiling crookedly. Dubnitz blinked, then gave a roar of laughter.

'Exactly! Exactly!' He caught Goetz a ringing slap on the back, nearly knocking him off his feet. 'Now, you have less than a day left in our foul little burg... what would you like to do?'

THE URCHIN RATTLED his cup insistently, his blue uniform grimy and fading. Dalla grunted and waved him away sharply, pulling the edge of her hood lower over her face as she did so. She sat slumped against the wall of a dockside tavern, watching the temple of Manann. It straddled the line between the more respectable bit of Marienburg's docklands and the rowdier areas.

Dalla made little distinction between either, finding it hard enough to process the fact that a city could be this size and still function. She was no awestruck babe, to be driven to fits of panic by the sheer number and size of the stone structures that surrounded her, but even now it was impressive. She shifted uncomfortably and pulled her already damp cloak tighter around her.

Her father had not wanted her to come, reasoning that it was too dangerous. Then, for him, life itself was too dangerous. Besides which, Dalla had her own duties to attend to... such as spying out the fattest vessels setting out across the Sea of Claws. The ones ripest for the plucking by her godi.

She spat. The godi was a vain, irritating man, but smart. Smarter than most godar, who, as a rule, seemed to think that diplomacy was what happened when you lost a battle. No, Eyri Goldfinger was smart. Cunning even, with the savvy of a salt-hardened sea wolf to temper his greed. He was greedy, no mistake there. He wanted everything the world had to offer. Even things that were manifestly not his to take.

Her grin surfaced like a shark's fin and swiftly vanished. She was the daughter of a gudja; Eyri would remember that now, and if he didn't, his missing fingers would certainly remind him. She spat to clear her mouth of the sudden taste of bile, and shifted her seat. Above her, a number of crows perched on a window, their croaking cries drifting down to her. She did not look up. Crows were the eyes of her father's enemy, even as her father used wolves and seals and, once, a fish.

Not all crows, true. But there were bound to be some here as everywhere. A particularly harsh caw caught her attention and she blinked, her vision momentarily dazzled by the sunlight glinting off polished metal.

'Einsark,' she hissed. One of *them*? Here? He was not clad head to toe in his gilded iron skin as the others had been, as the others always were, but he was one of them if the insignia he wore were any indication. Her hand clenched tight on the hilt of her sword and she forced herself to relax. No. Not here. Besides which, she still had a duty to perform.

But, perhaps she could kill two birds with one stone. She rose smoothly to her feet and started towards the wharf.

11

'NOT WHAT I had in mind, exactly,' Dubnitz said, looking up at what had once been the Order of the Blazing Sun's Marienburg Komturie. Now, however, it was little more than a mausoleum, its treasures moved to the Myrmidian temple and its inhabitants gone to Svunum. Like most Myrmidian komturies, it was circular, though not overly large, with sloping walls and a tiled roof quite unlike anything else in the Empire. Goetz knocked on the portcullis and turned.

'Don't feel that you have to accompany me,' he said. 'Besides, you'll get to see it soon enough, won't you?' Goetz said irritably.

Dubnitz snorted. 'Oh, but I do. It would look very bad indeed for two brothers of your Order to die under our noses, now wouldn't it?' Dubnitz said. He caught his helmet by the visor and struck it against the portcullis, setting it to ringing. 'A knight killed during an alley skirmish? Bad for all our reputations.'

'Worse for Athalhold, I think,' Goetz said, dropping

to his haunches and removing his glove. He ran his fingers across the stones of the street, his eyes narrowed.

'Hnh. You're likely right about that, true enough. What are you doing?'

'Looking for the – ah!' Goetz stood as the portcullis gave a shriek to rival that of the sea gulls circling overhead and began to rise. Dubnitz gaped as the iron-banded doors swung in, admitting them. Goetz gestured. 'After you.'

'What the devil was that?'

'Progress. Also, a way of ensuring that we're never locked out of our own keeps.' Goetz followed Dubnitz inside. The courtyard wasn't large, though it seemed more expansive, empty as it was. 'Arabyan, I'm given to understand. A bit of artifice they learned from the dwarfs. The sluice-gates are Tilean, however,' he said, gesturing to the steel shutters that lined the interior walls of the keep.

'And those are for…?'

'Boiling oil. Naphtha. Dwarf-fire. I understand the komturies in the Border Princes often let orcs into their central keeps and burn them alive as a matter of course. Best way to deal with the greenskins, really.'

'Your lot do enjoy their gewgaws, don't you?' Dubnitz said, not unkindly.

Goetz nodded. 'There's more to siegecraft than block and tackle.'

'Is that the one for throwing things or the one for hitting things?'

'Both,' Goetz said. 'We only use such things as the push-gate in cities, however. Only place the under-structure will support the pulley systems that–' He stopped as he saw Dubnitz's eyes begin to glaze over. 'Never mind.'

'It's –ah –it's not really honourable, is it?' Dubnitz said, swatting the sword on his hip. 'I mean, we burn out pirate nests readily enough, but to turn your own komturies into weapons…'

'The Second Duty,' Goetz said, shrugging. 'We do what must be done.'

'Myrmidia is a harsh one, no two ways there,' Dubnitz said, nodding to the statue that occupied a niche at the rear of the courtyard. Myrmidia at rest; her shield by her foot, her spear against her shoulder. Goetz looked at her and felt a moment of disconnect as his eyes met those of that inhumanly perfect marble face. He blinked and turned away.

'What?' he said.

'I said why did you want to come here?' Dubnitz said.

'To see what I could see,' Goetz said. 'The brothers left in a hurry. I want to know why they didn't come back.'

'And you think the answer is here?'

'No. But I wanted to get a sense of them,' Goetz said, looking at the other knight. 'A komturie is an extension of the brothers who inhabit it, by and large. It conforms to their methods and manner.'

'A house is a house is a house,' Dubnitz said.

'Not for us. Every hochmeister of the Order is expected to improve the defences and design of his komturie when he is made master. To make of it a monument to Myrmidia's influence. The latest works of literature and art and science. The latest engineering innovations.' Goetz turned in a circle. 'To let a house simply sit, silent and abandoned, is almost…'

'Heretical,' Dubnitz finished for him.

'Yes,' Goetz said. He shook his head. 'A funny word to use. Considering how often we're on the other end of it, I mean.'

'I had heard that the Grand Theogonist was on the warpath again about the "proper conduct" of his Imperial Majesty's knightly orders.' Dubnitz snorted. 'Lucky thing we don't have to bother with the old stirpot.'

'Nor do we, in truth.' Goetz shrugged. 'If the Empire rescinds its hospitality, we'll simply move the Order elsewhere. Unlike the Reiksguard or the White Wolves, we are not tied to Imperial demesnes.' He sighed. 'Still, it'll be a black day when it comes to tha–'

The portcullis chose that moment to crash down with a roar of straining metal, causing them both to whirl in surprise. 'By Manann's scaly nethers!' Dubnitz bellowed as the echo faded. 'Did you–'

'No. And it certainly shouldn't have done it on its own.' Goetz drew his sword and looked around. 'Wait – hsst!'

'What?'

'Listen!'

Faintly, the sound of boot leather slapping against stone came to them. Goetz looked up at the walls, his eyes widening. 'Oh no.'

'What? What?' Dubnitz growled.

'The sluice-gates!' Goetz grabbed the other man's arm and shoved him towards the stairs. 'Up! We have to get up! Go!'

With a grinding of stone on metal, the steel shutters of the sluice gates began to swing open. A moment later, boiling pitch sprayed out of them in tight arcs. Goetz hissed as some splattered his legs and he shoved

Dubnitz up the stairs, forcing him towards the second level of the keep.

'Why is there even still boiling pitch in there?' Dubnitz yelped as some splashed him.

'Dwarfen warming runes,' Goetz snapped. 'Work better than a cauldron any day!'

As they reached the top of the stairs, the streams of pitch abruptly shrank to a trickle and then tapered off completely. 'They must have run out,' Goetz said. 'There couldn't have been much in there to start with, not after all this time.'

The crossbow bolt skidded across the cheek-piece of his helmet and spun him around. He slammed back against the balustrade, dazed. Dubnitz spun, roaring. A second bolt caught the knight of Manann high in the shoulder, knocking him backwards. He clattered down the stairs with a sound akin to a crockery shelf going over. Goetz staggered upright, trying to spot their attacker. Across the expanse of the courtyard, a figure raced up the stairs to the next level.

'Dubnitz!' Goetz said. He looked back. The other man was on his back on the stairs, jerking at the crossbow bolt that stood at attention from the shoulder joint of his armour.

'I'm alive!' Dubnitz grunted. 'Barely a scratch! Get after him! I'm right behind you!'

Goetz darted after the assassin without further hesitation.

OLEG KICKED THE door to the bell tower closed and tried to catch his breath. He looked around, frowning. The bells, used to summon the knights to battle or prayer, had been silent since the brothers of the house had departed, and the engraved faces of Myrmidia glared at him from the dusty surface of each.

'It's not my fault,' he hissed, scratching at the puckered brand on his wrist. It burned like acid, and had since the previous evening when he'd failed to kill the knight. 'He's faster than the other one. Better,' he protested.

Something croaked. He swallowed and turned. The crow cocked its head and flapped its wings, its beak seemingly filled with a carnivore's teeth. But that wasn't right, was it? Birds didn't have teeth. Not normal birds at any rate.

'Myrmidia protect me,' Oleg murmured. The crow squawked and ugly black feathers rained down on him. They burned where they touched him and he shuddered away. 'I'm sorry! I'm sorry!' he said, backing away from the door and drawing his sword. He could hear the knight's boot heels thudding against the stone stairs.

The crow hopped across the bells, following him, its beady eyes watching him. He looked at the bird and said, 'What would you have me do? I can't defeat him. Once, maybe when I was younger, but not now... not here.' The crow croaked again, and the pain in his wrist intensified into something sublime.

He'd been left behind by the others when they'd gone. Left behind because he was too old, too weak to be of any help where they were going. Left behind to watch and wait and keep their trail hidden. He had done that, all of it and more. Now... now he would be rewarded for his faithful service.

'Oh. Oh yesss,' he grunted. He sank to his knees, his sword dropping from nerveless fingers. The crow flapped its wings and he crawled forward, opening his mouth. With a shudder of its feathers, the black bird thrust itself into the air and crossed the distance between them in an eye-blink. Then, in a moment of discomfort, it squeezed into Oleg's mouth and scrambled down his gullet. Oleg gagged and fell over, shuddering as the bird burrowed into him.

In moments, things moved beneath his skin, spreading outwards from the brand, growing and flaring. Bone quills pierced his flesh and he groaned. He raised his hands in supplication and tried to give thanks to the goddess for her blessing, but his skin had already pulled away from his jaws and the only sound he could make was a screech.

GOETZ PAUSED IN the doorway to the bell tower, listening for the telltale sound of a crossbow's mechanism as the scream faded. He eased the door open with his sword. He'd fancied he'd heard voices, just before that plaintive howl, but who would be up here with the assassin? The door swung open with a creak. He smelt bird dung, and heard the raucous croak of a crow. Slight shapes darted among the rafters of the tower.

'Where are you? Oleg? Brother Oleg?' Goetz said, sidling around the bells. 'Why have you been trying to kill me?' There was no answer. In truth, he hadn't expected one. Goetz turned, sweeping the tower with his gaze. Nothing. Were could he have gone?

The answer occurred to him almost a half-second too late as a swordpoint drove into the wood of the tower floor and the crossbowman dropped from where he'd been crouching atop the bell mechanism. He ripped his sword free and launched a salvo of strokes at Goetz, who back-pedalled furiously.

They traded blows for a moment, moving back and forth across the floor. Then Goetz caught the weight of the man's blade on the crosspiece of his hilt and twisted, sending his opponent's weapon flying. Before the man could react, Goetz pinned him to a bell, setting it to ringing dully. The assassin gagged and clutched at the sword, pulling himself forward as his hood slipped from his face.

Goetz jerked back as a bony beak snapped shut inches from his face. A thicket of fangs jutted crookedly from the protuberance and the red eyes set on either side of the triangular head blazed with madness and agony. Irregular feathers poked through the stretched and wrinkled skin and the thing's hands were more like the talons of a bird. Its claws scraped his fingers and he released his sword with a cry of disgust.

'What are you?' Goetz said, stumbling back.

'Blessssed,' Oleg hissed, yanking his sword out of his sternum and tossing it aside with a clatter. Claws extended, it leapt for him and he thrust up an arm to protect himself. Goetz stumbled under its weight as its malformed jaws snapped shut around his vambrace, piercing the metal. He drove a blow into where a normal man would have had kidneys and it screeched, swiping at him. The claws scored his helmet and the force of the blow sent him reeling against the wall.

The creature hunched towards him, circling, its head cocked in a distinctly avian manner. Beak-jaws clacking, it sprang again. Goetz spun aside and the creature hurtled over the edge of the tower and out over the courtyard. It fell with a shriek.

Breathing heavily, Goetz peered over the edge. Clawed fingers fastened around his helmet and he was yanked unceremoniously off his feet. Goetz grabbed hold of the creature's wrist with both hands before it could release him and they hung suspended for a moment.

It held tight to the stonework of the tower with its free hand and taloned feet. The bird-like head darted down at Goetz, pecking at his hands as it hauled him closer. Whipping back and forth, Goetz snatched out at it and grabbed its lower jaw in desperation. Its teeth slammed together on his hand and he screamed.

Planting the soles of his boots against the tower, Goetz twisted his hips and strained every muscle he had, wrenching the bird-man from its perch and sending them both hurtling towards the courtyard below!

12

AS THEY FELL, the creature squirmed closer, its snapping jaws aimed at his unprotected throat. Goetz grappled with it and tried to ignore the ground that was fast rushing up to meet them. Grabbing a handful of loose skin and feathers he yanked the creature forwards and crashed his head against its own, the metal of his helmet ringing hollowly as it met the monster's mutated bone. Then he shoved away from it, clawing desperately for any sort of purchase to arrest his fall.

His hand slapped into Dubnitz's waiting palm and the knight of Manann gave a roar. Before Goetz's full weight could settle, Dubnitz slung him up over the balustrade and against the wall of the second level in a massive display of strength.

The green-armoured knight sank to his hands and knees as Goetz fell flat, his face pressed to the cool stone, his shoulder and back numb from both impact and exertion. When Dubnitz looked up, his face was red and covered in a sheen of sweat. He made a sound like an exhausted horse and staggered to his feet. 'What in the name of Shallya's milky bosom do you call that?'

'Improvisational strategy,' Goetz groaned, sitting up. He tore off his glove and examined the hand the monster had bitten. Faint indentions beppled his palm, but the skin hadn't been broken. He breathed a silent prayer of thanks to whoever had sewn the chainmail inside his glove and then hauled himself up, using the wall for support.

'Not that,' Dubnitz grunted, rotating his shoulder experimentally. 'That,' he continued, hiking a thumb towards the courtyard. Goetz stepped to the edge and looked down. The creature looked like a broken doll discarded by a careless child. Its limbs were bent at odd angles, and it seemed deflated, emptied of all malice and ferocity.

'I don't know what that is,' he said, flexing his hand.

'It's a mutant, obviously. Some foul Chaos-thing.' Dubnitz tapped the broken-off crossbow bolt still protruding from his armour. 'Never knew one of them that could use a crossbow, however.'

'Or a sword,' Goetz said. He looked down at the body for a moment longer and then turned away. 'Speaking of swords, mine is still up there.'

Goetz led the way, ascending the stairs to the bell tower much more slowly than before. The door still hung open, but the crows were silent. Dubnitz stayed by the door as Goetz scooped up his sword. As he straightened, however, he thought he saw something. Something tall and foul, that glared at him from the shadows in the corner of the tower. Goetz froze, unable to move or speak as the form stepped towards him.

Eyes like dying embers fixed on his own and something hissed inside his head.

A band of sunlight chose that moment to strike the dusty surface of the nearest bell as the latter shifted on its frame. A deep, bone rattling toll sounded, shaking Goetz from his paralysis. The face of Myrmidia, engraved on the bell, blocked out those horrible eyes and Goetz stepped back, his sword raised.

The bell swung back revealing the retreating form of a scraggly crow. It hopped to the edge of the tower and took flight without a backwards glance. Goetz watched it go, then started as Dubnitz touched his shoulder.

'Everything all right?'

'I – yes. Fine. Everything's fine,' Goetz said, sheathing his sword. 'Did you set the bells off?'

'I thought you did,' Dubnitz said, looking at the bells curiously.

Goetz didn't reply. The two men retreated back the way they had come, followed by the sounds of the bells, which gave voice to a mournful rhythm.

'GET THOSE CRATES loaded!' Captain Feldmeyer of the merchant-ship *Nicos* bellowed. Feldmeyer was a thirty-year veteran seaman. Twelve of those years had been spent plying the coastlines of the Sea of Claws and his sun-darkened frame bore the scars to prove it.

The Sea had its secrets, and its dangers, resting as close as it did to the Sea of Chaos where the black arks sailed and worse things than kraken crawled in the deep. Feldmeyer had fought kraken before, and point-eared corsairs from Naggarond, and orcish reavers and Norscans gone raiding. His crew were a motley bunch, as diverse a lot as one could find on the Northern Seas.

Tileans, Estalians, Arabyans and Bretonnians crowded the decks along with men from a variety of Imperial provinces, moving about the tasks associated with a ship setting sail. Like their captain, they were veterans.

His first mate stalked past, scarred palm resting on the handle of the club stuffed through his belt. Feldmeyer whistled and caught the man's attention. 'Has our passenger arrived yet?'

'I have, actually,' Goetz said, stepping up the gangplank, his armour in a bundle on his back. 'Permission to come aboard, captain?'

Feldmeyer nodded and made a curt gesture, waving the first mate off at the same time. 'You're late.'

'You said sunrise,' Goetz said. He squinted upwards. 'And the sun has yet to rise.'

'Metaphorical sunrise,' Feldmeyer grated.

'Ah.' Goetz set his bundle down and rested a hand on his sword. 'You don't seem happy to see me, captain. Is there some reason for that? Have I given offence somehow?'

'No. Not you,' Feldmeyer said. He spat over the side and turned away. Goetz took the opportunity to look around, noting that he himself was the recipient of any number of similar covert glances. It took him a moment to realise that they weren't looking at him so much as at his armour.

But while it was understandable that a member of one of the Empire's knightly orders might attract some small attention away from the Empire's borders, the looks he was getting were anything but curious. Rather, they were the look a man might give an adder he had just stumbled upon.

He shook his head and turned to watch as the

green-robed priests from the temple of Manann began their rituals of blessing for the ship's journey. Dubnitz had explained that the Order of the Albatross, the ritual navigators of the temple, were paid a hefty sum to perform their rituals. The stink of sacred oils filled the air as urns containing ambergris and other concoctions were slopped across the deck and the sound of the deep rolling hymns of Manann, Stromfels and Mermedus filled the air.

The latter two brought a chill to Goetz's flesh, being songs of ill-omen and disaster. Holy statuary representing the three faces of the god, mounted on the three prongs of an overlarge trident. The priest who held it up was a muscular specimen, and wore a speckled breastplate emblazoned with an albatross in flight. As he paced the deck, stabbing the sea breeze with the trident, his fellows swabbed the deck with their holy oils, singing all the while.

Goetz stepped aside as oils spilled across the deck towards him and held his breath as the stink of fish paste and whale fat rolled over him. At the last, the burly priest thumped the deck with the butt of the trident three times and roared out, 'Manann! Bless this boat!'

'That's… an interesting blessing,' Goetz said tactfully.

Feldmeyer snorted. 'Manann is a god for little time with niceties.'

The priests tromped back down the gangplank a moment later and the ship set sail with the first breeze of morning. Goetz couldn't help feeling no small amount of relief. Two nights in Marienburg and he'd almost been murdered twice. Granted, the assassin was dead now, but he had a feeling that that wasn't the end of it. Ogg had demanded that he spend the night in the temple of Manann, and Abbot Knock had concurred. Oleg, or whatever – whoever – that creature had been had been disposed of by the servants of Morr, cremated in the cleansing flames of a marshland pyre, overseen by the Marsh-Watch.

'Hexensnacht' was all that Ambrosius had said to him as they watched the body crumble to ash. 'One week.' Goetz hadn't replied. He had been too preoccupied, wondering what awaited him on the island. Thinking of the attempts on his life brought him back to Svunum. In their history, they'd run up against Northern fleets more than once, being assailed by Norscan fleets at least twice in the last century. Add in the occasional attack by orc reavers or Chaos fleets come south, and Svunum had well earned a reputation for being the rock upon which many a dream of empire had broken.

An island fortress, built on a rock that straddled a major trade route. Goetz smiled at the thought. It was a common enough tactic these days, employed every-where the Order had a presence. Each komturie was a bastion of the finest that civilisation had to offer, but they were also gatehouses, blocking or opening the way to the civilised world proper. 'Or so we like to think of ourselves,' he murmured. Now it was almost over. The Order would be forced to abandon Svunum and all that they had built;and for what? A political ploy? A move in some game that he couldn't understand?

'What was that?' Feldmeyer said, joining him at the rail. The captain was frowning. It seemed to be his default expression.

'Never mind. Something I can help you with, cap-tain?' Goetz said.

'We make port in Svunum in two days. Be ready, for I don't intend to stay there any longer than necessary.'

Goetz turned. 'A man might think you had something against us, captain. Care to speak your mind?' Feldmeyer's frown deepened and he strode off without replying, bellowing orders to his crew. Goetz watched him for a moment. Then, shaking his head, he turned back to the ocean and quickly lost himself in its depths. Staring down, he watched the trail of foam ride along the lower half of the hull, contorting itself into a myriad of shapes. He looked up at the sails. The wind was good, insofar as he could tell.

Two days, Feldmeyer had said. Then what? He thought of Oleg again, and a slight shiver of revulsion coursed through him. Chaos was not an unfamiliar enemy. Not since that night in the Drakwald, and the sweetly singing thing that had almost devoured him. Beastmen too, he knew. The assassin had not been one of their kind, though. Had Oleg truly been a cultist, as Ambrosius said? A mutant? Was that what he was facing? Had Chaos taken Svunum? The thought sent a chill through him and the pain returned, caressing his nerve endings with delicate cats'-claws of agony. Sweat beaded on his skin despite the chill of the sea.

His wound had fully healed now. Before he'd left the city, Dubnitz had brought a priestess of Shallya to see him and she had seemed surprised that such a wound had closed so quickly. Now it was nothing but another patch of scar tissue to join the others. But the pain was still there. Still in his head. He wondered if it always would be… perhaps he was just as marked as Oleg had been. Just as 'blessed'…

Hands clenched, he looked towards the horizon.

The coastline was still visible, though only barely. It was a rare seaman who didn't hug the coast to some degree. Especially this near the Sea of Chaos, where worse things than pirates lurked in the coves. The Sea of Claws was little better. Goetz had heard that there were sea serpents there.

A speck cut through the air, and a half-familiar sound tugged at the edges of his hearing. 'Hunh.' Goetz rubbed his eyes, certain he'd seen something on their trail. A bird? Seabirds certainly weren't rare, even here, though Sigmar alone knew what they looked like a few miles south, at the edges of the Sea of Chaos. He dismissed the thought and pushed back from the rail, turning his attentions elsewhere.

DALLA WATCHED THE einsark board the merchant vessel and bared her teeth. With one of *them* aboard, it made the tub an even worthier prize. Eyri would not be pleased that one of the Svunum-filth was there, but her father would, sure enough. If they could question him–

'Pfaugh. Counting wolves before they've sprung,' she said to herself. The vessel was heading for Svunum, and the route was an open one. They could easily intercept it, provided she delivered the message in time.

The wharf was alive with the sound of commerce as she headed for Old Jarl's shanty-hall. Jarl had been a raider in his youth, but he'd since grown accustomed to the softer, Southern life. He ran a mead hall of meagre size and splendour down near the city's shore-gate. He also sold information on cargo convoys and other ripe prizes to proper Norscans; and, in a pinch, he could get you out of the city.

Jarl's was a dilapidated structure, and it smelt like a sty, but she breathed a sigh of relief as she slipped inside. It was as crowded as always, full of drunks of every race and description, and Jarl himself loomed behind the bar, looking like an overstuffed bear-skin that someone had crammed into a food-spotted doublet.

'Dalla?' he said, spotting her.

'Don't bellow so you old sea-cow,' she hissed, gesturing sharply. 'I need to borrow the cog.'

'The cog?' Jarl's frost-coloured eyebrows went up. 'Something important?'

'A pretty bit of pillage,' she said, flashing a grin. 'Nothing more. Eyri will reimburse you.'

'The day Goldfinger reimburses me is the day the dwarfs shave their beards,' Jarl snorted. 'I didn't hear of anything worthwhile leaving today. What ship?'

'None of your concern,' Dalla said, leaning over the bar. Though he outweighed her twice over, Jarl leaned back. 'The cog?'

'In use, I'm afraid,' Jarl said.

Dalla's eyes narrowed. 'What?'

'It's in use. Some of Tassenberg's boys are looking to use the river to–'

'I need that cog, Jarl!' she snapped, interrupting him. 'Is it still here?'

'Downstairs, but–'

Dalla whirled and darted for the privy where Jarl kept the entrance to his own private wharf. She jerked it open and slugged the man squatting inside. Booting him out, she struck the hidden catch and started down the slippery, foul-smelling stone stairs.

Jarl indulged in a bit of smuggling among his other

activities, and he'd chosen the location of his establishment carefully. Built over the bones of an old warehouse, it had access to both the river and the sea via an underground dock. Normally Jarl used it and the sturdy wooden cog moored there to bring in illicit merchandise, but every so often he used it to get something – or someone – out.

Ignoring the smell of the day's privy leavings that sat fuming in the nightsoil barrels set at calculated points, Dalla started down the makeshift corridor that led to the dock. She loosened her sword in its sheath as she moved.

She slowed as she heard voices. A group of street-ready toughs stood on the dock, discussing something in the flickering torchlight. Five of them in all, with the cog bobbing up and down just beyond. They were brutal looking creatures – Tassenberg's men, she recalled Jarl saying; Uli Tassenberg was one of the city's most ruthless purveyors of flesh. His men had kidnapped youths of both sexes from as far away as Cathay, though they usually stuck to those they could snatch near the river. Likely they were planning another raid now. Well, Tassenberg would just have to make do.

Dalla drew her sword and stepped out into the light. 'I'm taking the boat,' she said, loudly.

The men looked at her, then, as one, began to laugh. Before the echoes of that first burst of mirth had faded, Dalla was among them, cat-quick and deadly. Her sword was no rapier or sabre, but instead a chopping tool and as her wrists flickered and snapped it did just that. She hammered into the men with brutal efficiency, wasting neither words nor energy.

It was not unusual for women of her race to take to

the sword. They were not like the frail creatures of the South, afraid to even step outside without an armed escort. By the time she was thirteen, Dalla had killed two would-be suitors and joined four raids, earning her prizes honourably. The mail she wore and the sword she carried had been among the latter.

She had fought Kurgan and orcs and even the black-armoured elves who sometimes swept the coasts looking for easy pickings. She had fought them all and won, or at least survived. The street-toughs, surprised as they were by the ferocity of her assault, were no match for her. The stones of the floor greedily inhaled the blood. Kicking the last man off her blade, she turned as Jarl stepped off the stairs. He began to curse loudly.

'How am I supposed to explain this to Tassenberg?' he sputtered, his big hands clenching in fury. 'Those were five of his best!'

'I killed them. What is to explain?' she said, cleaning her blade on her cloak. 'I'm taking the cog.'

'And if I say no?'

Dalla stopped her cleaning and fixed him with a cold stare. Jarl hesitated. He looked around at the bodies and then at her and spat. 'Fine! Take the damn cog! Get out of here! And tell Goldfinger he owes me!'

Dalla didn't bother to reply. She untied the line and dropped into the cog. With broad, easy strokes of the paddles, she set out to sea.

13

BY THE TIME night began to descend, they had lost sight of Marienburg entirely.

Goetz had a hard time of it, enough so that he eventually abandoned his position above decks and retreated to the berth Feldmeyer had grudgingly provided him. He had never travelled by sea before, and it wasn't an experience he was not enjoying all that much.

Swaying in his hammock, trying to get comfortable, Goetz finally had time to appreciate the full joy of ocean travel. His stomach began to protest almost as soon as he stretched out. Eyes closed, Goetz mumbled a prayer and listened to the dull thud of water pressing against the hull.

He rose after a while, unable to relax. Sitting on the edge of his hammock, he stared at his armour where it lay in a heap across his bag. Grabbing his sword, he unsheathed it and laid it across his knees. Then, he began to sharpen it. The gentle scrape of the stone across the steel helped him ignore his stomach.

'It's sharp enough, I think,' a voice slurred.

'Captain,' Goetz said. Feldmeyer swayed slightly before plopping himself down on a box of fruit. A bottle of rum hung from his fingers and as Goetz watched, he tipped it back and took a swig.

'I hate you, you know,' Feldmeyer said, as he lowered the bottle.

'I got that impression, yes,' Goetz said, bemused.

'Damn knights. Always shouting orders and swinging swords. Killing people.'

'Yes, we do indeed kill people,' Goetz said. He slid the stone down the length of his sword again. Feldmeyer squinted at him.

'Why?' he said.

Goetz opened his mouth to reply, then shook his head. He looked back down at his sword. If Feldmeyer noticed that he hadn't replied, he gave no indication. 'It's a strange place, Svunum,' he continued. 'Strange people.'

'Who? The knights?' Goetz said.

'No. The others. Not... Norscans.' Feldmeyer made a face, as if he were searching for a particular word and it was eluding him. 'I like Norscans, mostly. 'S' why I trade with them. But I don't like them on Svunum.'

'Any reason in particular?' Goetz said carefully.

'No,' Feldmeyer said petulantly. He took another swig. Goetz waited for him to continue, but he remained silent. Eventually, a savage snore alerted him to the fact the captain had fallen asleep. Goetz rose and went on deck.

The first mate, a brawny man of indeterminate origins, started towards him and Goetz gestured towards the hold. 'He's down there. Asleep.'

'Sleeping it off, more like,' the mate said, with obvious affection. He sighed. 'I am sorry he disturbed you, sir knight.'

Goetz shook his head. 'I'm sorry I disturbed him. As I so obviously have.'

'Not you,' the other man said. He tapped Goetz's jerkin and the stylised sun emblazoned there. 'Your Order has a bad reputation out here.'

Goetz frowned, taken aback. 'What? Why?'

'Usual reasons,' the mate said. 'Fine line between pirates, privateers, merchants and smugglers. Hard times makes for hard men. The knights on Svunum don't make as pretty a distinction as we'd all like.'

'We do what must be done,' Goetz said, automatically. The mate looked at him, his broad face showing nothing. Goetz sighed. 'Yes, fine. I get your point. What have they done besides that?'

'Every so often they'll pressgang a crew and a ship. You don't hear much about them later. Some folk think they're building a fleet. Others that they're taking slaves to build up that damn great fortress they've got.'

'You've seen it?' Goetz said. The sky was growing light on the horizon as the chill of night began to retreat. A cold mist had settled across the water, and out in the darkness, something heavy splashed. Goetz looked away.

'At a distance.' The sailor shuddered. 'I'd not want to try and storm it, that's for sure.' He fell silent. Goetz didn't press the issue. Instead, he watched as the man carefully stuffed Moot-weed into a hand-carved pipe and lit the bowl. Soon he was puffing contentedly. 'We've been running this route for six years now, and it just gets bigger every year.'

Goetz held his tongue. It wasn't unusual, given the isolation and the nature of the threats they faced. The komturies that dotted the larger towns of the Border Princes did much the same. The mate continued, puffing on his pipe, 'It's almost a city these days, from the looks of it. Not that the captain lets us go ashore. Not that I blame him, mind.'

'The islanders are dangerous then?' Goetz said.

'One way of putting it, right enough,' the man said. 'They–'

'Ware! Ware!'

Both men turned as the cry echoed from the rail. It was echoed a moment later by the voice of the lookout at the top of the main mast. 'Ware! Dragonships!'

They came out of the mist rolling over the Sea of Claws like the great leviathans of legend – dragon-prowed and armoured. Instead of fire, however, they breathed arrows. Goetz twisted out of the way as the first volley thudded home. Some of the crew screamed in pain as the arrows bit flesh and punctured bone.

Goetz raised his head and saw that there were three of the dragonships and they were circling the *Nicos* like wolves, propelled by heavy oars that slapped the water like thunder-strikes. Raiders for the most part, the Norscans clung precariously to the precious few clean stretches of land between the sea and the Far North, where the Winds of Chaos blew. More civilised than the inland cousins who had formed the backbone of every invading army from the North for the past few centuries, they were no less feared by those living on the northern coasts of the Empire. While they might not have had the taint of Chaos in their blood, they were just as savage as any beastman or marauder.

'Arm yourselves!' the mate bellowed, thrusting himself back from the rail as more arrows thudded home in the deck. 'Up you sea-dogs! Up!'

'I'll get the captain!' Goetz said, heading below-decks. Feldmeyer, however, was already on his feet, seemingly sober. He swung a pistol towards Goetz as the latter descended. Goetz froze and raised his hands.

'What is it? What's going on?' the captain snapped.

'Norscans, captain. They appear to have taken an interest in us,' Goetz said, moving past him towards his bundled armour.

Feldmeyer gaped at him. 'What? No! It can't be!'

'It is. Now if you'll excuse me, I'd like to get dressed before our guests arrive,' Goetz said, unrolling the bundle. Swiftly he began to don his armour, snapping buckles and pulling straps with experienced fingers. When he had finished, he saw that Feldmeyer had already fled onto the deck. Goetz slid his shield onto his arm and drew his sword. He extended it, admiring the play of the lantern light across the blade for just a moment. Then, dressed for war, he clambered up on deck, his sword naked in his hand and his ribbons of merit fluttering in the sea breeze.

'You'll sink like a stone in that,' Feldmeyer said upon sighting him.

'I don't plan on having to swim for it, captain. You?' Goetz said, stabbing his blade point-first into the deck. He stood calmly, hoping no one had noticed the tension in his limbs or the slight tremor in his hands. A massed battle was always somehow more frightening than any brawl or skirmish. Perhaps it was the chaotic nature of the thing… even the best strategists only had the dimmest idea of how a given battle might go. The fewer participants, the easier to control things. To end them swiftly.

'This isn't right,' Captain Feldmeyer snarled.

'More men than you have likely made that claim in these waters,' Goetz said.

'No! You don't understand… it's not raiding season,' Feldmeyer said, glaring at him. 'They shouldn't be here!' He pointed an accusing finger at the boats circling them. 'Why are they here?'

'Offhand I'd say they've come to gut us and turn us into shark bait,' Goetz said. 'Look!'

More arrows swept the deck in a desultory fashion and then there was a crunch of metal on wood as a claw-footed climbing plank extended from the closest of the boats and thudded into the rail of the ship. A moment later, two more planks latched on at different points.

'Prepare to repel boarders!' Feldmeyer roared, pulling his pistol and his cutlass both. The first of the Norscans were over the rail a moment later, clad in furs and leather and wielding broad-bladed axes. Others beat the flats of their swords against their brightly coloured wooden shields as they hopped over the rail, and bellowed out savage hymns.

Then, with a roar worthy of any sea-borne leviathan, the battle began!

Goetz moved to meet the Norscans, his sword singing out to parry a looping axe cut even as he rammed his shield into its bearer's midsection. He shoved the man over the side and jerked back as a saw-edged sword chopped into the rail, spattering him with splinters. Goetz traded blows with the Norscan for a moment, then battered the man's weapon aside and chopped through the crude hauberk he wore, crushing his ribs. As the warrior dropped, an arrow skidded across Goetz's helmet, setting his ears to ringing.

A pistol barked nearby, sending the archer spinning into the water. Feldmeyer tossed the smoking weapon aside as he met the attack of another raider with his cutlass. Goetz didn't even have time to thank him before he was lost in the melee. The deck was already slick with blood as Feldmeyer's crew fought with desperate abandon against their attackers. One of the latter, naked save for a matted loincloth of wolf skin, bounded towards Goetz, howling and frothing.

The axe he carried flashed out in seemingly random patterns, chopping the air and the deck with equal ferocity. The Norscan howled like a wolf and his eyes were wide, his neck a mass of straining veins. Goetz had heard of such men – *ulfsarks*. Men possessed of a battle-lust that would make an orc's look puny. They fought until there were no enemies left, or they died.

'Myrmidia!' Goetz roared, blocking a blow that would have gutted him. 'Up, Talabheim! Haro, Talabecland!' The ulfsark paused, as if puzzled by the foreign battle-cries. Then he charged forward, snarling. His axe chopped whole sections out of Goetz's shield, rendering it down into so many useless splinters that he discarded it with a curse. The berserker came again, a web of spittle drenching his jaws.

Goetz met him and, for a moment, they traded ringing blows. In a spray of steel flinders, the berserker's sword shattered as Goetz swept it aside, and the berserker dove on him, digging for his face with the jagged stump of the sword.

Goetz's sword slid up into the man's belly and

surfaced from his back. The berserker jerked and gnawed the air as his spasming fists beat at Goetz. Then, with a groan, he went limp. Goetz heaved him aside and climbed to his feet. He shook his head, trying to clear it, and turned only to reel back as a wooden shield smashed into his face. Instinctively, he lashed out, trying to drive his attacker back. Shaking his head to clear it, he took a two-handed grip on his sword and fell into a defensive stance.

The Norscan was smaller and slimmer than the others. A youth perhaps, though his eyes had the hard glint of experience to them as they glared at Goetz through the slits in his helmet. The sword in his hand was of better condition than most and it flickered over the rim of his shield with startling alacrity. The tip sliced through Goetz's ribbon of rank and it fluttered away on the wind.

Goetz, rather than stepping back, moved into the blow, letting the second thrust glide over his shoulder. His own sword pierced the centre of the shield and he shoved his opponent back. With a twist of his shoulders, Goetz ripped the shield from his opponent's arm and flung it across the deck.

They circled one another after that, weaving a complicated pattern of strike and counter-strike. For every one blow that Goetz managed, the Norscan made three. Goetz's armour rang with the other man's lunges, but so far none had found a way past it.

They fought for what seemed like hours but was, in reality, only minutes. Sweating despite the chill rolling off the sea, Goetz stepped back, lowering his sword. The Norscan took a breath and lowered his sword.

'Good fight,' he said, in a surprisingly high-pitched voice.

'No such thing,' Goetz said. The Norscan looked at him with what might have been pity. Goetz frowned, feeling his anger surge. He sprang forward, gripping his sword in both hands. He chopped down. His opponent threw himself out of the way as Goetz's blade chopped into the deck.

The Norscan's sword darted in at Goetz's exposed side and he felt warmth blossom along his ribs. Panic burned through him and Goetz grabbed his foe's wrist, pinning him in place. The flat of his sword caught the edge of the Norscan's helmet and sent it flying.

A woman glared up at him, her eyes blazing with hate. Surprised, Goetz released her sword-arm and stepped back. 'What–' Goetz began. Then, a blow caught him on the back. A second numbed his hip. He turned awkwardly, and the haft of an axe smashed into his face, sending him crashing to the deck in a daze. Before he could even attempt to rise, a foot pressed down on his throat. He looked up at the woman through bleary eyes.

'I am Dalla Ulfarsdottir, Svunum-filth! Tell your master who it was who sent you to its bosom!' she snarled, raising her sword. Blackness claimed him a moment later.

'No!'

Dalla snarled as someone grabbed her wrist and wrenched her around. A stiff blow caught her in the jaw and sent her stumbling back. After nearly tripping over the einsark's unconscious form, she regained her balance and extended her sword.

'He must die!' she snapped.

'Agreed. But not like this,' Eyri growled. 'People – our

people – need to see him die,' he continued.

'There are enough here to witness it now!' Dalla snapped, gesturing to the men who had boarded the ship. Fully two-dozen Norscans stood on the blood-washed deck, their eyes riveted to the scene before them. She raised her sword and started forward. None of Eyri's crew made to stop her.

Her sword chopped down, but shivered to flinders inches from the unconscious man's skull. Dalla jerked back, her pale face crimson with rage. 'What–' The blood drained from her face as she caught sight of the elderly figure pushing through the crowd towards her.

'I seem to recall that you thought we could take him alive, daughter,' Ulfar said, poking her in the chest with his staff. 'Have you then changed your opinion?'

Dalla said nothing. Her hands curled into fists and she stepped back, allowing her father to move past her. With a grunt, the old man sank to his haunches and traced the already purpling bruise on the knight's skull with two fingers. 'His skull is cracked, but he'll recover.'

'Took a half-dozen blows to even get him off his feet,' Eyri said. 'He wears more armour than a Kurgan.' He spat a wad of phlegm onto the deck and sniffed.

'Not quite so much as that, I think,' Ulfar said. He traced the outline of the blazing sun engraved across the swooping curves of the cuirass and sighed. 'He's not from Svunum.'

'What?' Dalla said, picking up the fallen man's sword and testing its balance. 'But he wears their sign!'

'Mayhap they wear his,' Ulfar said. 'Regardless, he is not of them.'

'Perhaps he was going to join them? The others did, after all,' Eyri said, scratching his chin.

Ulfar stood with a groan and nodded tersely. 'Possibly.'

Eyri made a face. 'Don't play seer with me old man. Do you know or not?'

'We should kill him, just to be safe,' Dalla said, glaring at Eyri, who raised his hands in mock surrender. She looked at her father. 'At the very least it'll be a clean death.'

'Aye, because the manner of his passing is what's important here, isn't it?' Eyri said. 'No. I agree, he needs to die, but he needs to die where our people can gain strength from it. In the pit with the rest of the monsters.'

Ulfar looked away. 'I will not gainsay you, godi.'

'But…?' Eyri said, grinning crookedly. 'There's always a "but" with you, my faithful gudja.'

Ulfar looked at Dalla, and then up, at the rising sun. 'But nothing. Do with him as you will.'

14

THE ORC'S MAUL crashed down on him, driving him inches into the bloody soil. Goetz gasped and floundered, unable to breathe. The maul rose up, blotting out the sun, and the orc's piggy eyes narrowed in anticipation.

'This isn't the way it happened!' Goetz coughed, rolling aside just as the maul struck the ground with a dull thump. He tried to get to his feet, but his body felt brittle and broken. Another blow caught him on the hip and he rolled across the ground, his every nerve screaming in agony. 'It's not what–'

The orc laughed and the laugh became a snarl and suddenly it was no longer an orc, but a stag-headed beastman. Goetz made to rise, but arrows sprouted from his wrists and thighs like barbed roots, holding him in place as the creature trotted forward, his own sword raised to strike. Goetz thrashed in agony and the sky above him seemed to rupture and a face peered down through the clouds–

His eyes shot wide and he looked up into the Norscan woman's grim features. She rose from beside him as he sat up to the accompaniment of the dull clinking of chains. Goetz coughed and looked around. He was below-decks somewhere, in a cramped hold. Other bodies, chained as he was, lay scattered around. He had been stripped of his armour, save for the quilted undershirt, and bound in chains.

'Where am I?' he said hoarsely. He felt sick. Nauseous. His temples were pounding like a dwarfen smithy and his limbs felt loose and weak. The old pain in his side and back flared and he winced. 'Where am I?' he said again, trying for forceful, and afraid he only got desperate.

The woman – Dalla, he recalled – said nothing. Her knuckles were white where she gripped the hilt of a sword – his sword, he realised with a start. 'That's my sword,' he said.

'Mine now,' she spat, after a moment. 'Too good for the likes of you.' Her accent was atrocious, and it took him a moment to puzzle through it. When he had, he made a face.

'Says the pirate,' he said. Her boot lashed out, catching him in the chest. He slammed back against the wall and a groan escaped him. Every muscle in his body felt as if it had been dipped in acid, and his lungs struggled to pull in air. 'Perhaps I misspoke?' Goetz gasped, clutching at his chest. 'Privateer, perhaps? Would you prefer corsair?'

'We are not pirates. We are Norscan. We are the wolves of the sea, and everything in the sea is our prey,' she said, glaring at him. 'You are our prey.'

'Duly noted,' Goetz muttered. 'Any reason you chose us in particular?'

'What?' Dalla said, looking nonplussed.

'Only, it seems to me that obstacles to my goal are popping up at every turn,' Goetz continued. 'And I am not a believer in coincidences…'

'And what is your goal?' she said, sinking to her haunches and leaning against the sword, its point dug into the deck. 'Why are you here, einsark?'

'Einsark?' Goetz repeated, rolling the word around in his mouth.

She tossed her head impatiently. 'Iron-skin. Or brass-skin, in your case. Like the Kurgan or the dwarfs. You wear enough metal to crush a sane man.'

'My armour, you mean?'

'No. This–' she swatted the hauberk she wore. 'This is armour. What you wore was ridiculous.'

Goetz said nothing. He examined her through bleary eyes… she wasn't a classical beauty, not with the pale scars that cut across her cheeks and the bridge of her nose. Broad shoulders and slim muscles made her as far from the women he was used to as it was possible to get and still be of the same gender.

She drew his sword and sank to her haunches, pressing the tip of the blade against his throat. 'If I had my way, I'd–' she began, but was interrupted by a barked order from the stairs leading to the upper deck.

She rose and turned, replying in kind, her face flushing, though whether in anger or embarrassment, Goetz couldn't tell. Another Norscan stood on the stairs, his thumbs hooked into the wide, studded belt he wore over his furs. He wore a conical helmet and his dirty blond beard flared beneath it like a spade. He jerked a wide hand upwards and Dalla gesticulated with the sword, the tip coming dangerously close to Goetz's nose. Then, with what he could only guess was a curse, she stalked past the man without looking back.

The Norscan watched her go, then strode over to Goetz. He grinned down at the knight. 'She was about to kill you but good.'

Goetz blinked. 'Your accent–'

'I do a fair bit of trading along the coasts,' the Norscan said. 'Captain Eyri, that's me.' He swatted his chest with his palms. 'Or Eyri Goldfinger, around some fires. Chief Eyri, if you like.'

'Why did you attack us?' Goetz said.

Eyri eyed him speculatively, then said, 'Why not?' He shrugged. 'I'd watch yourself around Dalla, however. She hates you, brass-skin.'

'I've never met her before,' Goetz said.

'Wish I could say the same,' the Norscan said, squatting. 'Dalla is a bad one. A witch, like her skinny-shanks of a father no doubt. And she's got a temper.' He chuckled. 'Dead is dead, I say. It doesn't matter who – or how – it happens, unless there's profit to be had in the doing.'

'Why are you so concerned for my safety? I am your prisoner, am I not?'

'If Dalla kills you prematurely, I'm out no few coins,' Eyri said, rubbing his thumb and forefinger together.

Goetz felt a chill creep down his spine. 'I won't beg for my life,' he said.

The Norscan gave a roar of laughter and slapped a meaty hand against his thigh. 'Good! Or I might just let the witch-girl chop you up.' He fluffed his beard. 'You're marked for the pit as it is.'

'The pit?'

Eyri rose and beamed down at him genially. 'It's a

good death, as such things go. I caught a troll a few weeks ago. That'll be a fine fight to see, I think.' Chuckling, he turned and left the hold, leaving Goetz alone with his thoughts.

After a time, he took hold of his chains and tested their weight. Gathering his legs under him, he hauled on them, trying to pull them loose from their moorings. He set his feet against the wall and pulled, his muscles burning with exertion. He rolled his arms side to side. He knew how much pressure a given mooring plate could take, especially when fixed to wood. He couldn't break the chains, or the plate, but he could – there! There was a crack of wood and the mooring plate sprang off the wall, bolts and all. Goetz fell backwards onto his rear and sat for a moment, shaking. His head swam, and he shook it viciously, trying to focus.

'Impressive. Now you come with us.' Goetz spun as Eyri stepped down into sight, followed by four men. The Norscan clapped his hands together. 'Chains make noise, you know. And this is quite a small vessel.' He smiled and gestured. 'We're only a few miles out, so you may as well come up on deck.'

His men moved forward and Goetz sprang to meet them. He swung the chains out and caught one on the side of the head, sending him staggering over the other captives. As the other three closed in, Goetz swept the chains out, driving them back. With a jerk of his wrists he sent the chains looping around one man's hand and hauled back, yanking him off balance and into his companion. Goetz dodged past them and headed for Eyri, head lowered.

The big Norscan drew a polished club from his belt and brought it down just as Goetz reached him, dropping the knight to his knees. 'You've got spirit, I'll give you that. You are worth every penny I'll get for you,' Eyri said.

Goetz staggered as he was propelled up on deck. He fell, eliciting a round of laughter from the watching Norscans. As Goetz clambered to his feet, he caught sight of Dalla watching him from the prow, her expression unreadable. He turned as he was shoved forward and saw what was waiting for him beyond the rail.

The fog began to thin even as the drummers on the aft deck began to pound on the bear-hide drums. The inlet was a semicircle of rocky shore and scabrous, malnourished scrub pine that seemed altogether more menacing than it should have.

The village crouched on the rocky shore like a dog that had been whipped one too many times. The greasy smoke of a hundred cooking fires rose and rolled out over the water, bringing with them the stink of boiled fish and bear fat. As the dragonships scuffed along the shore, Norscans leapt over the sides and grabbed the great anchor hooks that dangled from the rails, dragging them through the surf towards the shore, where others waited with mattocks.

The anchor-spikes were driven into the shore by swift blows and the ships were dragged up out of the grip of the tide. 'Welcome to Eyristaad, brass-skin,' Eyri said, baring his teeth at Goetz. 'It's as good a place as any to find your way to the halls of the gods.'

15

GOETZ WAS DRAGGED through the streets, his chains looped around the axle of a trundle-cart. Eyri stood on the cart, gesticulating and bellowing to the crowd that bellowed back in reply. He held Goetz's cuirass over his head and angled it so that it caught the sun. The noise of the crowd seemed to double and clods of earth and other, less fragrant, substances smacked into Goetz's battered frame.

Goetz ignored the pelting and crowd both. He glared at Dalla, where the warrior-woman stalked alongside the trundle-cart, her fingers dancing protectively across the hilt of his sword. He shook his head and looked around. Eyristaad was small, as towns went. Less a town, really, than a collection of villages that had merged together around the mouth to an isolated inlet. Tradesmen and merchants shouted at the crowd and one another, hawking crude wares. Stray dogs ran yapping underfoot. Even the most remote outpost of the Empire had more a veneer of civilisation than this place. Abruptly, they came to a halt. The men guarding

Goetz knocked him to his knees and Eyri hopped off his cart. 'Well brass-skin, what do you think?'

'I've seen prettier pigsties,' Goetz said, trying for urbane politesse.

Eyri cuffed him. 'Be polite.' He tossed Goetz's cuirass into the mud at his feet. 'You can have it back now. Like as not, it won't do you any good.'

Goetz looked at his filth-stained cuirass and then back up at Eyri. 'What do you mean?'

'I told you, you're going in the pit.' Eyri squatted and tapped two fingers against the battered breastplate. 'It's rare we get one of your kind for an evening's entertainment. My people will want a show.'

'Give me my sword and I'll see what I can do,' Goetz said.

Eyri grunted. 'You'll take what you're given, brass-skin.' He stood and shouted an order. The crowd raised a cheer as Goetz was dragged into a wooden outbuilding. It was only when they were inside that Goetz realised that the entire structure had been built around a wide pit dug into the rock. It reminded him of the theatres in Talabheim, with raised viewing platforms surrounding a circular stage. Only these platforms were crowded with jeering Norscans, rather than clapping Talabeclanders.

His handlers cuffed him and sent him sprawling, and then laughed and joked in their guttural fashion. Blows, pokes and prods sent him reeling up the rough-hewn stairs, and the hiss of a blacksnake made him lose his footing. The whip snapped a chunk out of the rail and Goetz grabbed it and pulled hard.

The whip-man howled as he was jerked forward and Goetz sent him flying through the rail to land on the floor in a crumpled heap. Spear-butts and clubs were his reward and an exquisite jewel of agony blossomed in his side as the blows connected with his newly healed wounds. He half-fell on the stairs, and the Norscans growled and groused as they jerked him up.

As he was dragged along a creaking walkway, Goetz caught a glimpse of the pit. A pack of half-starved wolves surrounded one of the pale-furred bears he had heard occupied the mountains here. The fight was a bloody one, and as he watched the bear swatted a leaping wolf from the air, breaking its neck with one powerful blow.

He was unceremoniously tossed into a wooden cell and his chains were stripped from him with efficient brutality. His cuirass was tossed in as well, to land with a clang on the floor. Goetz got to his feet just as the door was slammed shut, leaving him alone. He snatched up his breastplate and began to buckle it on as he turned from the door, eyeing the cell's interior.

It was a squalid square, with sunlight pouring in through the holes in the slats. His engineer's mind began calculating the stresses and pressures needed to force an opening.

'It won't do any gut, yes?'

Goetz turned as a heap of rags unfolded into a battered heap of a man. Another Norscan, he was small by their standards, and he looked as if he had died and been dug up soon after. Bloodshot eyes met Goetz's, and the man smiled, displaying broken teeth. 'No way out, yes?' he said, in broken Reikspiel. 'Go nowhere, yes?'

'No,' Goetz said, and began to run his hand along the wall. In the neighbouring cell, something moved.

Something heavy. The adjoining wall suddenly creaked. Goetz scrambled away from it.

'No way out, yes? Ha – ha!' the Norscan wheezed.

'What is it? What's in there?' he said. The Norscan only shook his head and laughed harder. The wall creaked again. It was followed by a snort, and then a foul odour wafted through the cracks in the wood. Goetz gagged. On the other side of the wall, something gave a grumbling moan. Then the wall shuddered, as if it had been slapped by a huge hand.

Looking down, his eye caught a number of rusty brown stains on the wood. More stains ran along the wall. Blood, he was certain. 'Keep it fed, yes?' the Norscan cackled. 'Keep safe, keep it fed!'

'What?' Goetz was about turn as the Norscan slammed into him with frenzied strength. A broken chunk of bone, sharpened to a razor-edge, stroked his throat and Goetz made a desperate grab for the skinny arms. The man howled like a broke-back wolf as Goetz slung him around and planted him against the wall. The makeshift bone knife flew from the spasming hands even as cracks appeared in several of the boards that made up the wall. The thing on the other side gave a roar, and the Norscan shrieked in obvious terror.

Goetz eyed the cracks in consternation. If the creature got in here they wouldn't stand much chance. Another slap caused the floor beneath his feet to tremble. A red eye glared at him through a crack, and the slobbering sound that followed caused Goetz to shudder in revulsion. The Norscan clawed at his arms and tried to shove himself away from the wall. 'Keep it fed, keep safe! No escape, yes?' he whimpered, kicking weakly at Goetz.

Suddenly realising what the stains meant, Goetz hurled the man aside in disgust. 'Get away from me,' he snarled. The Norscan scuttled away, cowering in a heap in the corner. Goetz sank down in an opposite corner, near the door, and eyed both the madman and the wall behind which their monstrous neighbour lurked.

Outside the cell, he could hear the crowd roaring in pleasure as the bear snarled and wolves howled. As the noise reached a fevered pitch, Goetz, decision made, lunged to his feet and moved to the far wall of the cell. Through the gaps in the boards, he could see the town beyond.

'No no no no escape, yes?' the Norscan muttered, not looking at him.

'No. No escape,' Goetz said, grabbing two slats and working them loose. When he had created a gap, he shoved his way through and swung out onto the outside wall. Below him an armed guard paused to urinate in the alleyway between the pit and the next building along. Goetz grinned mirthlessly and dropped onto the man as he finished.

His weight drove the Norscan an inch into the mud of the alley, and Goetz grabbed the man's hair, shoving his face deeper into the muck. The Norscan flailed for a moment, then went still. Goetz rose, breathing heavily, and stripped the man's cloak from him. As an afterthought, he smeared mud across his cuirass, dulling it, and yanked the unconscious man's sword belt loose and draped it over his shoulder before snatching up his crude helmet.

His first thought was to find a boat, but he dismissed the idea. There was a distinctly nautical gap in his education, and leaving without looking for any survivors from the ship left a bad taste in his mouth. Moving swiftly, he pulled the helmet over his head, trying to ignore the crawling sensation that he was going to wind up with lice.

The village looked better from this side of captivity; people went about their business much the same as in Marienburg, albeit with a bit more crude humour. The women were freer with their bodies and mouths, hurling crude obscenities at children and grown men alike as the latter proved a bit too free with their hands.

He passed a stall selling skinned wolves for their meat, and a beast-master selling squalling malformed pups as their mother, a bony spike-covered brute whose ancestor might have been a wolfhound, snarled inside her cage. Mutation was rampant here, though not so much as the Sigmar-botherers of his childhood would have had him believe. Children ran and played in the muck, the same as in any city. He was forced to step aside for several of the latter.

He made it as far as the wharf before he heard the hue and the cry of his captors behind him. Cursing, he left the boats behind and moved into the shanty town. He didn't run, knowing it would only encourage pursuit. Instead he made it look as if he were searching houses, even as he kept an eye out for something that looked like a temple.

The Norscan idea of architecture lacked the sharp angles of the Imperial School of Measurement, but it made up for it with a 'bigger is better' ethic that made finding the temple of Mermedus easy work. It rose up from the shore like a pile of splintered keels and hulls, and it was both savage and impressive.

A stone carving of Mermedus, the dark mirror of Manann, rose up in front of it, crouching on its flippers. It, like its temple, was crudity manifest, but there was a raw power to it nonetheless. Mermedus had more in common with the brute-god Stromfels than with the more civilised Manann, but there was an eerie similarity. A wide mouth gaped from within a tangled beard, and shark-like rows of stone teeth protruded. The eyes lacked Manann's serenity, and were instead narrowed with predatory intensity. Mermedus clutched a wide-bladed sword and an anchor rather than a trident, and looked ready to use either to sweep aside worshippers and enemies both.

As he'd hoped, the slave-market had been set up in front of the temple, and men were being led up to the auction block in chains. More than just the unlucky crew of the *Nicos* were in evidence, and the crowd of customers ebbed and swelled as Goetz approached.

The slaver was an obese Norscan covered in tattoos, his thick ginger beard curled into greasy plaits. He bellowed out prices, insults and suggestions with seeming abandon as he jerked the chains and ropes that held his merchandise. There were men and women from as far away as Cathay, and even a few altogether more disturbing prizes. A Kurgan, covered in strangely-angled scars and blasphemous tattoos, roared out crude jeers at the guards who surrounded him with spears. They seemed nervous despite the chains that had been wrapped around the barbarian's thick frame.

Besides the Kurgan, there were a number of pale-haired Nordheimers, their pale faces slack with dull ferocity. Their hands and necks were trapped in wooden stocks and their feet were chained to the auction block. As Goetz watched, they yelled out oaths and cursed at their captors.

Anger boiled up in him as he drew closer, and he fought to keep his hand from his sword. Slavery of this sort was practically unknown in the Empire, especially in Talabecland, where even a peasant wouldn't hesitate to spit in a lord's eye if the opportunity presented itself. To see men chained and branded as cattle or merchandise roused a fury in him that he had rarely felt.

Forcing himself to stay calm, he looked around. There were too many people to risk a rescue. The crowd would pull him apart before he got ten steps. So what–?

He saw her a moment later, drifting through the crowd, her white limbs flashing in the grey light of the day. No one else saw her, that much he was sure of, for a woman as tall as that, as beautiful as that, would surely draw notice from a crowd as barbaric as this.

Eyes like pale flames met his and the pain in his back surged to life, coiling through his limbs and eliciting a grunt of agony. Black tears rolled down his cheeks and he resisted the urge to sink to his knees. He tore his eyes away from the goddess, ignoring the silent appeal on her lips, and crashed into a burly Norscan.

The man shoved him back with a bark. Instinct took over as pain thrummed through his mind. He swept his stolen sword out of its sheath and the crowd began to clear. Overhead, crows circled, croaking raucously. Men backed away from him, eyes wide. Someone yelled. Goetz shook his head trying to clear it.

The slaver's guards bulled their way through the crowd, clutching whips and hatchets. Goetz, barely able to see through the haze of agony consuming him, lunged for them. He killed the first with sadistic ease, gutting the man as he moved past. As the others gaped, he charged past them and up onto the auction block. The slaver growled and reached for his hatchet, but Goetz was quicker. His borrowed sword snaked out and cut through the chains that bound the Kurgan, freeing the brute. He howled joyfully and dove past Goetz onto the slaver, bearing the man down.

Goetz chopped through chains and ropes with abandon, freeing men as his head threatened to split open. Crows dove at him, their cruel beaks tapping at his stolen helmet. Flailing, he drove them back and jumped off the block.

'There!' someone shouted. Goetz spun, and saw Eyri and a group of his men running towards him. The Kurgan, having dealt with the auctioneer, headed them off, swinging a stolen sword as he howled out the praises of the Dark Gods.

A dozen spears punctured the barbarian's hairy hide, pinning him kicking and screaming to the ground. Goetz used the distraction to take the opportunity to flee. Armour and weapons rattled as Eyri's men pursued him. Not looking back, he sped away from the temple, clutching his head. The fire in his side made every step an agony, but Goetz ploughed on, crashing amidst the shanty dwellings that spread out around the temple.

Before him, the white shape of Myrmidia ran, almost tauntingly. She did not glance over her shoulder, or otherwise acknowledge his pursuit, and he plunged on after her. Above him, the crows kept pace.

The shacks and huts pressed close together, almost as if Eyristaad were seeking to entrap him in its streets.

He stumbled against a wattle wall, breathing heavily. Something that might have been panic filled him. It was hard to think with the pain...

Snarling, he kicked in a door and came face-to-face with the frightened features of a child and her mother. Goetz froze, the fury draining out of him on the instant. The woman babbled in fear, a boning knife held in trembling hands as she stood between him and her child. The fear on her face was out of all proportion to his entrance. Glancing down, he realised that the mud he had covered his cuirass in had come off and that the sigil of Myrmidia blazed brightly.

The woman stared at that sigil in a terror that he found inexplicably hideous. 'I–' he began, before realising that she likely didn't speak Reikspiel. He held up his hand, and kept his sword point dipped to the ground. 'I mean you no harm,' he said. 'I know that you can't understand me, but... I don't mean to hurt you.'

The woman kept up her babble, poking the air between them with her knife, and Goetz stepped back against the door frame, hoping to avoid a confrontation. Outside, he could hear boots rattling across the rocks. He yanked off his helmet and tossed it to the woman, causing her to drop her knife. Running his hand over his sweaty scalp, he looked at the door and tightened his grip on his sword.

'I know you're in there einsark!' Eyri called out. 'Come out, or we'll come in after you. There's no escape.'

Goetz stepped outside, his sword held loosely. Eyri stood across the narrow street. The chieftain was leaning against the wall, grinning, his brawny arms crossed.

A dozen men crowded the street, spear-points aimed at Goetz. 'Granted, you made the gods' own try, I have to give you that,' Eyri continued. 'Would you believe that no one has ever thought to escape that way?'

'No,' Goetz said. 'Unless your people are dimmer than has been claimed.'

'Well, fair enough,' Eyri said, pushing away from the wall and striding through his men. 'No, a lot of men try and escape. We always bring them back one way or another. It might please you to know that the odds on you have gone up. Everyone was quite impressed.'

'How nice,' Goetz said, wondering how quick he would have to be to get past the wall of spears surrounding him.

'I probably shouldn't have left you that armour. It made you bold.' Eyri was within an arm's length of Goetz and he sighed. 'Too kind for my own good, I suppose.'

'Yes, that is your problem,' Goetz said.

Eyri snorted. 'Come quietly, or come bloodily. It doesn't matter. I'd rather you conserved your strength, however. I need you healthy, you see.'

'I'm dead either way,' Goetz said.

'Wasn't it one of you Southerners who said "where there's life, there's hope"?'

'I'm not a man for philosophy,' Goetz said, gauging the distance. Eyri's eyes narrowed and he put a hand on the hatchet at his belt.

'Don't do it,' he grated.

Goetz let a grin flash across his face. 'Or what?'

Eyri paused, a perplexed look crossing his face. 'Err…'

'I hope you've invested in a nice afterlife,' Goetz said, his hand tightening on his sword-hilt. He was trapped, alone and without the prospect of aid. But he could teach these Norscans about how a Myrmidon died. Goetz tensed, preparing to lunge.

A pale hand extended over Eyri's shoulder then, fingers outstretched almost pleadingly. Goetz froze, his eyes widening. Her gaze was solemn and she gestured, and in his head, he heard the Litany of Battle recited.

'There is no trap a man cannot escape,' he said, straightening.

'What?' Eyri said.

'I give up,' Goetz said, tossing his sword down.

'You… surrender?'

'No. I'm engaging in a strategic withdrawal from the current impasse,' Goetz said, smiling crookedly. Eyri snatched up the sword and stepped back quickly as his men took Goetz's arms and bound him.

'Sounds like surrender to me,' Eyri grunted, as they stripped Goetz of his armour.

'Then your education has been sorely lacking,' Goetz said as they shoved him out of the alley. As he went, he glanced over his shoulder and saw the woman he'd frightened earlier clutching her child to her and watching him with a loathing that he could not understand.

They took him back to his cell, and he saw no more of the pale shape. He didn't know whether to be thankful or not. The agony that had enflamed his body had vanished as mysteriously as it had appeared, and his suspicions concerning it were growing stronger. He was reminded of the leash on a dog. The pain grew and flared at times when he looked to be diverging from some path he could only dimly discern. Was this the hand of Myrmidia? Or was it something else?

He was tossed back into the same cell that he had

escaped from, though the exit he had made had been repaired and reinforced during his absence. His cell-mate was missing, which was something of a relief.

Before he could muse farther, the cell door was jerked open and Eyri stepped inside, his thumbs tucked into his belt. 'Don't bother getting settled.'

'No?'

'No. I've decided you're too much trouble to keep around. I was planning to show you off for a special event, but well, you've ruined that.' His eyes narrowed and he glanced at the cracks in the wall. 'You've met your opponent already,' he said.

Through the open door behind him, Goetz saw several men move towards the adjoining cell with lit torches. 'He's a smart one. Not too stupid to be afraid of fire.' Eyri smiled. 'Already killed a bear, two orcs and some ugly thing we found that came down from the North and ate one of my thralls. The beast is a popular one with the crowd, if you can believe it. A merchant I know says he can get me one of those big lizards they have across the Southern Ocean for it to fight.' He cocked his head. 'You'll do until then, I suppose.'

'You expect me to fight it – whatever it is – bare-handed?' Goetz said.

'Still on about your sword?' Eyri grunted. He snapped his fingers and one of his men stepped forward, tossing a sheathed blade at Goetz's feet. 'Settle for this one. Its dwarf-made. Got a good bite to it, if you get close enough to hurt the beast. Better than the one you stole from poor Orgun.' He laughed. 'Best thing about having a troll... no matter how much it gets torn up, it'll be fierce as frost for the next fight.'

Troll. The word sent a chill of fear down Goetz's

spine. At least now he knew. He scooped up the sword and slid it a little ways from its sheath. It had seen hard use, that much was obvious, and there were rust-coloured stains on the hilt. 'How many men have used this same sword?' he said, glaring at Eyri.

'A dozen I'd say. None very well though.' The Nor-scan stepped aside as more men stepped into the room, clutching spears and shields. 'Maybe you'll do better, eh?'

Goetz was herded out onto the catwalk. The crowd around the pit seemed to have grown. Planks were extended and he was forced down one at the point of his escorts' spears. He drew the sword and tossed aside the sheath, testing its weight.

It was well-made, but the blade was too heavy. Like as not, it had been made for a dwarf though there were precious few swordsmen of note among that race. He tested the blade's edge along his forearm, slicing threads from his sleeve. It would do.

Dead wolves littered the floor of the pit, and the bear was slumped not far off, black-fletched arrows jutting from its hairy carcass. The smell was atrocious, and Goetz swallowed back the bile that burned in his throat.

'Don't worry, brass-skin, if you win, we won't stick you. The bear is for tonight's feast, just like the wolves. If you survive, you'll live to fight another day!' Eyri called down.

Goetz said nothing. A hundred faces or more glared down at him, and jeers and catcalls rained down. He had never encountered such hatred before. Such raw fury, as if he were some foul thing of Chaos. He tight-ened his grip on his borrowed sword and waited.

The troll did not walk down a plank. Instead, it was driven off the catwalk by burning brands and boar-spears. It tumbled to the ground in a flailing heap. Long ungainly limbs unfolded and it shoved itself up, its wide head rocking back and forth on a deceptively spindly neck. With skin the colour of slate it almost blended into the rock floor of the pit. Immense bat-like ears unfurled and twisted on a malformed skull as Goetz's boots slid across the rocky floor.

The creature looked almost ridiculous, if you discounted the muscles that lined its limbs and the size of its jaws. The dull eyes took in the bear the wolves and the crowd and then, at the last, settled on Goetz. Worm-like lips wrinkled back from tombstone teeth as the troll caught sight of him. It snuffled the air, then gave a grunt. Goetz tensed. If the beast caught hold of him, that was it. He raised the sword even as the troll began to amble forward. The trot became a lope, the lope became a run, and then the monster was hurtling towards him like a veritable avalanche. Jaws gaping, it stretched impossibly long arms towards him.

Goetz ducked, sliding under the grasping paws, and slit the beast's belly. Loops of foul-smelling intestine spilled out, tangling around the creature's stumpy legs and it staggered, whining. Goetz circled it, and darted in, hoping to hamstring it.

A backhanded blow caught him on the side of the chest, denting his armour and sending him skidding across the pit. He crashed into the dead bear and his sword went flying from his grip. The troll gathered up its intestines and hissed, swinging towards him. Knuckling the ground with its free hand, it rushed towards him in simian fashion, head swinging from side to side, jaws champing spasmodically.

Goetz climbed over the bear's bulk and grabbed the hind legs of a stiffening wolf. With a grunt he heaved it up and swung it around, cracking the troll in the snout with the wolf's mangled skull. The troll stumbled off balance and Goetz threw himself towards his sword. His breastplate drew sparks from the stone as he skidded across it and his fingers wrapped around the pommel even as he felt the troll's approach. A knobbly fist crashed into the ground as he rolled aside. Desperately he chopped at the arm, hacking through the thick wrist. The sword quivered in his hands as it chewed through inhumanly thick bone.

The troll reared back, shrieking. Foul ichor sprayed from its stump. Goetz took the opening offered and plunged his sword to the hilt in the creature's chest, angling for where he hoped its heart was. The blade scraped bone and hot fluid coursed down Goetz's arms as he twisted the hilt, wedging the weapon in place. Coughing, he stepped back. The troll had a puzzled look on its face as it bent double, mouth opening.

Realising what was about to happen, Goetz threw himself out of the way as the troll vomited a blistering tide of bile. The substance charred the stone black where it landed, and Goetz scrambled backwards. The troll stumbled around in a circle, its one good hand pawing at the sword-hilt trapped by its already healing flesh.

Breathing heavily, his muscles aching, Goetz got to his feet. The crowd had gone silent now. Swiftly, he unbuckled his breastplate and let it hang loose in his grip. Then he scraped its edge across the ground once. Twice. Flipping it up, he grunted. It would have to do.

'Nothing for it,' he murmured. The troll shook its head and jerked on the sword again. Black blood gushed from its mouth and it fell to one knee. Unable to extricate the weapon, its struggles only caused it to wound itself further. Eventually, however, the blade would simply dissolve, courtesy of the troll's acidic internals. It might take hours or minutes.

Goetz gripped the breastplate tightly, the straps wrapped around his forearm. It was awkward, but it would do the job. If not–

'We do what must be done,' he said, taking little comfort in the mantra. Then he cried 'Myrmidia!' and charged towards the troll. As he drew within arm's reach of the beast his feet left the floor and he smashed the cuirass into the beast's face. It fell back in surprise as his weight carried it down onto its back. Lifting the breastplate over his head, he brought the edge down on the troll's throat again and again. He slammed the chunk of metal down until his shoulders were on fire and his arms screamed in agony.

The troll lay still as he finally stood. Straddling it, he looked up at the platform where Eyri stood with wide eyes and a gaping mouth. 'That for your bloody troll,' Goetz said, his voice loud in the silence.

A moment later the troll lurched up, spilling Goetz onto the floor. With his breastplate jutting from its throat and his sword from its breast, it brought a fist and a swiftly healing stump down between his legs. Goetz raised his arms and closed his eyes.

When no blow fell, Goetz cracked an eye. The troll had fallen once more, and its head lay some distance away.

'Well met, brother,' someone said. Goetz twisted,

looking up. Three men in armour stood over him protectively. They wore dark furs over their armour, mud and clay had been slathered over the plates, obscuring any insignia, but their ornate helmets bespoke their origins as well as any symbol. The one who'd spoken offered his hand to Goetz. In his other hand was the dripping axe that had decapitated the troll. He chuckled as Goetz gaped at him.

'Don't look so surprised, brother. Surely you know by now that the Knights of the Blazing Sun look after their own.'

16

THE KNIGHT REMOVED his helmet, revealing handsome, hawk-like features. Pale blue eyes examined Goetz and then flickered to the troll. He clucked his tongue. 'Such ill-treatment of your armour, brother... What would your hochmeister say?'

'We do what we must,' Goetz said, accepting the helping hand.

'Including experimenting with non-traditional weaponry,' one of the other knights said, chuckling. 'I remember when we got stable duty for that sort of thing.'

'Times change, Brother Opchek. Circumstances as well, eh brother?' the first knight said as he pulled Goetz to his feet.

'Goetz. Hector Goetz. I – who are you?'

'Salvation come on the wing,' Opchek said, tapping a finger against the winged figurine of Myrmidia that crouched atop his helmet. 'Another tradition.'

'And a good one. I am Balk, hochmeister of the honourable komturie of Svunum. The quiet one here is
Brother Taudge. And it's a lucky thing we happened
to be passing by, eh?' Balk said, turning his blue eyes
towards the viewing platforms. 'Ho Eyri! Who said you
could kill one of our Order, eh?'

Eyri's normally ruddy face had gone pale. The Norscan stepped forward, his fists dangling at his sides.
'Who we take and what we do with them is no concern
of yours, brass-skin!' he barked. 'And who said you
could kill my troll, then?'

'It'll recover, more is the pity,' Balk said, kicking the
head aside. The troll's eyes blinked alarmingly. 'That's
more than I can say for you, however.'

'Is that a threat?' Eyri said, raising his arms. 'Here?'
Along the platforms, Eyri's men raised bows.

'A warning,' Balk said, apparently unconcerned.
'We'll hang you eventually, Eyri. But not today, if you
play nice.'

Eyri grimaced. Then he gestured, and the bows were
lowered. 'What do you want, Balk?'

'Him,' Balk said, gesturing to Goetz.

'Take him and be damned!' Eyri snapped. 'Now
leave my steading.'

'Gladly,' Balk said, smiling brazenly up at the Norscan. 'The smell of fish and filth is getting too much to
bear anyway.'

They trooped up and out, the glares of Eyri and his
men following them the entire way. 'How did you
come to be here?' Goetz said as they stepped out of the
pit's stifling confines and onto the street.

Balk smiled. 'At so fortuitous a moment, you mean?'

'Yes, I suppose so.'

'Pure happenstance, I assure you.' Balk gestured to the buildings around them. 'We visit every few months or so to buy slaves.'

Goetz nearly choked. 'What?'

The three knights laughed. Opchek slapped him on the shoulder. 'Don't look so dismayed, brother. We buy them and free them.'

'We go where we are needed, eh?' Balk said. He looked around. 'And we are most certainly needed here, I think.'

EYRI WATCHED SOURLY as his men cleaned up the troll. Balk had been correct – it would heal, eventually. But it would be several days. He spat and turned away, stopping short as the tip of Dalla's looted sword pricked his nose.

'You had them,' she hissed. 'You had them and you let them walk out of here!'

'Aye,' Eyri said, using two fingers to carefully push the blade aside. 'What would you have had me do? Cut them down where they stood?'

'Yes!'

'No,' Ulfar said, stepping out onto the platform. He extended his staff and gently shoved his daughter to the side. 'Godi Eyri was correct to do as he did. He was thinking of his people. Of the good of Eyristaad.' Ulfar watched the men tossing bits of troll into its cell for a moment, then turned back. 'Even if he does play the fool sometimes.'

'I caught that troll fair and square I'll have you know,' Eyri said. 'People love that troll. I love that troll.'

Dalla snorted. Ulfar chuckled. 'Regardless, it was a dangerous game you played. Be glad you didn't lose more than a bit of face.'

'I can weather the loss. As long as I get to take the cost out of Balk's smug face,' Eyri said, making a fist. 'I'll call it even then.' He looked at Ulfar. 'And when are we getting to that, old man? My men are restless.'

'Soon enough,' Ulfar said. 'Once the godar have gathered here, we will speak more.' He looked up, his attention drawn to the outermost wall of the pit. A scraggly crow watched them, head cocked so that one black, shiny eye was fixed on them with unblinking intensity. Ulfar sniffed and flicked his fingers. A stiff breeze swept up dust and grit from the pit floor and flung it at the bird, driving it into the air with a squawk.

Dalla watched it flap away, her fingers clenching nervously around the hilt of her sword. Ulfar met his daughter's gaze and smiled benignly, patting her arm. Then he turned and left the platform, having said his piece. Eyri watched him go and then looked at her. 'He knows more than he's telling, your father.'

'Always,' she said. She drew her sword a little ways from its sheath before slamming it back down. 'He's wrong about this.'

'Oh?'

She looked at him. 'Don't play the innocent with me, Eyri Goldfinger.'

'Don't call me Goldfinger, Ulfarsdottir,' Eyri shot back. 'What? I suppose you'd take a few men and see that they never reached their galley, aye?'

'Maybe.' Dalla hesitated.

Eyri cocked his head. 'Or maybe you'd even have men lying in wait. Knowing, as you would, that they'd come running, the brass-skinned dogs, once their daemon-spies told them who we had.'

Dalla stared at him for a moment, then chuckled. 'I wondered why you waited as long as you did to feed him to the troll.'

Eyri tapped the side of his nose. 'I am godi for a reason, girl. Never forget that.'

'Don't call me 'girl', man,' Dalla said. 'Where?'

'Where do you think?' Eyri spread his hands and smiled.

'TRULY A TREACHEROUS people,' Balk said. 'Don't you agree, Brother Goetz?'

'I'd heard the opposite, actually,' Goetz said. 'I'd heard the Northmen held personal honour in high regard.'

Opchek grunted. 'They do. They just don't think it applies to us soft Southerners, you see.' He slapped his hands together. 'That they include Kislev in that sweeping generalisation is proof of their ignorance.'

Goetz eyed the other knight's dangling mustachios and fought back a grin. 'I see.'

'I don't think you do,' Balk said genially. 'But experience is the best teacher, I've heard tell. We'll see you blooded yet, brother.'

'Where are we going?'

'We have a galley waiting,' Balk said.

'More a tub really,' Opchek said, nudging Taudge. The knight, who had not spoken the entire time, grunted softly in acknowledgement, but said nothing. Opchek made a face. 'You'll have to forgive Brother Taudge. He's under a vow of being a humourless stick.'

'Maybe I just don't think you're very funny,' Taudge said, his voice a hoarse rasp.

'Impossible,' Opchek said, winking at Goetz. Then

he said, 'How did you come to be here, Brother Goetz? Just out of curiosity.'

'I was coming to see you, actually,' Goetz said, after a moment's hesitation. 'You are from the chapter house on Svunum, are you not?'

Balk stopped so abruptly that Goetz nearly crashed into him. 'Coming to see us? Why?'

Goetz stepped back, suddenly aware that he had neither weapons, nor armour. 'At the Grand Master's command,' he said.

'The–' Balk stopped. 'Why?' he demanded.

'He feared for you,' Goetz said, skirting the truth. 'It has been some time since your last report and with one thing and another…' Goetz gestured helplessly. 'He feared you might have been overrun.'

Balk eyed him for a moment and then let out a breathy chuckle. 'Of course he did. You hear that, brothers? A few messengers get waylaid and the Grand Master loses confidence in us.'

Goetz flushed. 'I wouldn't call the murder of a brother of our Order a simple matter of being waylaid, hochmeister,' he snapped.

'Murder – what?' Balk said, looking shocked.

'Oops,' Opchek interjected. He made a surreptitious gesture. 'I thought Goldfinger was being too pleasant.'

Goetz looked past Balk and saw that their path to the quay was barred by a dozen men. He recognised several of them from Eyri's vessel. Balk clucked his tongue. 'This is unfortunate.' He looked at Goetz. 'You see what I mean, brother. Treacherous.'

'Sneaky, even,' Opchek said, loosening his sword in its sheath. Taudge did the same, his grim face growing even more so.

'What is the meaning of this?' Balk said, stepping out in front of the group. He kept his hands well away from his weapons, but Goetz had little doubt that he could have them to hand quickly enough.

One of the Norscans barked something in his own tongue, and gestured with the long-handled axe he held in one hand. Balk replied in the same tongue and then looked at the others over his shoulder. 'Eyri is a sore loser. I'd wager he set this up. Be ready…'

'He's going to try and kill us in the street?' Goetz said, his hands clenching uselessly.

'No. He's going to try and make us kill him,' Opchek murmured. 'How quick on your feet are you, Brother Goetz?'

'Quick enough,' Goetz said, eyeing the closest of the Norscans.

'I hope so.'

The first clod of dung struck Taudge in the face. The knight twisted aside and clawed at his eyes, cursing virulently. More clods struck the others, sliding across their armour and leaving grimy patinas in their wake. Opchek cursed and made to start forward, but Balk held him back with a look. A crowd had gathered now; jeering, cheering Norscans, all hurling dung and curses with equal fervour.

Something hard struck Goetz in the cheek and he staggered. Another rock caught him in the small of the back and he fell against Opchek. The latter caught him and spun him around, placing his armoured form around Goetz protectively. 'Do something, Balk!' Opchek snarled.

'Just keep moving forward,' Balk said, moving towards Eyri's men steadily, his visor flipped down. 'If we attack, they'll be on us like wolves.'

Goetz suddenly realised what Eyri's plan must have been. If Balk and the others reacted in a hostile manner, the Norscans could claim they were only defending themselves when the rest of the Order came calling. A shabby fiction at best, but Eyri didn't seem altogether too concerned about such niceties.

As they pushed on through the swelling crowd, one of Eyri's warriors got too close and jammed the butt-end of his spear into Taudge's side, knocking the knight off his feet. Immediately a half-dozen Norscans fell on him, striking out with fists, clubs and knives.

'That's torn it,' Opchek barked, and drew his sword. It came free of his sheath with an evil hiss and looped out in a glittering arc. Men screamed as the blade danced across their extended arms and legs. Goetz immediately set to pulling Taudge to his feet. Balk turned back and drew his axe, blocking a blow meant for Opchek and gutting the man who'd made it.

'Nothing for it now,' Balk said. 'Kill them all.'

'I was hoping you'd say that!' Opchek said exultantly.

Getting Taudge to his feet took no small amount of effort. Besides the weight of his armour, he was solidly built. As Taudge stood, a Norscan darted towards them, roaring, an axe raised over his head. Goetz snatched the other knight's sword out of its sheath and lopped the head off the axe as it fell towards them. The Norscan looked at his beheaded weapon stupidly for a moment, then tossed the haft at Goetz and snatched for a dagger at his belt. Goetz didn't give him the opportunity to draw it. He batted the axe handle aside and sent its owner's head to join the blade in the dust.

More of Eyri's men were forcing their way through

the crowd now, armoured for war. It was well-planned as ambushes went, and for the life of him, Goetz couldn't see how Balk intended to escape. He blocked a blow and thrust an elbow into his opponent's face. A hand fell on his shoulder and Goetz whirled. Iron fingers fastened on his hand.

'My sword, if you please,' Taudge said. Goetz gave him the blade and stooped to pick up a fallen one. Before he could grab one, however, Balk grabbed the crook of his arm and shoved him forward.

'Get to the docks!' the knight growled. Impossibly, the three men had cleared a path for them all through the crowd. Bodies and blood covered the ground and the survivors were drawing back. Arrows hissed off the rooftops, and Opchek chopped a number of them out of the air.

'I'll say this for them... they're determined!' the Kislevite said, laughing.

Goetz stumbled ahead of the trio, heading in the direction Balk had shoved him. A boat was waiting in the harbour, smallish and protected by a fourth knight, whose eyes widened as the group approached.

'What–' he began as Goetz stopped in front of him.

'No time! Into the boat!' Balk snapped. He jumped down off the dock into the coracle and hefted a large flag. As Goetz climbed down after him, he raised the flag and let it unfurl in the sea breeze.

Opchek slapped Goetz on the shoulder. 'Grab an oar, brother! Pull like your life depended on it!'

'Because it does,' Taudge added. Goetz grabbed one of the four oars and, despite the ache in his muscles, began to pull. The coracle slid away from the dock as their pursuers closed in.

'What good is waving a flag going to do?' Goetz said.

'You'll see,' Opchek said cheerily.

The crack of the waves slapping against the hull of the coracle was suddenly overwhelmed by a thunderous roar. Then another, and another. Five times in all, and with every belch a section of Eyristaad's waterfront disappeared in fire and death. Goetz dropped his oar and slapped his hands to his ears as he watched bodies and broken wood alike tossed into the air the way a child might toss a toy. He turned and caught sight of a long, heavily built galley sliding out of the cold fog, black sails fluttering in the breeze.

'Ha!' Balk crowed as he dropped the flag. 'Show those heathens the light of righteousness!' he roared, striking the air with his fists. More thunder rolled across the choppy surface of the sea, battering the shoreline.

'Blow them to hell more like,' Opchek said, resting his oar across his knees. 'You did us a good turn back there, brother,' he continued, looking at Goetz. 'Saving sourpuss like that.'

Taudge grunted and looked away. Goetz shrugged and then winced. 'We do what must be done,' he said, rubbing his aching shoulder.

'That we do, Brother Goetz,' Balk said, sitting down in the prow of the coracle. 'That we do.'

17

Svunum was a striking sight, even at a distance. Square stone towers rose up seemingly out of the very rock of the island, as if they had been birthed rather than built. The harbour nestled in a curve of the shore, and entrance to it was blocked by a number of great stone pylons which jutted from the water like the fangs of some immense sea-beast. A heavy chain had been threaded through the holes carved into the pylons and as Goetz watched, the chain was rendered limp and subsequently retracted out of the path of the galley.

'In the best traditions of our esteemed Order, Svunum is something of an ongoing project,' Balk said, sipping from a cup of iced fruit juice. The secrets of iced drinks had been brought back from the Crusades in Araby, along with the more material treasures used to fund the nascent Order.

Goetz and Balk sat on a raised platform on the aft deck, beneath a fur-lined awning. Balk had stripped off his armour and now sat in a thick bearskin robe on a chair made from tusks and sinew. Goetz wore a similar robe, and had it pulled tightly around him to ward off the chill.

'I can see that,' Goetz said, admiring the ingenuity that must have gone into crafting and depositing the pylons. 'Someone has read Mario Flavia's treatise on naval combat.' He gestured to the pylons as the galley slid past. 'Not to mention Hellestrome's pamphlet on ship-board artillery,' he continued, motioning to the ten slender brass-barrelled cannons that lined the rails, five to either side.

'I see the Order's standards haven't diminished since I came out here,' Balk said, chewing a sliver of ice. 'We've made a few innovations of our own as well, to be sure.'

'I'd be interested to see them,' Goetz said carefully.

'In due time, brother,' Balk said, smiling. The expression faded. 'What you said earlier… about a murdered brother…'

'Athalhold. From the Bechafen Komturie,' Goetz said. 'He was sent to – he was my predecessor in this mission.'

'The mission to check on us, you mean?' Balk said carefully.

Goetz heard the care in his words and decided to take the hint. There was no reason to antagonise his saviour with Marienburg's demands. Not yet anyway. 'Yes,' he said.

'How did he die?' Balk said, his eyes never wavering from Goetz's own.

'Murdered.'

'By who?'

Goetz hesitated. Then he said, 'Cultists. Followers of the Ruinous Powers.'

Balk sat back, almost slumping. He sighed and hung his head. When he looked up, his expression was ragged. 'Another brother gone. We will tip a goblet to him and carve his name upon a Martyr's Niche in the komturie.' He shook himself and said, 'I had no idea, brother. I thought that we were being ignored. If I had known… well.' He waved a hand. 'For now, I can but extend the courtesy of our komturie to you. Make yourself at home.'

Goetz sat back on his stool and took in the galley as an excuse to avoid Balk's haunted gaze. A long vessel, it stood in contrast to the more bulky dragonships of the Norscans despite the similarities in design. There were forty knights aboard, though only a few wore armour. The rest had stripped themselves down to their trousers as they bent forward over their oars, though their swords and shields remained near to hand.

The rail was studded with heavy iron plates, each of which bore a face that Goetz assumed was Myrmidia's, though the engraver had obviously never seen a lithograph or a statue of the goddess. Braziers filled with incense hung from the mast and from the deck railings, filling the air with a warm, calming scent.

Those knights who were not at the oars moved across the deck seeing to other duties – some stowed the guns, while others brought water to the rowers.

'I'm curious,' Goetz said, turning back to Balk after a moment. 'The Norscans seem to bear our Order a grudge.'

'That's a polite way of putting it,' Opchek said, striding up onto the deck. The big Kislevite had his helmet tucked beneath his arm and his bald head gleamed in the faint sunlight. 'They bloody hate us might be more accurate.'

Balk grunted. 'True enough, unfortunately.' He looked at Goetz speculatively. 'It's not so complicated, brother. We have had to undertake a more – ah – proactive approach to dealing with our neighbours to the North, I'm afraid.'

'Proactive?'

'Punitive,' Opchek said merrily.

Goetz frowned. 'You mean that what I saw today–'

'Was a taste of something that jumped-up pirate Goldfinger has had coming for months now,' Balk said, nodding brusquely. 'In truth, we were scouting his defences. Eyri has become much bolder than he ought to be, and I wanted to know why.'

'And did you find out?'

Balk smiled crookedly. 'No. We got a bit distracted.' Goetz flushed. Balk held up a hand to forestall his reply. 'No offence meant or blame attached, brother. But you did pick a rather busy time of year to visit us.'

'I'll make a note of that for next time,' Goetz said.

Scribes and other functionaries, clad in the livery of the Order, were waiting for them at the docks. They instantly besieged Balk, waving papers and shouting questions. Opchek took Goetz's arm and guided him out of the way.

'Come lad, let our fearless hochmeister handle this most dangerous of foeman by himself.'

'I wasn't expecting it to be so busy,' Goetz said. He continued on quickly. 'Not that it shouldn't be, but…'

'We are out on the fringes, aren't we?' Opchek said. He chuckled. 'Or so it must seem. In truth, I believe we are one of the busiest komturies in the Order.' He gestured at the ships in the small harbour. There were over a dozen vessels of various sizes – merchantmen, galleys and sloops, flying half a dozen different flags. 'We've made ourselves over into something approaching a port-of-call for the local money grubbers.'

'And what do the authorities in Marienburg make of this?' Goetz said.

Opchek laughed. 'Oh they're fit to be tied I expect!' He tapped the side of his nose. 'What are they going to do about it then, eh?' He gestured to the towers. 'We are the most heavily fortified area for miles around. We keep the trade routes open, save for when there's reason to close them.'

'And is now one of those times? Is that why the vessel I was on was taken so quickly? And so close to Svunum?' Goetz said carefully. Opchek stopped and turned, frowning.

'No. That is a different matter entirely. And one I'll thank you to hold your tongue on until such time as Hochmeister Balk chooses to illuminate you.'

Goetz raised a hand in surrender, and Opchek's smile returned. 'Besides, there are more pleasant discussions to be had. We can–'

A crow croaked, interrupting Opchek. They turned to see a slender figure standing behind them, swathed in a robe of feathers and fur, with a crow perched on its shoulder. A smooth face peered out from under the peaked hood and two dark eyes peered out of a mask of intricate tattoos to fix on Goetz.

'Ah, our hostess,' Opchek said softly. Almost reverently.

'Who?' Goetz said, confused.

'The lady of the island,' the other knight murmured, sinking to one knee. Goetz hesitated, and then followed suit. Slim hands threw back the hood and a smile curved across the woman's face. She was young, perhaps a year or two older than Goetz himself, with a curious cast to her features. The dark tattoos coiled across her cheeks and brow like a lover's fingers, and Goetz was uncomfortably reminded of the woman in his dreams, her face caressed by dark feathers.

'Myrma,' she said softly, reaching up to stroke the crow. Goetz felt a chill go through him. He turned slightly and met Opchek's gaze.

'You feel it, don't you?' the Kislevite said.

'Of course he does,' Balk said, approaching them, followed by his scribes. 'How could he not? How could any true servant of the Order not?'

'What?' Goetz said, getting to his feet. Myrma looked away, a half-smile curling across her face. 'Who is she?'

'Better to say what is she,' Balk said, inclining his head to the young woman, who returned the gesture. 'To which I answer, a blessing from the goddess on our endeavours.'

Goetz tore his eyes from Myrma. 'Endeavours?'

'Later,' Balk said. 'First, we must get you settled, brother. Our komturie is open to you, and I hope you will indulge in our hospitality.'

The crow took flight from the woman's shoulder. Goetz watched it fly, and then turned to Balk. 'Nothing would please me more,' he said.

SMOKE ROSE INTO the cold air, meeting the rain as it came down, mingling into a grey sludge that coated the ruins of the wharf. Dalla rested her chin on the pommel of her sword and watched as Eyri's men searched for survivors.

'Foolishness,' her father murmured, his eyes on the sea.

'You did warn him,' Dalla said bluntly. Her fingers played across the intricately wrought hilt of the sword. It was a beautiful thing. Heavy, but somehow light at the same time. 'Is it your fault if Goldfinger is too stubborn to listen to the advice of his gudja?'

'Maybe if the gudja's advice had been less cryptic, the godi might have listened!' Eyri snarled, stalking forwards with a naked sword in hand. He was covered in ash, soot and blood, and his eyes were wide and fierce.

'Sheathe your sword, Goldfinger!' Dalla snapped, rising cat-like to her feet. She extended her own sword and batted Eyri's aside contemptuously. 'No man threatens my father.'

'I'll threaten who I damn well like, wench!' Eyri roared, swiping at her. Their swords met and Ulfar's staff came down on them, sweeping them from their hands.

'Enough,' the old man said harshly. 'Maybe you will listen now, godi… now that you have seen what our Enemy is capable of.'

Eyri stooped to snatch up his sword. 'This was your idea of a lesson, old man?' He glared at Ulfar. 'Did my men die so you could show me what a fool I've been?'

Ulfar met his glare silently. Eventually, Eyri looked away. He made a snort and sheathed his sword. 'What now?'

'Now, you do as I asked earlier. You call a meeting of the godar. A council of war,' Ulfar said, looking off in the direction the galley had gone. 'We must prepare for the storm to come.'

As Eyri stalked off, Dalla looked at her father. 'Is it truly that bad then?'

'No.' He smiled slightly. 'It is worse.'

'Your comforting skills leave something to be desired, father,' Dalla said. Tenderly, she brushed a few specks of soot out of his beard. He batted at her hand irritably.

'That was your mother's job.'

'No. Mother's job was to take care of you, old goat,' Dalla said, grinning. The grin faded as she said, 'He fought well.'

'Who?'

'The einsark,' Dalla said. 'For a Southerner, I mean.' A note in her voice caused her father to look at her.

'Yes. His kind are born to the blade.'

'Not this blade,' Dalla said, slapping her looted sword. 'It's mine now.'

'For how long?'

'What?'

'I am reminded of a story,' Ulfar said. 'A thane of some standing gave, as a gift, a fine dwarfish blade to the maiden he wished to marry. She, in her turn, gave it back to him, though not entirely in the manner he'd intended.'

'She killed him?'

'No. Though he did learn that swords do not make proper gifts,' Ulfar said. He looked at her. Dalla blinked.

'I took this sword from him. He did not give it to me.'

'Yes.' Ulfar turned away. 'Maybe the story is not similar at all.'

Dalla was about to reply when she caught sight of

the gathering crows perched on the still-smouldering remnants of the destroyed buildings. 'Father…'

'I see them. Rest easy. They are naught but ordinary scavengers,' Ulfar said, leaning on his staff. 'Our foe has turned his eyes from us for the moment.' He sighed wearily and looked up at the circling birds. 'I do not know why, but I can but hope it will last long enough for us to act…'

18

GOETZ WAS BACK in the Drakwald and avian furies spun around him in a black kaleidoscope, shedding rotten feathers as they tore strips from his flesh. His sword was broken and his armour was held on by ragged strips of leather, and neither did him any good. The witch-light made the trees look sickly as he spun, lashing out blindly at the bird-shapes that left ragged canyons in his battered flesh. Staggering, he tried to find escape, but there was none to be had.

Goetz stumbled and fell, sinking to his knees, blinded. Fingers gripped his chin and jerked his head up.

'You were poisoned,' Myrmidia said. 'Poisoned.'

Goetz snapped awake, covered in sweat.

'You were dreaming,' someone said.

Goetz turned sharply. The young woman called Myrma sat on a stool in the corner of the room he'd been given. She stroked the feathers that lined the edge of her robes. 'How did you get in here?' he pressed.

'I go where I am needed,' she said. She stood and left the room as silently as she had come. Goetz waited until the door had shut and then stood, shrugging into a robe. He shuddered slightly, though whether from the chill in the room or the lingering echo of his dream, he couldn't say.

He went to the window, rubbing the scars on his back as he went. Were these dreams the product of whatever poisons remained in his system? Or was it something else? He leaned against the sill and turned, looking for the lithograph of Myrmidia that should have been on the wall somewhere.

As he'd noticed last night, there was neither image nor icon anywhere to be seen. The thought made him uneasy and he turned back to the window. He could see the sea from where he stood, and he could hear the sharp snarl of the waves crashing against the rocky shoreline. Svunum was not beautiful, save in the most savagely aesthetic sense. Kleerman or Pattilo would have made much of this place, with their love of the darker end of the colour spectrum.

Still, he wasn't here to think about painters. Goetz pushed away from the window and dressed swiftly. What had been built here was far more impressive than he'd been led to believe by Grand Master Berengar. Even the Talabheim Komturie paled in comparison to this citadel.

Goetz left his room and moved through the torch-lit corridors. He wrinkled his nose at the smell of pitch emanating from the torches and moved towards the stairs, hoping to find open air. Taking them up, he moved out onto the battlements, his hands behind his back. Above, the moon rode through dark clouds. The wind whipped at him as he stepped out of the shelter of the doorway and he stumbled slightly. He rubbed his arms as the cold bit into him and he moved towards the edge.

'Couldn't sleep?'

Goetz frowned as Balk turned towards him. The hochmeister smiled thinly. 'After the beating you took, I thought you'd sleep like the dead.'

'I feel fine, hochmeister,' Goetz said, flexing his hands for emphasis. 'The girl – Myrma – was in my room.'

'Ah. You should feel honoured,' Balk said, looking out towards the sea.

'Who is she?'

'I should have thought that that would have been obvious,' Balk said, not looking at him.

Goetz let the comment go unanswered and joined him at the wall. 'I wasn't aware that this island was inhabited,' he said, recalling what the first mate onboard the *Nicos* had said. Balk chuckled.

'You mean that the Grand Master wasn't aware, don't you?'

Goetz said nothing. Balk glanced at him, and then went on. 'When our Order was gifted with this island, it was without the permission of its owners.'

'The merchant-princes?'

'*Pfaugh*,' Balk said, making a sharp gesture. 'Those money-grubbers? No. No, there were folk here then, and long before. A primitive people, but touched by grace despite that.'

'Norscans?'

'No.' Balk's face twisted slightly. 'Not Norscan. Not

precisely at least. They call themselves Svanii, after the island one assumes. Quite a surprising folk. Our first meeting was an interesting one, albeit a bit bloody.'

'They fought?'

'Oh my yes. But our Order held firm. And in the end, we followed Myrmidia's teachings and brought civilisation to the savages,' Balk said, motioning to the fortress. 'They are still here and they serve our Order as faithfully as any knight.'

Goetz shook his head. 'And her?'

'Ah, there we have an interesting story,' Balk said. 'She is a priestess. I suppose that is as good a word as any.' He scratched his chin, smiling slightly. 'They worship a goddess, you see. One of the old ones, before artists, poets and philosophers made them palatable for the common herd. They call her the Young Crone, or the Maiden of Wisdom.' He tapped the side of his nose. 'A war-goddess, as well as a goddess of knowledge.'

Goetz felt a chill that had nothing to do with the wind blowing off the sea. 'Coincidence?' he said.

'Do you believe in coincidence, Brother Goetz?' Balk said, turning to him. 'Or do you believe in something greater? Why else would you have joined the Order?'

'Obligation,' Goetz said softly.

Balk looked at him. 'Faith is no burden, brother. It is the armour that defends us and the sword that pierces the darkness.' He turned back and pointed a finger at the sea. 'That darkness.'

'Norsca?'

Balk spat. 'Yes. Norsca. A weeping tumour on the shank of the world. That. That is why we are here, brother!' The hochmeister clapped his hands together. 'The Norscans are the wolves at the gates of the world, and we have been placed here to bar their entry.' He smacked a fist against the parapet. 'Chaos surges across the mountains of the Old World in ever increasing numbers, brother, their daemonic ranks swelled by the Northmen. They worship the Ruinous Powers as gods, brother! Gods! And they follow them as zealously as... as...'

'As we do Myrmidia,' Goetz said.

Balk swung around, and for a moment, Goetz thought the other man might fly at him in a rage. Then, Balk began to laugh. 'Exactly. Exactly!' he said, clapping his hands against Goetz's shoulders. 'And that, brother, is why we must be the ones to face them.' He sighed and crossed his arms. 'We can end the Long War with a single mighty stroke. And we can do it from here.'

Intrigued, Goetz said, 'Is that why the Marienburg brothers abandoned their komturie to come here?'

'In part, yes. But we have days yet,' Balk said. He moved past Goetz and headed for the stairs. 'Get some rest, brother. Tomorrow will be busy.' Goetz wanted to call to him, to stop him, but he refrained. He was a guest here, and Svunum seemed to lack that easy familiarity that so characterised his own komturie.

He couldn't blame them. He looked out over the Sea of Claws and tried to pierce the icy fog that covered it. Balk had a grudge, that much he was certain of. Justified or not, it was a bit disturbing. He wondered what had caused it... what had given birth to the raw hatred he'd seen blossom in the hochmeister's eyes when he'd spoken of Norsca?

More importantly, what had it grown into?

* * *

'Up, LAD!'

The boot struck the side of Goetz's bed and he sat upright. Weak grey light came in through the windows and the sound of gulls echoed loudly off the stone. Ivan Opchek had flowing moustaches and a face like an apple. Older than Goetz, he radiated good cheer. He grinned down at Goetz and tossed a sheathed sword onto his blankets. 'This looked to be about your size, so I took the liberty of bringing it here.'

The Kislevite hooked the stool with his foot and sat down, swinging his legs up onto the bed. He tore a chunk out of the loaf of bread he held with his teeth and chewed noisily. 'Can't have you wandering around without a proper sword or armour.' He ripped the loaf in half and tossed the unchewed section to Goetz, who caught it.

'No butter?' Goetz said.

'Am I your maidservant?' Opchek leaned back and looked away as Goetz dressed and buckled on the sword. He drew it and sighted down the blade.

'Good balance,' Goetz said. 'Bit lighter than I'm used to.'

'Our weapon-smith is a bit of an artist,' Opchek said.

Goetz looked at him. 'You have a weapon-smith? Here?'

Opchek snorted. 'And an armourer and a blacksmith or three. We also grow our own vegetables and bake our own bread.' He waved his half-loaf at Goetz for emphasis. 'Isn't your own komturie self-sufficient?'

'Yes, but not quite on this scale.' Goetz sheathed the sword. 'Good bread though,' he said, taking a bite.

'The secret is in the yeast, I'm told.' Opchek hopped to his feet. 'Our ever-attentive hochmeister would like to see you.'

'Am I in trouble?'

'Depends on your definition of trouble,' Opchek said. 'He's quite taken with you.'

'He seems like a good man,' Goetz said noncommittally. He recalled the previous night, and the expression he'd seen on Balk's face. 'Dedicated.'

'As we all are,' Opchek said wryly.

'You make it sound like a bad thing.'

'*Heh*. I worshipped Ulric once. Wore the fur cloak and the wolf's head, damn me if I didn't,' Opchek said, stroking his moustaches. 'Dedication can lead a man down ugly paths.'

'There's a difference between duty and fanaticism,' Goetz said.

'Oh aye. Indeed there is. The question is can you tell the difference?'

'You're one to talk.' Taudge pushed himself away from a wall and joined them. 'You wouldn't know dedication if it attacked you in a dark alley.'

'Well obviously,' Opchek said, winking at Goetz. 'It being a dark alley and such.'

Taudge shook his head. 'Idiot.'

'Possibly,' Opchek said. 'Joining us on our constitutional?'

'Yes,' Taudge said tersely. Goetz was about to say something when they stepped out through the gatehouse door and he caught sight of Svunum in the morning light. He hadn't fully appreciated the sight the day before. He stood, dumbstruck.

'It's a sight to behold, is it not?' Opchek said. 'Fairly takes your breath away. Or that might just be the smell of the nightsoil containers.'

Goetz didn't reply. He looked down at the town that

pressed close to the walls of the komturie with the faintest sense of unease. It was a bit like looking back into the history of the Empire. Crude huts battled for space with more modern-looking dwellings, and every man and woman went armed, as far as he could see.

The town encircled the section of the komturie that did not rest on the steep sea-cliffs, spreading out in a sickle-moon shape. It bustled with activity, and the smoke of a hundred or more cooking fires wafted up into the air, carrying with them the mingled scents of spices both familiar and otherwise. It was no primitive fishing village, but a town, full of life, noise and colour. In short, the very last thing he had expected.

'I can't believe it,' he said after a moment.

'Why not? You've seen isolated backwaters before haven't you?' Opchek said from behind him. 'This one just happens to be a bit better taken care of than most.'

'Still, to be so– so–'

'Pure,' Taudge said. The other knight had stopped nearby, hands behind his back.

Goetz looked at him. 'I was going to say large.' He ignored the other knight's glower. 'They seem to have adapted to your presence well enough. The Svanii, I mean.'

'After we killed a hundred or so of them, way back when,' Opchek said. He had picked up a chunk of driftwood in his hand and began whittling it to a point with his dagger. 'They became very quiet after that.'

'Wouldn't you?' Goetz said mildly. Opchek laughed. Taudge bestowed a disapproving gaze on both of them.

'Fools, the pair of you,' he said. He gestured to the village. 'It is a sign of Myrmidia's blessings that we were sent here, to this untainted land, to spread the word of her coming!'

Goetz blinked. 'I wasn't aware that the goddess was going anywhere, let alone coming here,' he said.

Opchek coughed. 'What he meant to say was–'

'I think I heard him quite clearly, thank you.' Goetz ignored the Kislevite and faced Taudge. 'What do you mean, brother?'

Taudge made a face. 'I simply meant that we are bringing the light of her to these people.'

Goetz glanced at Opchek, who looked away. He stepped back. 'You don't like me very much do you, brother?'

'It is not a matter of like or dislike,' Taudge said. 'I do not know you. And you have a quick tongue, a trait I find annoying in even those I do know.' He glared at Opchek, who made a rude noise. 'Come. See for yourself what I meant,' he said, starting down the slope towards the village.

Goetz looked at Opchek, who gestured with his driftwood. 'After you, brother. I've seen it before. And that's why I brought you out here anyway.' They started after Taudge. The knights were apparently a common enough sight and several times Opchek and, to a lesser extent, Taudge, stopped to make conversation with the locals. They were a people not entirely dissimilar to the folk of Talabecland, with the slight oddities of feature any isolated region might eventually come to favour. Dark tattoos covered what flesh was visible beneath their rough clothing, and several times Goetz found himself staring blankly at the weaving skeins of ink that crawled across a cheek or forearm. If any of the locals took offence, they didn't show it.

'They get the ink from octopuses, apparently,' Opchek said after he caught Goetz looking.

'I wasn't aware there were any such creatures in the Sea of Claws,' Goetz said.

'Neither was I until one tried to eat one of our galleys,' Opchek said. 'Big as a whale and twice as tasty, once we'd given it the business.'

'You ate it?'

'It's not exactly good farmland hereabouts.'

Goetz shook his head and turned to watch a bevy of knights, stripped to their trousers and boots, pull down a shack with equal parts of rope and virulent swearing. 'What are they doing?'

'Improving the view,' Taudge said with evident satisfaction.

'What?'

'We're in the process of rebuilding the older structures in the village as it expands. Can't have it becoming a sty like Eyristaad now can we? Or Marienburg for that matter,' Opchek said. He motioned around with his driftwood chunk. 'We'll have a suitable little city here soon enough.'

'Besides which, it gives the brethren something to do when they're not fighting,' Goetz said. 'Right?'

'Your intuition does you credit, brother,' Balk said, stepping out from a doorway. Goetz started in surprise. Balk jerked his head. 'Come, she wishes to see you.'

'Who?'

'Who do you think, brother?' Balk said, half-smiling. 'Our hostess. Now come, it wouldn't do to keep her waiting.' The hochmeister started off, leading them deeper into the village. People stepped aside for him, heads bowed. Some made the sign of Myrmidia, Goetz noticed. Thumbs hooked together and palms spread like the wings of the goddess's messenger-crows. Thinking of the birds caused him to look up. Hundreds of the birds circled above, alighting on rooftops or skimming across the street. The sound of their croaking provided a disturbing counterpoint to the sounds of routine industry.

'I know what you're thinking – why'd it have to be carrion-eaters?' Opchek said slyly, tilting his head so the others couldn't hear. 'Crows go everywhere, see? And they can get into anything. Only animal that might be better at ferreting out knowledge and secrets are rats, and even Myrmidia, bless her name, probably can't stand those little buggers.' He sniffed. 'That's my thinking anyhow.'

'There are enough of them around,' Goetz said, still watching the birds.

'More every day. The Svanii look on it as a good omen.' Opchek shook his head. 'I don't see it myself, but as Myrmidia wills it, I suppose.'

'She will be pleased to hear that you have no objections, I'm sure,' Balk said without turning. Opchek made a face at his hochmeister's back and Goetz fought to restrain a chuckle. They stopped a few moments later before an incongruous hut that sat at the farthest edge of the village. The hut sat on a circular wooden platform which itself sat upon legs made of what looked to be repurposed ship's masts. Crows lined the roof and waddled across the platform. There was a strange smell on the air that had nothing to do with either the birds or the sea.

'It's a sort of mould that grows on some of the rocks around here. They burn it and it puts off an odd odour,'

Opchek whispered. Balk lifted the tanned hide curtain that blocked off the hut's doorway and extended his hand.

'She waits within, brother,' he said.

'Try not to embarrass us,' Opchek added.

Goetz ducked his head and stepped inside. The strange smell enveloped him and he fought back a cough. Two knights, clad in their burnished plate-mail, knelt before the woman, Myrma. As Goetz watched, she lifted a crude ladle of water and poured it over them, murmuring the entire while. The water crawled across the armour and dripped down and as one the knights rose. They filed out past Goetz without a word.

'They go hunting,' she said, without waiting for him to ask. She dropped the ladle back into the bucket near her seat.

'For what?'

'Their enemies. Your enemies,' she said, smiling. She leaned back in her seat and spread her arms. She was wearing only a thin robe and Goetz suddenly felt uncomfortably cramped in the tight confines of the hut. To distract himself, he looked around. With some surprise, he suddenly realised where all the images and lithographs of Myrmidia had gone. They lined the circular walls and ceiling of the hut, plastered together like tiles. The goddess's face stared down at him from every conceivable angle.

Goetz felt suddenly light-headed and stumbled. 'Sit,' Myrma said softly. 'You are still weak.'

'I feel fine,' Goetz said, sinking down. A flare of pain cut off his protest and he grunted. He fell forward and caught himself inches from the floor. His side felt as if it were on fire.

'Yes?' she said, rising from her seat. She glided forwards on bare feet and placed a hand on his side. He hissed as red blossoms of agony burst at the corners of his eyes. 'Take off your shirt.'

'I do not think–'

'You are ill. Take it off,' she said, her voice steady and warm. Goetz did as she asked, his movements awkward and stiff. The scars on his side were inflamed and as she pressed her fingertips to the edges of them, pus leaked out in thin streams. 'Poison,' she said, the word reverberating oddly in his head. The world seemed fuzzy at the edges and he shook his head, trying to clear it.

'They said there was nothing there,' he said.

'They say many things. Believe your eyes, not the words of others,' she murmured. She drew something from within her robe – a feather with a sharpened quill. Goetz couldn't stop himself from cringing slightly as she jabbed it into his wound. He wanted to pull away, but the eyes of the multitude of Myrmidias that looked down on him seemed to hold him in place.

The quill dug into the soft scar tissue, peeling it away. More pus leaked out and the pain intensified. Goetz groaned. His vision went black at the edges and he felt himself falling forward.

Then, beneath his face, damp grass. He opened his eyes and saw the hatefully familiar glare of the witch-fire and heard the stamp of beast-hooves between the twisted trees of the Drakwald. He pushed himself up, his movements loose and slow, as if he were underwater. Automatically he reached for his sword but it wasn't there.

The fire roared up and he turned. A woman stepped

out of the flames, her armour gleaming with an eerie light. 'Poisoned,' she said. 'You were poisoned.' She extended a hand and Goetz reached for it even as a storm of crows exploded out of the dark between the trees and sped around him in a cyclone of digging beaks and flashing talons. Amidst the feathers, he thought he caught a glimpse of the woman's face, before it became something else. Someone else. Goetz threw up a hand as the face expanded, passing through the black feathers even as it somehow *was* the feathers and then the great mouth was closing on him and he screamed.

He sat bolt upright, his breath burning in his lungs and his stomach churning. Twisting, he looked down at the poultice that had been placed on his wound and bound with strips of cloth. Myrma had resumed her seat, her robe loose where she had torn strips off to make the bandage.

Goetz staggered to his feet, sweat dripping from his face and chest. 'What did you–'

'You are ill. We will speak later. Rest now,' she said gently.

Bewildered, Goetz walked drunkenly towards the curtain and stepped out into the light of day. Balk was there to catch him as he fell.

'I told you he was going to embarrass us,' he heard Opchek say, even as consciousness fled.

19

Goetz awoke to the smell of cooking fires and the night breeze. He had had dreams, but he could not, for the life of him, recall them. Head full of muggy, half-formed thoughts, he left his room and wandered until he came to the battlements of the komturie. The battlement was circular and composed of equal parts stone and wood. There, he found Opchek, sitting in a chair, his booted feet propped up on the stone buttress. 'The wood comes from the Drakwald. We had it shipped in special. Resists fire like nothing I've ever seen,' Opchek said, taking a swig from a jug of wine.

Goetz looked down, his skin crawling slightly as the bad memories pressed tight to the door of his mind. Angrily he shook them aside as Opchek offered him the jug. He took it and gulped a swig down before handing it back. 'The Drakwald?'

'Oh yes. Absorbs sound and vibration as well. Keeps the stone from shifting under the recoil of the cannons,' Opchek said, seemingly oblivious to Goetz's discomfort. He gestured to the trio of wide-muzzled cannons resting on a raised platform. 'We have nine of these, acquired over the past twenty years, I'm told. Beautiful, aren't they?'

'The cannons… how were they crafted?' Goetz said. 'Surely there are no engineers here?'

'Not unless you count us, no. I don't know about you, but I'm lucky if I can get a trebuchet working. And the College of Engineering is notorious about keeping their secrets, especially where these sorts of things are concerned, selfish beggars,' Opchek said. He patted one of the guns affectionately. 'No, we bought most of these with honest gold from the dwarfs. A few are from Tilea as well. The light guns we use on the galleys were bought wholesale from some bankrupt duke from across the Black Mountains.'

Goetz blinked. While such purchases weren't unheard of, the Imperial Assessor's Office frowned on the private purchase of powder weapons. 'And the Imperial authorities didn't interfere?'

'Marienburg is no longer under Imperial authority, brother. Don't you read your history books?' Opchek smiled. 'We bought them through third parties regardless. Had them shipped in pieces and reconstructed them here. And soon enough we'll be able to manufacture our own – albeit crude-copies. The Svanii, bless their savage little spirits, take to the manufacturing arts like a fish to water.' He knocked a knuckle on the cannon barrel and chuckled. 'Best idea old Greisen had. He was a clever one, always with the cunning plans. Shame the Norscans put an axe through his twisty brainpan.'

'So it wasn't Balk's idea?'

Opchek snorted. 'Conrad is a bright one, and as dedicated as the day is long, but this komturie has been a work in progress back since the Order was first gifted it sixty years ago. Balk just happens to be the one with the drive to implement some of the – ah – bolder strategies in our war-book.' Opchek sighed and looked out at the sea.

'You don't sound happy about it,' Goetz said.

Opchek looked at him. 'I'm neither happy nor unhappy, brother. I have faith in the doing, and the reasons for it and that's enough for now.'

'Didn't you tell me earlier that faith could lead you down the wrong path?' Goetz said, his tone teasing.

Opchek chuckled. 'So I did. So I did.' He leaned on the battlement and thrust his bullet-shaped head out over the water. 'It's a grand thing to be a part of a crusade.'

'Is that what it is?' Goetz said.

'Of course. The Northern Crusades, they'll call it when it's done,' Opchek said, taking in a deep lungful of sea air. 'It'll be a glorious tale, depicting how we brought civilisation to these savage climes. I'll get three stanzas, myself.'

'Will you?'

'Oh yes. Possibly four.' Opchek glanced at him slyly. 'You'll make do with one, I think. Being much younger, you understand.'

'Do you truly believe that she's the Goddess incarnate?' Goetz said suddenly. 'That Myrma is Myrmidia come again?'

Opchek paused and let out a long breath. 'The Tileans say that she came to the mortal world before, to lead them out of their darkest years. She appeared as a shepherdess and rose to command an empire second only to Sigmar's or that of the Dragon-Emperor in far Cathay in the annals of the Old World.'

'I'm not asking what the Tileans think,' Goetz said. 'I'm asking you.'

'Faith,' Opchek said, turning around. He crossed his arms and looked steadily at Goetz. 'I suppose you can be forgiven for being suspicious. You weren't here for it. For any of it.'

'Any of what?'

'This,' Opchek said, indicating the komturie. Seeing the look of confusion on Goetz's face, he smiled and went on. 'There's been a Myrma here since the beginning. You recall what Conrad told you earlier? About their goddess?'

'Yes,' Goetz said.

'Well, that's not the whole story.' Opchek hesitated, as if debating what to say next.

'What is then?' Goetz pressed.

'Sixty years ago, our Order arrived here. And the Svanii weren't shy about showing us how unwelcome we were. So we killed them in droves, in endlessly clever ways until, finally, we shattered them. And in the shattering, we discovered that they worshipped a goddess.'

'Myrmidia?'

'Then, possibly. Now, certainly,' Opchek said. 'A goddess of battle and wisdom regardless. A goddess who spoke through those blasted geyser caves, her words hidden in poison smoke and herbs. And then Kluger, the hochmeister before Greisen, met with the first Myrma–'

'The first? How many have there been?'

'Five? Six?' Opchek said. He caught Goetz's look and smiled sadly. 'It's the caves, you see. The gases.' He tapped his chest. 'They eat away at the lungs and the brain. The one Kluger met was on her last legs. She passed away as peace was made and her daughter took over. The daughters always take over.'

'What of the fathers?'

Opchek shrugged. 'Who knows? They're so inbred that I'm not sure it matters.' He snorted. 'Granted, they freshen up the bloodline with captives every so often, but it's a drop of clean water in a Marienburg canal, if you get my meaning.'

Goetz grimaced. 'I think I do, yes.'

'They drove mutants into the caves, you know,' Opchek said. 'When they cropped up, which was often, considering what sort of debris the Sea of Claws drags ashore from the Sea of Chaos, they drove them into those gas caves. We used to have mutant hunts, in my first years here. Until we killed them all.'

Goetz felt a chill at the casual way Opchek said it, though he was careful not to show it. Kislevites were known to have little sympathy for those touched by Chaos. 'What happens if they're born now?' he said.

'There are none, apparently.' Opchek shrugged. 'They haven't had a sour birth since we killed the last of the wild mutants.' He looked steadily at Goetz. 'The blessings of the goddess, Conrad says.'

'Do you believe that?'

'I believe my eyes,' Opchek said slowly, hooking his thumbs into his belt. 'I haven't seen any freakish specimens since then. Ergo, they don't exist.'

'A bit of philosophical fallacy there,' Goetz said, chuckling.

'I'm allowed, I think.' Opchek slapped him on the shoulder. 'A fluid philosophy allowed me to shuck the wolf-skin for the eagle, after all.'

'I wasn't aware knights could do that,' Goetz said.

'I wasn't aware we couldn't,' Opchek said. 'Besides, it seemed the done thing after I punched the Ar-Ulric in the snout.' He grinned and rubbed his knuckles. 'The Brethren of the Wolf are a humourless bunch, unfortunately.'

'And we're full of jest and cheer?' Goetz said.

'Depends. Taudge, for instance, has a stick so far up his fundament that there are leaves growing out of his head,' Opchek said. He looked past Goetz. 'Hello Taudge.'

'Brothers,' Taudge said, frowning. 'What are you doing up here?'

'Getting some air,' Goetz said. 'I was thinking of taking a walk. Opchek was kind enough to join me. Care to come along?'

'Someone must,' Taudge said, falling in alongside them. 'If only to keep you both out of mischief.'

'How long has Balk been hochmeister?' Goetz said, as they left the keep.

Opchek looked at him sidelong. 'Any particular reason you'd like to know, brother?'

'Call it curiosity.'

'You'll have to try harder than that, my lad.' Opchek made a face. 'Did Berengar send you to check on us, or spy on us?'

It was Goetz's turn to make a face. 'Does it matter? I'm here now. You may as well answer me.'

'Ha! Fine. A year. No more,' Opchek said, holding up a finger. 'When old Greisen popped off, Balk was made hochmeister. Only one who wanted the job, honestly.'

'Others had more seniority?'

'Oh several. Me, for instance.' Opchek brushed a thumb along his moustaches.

'How did Greisen die?'

'Norscans,' Taudge said. 'They swept down out of the North in those serpent-boats of theirs and attacked our galleys. Killed a third of the brothers.'

Goetz's eyes widened slightly. 'What happened?'

Taudge glanced at him, then at Opchek. 'He doesn't listen too well, does he?'

'He's young. All those questions are blocking his ears.' Opchek laughed. 'Or maybe he'd like you to elaborate, my taciturn friend.'

Taudge glared at the other man, but went on regardless. 'Greisen was a diplomat,' he said, almost spitting the word. 'He made alliances with several packs of those mangy sea-wolves against the others. We were reduced to sea-wardens, keeping the peace among feuding pirate bands.' His eyes glazed slightly as he looked back into his memories. 'And then–'

'They betrayed us,' Balk said.

Taudge and Opchek flinched, as if caught out at some illicit activity. Goetz looked at the hochmeister, who had appeared almost as if out of nowhere. 'Why?' he said.

Balk's face was like something carved from marble. 'Because they are treacherous by nature. And savage by disposition. Hochmeister Greisen thought he could deal with them as one would deal with civilised men and, for that, they impaled his body and left it to rot on the shore, alongside a good many of our brothers.'

'And that's when you called for help,' Goetz said. 'From Marienburg.'

'We needed to teach them a lesson,' Balk said. 'We still need to teach them a lesson.' He smiled suddenly, the expression rippling across his face like cracks across ice. 'Which leads us to here. Today. And you,' he said. 'Come. I want to show you something.'

He led Goetz up onto the stone platform and gestured to the docks. 'Look.'

As with the previous day, there were a number of ships in the harbour. Only now they all flew the same flag. Gold on black, and a woman's face, wreathed in solar flame. As Goetz watched, men crawled across the ships, attaching armour plates and building what could only be gun-decks similar to the ones on the galley that had brought him here.

'What are you doing?' he said, despite already knowing the answer.

'What we must,' Balk said, smiling triumphantly. 'And what you see is just the beginning. Our fleet will stretch from horizon to horizon when we're done. But for what comes first, we only need these.'

'First?' Goetz said. 'What comes first?'

'Eyristaad,' Opchek murmured. 'Won't he be surprised, the stumpy little thief?'

Goetz looked at him and then at Balk, realisation slowly setting in. 'You were scouting his defences,' he said.

Balk turned away, his hands clasped behind his back. 'It's the perfect staging area. Whether he knows it or not, Eyri Goldfinger has built a settlement on the perfect point by which to invade Norsca. The rivers, you see,' he said, glancing at Goetz. 'We have a number of ships which can sail up those rivers as easy as an eel. And once they are armoured and armed, there will be nothing that can match them, save the daemon engines of the far north.' Balk's eyes narrowed. 'And I have it on good authority that we will be ready for them before too long.'

Goetz turned as the words left Balk's mouth. Myrma stood nearby stroking the feathers of the crow perched on her shoulder. She cocked her head and smiled and he felt a flush of heat spread through him. Instinctive wariness warred with fascination. Shaking his head he turned back. 'This – it's impossible!' he said.

'No, merely improbable.' Balk's smile faded. 'And worthwhile. Think of it brother! The North, civilised at last! Brought from heathen darkness into the light of our goddess!' His voice rose an octave. 'And then – then with the Norscans, we will sweep east, into the Chaos Wastes themselves. We will drive every daemon and daemon-worshipper off the edge of the world.' Balk chuckled. 'Oh, it will take generations, to be sure. But we do not lack for clarity of purpose, or dedication, do we brothers?' he said, looking at the others.

Taudge inclined his head and Opchek gave a hearty laugh. 'Nor do we lack for weapons and artillery!' he said, crossing his arms over his barrel chest. 'Either of which I'll take over purpose and dedication any day.'

Balk frowned, but before he could respond, Goetz said, 'Why haven't you informed the Grand Master of your plans?'

Balk's face lost its humour. 'Why? Who says I haven't? I've sent letters. Missives. A pigeon, even!' he snapped, his face flushing. 'Did Berengar ever respond? No! Not even when Greisen died!'

Goetz was tempted to take a step back in the face of such fury, but he held his ground. 'He says he has received nothing. That's why he sent Athalhold.'

Balk hesitated at the mention of the dead knight's name, but he regained the initiative quickly enough. 'He says. He says! He says one thing and sends a spy. Because that's what you are, brother... a spy,' Balk snarled, jabbing a finger at Goetz. 'And not the only one, I'd wager.'

'Hochmeister–' Opchek began, trying to interpose himself. Balk thrust out an arm and shoved him back.

'No,' Balk growled. 'Let him speak.'

'I already explained why I was coming here,' Goetz said, feeling himself growing angry. He thought of Athalhold and of the assassin, of everything that had occurred and his fists clenched. 'If I were a spy, would I announce myself?' Of course, if I weren't a spy, I'd have mentioned that the Marienburgers want you off this rock and soon, he thought, somewhat guiltily. He had been so preoccupied with what he had discovered, not to mention the injuries he had sustained, that he had failed to mention it to Balk. Now, as he paused to think about it, he wondered whether he should.

'Would he ask so many questions?' Opchek said, glaring at them both. 'And would we keep secrets from our own Order?' He made a sound like an aggravated bull. Balk's scowl switched from Goetz to Opchek. Then it faded and he laughed bitterly.

'No.'

Goetz stepped back. 'I never intended to accuse you, hochmeister,' he said. That at least was the truth. He had no evidence that Balk was involved in anything. As far as he knew, it had been the Norscans who were behind things, using catspaws to assure that the war between them and Svunum stayed private.

'Or I you,' Balk said, extending his hand. Goetz hesitated, and then they clasped forearms.

'WE WILL BLOCK the surf with their bodies!'

A roar of assent filled the smoky hall and Dalla flinched as the wave of noise rolled over her. A dozen godar sat around the immense mammoth-bone table Eyri had scrounged up from somewhere. Ringed around the table, the followers of each man bellowed and shouted across at one another.

The alvthing was as ancient a tradition as any in Norsca. The gathering of chieftains, only able to be initiated by one of their own or a man of sufficiently high renown, such as her father. Here, each man had a voice equal to every other, and it was in such councils that the important matters were decided. When the Kurgan rode to war, it was at an alvthing that the men of the southern coasts decided whether they would follow the banners of the *Aesgardr* to war with the Empire across the sea. When their shared shores were invaded, it was at an alvthing that recriminations were planned.

It reminded her of nothing so much as a beach full of bull seals in the rutting season. Thalfi Utergard was the primary cause of the noise, capering across the table as he was, punching the air with his ham-sized fists, the plaits of his greasy beard slapping against his hauberk. 'Just as we did before, we will turn the sea to wine with their blood!'

'Somehow, Thalfi, I don't think they'll be falling for that trick twice,' Eyri shouted. 'Now get off my table!'

'Goldfinger is right,' another chieftain said, even as

he used his staff to sweep Thalfi's feet out from under him. The big godi fell onto the table and was hauled off by his men, who snarled at his attacker like wolves. The other godi made an insulting gesture and turned to Eyri. 'As much as I hate to say it, you are right. They will be more cautious.'

'Your common sense is appreciated, Lok.' Eyri rose to his feet and leaned forward on his knuckles. 'The rest of you kindly shut up.' He swept the gathering with a flinty gaze. 'You've seen what's left of my harbour, I trust.' He thumped a fist on the table. 'Well, that'll happen to each of you unless we do something about it here and now!'

'The way I understood it, you had one of theirs in a pit with that man-eating pet of yours,' another godi said. He was called Kettil Flatnose, for obvious reasons. His handsome features were marred by the offending protuberance, broken and squashed at some point and time in the past. He stood, and the Imperial coins threaded through his hair clattered as he moved. His armour was of better quality than any other man in the room, save Eyri, and he wore a torc around his throat. 'That's why they blew the helheim out of you.'

'Aye, if you hadn't provoked them we wouldn't be here now,' another chieftain piped up, rubbing an amulet shaped like a golden frog's face between his fingers. Hrothgar Olveksan, Dalla knew. The only man among the chieftains gathered here who'd been across the great ocean and seen the green and deadly land there. His people paid for their purchases with the gold of the ancients. 'You always were a troublemaker, Eyri Light-Finger–'

'Don't call me that!' Eyri hissed, his hand going to

the long knife at his belt. 'I'm no thief!'

'And a liar as well,' Kettil said in his curiously nasal voice. 'Next you'll be trying to explain that you didn't *mean* to break my nose or that your shield got away from you.'

'Are you still going on about that?' Thalfi said. 'You ask me, he did you a favour!'

'No one asked you, oaf,' Kettil said, ignoring the other chieftain.

'Oaf? Oaf!' Thalfi said, his hand dropping to the hilt of his sword.

'Oaf,' Lok said, swatting Thalfi in the jaw with his staff. Lok was the oldest of the chieftains gathered there, and his plaited hair was as white as snow. It contrasted with his sun-darkened features. He wore heavy robes and a suit of archaic chainmail. His staff was topped with the broken and lashed pieces of an orc's skull, which made it almost as deadly a weapon as any sword.

Thalfi fell heavily, dazed and nearly senseless. His men went for their swords, but Lok's interposed themselves. Lok slammed his staff against the table. 'Oaf I call you, and oaf you are.' He looked around the hall. 'All of you, in fact. I would hear the words of Ulfar Asgrimdalr, gudja to godi Goldfinger!' he roared, sweeping his staff out to indicate Dalla and her father, where they sat out of the way. The other chieftains fell silent as her father stood.

'I thank you, Lok Helsgrim,' Ulfar said, stepping forward through the formerly raucous crowd and moving towards the table. 'I thank you and I ask that you all listen to me. I have ridden the waves of the daemon-sea and seen the ghosts that cling to the night-winds, and felt the talons of that which drives our enemies forward.' He raised his staff. 'She returns. And with her comes an ending. Our ending, unless we strike, and strike now,' he thundered, slamming the butt of his staff on the floor. The sound was loud in the silence.

'And where is your proof?' Kettil said, sitting back in his chair. 'Our gudjas have said nothing of this to us. Our priests remain silent.'

'Your priests are whipped dogs,' Ulfar said. 'You have bent them to see only that which benefits you.'

Kettil flushed. 'And if what you say is true, would not they then have spoken of it, considering the implications?'

Hrothgar laughed nastily. 'There are only implications if we join Light-Finger in this mad enterprise.' He stood, one hand on his sword-hilt. 'Also, we all know the grudge Asgrimdalr bears the einsark. Now, as he enters his twilight, it is not so strange that he wants one more chance to claw their guts?'

Ulfar tensed. Dalla half-rose from her feet, her lips peeling back from her teeth. Without turning, Ulfar swung his free hand up and gestured for her to sit. 'Aye, they owe me *weregild*. As do you, Hrothgar Olveksan.'

'I? I owe you nothing old man,' Hrothgar blustered.

'Oh but you do. For did you not take tainted gold to kill the einsark commander? And like a rock rolling down hill, did that one death not result in the deaths of hundreds as the brass-skins sought vengeance? Including those of my wife and sons?'

Hrothgar stood abruptly, clawing for the hatchet shoved through his belt as Eyri went pale. Dalla was faster, however, lunging past her father. She was up on the table and across it even as the chieftain yanked his weapon clear. Her sword sang a moment later and the hatchet fell to the table with a dull thud, accompanied by a flopping hand. Hrothgar shrieked and stumbled back, clutching his gushing stump. Kettil reacted with a curse and grabbed the other man's arm and forced the pumping wound into the nearest torch flame, cauterising it with a hiss.

As Hrothgar collapsed into the arms of one of his men, Kettil turned on Dalla. 'You dare? You dare strike a godar under the roof of an alvthing?' He looked at Eyri. 'Perhaps you meant the same for us all, eh?'

'What?' Eyri stood, his face red. 'You go too far!'

'And just how did you take this steading anyway? The same way you meant to take ours I think!' Kettil snatched up Hrothgar's hatchet and gesticulated with it. 'I knew you couldn't be trusted, Light-Finger!'

'Enough,' Ulfar said. His voice was mild, but it reached every ear in the room. Kettil paused in mid-rant and swung around.

'What will it take to convince you?' Ulfar said.

'A sign from the gods themselves,' Kettil snapped. 'Nothing less than that, old man.'

'Then you will have it,' Ulfar said. He looked at Dalla, who still crouched on the table, her sword out and dripping red. 'A challenge, my daughter.'

Dalla spat at Kettil and stood. 'A challenge.'

Kettil eyed her sword and went pale. 'But–'

'You wanted a sign, Flatnose,' Lok said, smiling grimly. The old man rose. 'If you win, this alvthing concludes as it began, with nothing changed. If Dalla Ulfarsdottir wins, however, we go to war!'

* * *

BALK STIRRED HIS axe through the water that had collected between the fang-like rocks. In the ripples, he
saw the images of what had been. Memories were his
burden to bear, heavier even than his armour. A thrill
of guilt flared through him and he fought it down.

'He fought well,' he said, after a moment. 'Precise.
Efficient. He is a credit to the Order.' He looked at
the priestess, squatting over her vent, her head hung
low after the effort of bringing the visions to life. She
looked up at him through her curtain of hair and
grinned. If she noticed Balk's shudder at the sight of
her teeth, she gave no sign.

'Yes,' Myrma said. 'He is blessed by the goddess,
though he knows it not.'

Balk made a face and his grip on his axe tightened.
She could practically see the thoughts that flashed across
the surface of his mind like lightning. An almost incan-
descent fanaticism and lust for vengeance, coupled with
a stubborn determination and iron resolve. He did his
ancestors proud in that way, she knew. Such men had
been instrumental in giving her people the time they
needed to escape Sigmar's wrath. 'Yes,' he said. He hesitated a moment, and then said, 'Should we–?'

Myrma cocked her head and eyed him with an
amusement she didn't let show on her face. 'At your
command, Master Balk…'

'Wait!' he said, throwing up a hand. 'Just – just wait.
Give me a moment to – to think.' He looked away. 'I
need to think.'

'Of course. But–'

'I said that I need to think!' Balk roared, startling the
crows that perched on the rocks. They fluttered into the
air croaking and scattering feathers.

'Do you still think he is a spy? Like the other?' she needled. It pleased her no end to point out his hypocrisy, though doubtless he did not notice it. He was far too preoccupied to be so self-aware. His schemes were brittle things, like the footsteps of a calf: easily disrupted and tripped up, easily butchered, easily supplanted by better things, stronger things.

'Yes. No.' He shook his head, like a bull beset by a nettlesome fly. He looked at her. 'No. If Myrmidia has taken him to her bosom, I will think no ill of him.' Of course he would think so, with his mulish devotion to the Slaughter-Woman and her glib pronouncements. Myrma fought to keep her face blank.

She rose and shrugged. 'Then do not.' She waved a hand. 'Go. Make ready for war, master.'

'But–'

'Myrmidia thirsts for the blood of our enemies.' she said, pressing her hands against his breastplate. She bent her fingers, scraping her nails down across Myrmidia's symbol, now caked with mud and oil. His armour was dulled and stained, as was the armour of every knight on this island, and the hated sigils were hidden. 'Take him with you, show him the rightness of the goddess's cause or else all that you have worked for will be endangered. What will he do, your fallen Grand Master, if he learns of our true goal… of the goddess's design?'

'Berengar,' Balk said, his face becoming grim. 'He'd wipe us out in a heartbeat; he'd bring the full weight of the Empire down on us.'

'So he will, if Goetz does not join us.' She smiled slightly and continued, 'You go where you are needed…'

'And we do what must be done. Yes.' He looked at her, his face set in grim lines. 'I will make him see.' He reached out and touched her face, almost fearfully. 'I wish it had been me. I thought it would be. I thought…' He pushed her back gently. 'Thank you for showing me what I must do, my lady.' Then he turned and stalked away, his back ramrod stiff. When he had gone she sighed and sank back onto her haunches, a grin on her lips. The island rumbled softly beneath her as the volcanic vents belched and simmered.

'Exactly as you said, mistress,' she murmured. 'Balk is not the one, but he has brought him to us sure enough. He has brought us our Myrmidon.' She chuckled, and the crows perched in the nooks and crannies of the cavern echoed her.

She had nearly exhausted herself days earlier, ensuring that the fen-dwellers hadn't killed the knight. 'Goetz,' she said, rolling the name around on her tongue. He was marked by the Great Mutator, his body riven with poisons that were as insidious as they were undetectable.

That those poisons hadn't yet begun their fearful work on him was either a testament to his strength, or to the hand of the Father of Illusions. Her queen had whispered the secret skeins that clung to this man to her… not of destiny, but of place and position. He was a cog, shaped and placed to fill the hole of another, but ill-fitting for all of that. Plans within plans which had been dislodged by still other plans. In her mind's eye, she saw a screaming thing, writhing in a blister-burrow within the tainted heart of the Drakwald. Another child of the Lord of Labyrinths, birthed to meet the wrong man. She grinned, baring her filed teeth in an agony of ecstatic contemplation.

A push here, a pull there, and Old Father Fate wove strange circles. None of which was stranger than the one now encircling the man known as Hector Goetz.

As one, the crows set to croaking, and in their cacophony she heard a voice purring assent. Yes, Goetz was marked for great things indeed. She glanced towards the bulging pods that nestled in the corners and crevices. They seemed to flex and moan as her gaze touched them and her smile threatened to split her face as she glanced down at the piles of discarded, dwarf-forged armour that nestled at the foot of every pod. Birthed as they were from the cast-off shells of dead men, they were growing into something wonderful indeed.

20

'INVASION?' GOETZ SAID.

'Invasion,' Balk repeated, tapping a finger against the mast. They stood on the deck of one of the black-sailed galleys preparing to launch. Balk looked out over the Sea of Claws, his face set in an easy smile. 'Specifically an invasion of the southern coast of Norsca.'

'That's a bit…' Goetz trailed off, looking around as preparations were made for casting off with the evening tide. It was a far brisker sort of affair than he had witnessed in Marienburg. The crew, composed mostly of Svanii, moved with a sharp efficiency that bespoke both unfamiliarity and eagerness.

'Grandiose?' Balk said.

'I was searching for a less insulting word. Rhetoric was among the subjects I was taught.'

'Ha! Yes.' Balk grinned. 'It is grandiose. Epic, even. Worthy of a saga or three, as the Norscans would say.'

'Why?' Goetz said. Balk had taken him into his

confidence soon after their argument. The man was mercurial, his moods changing like the tides. Goetz was coming to understand why Berengar had been concerned, though he was careful not to let it show on his face.

'It needs to be done. And the goddess commands. Isn't that enough?'

Goetz said nothing. Balk went to the upper deck and sat in the chair mounted there. He pressed his fingers together and rested his chin across them as Goetz came to a halt in front of him. He frowned. 'I sense trepidation.'

'There are rumours. In Marienburg…' Goetz said.

Balk sighed and leaned back. 'Still you doubt me?'

'It's this plan I doubt,' Goetz said. 'Do you think you can hold Eyristaad? With the men you have now?'

'I could hold half the Empire with the men I have now,' Balk said primly. 'But, fine. Why not see for yourself?' He leaned forward. 'Come with us. I intend to begin as soon as we're ready to cast off. We'll put Eyristaad to the torch and build a new beginning on the ashes. Then, maybe, you'll begin to see things my way.'

Goetz nodded slowly. 'Perhaps.'

'Besides, I assume you'll be wanting a bit of repayment for the trouble they gave you,' Balk said.

'I try not to hold grudges.' Goetz watched as the Svanii laid in sail and tied off ropes with simian-like agility. With their savage tattoos and grunting language, they reminded him of nothing so much as feral children. Then he would catch sight of a weapon or a coiling scar and he would be reminded that they were anything but. Smaller and slimmer than the Norscans they were related to, they nonetheless possessed a similar brute vigour that Goetz couldn't help but be impressed by.

'The dwarfs have a saying… "Cherish your grudges as your children, for both will only grow stronger with time",' Balk said.

'Not exactly something to look forward to,' Goetz said.

'Really?' Balk said, looking at him in mock surprise. 'Quite a wise folk, dwarfs.' He stood. 'Still, you take my meaning. We leave in an hour. I'd like to have your sword with us.'

Goetz watched him leave. 'Stay or go?' he mused. What would the Grand Master say? he wondered. He looked at the harbour and the galleys that populated it, and wondered what Ambrosius's fleet would think when it arrived to kick Balk's men off the island. He smiled grimly. What was it the abbot had said? 'We are playing dice with the gods,' he said. 'Is that what I'm doing?'

He went to the rail and leaned on it, looking at nothing. 'Use your brain,' he muttered. Neither Ambrosius nor Berengar for that matter had seemed to be aware that Svunum was inhabited… had the hochmeister hidden that from them? Or had Balk's predecessors merely not thought it worth mentioning?

'Not worth mentioning,' Goetz said. He watched cogs bearing Svanii warriors bob towards several of the farther galleys. Armed and eager, they shook their spears at him and he waved half-heartedly. 'Not at all, eh?'

An armed encampment. Not merely a hundred or so knights, but an armed, aggressive population, divinely motivated and well-led. It was like something out of an epic saga of the time before Sigmar.

That's likely how Balk wanted to think of it at any rate. Goetz thought of the armies said to populate the Chaos Wastes to the north and wondered at the parallels there instead. It wasn't a pleasant thought, and it stirred up memories of the bird-masked assassins who had tried to kill him in the temple of Myrmidia.

Thinking of them naturally led him to meet the gazes of the crows perched on the rail and on the ropes. The birds eyed him with disturbing intensity and his hand found the hilt of his sword. No, not his sword. His sword was still in Eyristaad.

'Balk said he needed my sword,' he said to the crow watching him from the rail. 'Only I don't have my sword, do I?'

'Perhaps you'd like to get it back, hmmm?' Goetz didn't turn as the woman slid off the rail and came to stand behind him. The crow on her shoulder fluttered its wings in agitation and she cooed softly to it before turning back to him. 'Losing a good weapon is like losing a limb.'

'I didn't realise you were there,' Goetz said, glancing at Myrma. As lovely as she was at a distance, there was something frankly unnatural about her beauty close up. It was as if her face shifted, forcing you to focus on each aspect of her features individually. As if there was more than one face there, striving to be seen.

'That is because I did not wish you to,' she said. 'You interest me.'

'And you interest me,' Goetz said. It was the truth. Though not for the reasons that a woman usually interested him. 'You speak the tongue of my people well. The brothers here educated you?'

'They educated all of my people. We have learned the arts of the sea and metal from them over several generations,' she said. She reached up and stroked the crow's beak. Its glittering eyes bored into Goetz's own, and he made a game attempt at ignoring it. It reminded him unpleasantly of the bird that had attacked him the day he'd arrived in Marienburg.

'Where I come from, Myrmidia is associated with the eagle, not the crow,' he said, more for something to say than any other reason. She wielded silence like a flail, and it scraped raw runnels in his temper.

'Eagles are great warriors. But the crow is a survivor,' she said. 'As are we.'

Something about her gaze made him nervous. 'I have not yet thanked you for what you did for me,' Goetz said, tapping his side. She smiled and inclined her head.

'It was nothing. Payment on a debt yet to be owed,' she said. Goetz was about to ask what exactly that meant, but she continued on before he had the chance. 'Your faith is like water. It has not the solidity of Balk's or the others. Why?'

'What do you know of my faith?' Goetz said, feeling slightly insulted.

She laughed and Goetz felt his flush deepen as the sound danced along his spine. 'I know it is a hard thing, and not comforting. Like the sea, it rises and falls and it is cold. Your faith does not warm you, Hector Goetz. It drags you down.' Goetz turned away. He scowled out at the sea.

'In your heart, in your soul, you do not believe,' she said. He glanced at her out of the corner of his eye and her face seemed to bulge and shift oddly. He whirled and she met his confused gaze calmly. 'Despite everything, you do not believe.'

'I believe,' he said hoarsely.

'You do not. But you will,' she said. Then she left him where he stood, gaping after her.

GULLS BANKED AND spun through the grim grey air. Torches were lit and a hue and cry went up all across the steading as word of the challenge spread. Eyristaad was crammed with people, each of the godar having brought a retinue worthy of their esteemed status. Those merchants who made the steading their home were pressing their wares on the newcomers with glee. The slave-market especially was doing a booming trade.

Dalla ignored all of this, preferring instead to focus on her swordplay. The gleaming blade caught what little light there was as she moved through a series of exercises she'd learned from a travelling Cathayan mercenary. Her mimicry was crude at best, but she found the movements soothing. She wondered if the einsark felt the same way when he practised. Thinking of that made her think of him.

He was a warrior, no two ways there; and a good one. There were not many men who could put a troll down with only a sword, yet he had done it. It made him... interesting. She pivoted and slashed, pushing the thought aside.

'Foolishness,' Eyri muttered, watching her. Dalla ignored him.

'Necessary,' her father corrected.

'And if she fails?'

'She won't,' Ulfar said, hunching forward as a chill wind rippled through the steading. 'She can't.'

'Cheerful as ever,' Eyri said, pulling his cloak closer

about his squat form. 'Kettil is good. Better than most.'

'And I am better than that,' Dalla said, stabbing her sword point into the ground. 'Or have you forgotten?' She motioned towards his hand, with its missing fingers. Eyri frowned and looked away.

'Kettil won't be drunk. And he won't be trying for a kiss, woman.'

'You've seen me fight, Eyri. Is it concern prompting your words, or are you hoping to frighten me off?' Dalla said.

Ulfar chuckled. 'Is that it, godi? Do you yearn for failure so that you might have an excuse to let things lie?'

'I am no coward!' Eyri snapped.

'No one said you were,' Dalla said. 'Merely that you might want to shirk your responsibilities. That we do know you do.'

'Mind your tongue.'

'Mind yours,' Dalla said, yanking her sword free of the soil. Once more she admired the balance of the thing. In all ways it was an improvement over any other blade she had held. She gave a few swipes and turned as the sound of drums started up. The beat was steady and deep and the crowd fell silent as Kettil Flat-nose stepped into the circle of torches. He carried a long-handled axe in one hand and a round shield on his other.

Dalla scooped up her own shield and trotted forwards to meet him. The sun was a distant promise on the horizon. She took a final, cleansing breath, and slapped the flat of her blade against her shield's rim. 'Well? Ready to get on with it, Flatnose?'

Kettil winced as she slapped her shield again. 'I'll give you one last chance, Ulfarsdottir… renounce your challenge and no man here will mock you.'

'Whereas every man will mock you, eh? No, no, I think we shall see this through, Flatnose,' Dalla said. Dirt skidded beneath her foot as she lunged, the tip of her sword scoring a line across the face of Kettil's shield. He jumped back like a scalded cat and his axe looped out. She deflected it with her shield and jabbed his leg, causing him to yelp.

He was only off balance for a moment, however. Jerking his leg back, he chopped out with his axe, cutting a divot out of her shield. Her arm ached from the force of the blow. Pretty as he was, Kettil was also a strong man and an experienced warrior. She went for his leg again, drawing blood this time. The edge of his shield dropped, punching her sword to the ground and the handle of his axe connected with her head. Stars burst in her vision and she only just avoided the next blow. She threw herself aside and scrambled to her feet as he came at her in a rush.

They traded blows for several minutes. Dalla hopped back and took a breath as he overextended himself and stumbled.

'You fight well,' he grunted, wheezing.

'For a woman?'

'For anyone,' he said. 'But it will avail you little. I am stronger.'

'We'll see,' Dalla said. She stamped forward, her sword licking out to draw a line of red across his cheek. He jerked back with a snarl and her blade gouged a line across his neck before scraping against his hauberk. She spun and chopped into the side of his shield, using the momentum of the blow to rip it off his arm. Off balance, he dropped his axe and fell.

Dalla kicked the shield off her blade and advanced. 'Surrender, Flatnose. Your people need their godi.'

'If their chieftain can't defeat a woman, even a woman as skilled as you, then he doesn't deserve the title,' Kettil said, scooping up his axe and cracking a blow against her hastily interposed shield. It cracked at the point of impact and her shoulder screamed in agony. Dalla ignored the sensation and drove forward, slamming the crumpling shield against Kettil's chest. She shoved him back into one of the torches and he went tumbling, the flames licking at him.

He tossed his axe aside to beat at the flames and she raised her sword in triumph. Before she could say anything, however, an explosion rendered all of her efforts moot.

The first was followed by a second, a third and a fourth. Wood splintered and toppled as already abused structures collapsed in the orange glow of newly born fires. Crouching to avoid flying debris, Dalla looked in incomprehension at the sea. Four black-sailed galleys drifted past the steading, their decks awash in bronze dragon-maws that belched death and ruin.

21

'Ha! That got them running!' Opchek said, pounding the rail with a fist. He, along with Goetz and a dozen others, waited to descend into the sleek boats that would take them ashore.

Goetz didn't share the other man's enthusiasm about either the destruction being wrought or the rest of it. He held tight to the hilt of his new sword and scanned the shore, almost hoping for some sign of organised resistance.

The galleys had anchored themselves parallel to the shore and presented a solid wall of armour and gun muzzles. The latter roared as swiftly as the Svanii manning them could load them and light the fuses. 'They seem quite enthusiastic,' Goetz yelled, trying to be heard over the roar of the guns.

'Considering how often the Norscans raided their shores before the Order took up residence, can you blame them? These folk cherish their feuds almost as much as the dwarfs.' Balk said, crossing the deck towards them. As with Goetz and the other knights, the hochmeister was clad in the full panoply of field-plate, with a towering helmet and a wide shield that bore the same emblem as that on the sails of the galleys.

Goetz looked up at the sails and the design on the shields that surrounded him. It was just familiar enough for the alterations to strike him as alien and strange. 'Eyes front, Hector,' Opchek said, bringing the side of his fist down on Goetz's shoulder. The big Kislevite had taken to calling him by his given name in the aftermath of his disastrous visit with Myrma. 'We're ready to go ashore.'

Awkwardly the knights clambered down the wood and rope ladders into the waiting skiffs. Each skiff could hold ten fully armoured knights as well as the same number of livery-clad Svanii, each of whom carried a hatchet, spear and shield and were already waiting for the former.

Goetz couldn't help but flinch as the cannonade continued, pounding the shoreline. Opchek grinned at him as they both settled into a crouch at the prow of the skiff. 'It'll take some getting used to, but goddess help me I do so love the smell of a good barrage.'

'I've never seen it so – so concentrated,' Goetz said, ducking as the telltale whistle of another round filled the air. 'I've been in battles before where it was used, but this…'

'Aye, I once fought alongside the Ironsides during one of the Countess Emmanuelle of Nuln's interminable forays into territories not her own. If we had a few of those hand-cannons, we'd be near unstoppable. As it stands, this pounding is only as good as our follow-through,' Opchek said. 'Speaking of which…'

The skiff crunched as it slammed ashore, propelled ashore by Svanii muscle. The spearmen clambered out and formed a rough line. They knelt, spears extended and shields raised. The knights stopped just behind them. There were only a few Norscans on shore, and these immediately charged forward, howling out their barbaric war-hymns at the top of their lungs.

Goetz could not fault them for their courage. It took a certain kind of bravery to charge headlong into a bristling wall of spears, and each of them possessed it in abundance. Balk, however, did not appear to share that respect.

'Spears… UP,' Balk snapped. The Svanii raised their spears and waited. The first Norscan to reach them crashed gut-first into a waiting spear, unable to halt his rush in time. The second and the third ploughed past him, almost leaping over the Svanii in their eagerness to come to grips with the knights behind them.

'Leave them! They're mine!' Balk snapped, as Goetz moved forward. Balk's axe thundered home into the hairy skull of the first man to reach him and he back-handed the second with his shield, knocking him flat. The other knights reacted then, with five swords striking out to pin the Norscan to the shore. Balk whirled on his men, his eyes blazing with rage. 'I said he was mine!'

'Plenty to go around, Conrad,' Opchek said, gesturing with his sword. Out of the smoke boiling across the shore, indistinct shapes moved. Goetz turned and saw that the other two skiffs had beached themselves. Little under fifty men, facing the goddess alone knew how many.

'Crossbows would have been nice,' Goetz said as they started forward.

'A lot of things would have been nice,' Opchek said. 'A jug of wine, a bit of good Ostermark cheddar, maybe a pretty girl.' The Norscans charged onto the shore in a disorganised mass. Opchek raised his shield and glanced at Goetz. 'A lot of things.'

The Norscans slammed into them with a roar.

DALLA SWUNG HER arm, trying to work some feeling back into it. Nearby, Eyri barked orders at his men, trying to organise the steading's defenders. The other godar were doing the same, bullying their followers into warbands.

'What is going on?' Hrothgar said, looking around wildly. He was still pale from blood loss, and his stump had been bound tightly and strapped to his chest. 'What is it?'

'While we argued about seeking out trouble, it came looking for us,' Lok said. He looked at Eyri. 'My men are yours. We stand or fall together, Goldfinger.'

'Wonderful sentiments,' Kettil said. He had acquired a new shield and he tested the edge of his axe against the rim. 'Of course, it's not like we can escape, eh?'

'Escape? Who wants to escape?' Thalfi roared, raising his sword and axe. 'Let us wreath them in their own intestines!'

'We'll have to get through their armour first,' Eyri snapped. Dalla's eyes widened as she saw a group of his men coming forward, their arms straining as they held tight to the chains attached to Eyri's troll. The beast had been crammed into a suit of crude armour and it roared and jerked as they hauled it forward.

'And your plan is to use that?'

'No, I intend to give it to Balk as a token of my esteem,' Eyri said acidly. 'Get that brute going in the right direction damn you!' The latter was directed towards his men. The troll had obviously smelt the fire and the blood and it was growing far more agitated – not to mention animated – than Dalla had ever seen it. A chain whip snapped out, flensing the creature's rubbery skin.

With a berserk scream, the beast tore itself free of its handlers and charged towards the beach with a simian motion. It crashed through a lean-to, scattering squawking hens and tossing animal hide and wooden scraps in every direction.

'Troll's loose,' Dalla said unhelpfully. Eyri glared at her.

'Yes. Thank you. Shouldn't you be doing something useful?'

'I intend to,' Dalla said, slapping her sword against her shield rim. She glanced at Kettil. 'Come, Flatnose. The world's black rim calls for walkers.'

'I don't intend to die here, witch,' Kettil said, falling into step with her. His men followed suit.

'Good. Neither do I,' Dalla said, baring her teeth in a feline grin. The other chieftains joined them, striding forward with weapons in hand, their *einjhar* gathered about them in a protective mob. Thalfi began singing a bawdy tune, belting out the verses with more enthusiasm and volume than ability.

A flash of brass caught her eye through the smoke. Spear-points pierced the cloud of ash and embers and she shrieked in anticipation. Then, still shrieking, she began to run towards her enemies.

22

GOETZ NEARLY FELL as the rocks of the beach shifted beneath his feet. He smashed the edge of his shield into the Norscan's wide-open mouth, cutting off his war cry. As the man staggered, clutching at his bloody mouth, Goetz chopped him down. Stepping over the body, he rejoined the group as they moved up into the settlement.

'Some fun, eh?' Opchek said, shaking the blood off his sword.

'No,' Goetz said.

'Could be worse,' the Kislevite said. 'You could be dead.'

'True,' Goetz said, raising his shield even as a drizzle of arrows pounded down upon them. The entire group halted with well-trained precision and sank down, shields raised. Goetz winced as three arrows hammered into his shield, the broad head of one scraping across his vambrace. He looked at Opchek. 'Crossbows,' he said. 'Those would have come in handy.'

'The Svanii aren't what you call natural archers,' Balk said as the group rose. 'Besides, until we have a bowyer and a fletcher in residence, I'd rather not rely on anything we can't build or repair ourselves.'

'Says the man wearing dwarf-made armour,' Goetz said. Balk looked at him, his features unreadable behind his visor.

'Yes, well, we'll soon have an answer for that,' he said. Then he turned away, leaving Goetz puzzled.

'What did he–' he began, glancing at Opchek. His inquiry was interrupted by another blanket of arrows. 'The houses. They've got archers on the rooftops,' he said.

'Smart,' Opchek said. 'Someone's thinking.'

'Yes. Me. Let's go,' Goetz said, shoving his way out of the group and trudging towards the closest houses. He paused only to snatch a torch from the hand of a startled Svanii. Opchek hurried after him, positioning his shield over both their heads as they moved.

'What are you planning?' the other knight said. 'Whatever it is, it better be worth it!' he continued as an arrow glanced off his shield and scuttled down across his arm.

'Trapner's *On Clearing Redoubts*, page fifteen,' Goetz said, hurrying towards the closest doorway. 'Fire is the invader's closest ally.' Without slowing, Goetz kicked in the door. The driftwood cracked and split from the blow and he shouldered his way in, using his shield as a prise-bar.

'These huts are too damp to light! Not like this anyway,' Opchek said, following him inside. They could hear men running across the roof above. Goetz kicked over a clay urn full of whale oil.

'Did you know that they use this oil in lamp wicks?' he said, touching the burning end of the torch to the oil. It caught with a crackling hiss. Goetz tossed the torch to Opchek and hefted the urn, splattering the dregs of the oil all over the room. Letting the urn fall and shatter on the floor, he stepped back as the flames spread hungrily. Foul-smelling smoke spread towards them.

'Wonderful,' Opchek coughed. 'Now what?'

'Now we repeat,' Goetz said, gesturing to the sagging wall. 'It's not all stone.' Without waiting for Opchek, he charged at the wall and crashed through, scattering chunks of loose stone and dried mud. Off balance, he crashed through the next wall and fell into the hut. He was on his feet in a minute, face to face with a Norscan who had dropped through the thatch roof. Goetz slammed his shield into the startled warrior, pinning him against the wall. 'Opchek!' he called.

'Busy!' Opchek cried out as he backed through the hole Goetz had made, duelling with a gigantic swordsman. The Norscan growled and battered through Opchek's defences, and the Kislevite cursed as he lost his grip on his sword. Opchek made do, shoving the torch into the man's face and setting his beard and hair aflame. The Norscan screamed shrilly and clutched at his fiery skull. Opchek kicked him back into a set of raw-edged shelves. Urns splattered and the fire leapt from the dying man to the floor and the ceiling.

Goetz, meanwhile, jammed the edge of his shield up under his opponent's chin. With an almost apologetic grunt, he jerked the curled rim of the shield to the side, tearing a ragged hole in the man's throat. He stepped back as the body toppled forward, twitching.

'Did you sharpen that?' Opchek said incredulously. Goetz shrugged.

'You never know when you're going to have to improvise. First Litany of Battle…'

'Always be prepared, yes,' Opchek finished, shaking his head. 'Still…'

'You're obviously not familiar with Brother Helmeyer of the Talabheim Komturie,' Goetz said. He tapped the surface of his shield. 'He puts murder holes in his shields. He mounts two of those nasty little repeating crossbows the elves like so much on the inside.' Goetz headed for the door, shaking his head. 'That's much worse, I should thi–'

The grey arm and boulder-sized fist pounded through the door, narrowly missing Goetz's head. He staggered back, eyes widening as the door was ripped from its hinges and a familiar, horrible visage leered at him. 'Troll!' he shouted.

'What?' Opchek said.

Goetz had no time to reply as fingers like boat hooks pierced the surface of his shield and wrenched him off his feet. He was slung through the wall and into the street by one whip-like motion of the monster's arm even as it splintered the support beam for the shack, bringing it down. Goetz hit the ground and bounced. When he rolled to a stop, breathing heavily, he saw the troll batter its way free of the burning wreckage of the hut as Opchek staggered to his feet. The Kislevite levered a ruined roof beam off himself only to find the troll bearing down on him.

'Out of the way!'

Opchek dove aside as Balk and Taudge and a squad of Svanii charged out from between the burning buildings. Taudge met the beast with a bellow and smooth lunge. His blade slid through the creature's belly and became snagged on something in its ponderous gut. It brought both fists down on the knight, dropping him insensate on the street.

'Off him, monster!' Opchek said, cutting at it from the side. A second later, he went down like a sack of bricks, hammered flat by the slightest swat of the creature's paw. Two Svanii died next, torn into pieces by the blood-maddened monster. Goetz and Balk went after it from either side. Goetz cursed as his sword edge met the troll's armour and skidded off in a shower of sparks. Balk had more luck, his axe whirling around to lop off one of the creature's hands.

It howled in agony and punched the hochmeister with the gouting stump, knocking him off his feet. A splayed foot thudded down inches from Balk's head as he desperately rolled aside. Goetz lunged, driving his sword home through a gap in the badly fitting armour. The troll reared back, grabbing for him. Goetz avoided the clumsy movement and twisted his blade, causing the beast to double over and vomit. The rocks sizzled and hissed as the acidic bile turned them into sludge.

Ripping his sword free, Goetz immediately brought it down on a gangly arm, severing it at the elbow. His sword rebounded off the rocks and he twisted, chopping upwards into the creature's belly, opening it in a burst of slippery flesh and foul gases. The troll screamed like an oversized child and brought its spurting wrist thudding across his head. Goetz fell to his knees, dazed.

Balk's axe flashed, splitting the troll's head in two. It groaned and slumped, body twitching. Yanking his weapon free, the hochmeister helped Goetz to his feet. 'Nicely done, brother,' Balk said, flipping up his visor.

'As you say, hochmeister,' Goetz said. 'Look out!' He drove his shoulder into Balk, knocking the other man aside. The thrown spear tore a furrow in Goetz's cheek and he pitched backwards, one hand clapped to his face.

The Norscans roared out brutal war-songs as they charged down on the group. On his back, Goetz saw that these men were more richly attired than any other Norscan he had seen. Then he caught sight of Eyri Goldfinger's squat shape and he pushed himself to his feet, eager to come to grips with his former captor.

Snatching up his sword, he dove into the melee. He parried a blow that would have finished a wounded Svanii and swept his attacker aside and out of the world. Spears dug for his blood and he chopped them to kindling. Using shield and sword, he forced himself a path through the Norscans. Weapon points blunted and chipped on his armour and their swords broke on his own when they met. The best armour that the elder race could produce met crude Northern iron, and the latter was forced to retreat.

For a moment, Goetz thought he saw a pale form sliding through the press of combat. A woman's face, sharp and beautiful turned towards him through a space between the spears and swords, her mouth open in what might have either been benediction or warning. A glowing spear gestured and Goetz's hackles prickled as he was forced around.

The movement saved his life. An axe that would have split him crown to groin bounced off the turf. Goetz struck back, gutting his attacker with a surge of desperate strength. Just as suddenly as that, he found himself in a cleared space. Bodies surrounded him, and his armour was no longer gleaming, instead coated in the excrescence of slaughter. Men pressed away from him, their eyes wide. Only one in particular held any interest for him.

The old man stood amidst the slaughter like an old tree weathering a storm. Spear-points shivered to pieces before they got too close and swords shattered on his withered shoulders. He stood calm, his face twisted in an expression of concentration. Goetz fancied that he could see the faintest pulse of an arctic-hued nimbus surrounding the shaman. With a shout, the old man lifted his staff and struck the ground. Warriors were thrown off their feet as the ground shuddered and heaved. Goetz kept his feet, but only barely.

He pushed through the melee towards the old man. If he were some sort of barbaric sorcerer, then he was far too dangerous to leave alive. Though Goetz bore him no personal malice, he had to die. As if sensing these thoughts, the old man glanced at him and Goetz felt a shock of something like recognition.

'What–?' he began. Then a spear-point darted for him and he was forced to turn aside to parry it. 'Captain Goldfinger,' he said, pointing his sword at the spear's wielder. 'Or is it Chief Goldfinger?'

'Sir Knight,' Eyri said, hesitating. 'I wondered if you'd pay us another visit.'

'Happy to oblige,' Goetz said thickly. He spat out the blood that had collected in his mouth from the wound on his cheek and started forward. 'I owe you for that rap on the head. For the crew of the *Nicos*, and for trying to feed me to a troll.'

'I seem to collect debts like a whorehouse collects lice,' Eyri said. He struck out, the spear in his hands piercing the battered face of Goetz's shield and driving him back a half-step. The Norscan was stronger than Goetz had given him credit for. Eyri's thick arms bulged with muscle as he shoved Goetz back another step.

Setting his feet, Goetz strained against his opponent, putting his weight behind his shield. Suddenly, Eyri stepped back, releasing his spear. Goetz stumbled forward, nearly toppling. A hatchet chopped out and he only narrowly avoided it, jumping back and losing his shield in the process. Eyri advanced, drawing a second hatchet.

'Come on then, einsark!' Eyri crowed. 'Come and take your debt!'

'I think mine takes precedence,' Balk said as he brought his axe around into Eyri's belly. The Norscan was driven into the air for a moment by the force of Balk's blow and he flopped to the beach with a limp finality. Balk stalked forward, swinging the axe up. 'It was always going to end this way, Eyri. There's only so long you can stand in the path of a goddess.'

A hurtling form caught the hochmeister in the back before he could deliver the deathblow and he staggered. A shield-rim caught him on the side of the head, shattering as it impacted with his helmet. Balk was thrown off his feet, senseless. The sound of the blow snapped Goetz out of his reverie and he charged forward. Balk's attacker spun to meet his charge and their eyes locked over their crossed swords.

'You,' Goetz said.

'You!' Dalla growled. 'Again, you!'

Goetz forced her sword aside and rammed her with his shoulder, sending her flailing backwards. 'Always me,' he said, stepping forward. 'That's my sword you have there.'

'Then come and take it,' she said, scrambling up, waving the blade between them. 'Have the full measure!' She sprang forward, faster than he could track, and tried to drive the sword through his chest. Goetz tried to parry and was thrown off balance as his weapon shivered asunder at the point of impact. With a triumphant cry, Dalla capitalised on his predicament, chopping down on his exposed side. He twisted desperately and caught the descending blade with both hands. Metal rasped against metal as he halted the tip only bare inches from his chest. Straining, he pushed the weapon up. Blood ran down the insides of his gauntlets. Eyes wide, Dalla tried to force it back down.

Goetz shoved the blade aside and it sank into the ground. Rising, he drove a fist into the swordswoman's belly, knocking her down. She curled around the blow and made a whooping sound as she tried to suck air into her lungs. Goetz uprooted the blade and jabbed the tip between her eyes.

'Yield,' he said.

'I know no such word,' she spat, and made to rise. Goetz shook his head and stepped back.

'I'd rather not kill you,' he said.

Dalla uttered a wordless snarl and pulled her legs under her, preparing to spring. Goetz tensed.

The haft of the axe connected with the top of her head with a decidedly audible *thump*. Dalla pitched forward and didn't move. Balk grinned at Goetz. 'For shame, brother. You should know that she-wolves are more dangerous than the males.'

'I've traded blows with her twice now,' Goetz said, looking down at the unconscious woman.

'And?'

'And nothing. I can't seem to kill her,' he said.

'Didn't look like you wanted to,' Opchek said. He gestured over his shoulder. 'They're regrouping, Conrad.'

'Eyri?' Balk said, looking around.

'Gone. They've retreated, but listen…' Goetz did. Faintly, on the wind, he could hear the wail of horns.

'What is that?'

'Reinforcements. Damnation.' Balk frowned. 'There were more of them here than we figured. Why?'

'Questions for another time. We've shown our strength. Now it's time to go before they show theirs.' Opchek began shouting orders. 'Grab the wounded and then gather up the prisoners and the loot!'

'Loot?' Goetz said, hesitating. 'I thought we came for the town?'

'Call it a consolation gift. If we can't have it, we'll take what we can and burn what we can't, eh Conrad?'

'Yes,' Balk said distractedly. He was looking down at Dalla, his finger running gently across the curve of his axe. Goetz watched him and Balk, as if noticing the other knight for the first time, shook himself and said, 'Take her.'

'Why? She doesn't look like she can pull an oar,' Opchek said.

'You're making a habit out of questioning me, brother,' Balk said, letting the head of his axe tap gently against Opchek's breastplate. Opchek blanched.

'Right. Take her with us. Wonderful idea, hochmeister.'

Balk smiled serenely. 'That's better. We must maintain discipline, eh brother?' he said, looking at Goetz. 'Now… let's take a page from Brother Goetz's book and burn this sty to the ground, shall we?'

'IS HE DEAD?' Thalfi Utergard said, looking down at Eyri. The big man was painted red from crown to sole, though none of the blood seemed to be his. There were some who said Thalfi was ulfsark, and looking at him, his fellow chieftains could believe it.

'I'm not dead,' Eyri groaned. He patted his armoured torso gingerly. 'Gromril. Won it in a game of draughts from a trader a few months ago.'

'Are you sure you're not dead?' another chieftain said warily. 'Axe might have crushed your lungs. You could be suffocating even now…'

'I'm not dead, Grettir Halfhand, no matter how much you might wish,' Eyri growled. 'Someone help me up.'

'If you're not dead, what do you need our help for?' Halfhand said. He was nearly as big as Thalfi, with a ginger-coloured spade-shaped beard that had been greased with bear fat and twisted into spikes. One hand was covered by a modified knight's gauntlet, its gleaming surface covered in hammered runes.

'Up, Goldfinger,' Lok Helsgrim said, extending his staff. Eyri grabbed it and the old man hauled him to his feet with little apparent difficulty. 'The gods were watching out for you, trickster.'

'The gods help those who help themselves,' Eyri said. He looked at Ulfar, who sat hunched on a rock nearby, watching Eyristaad burn. 'Old man, I–'

'They took her,' Ulfar said.

Eyri shook his head. 'She saved my life.'

'And she likely paid for it with her own.' Ulfar stabbed his staff into the ground and levered himself to his feet.

'I–I'm sorry,' Eyri said, sounding as if every word pained him.

'Don't be. She still lives. And while she lives, we have not lost.' Ulfar took a deep breath and turned to look at the assembled chieftains. 'We have a day until the Witching Night. One day until the force that drives the einsark is freed once more to tread our shores.'

'And if what you say is true, what then?' Kettil Flat-nose said as a thrall tied a bandage around his bicep. 'What do you want of us, old wolf?'

'Ships and men,' Ulfar grunted. 'We will raid that hell-rock and kill every living thing on it. As we should have done before.'

'And why would this time be any more successful?' Hrothgar Olveksan wheezed.

Ulfar turned a red gaze on the wounded chieftain who shrank back, cradling his bandaged stump protectively. 'My daughter won her challenge. Do any here deny that?' Ulfar said.

'None deny that,' Lok said, casting his own glare around. 'But mayhap the deed must be done carefully, eh?' He frowned. 'We need to–'

A shriek cut him off. The chieftains and their men spun as a dark blotch dropped out of the sky. The blotch spread and split, becoming a murder of crows. The crows dove upon the gathered warriors, pecking and clawing. Lok swung his staff, swatting feathered bodies out of the air.

'What in the name of Olric is this?' the old man growled.

'Our foe is taunting us!' Ulfar said. 'Look out!'

Lok howled as one of the birds fell upon him even as its form bulged and ballooned into something else. Flames crawled from its beak and enveloped the old chieftain, consuming him in weird fires. Lok's strong form heaved and thrashed as the flames crawled across him, changing him in unutterable ways.

The other chieftains watched in horror as Lok's body expanded past the stretching point of his weathered flesh. Red, wet muscle became crusted carapace and his stern face dissolved into something at once reptilian and arachnid. Lok screamed as segmented limbs burst from his torso and then it was Hrothgar's turn to scream as those spiked, jointed limbs tore into the wounded godar, ripping him limb from limb.

'Dark Prince's Pleasure!' Kettil spat, swinging his weapon at the thing that had been Lok. 'What's happened to him?'

'It's obvious isn't it?' Eyri snapped. He looked at Ulfar. 'Can't you do something old man?'

'Nothing but put him out of his misery,' Ulfar growled.

The chieftains and their men fell on the squirming, squealing thing that had been the most respected member of their group and their weapons flashed amidst the feathered storm of crows that still squawked and spilled through the air.

Ulfar ignored the battle, his eyes seeking out the bloated shape of the fire-breathing creature that had changed Lok. It waddled along the beach like a cat caught in a sack, purple shimmering flesh showing through its feathers. Its neck bulged and it breathed more fire, this time enveloping one of Eyri's men.

The man screamed and burst apart as the flames wreathed him, his gutted form writhing like an over-sized starfish. Ulfar moved swiftly, his old bones creaking in protest. His staff shot out and a cleansing cold flame consumed the mutated man, reducing him to ash. Whirling, he caught the waddling crow across the skull with the weighted tip of his staff. It flopped around alarmingly, and twisted towards him with serpentine elasticity.

Ulfar pinned the creature in place and sent his power coursing through the staff. The daemon, a minor petty thing, writhed and shrieked, its true fungous nature bursting into visibility through its shell of feather and bone. It spat coloured flames in weak spurts as he ground it into the shore. Crows clawed at him, pecking and gouging. The daemon squirmed and dissipated, its essence scattered back to the spirit-sea.

Lok – the thing that had been Lok – had sunk to one rubbery knee as Thalfi hacked at it with a broken sword, roaring a battle-song. Bilious blood spilled from the rents in its carapace, and its limbs flailed, hurling men about. It screamed out imprecations in a dozen languages, some not meant for human ears, and heaved itself up as Ulfar confronted it.

'My friend,' Ulfar said softly.

'No friend, Asgrimdalr,' a horribly familiar voice spat from between the creature's clicking mandibles. 'Only death…'

'Not mine,' Ulfar said, gripping his staff tightly. He felt tired. The creature shrugged off its attackers and reared up.

'You will die, old wolf. I will have your pelt for my cloak,' the thing said, speaking in a woman's voice now. The same voice that had taunted him with the deaths of his wife and child at the hands of the ein-sark. The same voice that had tormented him above the island only days before. 'I will peel your soul like scales from a fish and devour it raw.'

'Myrma,' Ulfar said. 'You have lost your beauty, queen of rocks and corpses.'

'My–?' The mutated thing hesitated and then shrieked wildly. Its hooves tore the earth as it charged towards him. Ulfar met it, shedding his frail flesh like a cloak and greeting the foul thing with fang and claw.

Clothed in the skin of a great white bear, Ulfar wrapped powerful paws around the creature and ripped it off its feet, scooping it up and crushing it to his hairy breast. Claws and spikes dug into his trans-formed flesh but he ignored the pain and roared. Ursine muscle flexed and the carapace splintered, spill-ing acidic blood across the rocks.

Savagely, he bit off the struggling thing's head and spat it out. A canny warrior pinned it to the ground with a spear. Ulfar let the body fall and spread his paws. He roared again, casting his challenge into the wind. He turned, dropping to all fours and then into his old skin. He rose, naked and wrinkled, and looked at the chieftains. None of them met his eyes and he grunted and spat a wad of phlegm and blood.

'I will have my weregild, men of Norsca. Will any here gainsay me?' he said.

As one, the godi raised their weapons and uttered a hoarse cheer. Ulfar let the sound wash over him and turned to face the sea, satisfied. 'I am coming, Myrma,' he said. 'I am coming for my daughter, mistress of curs.'

* * *

MYRMA'S EYES SPRANG open and she spat blood as the tang of the old wolf's power filled her mouth. Hawking and retching, she toppled over. She cursed and raved and clawed at the stone until she could muster the strength to rise. The years had not dimmed his might, no matter how much she might have hoped otherwise. Or perhaps she was simply growing weak.

One of her daughters helped her to her feet, and Myrma fondled her, testing the firmness of her flesh. The girl flushed, though more from fear than embarrassment. Which was as it should be. 'Tomorrow,' Myrma croaked. 'You will join her.' The girl tried halfheartedly to pull away, but Myrma's grip was firm. Even knowing it was their lot, some still tried to resist, however token an effort it might be. It was the nature of her people to do so, to rail against fate.

She shoved the girl into the arms of her initiates and they locked their arms around her. 'Prepare her,' Myrma said, hobbling towards one of the tidal pools. She leaned heavily on her staff and glared at her reflection. Her hair was going silver, and her face was lined with what another might have called exhaustion, but which she recognised for what it was: decay. Entropy. That was the price of her power; the more she expended, the more her physical form withered. It was a small thing, as such payments went, and her mistress had seen to it that she had a ready supply of skins with which to clothe herself, but still, it was too soon.

She was more powerful than Asgrimdalr, but the old wolf had a daemon's stamina. Pickled as he was, he would take more than she dared give to kill. Still, it had been worth the effort. It had been too long since she had tasted direct battle and her fingers curled like talons as she indulged in a pleasant reverie. His strength, cracking the bones of the spawn-thing, had been delightful. The feel of his teeth – ah!

The island trembled and she pushed the pleasurable sensations aside. Her mistress was a jealous one, and would not tolerate her priestess feeding the Dark Prince. She rubbed her arms and turned away, seeking out the black pods. They clustered like barnacles now, growing larger. They would burst in a matter of hours. A day, maybe less, and they would be ripe for the Witching Night. She stroked the closest of them, feeling the warmth of its hairy shell beneath her fingers. Her toes touched the cold metal of the fertiliser and she looked down at the breastplate, with its decorative sun. A woman's face stared up at her from the within the stylised corona and she grimaced and spat.

'Out of weakness, comes strength,' she said mockingly. 'Your weakness, our strength, false goddess.'

23

As THE GALLEY slid away from the shore, Goetz watched Eyristaad burn. He held tight to his sword, happy at having regained it despite the circumstances. Somehow it didn't seem right. Conquest Goetz understood, though he rarely approved. But this – this was seemingly destruction for destruction's sake.

'Are we knights?' he murmured, feeling a pang for having started the fires in the first place.

'It's an Unberogen word, you know,' Opchek said, coming up behind him. The Kislevite was chewing on a strip of dried jerky. 'Or it was.' He offered the jerky to Goetz, who shook his head. 'Battle always makes me hungry,' Opchek went on.

'It has the opposite effect on me. What is an Unberogen word?'

'Knight. It originally meant "servant" or some-such.' Opchek chewed and swallowed. 'Which is quite appropriate, when you think about it. We are servants, and of a higher power, no less.'

'Are we?' Goetz said.

'You doubt it?'

'Somehow I don't think Myrmidia would be in favour of burning a village full of innocents,' Goetz said, his tone turning harsh. Opchek grunted.

'Who's to say? Gods are funny things, Hector. Who can say what they want or don't want at any given time?' Opchek cocked his head. 'Besides, it was a practical military decision.'

'Was it?'

'Definitely. They'll be too busy putting out those fires to worry about following us. I don't know if you noticed, but there were more ships there than there should have been this time of year.'

'Meaning?'

'Meaning, we aren't the only ones who are up to something,' Opchek said, tapping the side of his nose. 'The Norscans are a sneaky bunch. Wouldn't be the first time one of their chieftains has whipped them into a frenzy.'

'They didn't seem that frenzied to me,' Goetz said pointedly. 'More like any Imperial peasant trying to defend his home.'

'Are you honestly comparing the citizens of your Empire with a bunch of fur-clad barbarians?' Opchek said. 'Even we Kislevites are more civilised than those savages, and we still wrestle bears!' He caught Goetz's look and continued. 'Not me, you understand. It's foolishness. Bears don't really wrestle anyway.'

'No?'

'No. They grapple,' Opchek said, spreading his arms

and growling. Goetz couldn't help but smile.

'Be that as it may, my point stands, I think.'

'If you had a point, I might agree,' Opchek said. 'You're a knight, Hector. And they are your enemy. Do not do them the discourtesy of viewing them as anything less.'

'Now I believe you were a servant of the White Wolf,' Goetz said. 'That sounds like something a follower of Ulric would say.'

'A man can follow more than one god. And don't forget, Myrmidia is a war-goddess. She may have more interests than spilt blood, but she is still the Patroness of Battle.' Opchek made a fist. 'We must smash the fortifications to rebuild the city.'

'You don't have to recite the fifteenth catechism at me.' Goetz rubbed his face. His face ached from the cut that split his cheek wide, exposing his jaw. Opchek had proven to be a competent battlefield surgeon and had cleaned the wound and sewed it shut with leather. The Kislevite slapped his hand.

'Don't touch it. It'll go sour.'

'I'm going to have a scar.'

'And a handsome one at that. You're lucky it didn't peel away from the bone. Then you'd have people asking you what you're grinning about all the time.' Opchek laughed. 'I–' A scuffle interrupted him and they both turned from the rail. A trio of Svanii was dragging a prisoner up onto the deck.

The Norscan roared in fury as the Svanii threw him against the mast. He was a big man, and bare-chested. They lashed his hands and feet tight, pinning him in place. He bellowed and struggled, trying to free himself but to no avail.

One of the Svanii bowed to Balk, and proffered a knife. Balk inclined his head and waved the man off. He spoke rapidly in Svanii and the natives gave a barbaric cheer. Goetz felt a sinking sensation in his stomach as the one wielding the knife turned back to the mast-bound captive.

'What are they doing?' he said. His throat felt dry.

Opchek didn't look at him. 'Making an offering to Myrmidia.'

When the knife went in the first time, the Norscan did not scream. Instead, he spat full in the face of the closest Svanii. When the knife blade reached his ribs, he tensed, grunting in agony. At a bark from the knife-man, other Svanii crowded forward, holding the Norscan still. The knife sliced easily through muscle and meat. Bones snapped and popped wetly as eager fingers dug into the gaping wounds. Now the Norscan screamed.

'No,' Goetz said. 'No!' He grabbed the hilt of his sword and started forward. Opchek made a grab for him, but was too slow. Goetz had his sword out when Balk stepped between him and the mast, the latter's axe hanging loosely in his hand.

'No further, brother. This is a holy moment, and it cannot be interrupted.'

'Holy? This is an abomination!' Goetz sputtered. 'They're torturing him!'

'So they are. Do you think his kind haven't done worse?' Balk said softly. 'They have raped and pillaged the coasts of the Old World for centuries, putting towns and temples alike to the sword.'

Behind Balk, the Norscan's screams had risen in pitch, becoming animal squeals. Goetz made to shove the hochmeister aside. The axe came up and the flat of the blade rested on Goetz's shoulder, its edge within a razor's distance of his neck. Balk continued speaking quietly, as if Goetz hadn't interrupted them.

'They are a treacherous people, brother. Daemon-ridden and corrupt. They bathe in foetid pools that glow in the night, and make offerings to twisted idols. They venerate the mutant, the beastman and the marauder. They are not human. They are not worthy of your blood or your sacrifice.'

'I–' Goetz didn't take his eyes off Balk. The other man's face could have been carved from marble, so serene it was.

'Make no mistake, if you interfere with our allies, I will stop you,' Balk said. The axe slid forward, and the edge shaved off a few stray bristles on Goetz's cheek. 'It is a holy moment. One the goddess herself approves of… see?' he continued, gesturing.

The Norscan would have hung slack in his bonds, had not the Svanii been there to hold him upright. His back had been reduced to red ruin and his ribs had cleaved from his spine and spread away from the rest of him. Goetz felt a wave of bile rise up in his throat as one of the Svanii reached inside the dying man's back and carefully, almost gently, pulled his lungs free.

It looked, for all the world, like some great red bird. An eagle, or even a crow. Goetz turned away. The Norscan was dead, of either blood loss or suffocation. He caught a glimpse of white in the crowd. A swaying shape that moved through the men slowly, almost mournfully. Ancient eyes met his own, and the warmth of her gaze filled him with a sense of shame and regret.

'Do you see her,' Balk whispered. 'Do you see her,

brother? She walks among us, to show us the way.'
He sounded ecstatic, like a doomsayer crouching on a
plinth in the Square of Sigmar in Altdorf, terrified and
excited and certain, oh so certain.

Goetz felt no certainty. No excitement. Only a
dull ache. The woman-shape wove between the men
unseen, and something that might have been a spear
rose and pointed at him, and he saw those eyes again,
blazing brighter and brighter, making him feel smaller
and smaller. The harsh croaking of crows broke him
from the trance. He tore his eyes away from the now
empty spot and looked back at the mast.

The crows had gathered to feast. Balk raised his
axe. 'Myrmidia! Myrmidia!' The gathered knights and
tribesmen echoed the cry. Goetz alone was silent. It
was only a few minutes later that he realised that Balk
hadn't been looking at either the dying man or the
white shape when he'd spoken.

After they reached the safety of the harbour and
docked, the prisoners were herded down the ramp and
onto the docks in a rattle of chains. The Svanii cluster-
ing on the wharf raised a cheer. Rocks and fruit flew
with abandon until Balk roared out something and
the crowd began to scatter. Goetz was reminded of his
own treatment at the hands of the Norscans. He didn't
feel any pleasure at the thought of them now undergo-
ing the same treatment.

The body of the sacrifice was left strapped to the mast
for the crows and the gulls. Goetz resolutely ignored
it, trying not to think about what he'd seen. It wasn't
as easy as that, however. Pain crept through his face,
making every expression an experience in agony, and
with every twinge he was reminded that there was a

difference between death in battle and death after the fact.

They were better than this. They had to be. Had the goddess truly approved? Was he just squeamish? He wanted a sign. Something. Anything. Something to tell him which path was the right one. What would the Grand Master do? What would he think? He watched the knights and their allies disembark, and wondered if this were a noble army of civilisation or something else.

He caught sight of the warrior-woman in the crowd of captives. Their eyes locked for a moment, and a thrill of something passed through him. She looked defiant, even now. Like a panther in a cage.

Goetz glanced back at the galley, and the body lashed to the mast. His face hardened. 'Sign enough,' he muttered. 'Thank you, my Lady.'

'You are welcome,' Myrma said, appearing at his elbow. Goetz turned to find Balk and the priestess standing behind him. The latter looked as tired and worn as any warrior. Balk slapped his gloves into his palm and smiled wearily.

'Well, brother? What say you? Do you see now why we need more men?'

'I see,' Goetz said. 'Opchek said there were more of them there than you were expecting.'

'Yes. They are gathering for war. War against us,' Myrma said, her lips tightening. Her eyes flashed, and for a moment Goetz was again struck by her resemblance to his patron goddess. But beyond that initial similarity, there was something else, some fundamental flaw in her proportions that he hadn't quite noticed until now. What was it? What was he seeing?

'Which is why you need to do as I've asked, brother,' Balk said. 'We need to bring the full force of the Order to bear on these savages.'

'I… understand,' Goetz said, keeping his face blank. 'I will compose them tonight. But in the meantime, are we capable of withstanding a siege?'

'Hopefully,' Balk said. 'Why, brother? You have a suggestion?'

'Several. Siege-craft was a specialty of mine.' Goetz hesitated. 'That is, if I'm not overstepping my bounds.'

'Ha! Hardly,' Balk said, smiling broadly. 'I look forward to it! But first–'

'The letters,' Goetz said, nodding. 'Do not worry, hochmeister. I will make them my priority.'

'Very good. Now, I must see to the dispensation of the prisoners. I have a feeling we're going to need the extra labourers. My lady?' Balk said, looking at Myrma. She did not look at him as she shook her head.

'I will stay. I wish to speak to Hector.'

A dark expression flashed across Balk's face, but then vanished as quickly as it had come. 'As you say.' He left with a swirl of his fur cloak. Goetz watched him go, and then turned to Myrma.

'Speak,' he said.

Her eyebrow quirked. 'You sound angry, Hector.'

'What I am is of no concern to you, surely,' he said. She frowned.

'Rude too.'

'What do you want?'

'To talk. To help you.' Her fingers stroked the edges of the rawhide thong that held his cheek together. He jerked his head away.

'I'm fine, thank you.'

'I helped you before, didn't I?'

'I don't know.' Goetz stepped away from her. Her hand shot out, snagging his wrist with surprising strength.

'The poison is still in you,' she said, and he felt a jolt in his side. He flinched and the leather in his face pulled tight, eliciting a grunt from him. 'You should let me help you.'

'I can manage, I think. I have letters to compose,' he said, pulling his wrist free. Without waiting for a reply he headed away from her, one hand clutching his side.

DALLA GLARED AT the einsark as she was dragged away from the ship. He was speaking to the – no, not a woman. She knew what that creature was, even if the brass-skins appeared to be oblivious. Her father had described the hag-queen of Svunum often enough.

Lagging slightly, she watched as the knight stalked away from the hag, limping slightly. A strange sense of relief flooded her, only to be angrily shoved aside as the witch met her eyes. The woman grinned, bearing filed teeth, and Dalla turned away. Beneath her tattered hauberk, the amulets her father had crafted for her seemed to burn white-hot against her skin.

Hopefully that meant they were working. Keeping her invisible to the eyes of the hag's daemon-familiars. She rattled her chains in frustration. There was nothing that would please her more at the moment than getting her fingers into the soft flesh beneath the hag's jaw, but such was not to be.

Instead, all she could do was hold her peace and bide her time. There would come an opportunity for escape. And when it did… She fought to keep the lupine grin off her face. It became easier when the hiss of a lash split the air. The tattooed savage garbled something at the prisoners and snapped the whip again.

Dalla hurried, not wishing to feel the sting of the whip. She saw familiar faces among the group. The raiders hadn't been picky… there were women mixed in among the old and the far too young and there were a number of warriors, most bearing wounds. One man saw her looking and grinned, baring broken teeth. She recognised him as one of Flatnose's jarls.

'Ho, Ulfarsdottir. We are swimming in a sea of dung now, eh?' he rasped. Blood leaked out from between the fingers pressed to his shoulder.

'Yes, but I intend to make for shore as soon as possible,' Dalla said. 'Are you with me?'

'Oh aye. I saw you bash Kettil… any woman who can fight like that I'll follow to Hel itself.'

Dalla snorted. 'You must follow a lot of women,' she said.

'A fair few,' the warrior grunted. 'You have a plan?'

'Not yet.'

'Best hurry. I'd hate to bleed to death before I get a chance to strangle one of these cannibals with his own tongue.' He pulled his hand away from his wound and grimaced.

They were harried away from the harbour and out past the town towards the rocky reaches of the island shore. Scrub trees and bedraggled weeds clutched at them as they were forced towards the mouth of a cave. A foul smell, like rotten eggs, emanated from it and Dalla pressed her hands to her mouth as they were herded inside.

More Svanii were waiting there, though these were

not the tanned warriors who had escorted them. These were pale wraiths, covered in tattoos that looked like fish scales and they wore wooden masks shaped like beaks and feathered cloaks. They took over escort duties with a smoothness born of practice. They carried weapons crafted from what looked like volcanic glass and moved through the stinking darkness with sure-footed grace.

The captives were led down a flight of stone slab-steps. The smell grew fouler and the air tasted of sulphur. Vents in the rock belched witch-light and noxious clouds that made Dalla's eyes water. Her vision played tricks on her, and she thought she saw flat shapes hunching along the roof of the cavern.

Finally, they came to a large grotto which echoed with the roar of the sea. The thunder of waves was amplified by the shape of the cavern, and a sea breeze battled with the stink of the gases, making the air semi-breathable.

They were forced at spear-point into a pen – one of many in the grotto – constructed of bone and other, less pleasant substances. There were cages of smaller size hanging from the great fangs of rock that occupied the upper reaches of the cavern, all of them crammed with prisoners, most in some state of malnutrition.

Dalla considered making a lunge for the nearest guard, but knew that she wouldn't get far, even with help. No, she would have to wait until a better opportunity presented itself.

'As cunning as ever, my daughter.'

Dalla froze, not quite believing her ears. She opened her mouth.

'No. Do not speak. Do not draw the attentions of any that might be listening. Look up.'

She did, as casually as she was able. The dim shapes she had spied before suddenly sprang into stark focus and her blood chilled. Flat, plate-shaped multi-hued *things* clung to the grotto ceiling like bats. They constantly moved, shoving and jostling like puppies at the teat, their circular maws clinging to the rock as if they were leeching strength from it.

There were other shapes than just those. There were cackling pink things as well, like stretched and boiled infants capering back and forth invisibly around the pens and the captives within, reaching out to pinch at the captives with ethereal fingers. She watched a man so molested shudder, as if a chill had passed through him. Past the pink things were fungoid creatures that glided along on flat disk-like feet, trailing spurts of rainbow-hued flame. One drew too close to the pen she was caged in and she felt her amulet burn. She placed fingers to it and looked away as the thing glided past.

'The children of Old Father Fate, daughter. They are held to this place by she whom we bound here. The Black Crow-Queen and her mad court.' Her father's voice was soothing and she felt the fear that had filled her upon sight of the creatures fade. 'And they will be free again, come the Witching Night.'

Dalla's hands clenched. Her father's voice began to fade. 'We are coming, daughter. And we bring sword and fire.' And then he was gone. Dalla leaned against the bars of her cage, eyes closed. As her father left her, so too did the vision he had bestowed. It was almost worse not seeing the daemons. She shook her head.

She had other things to worry about. She turned and her eyes met those of several of the men. The one she had spoken to earlier nodded. Slowly they drew together amidst the crowd, and Dalla began to speak in soft tones.

24

BLACK SAILS SET off in the night. Goetz watched them from the library window, a half-finished letter sitting on the desk behind him. Three slim galleys, sails unfurled to take advantage of the night-wind, sped out of the harbour.

He turned away from the window. The library was big, bigger than that in the Bechafen Komturie, incorporating as it did the accumulated knowledge of two houses. The shelves were overflowing and piles of books, stacked sloppily, hugged the bulk of the floor space. Most had the look of books that had been placed and left, if the sheen of dust was anything to go by.

Too concerned with their crusade to read, perhaps. He sat down at the desk and stared at the letter. It contained neither plea nor explanation. Instead, it was a condemnation. One likely to have heads on the block and bloody consequences. His skin crawled at the thought and he pressed his hand to his side. The pain had not abated. Nor did he think it would. Not this time.

In the Order, they were taught to think first above all else. To scrutinise, ponder and decide. The key to strategy was to consider the possible variables and create a plan of action flexible enough to accommodate random happenstance, and yet firm enough to deal decisively with the enemy. Watch and wait was how old Berlich had put it. Goetz felt a pang. He could have used his old hochmeister's advice.

He was neither novice nor naive, but still the situation confused him. There were too many elements to the thing, too many instances of seemingly random happenstance that he knew – *he knew* – were anything but. Every instinct he had screamed warnings at him.

Goetz looked around the library, scanning the faded bindings. Unlike in other komturie libraries there were no icons here, no representations of ancient heroes or even of the goddess herself. It wasn't just the library which was barren… for such a divinely inspired bunch, the brethren of the Svunum Komturie were not fond of displays of devotion.

Unless you counted blood sacrifice, of course. Goetz frowned. Surely the goddess did not truly demand blood; but then, how to explain what he'd seen? Had he seen anything?

He sat down and scraped his palms over his scalp, trying to think. Who was it who'd said that Sigmar's wrath was turned aside by the blood of mutants? Wasn't that simply a form of blood sacrifice? What was the difference, in the end, between the blood of one enemy and the next?

'Are the gods so picky then?' he said, his voice

surprisingly loud in the silence of the library. He gripped the medallion Abbot Knock had given him and rubbed his thumb over the embossed spear and shield. The tools given to man to defend his nascent civilisation, the one to prod and the other to ward.

Was that what this was? Civilisation in the offing? In the beginning, there was fire and there was blood that was what the *First Book of Sigmar* said. His fingers tightened around the medallion and he turned back to the window. Something pale and grave looked back at him in place of his reflection. The face was the same as the apparition he'd seen on the beach and on the boat, and its gaze bored through his own and into his mind beyond. The mouth opened but all he heard was the cry of birds.

Goetz closed his eyes and backed away from the glass, his fists clenched. 'I don't know what you want,' he said. Then, louder, 'I don't know what you want!'

The face grew larger, expanding through the glass. It seeped through the brick, spreading like a mist. Cold crept through his limbs and he tried to turn away, but he found himself unable to move. The medallion burned on his chest and in his head he saw chained figures shoved down gangplanks and into dark holes.

He saw fire and death, and the komturie felt as if it were collapsing around him. 'You see?' a rough voice said. Goetz spun and saw the old shaman sitting not five feet away, hunched against his primitive staff, his ancient eyes locked on Goetz's own. Though he'd only seen the old man at a distance before, Goetz easily recognised him.

'I'm dreaming again,' Goetz said, forcing himself to relax.

'Are you?' the old man said.

'I must be. Otherwise you wouldn't be here.'

The old man smiled. 'As you say,' he said. 'I am Ulfar Asgrimdalr, gudja of Goldfinger, father of a wayward daughter.' He gestured to Goetz's sword, where it sat sheathed on the desk.

'Father... her?' Goetz said, slightly shocked. 'She's your daughter?'

'Every daughter has a father. Should mine be any different?' Ulfar smiled and leaned forward. 'You are brave and strong.' He frowned. 'But for how much longer, hmm?'

'What?'

The staff swung out, the tip motioning towards the scars on Goetz's side. Instinctively he looked down. A thrill of panic went through him as he saw the black lines radiating from the wound point and staining his shirt. 'Those weren't there before,' he said hoarsely. He pulled up his shirt and reached out a finger to touch the puffy flesh around the wounds, but a grunt from his visitor stopped him.

'Do not touch it,' Ulfar said.

'Why?'

'It would not be wise. What causes pain in one world, can cause death in another.'

'Death?' Goetz said. 'Who are you? Why are you here?'

'I told you who I was. As to why I am here... ah. I owe you a debt, one I am here to repay.'

'Your daughter,' Goetz said. Ulfar nodded.

'You could have slain her. Others would have.' Ulfar smiled, his strong yellow teeth surfacing in his white beard and then fading. 'Thus, I owe you, boy. And

Ulfar Asgrimdalr always repays his debts.'

'And how do you intend to do so?' Goetz said warily.

'I intend to save your life. And hopefully your soul in the bargain,' Ulfar said solemnly. He cleared his throat. 'Our gods are old and hard and wild, like the wind in the great troll-peaks. They do not give, but instead take, even as we take from the soft Southerners. Our gods raid us for blood and souls and we give to them freely enough. But sometimes they want more than even we are prepared to give. Sometimes their messengers come and take and take and take and we are left empty and hollow like a drained tun of wine.' The old man shifted in his seat, and his eyelids drooped as if gravity were warring against him. They sprang open a moment later. Goetz stepped forward.

'Are you–?'

'I am fine. It is wearying to speak like this.' Ulfar took a breath and continued. 'We worship many gods, and among their number are counted aspects of those you call the Ruinous Powers, though in our tongue they are less ruinous than capricious. The Wolf-Father, the Crow-Brother, the Laughing Prince and the Shaper-of-Things, these are just some of their names and faces. They are each unto themselves a pantheon, warring and growing in high Aesgardr – the Wood Between Worlds.' He sucked on his teeth for a moment, as if the taste of the words to come were not to his liking in the least. 'They pluck champions from among us, the way a man might pluck a pup from a litter. They raise them up and dash them down. But there are others…'

'Others?' Goetz prodded. Ulfar smiled bitterly.

'Daemons,' he said, in perfect Reikspiel. Goetz could not repress an instinctive shudder as the word hung heavy in the air. Ulfar went on. 'That is what your people call them, aye?'

'Yes,' Goetz said, his mouth suddenly dry. 'That is what they are.'

'They are what they are, no more, no less,' Ulfar responded with a shrug. 'Some are worse than others.' He thumped his staff on the hard stone floor, and the echo caused Goetz's bones to quiver. 'Some are more dangerous than others. More cunning. More foul.'

'What are you trying to tell me?'

'My gods speak to me. Your goddess speaks to you.' Ulfar paused. 'And something else…' He cocked his head, as if listening. Goetz followed suit. He heard nothing. He hadn't really expected to.

'I have never heard Myrmidia,' Goetz said. Ulfar looked at him with what might have been pity.

'That does not mean she has not spoken.' He tapped an ear. 'The deaf cannot hear. That does not mean we do not speak, eh?'

Goetz got the point. Annoyance filled him. 'I think I would hear a goddess if one spoke to me!' he retorted.

'Not if someone else was speaking too loudly,' Ulfar said and thumped the floor again, more loudly this time. Goetz hissed as his body was suddenly wracked with pain. Gasping, he ripped his shirt open and stared down at the scars on his side. The pale tissue bulged and puffed like some sort of deranged fungus. Beneath his skin, something sharp and dark moved.

The tip of Ulfar's staff jabbed out, catching him in the side. Goetz fell to the floor with a scream. Blood flowed between his fingers as whatever was inside him thrashed. A black beak pierced his flesh and the scars gaped wide and the crow thrust itself out into his room, wet and foul. Goetz rolled away desperately, leaving a trail of blood behind.

The crow hopped after him, croaking. 'Poisoned,' it said, in a woman's voice. 'Poisoned.' As it drew closer, however, its voice changed, becoming deeper and harsher. 'Poisoned,' it said, talons clicking across the floor. 'Poisoned.'

'Poisoned,' Ulfar said, sweeping the bird aside with his staff. It struck the wall with bone-snapping force and tumbled to the floor, twitching. Goetz looked at Ulfar, then at the bird.

'What–' he began.

'Hush,' Ulfar said. 'Come out, come out, wherever you are, old hag.'

Before Goetz's horrified eyes, the bird's corpse twitched. Then, a number of white maggots poked through its feathered breast and wriggled into the air. The maggots extended further and further until, with a start, Goetz realised that they weren't maggots at all but fingers.

The fingers bent and tore at the feathers, spreading the wound they had emerged from, even as the bird had previously torn its way out of Goetz. The carcass flopped wide and something far too large emerged, rising up and up, its pale white head brushing against the ceiling.

'Asgrimdalr,' it said, the words slipping from between ash-black teeth and riding on a waft of carrion breath. 'I find you slinking around her temple like an alley cur. Appropriate…'

'Myrma. Old charlataness. Troll-wife. Still hiding in the skins of your betters?' Ulfar said, standing between the thing and Goetz.

'I have many skins now. My Master, my Mistress, they give me so many to wear in her service, in His schemes,' the thing replied, drawing its feet from within the bird one at a time with an almost dainty grace.

It looked like a woman as seen in the surface of warped glass. Too-long limbs stretched from a bloated torso and a head like a chopped mushroom bobbed on a stalk like neck. The feet were wide and splayed, almost like flippers. Tattoos covered the entirety of its naked form, the ink almost dripping down its limbs and face. Eyes bright like balefires gleamed above a mouth full of rotten teeth. In the drift of its words was the scream of a flock of birds and every movement made a sound like the rustle of oily feathers.

Man and monster faced one another, and Goetz, bleeding like a stuck pig, could only watch helplessly. He tried to get his feet under him, but he was weak. He felt feverish and sick, and the hole in his side wasn't helping. Holding his arm tightly to his side, he began to crawl away. If he could find some weapon, any weapon…

'He is mine. They are all mine,' Myrma gurgled. 'They have heard her song and have joined the Great Game.' Black teeth clicked and its eyes flickered to Goetz, who froze. 'He will join too.'

'The game of gods is for them alone. Not for mortals,' Ulfar barked.

'Says one who interferes,' Myrma countered, advancing. Her too-long arms shot out, grasping for the old man. Ulfar evaded the clutching talons and jabbed his staff into her stomach. The creature squealed and caught the staff, wrenching it out of Ulfar's hands.

'You'll interfere no more though!' She swung the staff up as if to crush Ulfar's skull, but suddenly in the old man's place a great white-furred bear reared back and swept out a crushing paw.

She shrieked as the paw sent her flying. But even as she flew, she changed, shedding her skin like droplets of water. Her shape twisted into that of a malformed hound and she sprang at the bear. The two beasts roared and thrashed, tearing at one another. Even as they fought, however, they both lost cohesion, becoming so much vapour. Goetz closed his eyes as the mingled vapours suddenly swept over him and when his eyes sprang open, the cacophony of birds filled his head. A murder of crows flew past the window, their dark shapes merging with the night as they shot upwards as if in pursuit of something white. Goetz took a breath and felt the chill fade.

His body hurt all over, but the agony of his wound had become a dull thing, pushed to the back of his head. The old man – Ulfar – had done something to him. He had tried to protect him from – what?

Goetz felt bile rise up in his throat as he considered what he had seen. If he believed it, then this island was lost, not just to the Order, but to humanity. He leaned over the desk and looked at the half-finished letter. How long had it been? How many days were left until the Marienburg fleet would arrive? When was Hexensnacht? Casting a glance at the window, he knew the answer to that. Both Mannslieb and Morrslieb were almost full, which meant Hexensnacht was tomorrow night, if he was any judge. The fleet was already on its way, and the blessings of Myrmidia on them.

He knew what he had to do.

He left the library and moved through the silent corridors, heading down towards the sound of the sea. There were Svanii on sentry duty in the courtyard, but when they caught sight of his arms and armour, they stepped aside respectfully.

'Master,' one said in oddly accented if passable Reikspiel, nodding. Goetz stopped and looked at the man. He was, like all the Svanii, slightly smaller than the average Imperial citizen, though much broader. Round, slightly brooding features dominated by a crudely shorn bristle of dark hair and facial tattoos that reminded Goetz of a flock of startled birds. The man blinked nervously as Goetz peered at him.

'Something we can help you with, master?' the other sentry said, smiling ingratiatingly.

'The prisoners. Where are they held?' Goetz said.

'Ah–'

'Hurry now!' Goetz barked. 'The goddess commands!'

The two men exchanged glances and then one said, 'In the sea-caves, master. With the others.'

Goetz nodded his thanks and stepped past them, wondering whether they would alert someone as to what they had seen. Possibly, though it wouldn't matter. Goetz left the komturie behind, his skin crawling with every step. Outside of the fortress-monastery's protective embrace he felt as if he were being stalked by something monstrous. The worst part was that he knew it was true now.

He could not say why he had so readily believed the old man. Everything he saw in the library could have been a sorcerous illusion easily enough. But in his gut, he knew it hadn't been. The old man had been trying to warn him. Even as, perhaps, Myrmidia herself had.

Which meant what, exactly, a small part of him murmured. What of your sceptic's faith now?

He grunted and pushed aside that latter thought. This was no time to consider the philosophical ramifications of divine intervention. Before tonight was out, he was likely going to have to spill the blood of men who were his brothers.

Crows perched on the lintels and rooftops of the Svanii village, watching him as he moved through the ill-lit streets towards the wharf. There were more birds in evidence than he thought the island could support. Doubtless Balk would say it was a sign of the divine.

Balk. How much did the hochmeister know? Was he a pawn of a sorceress? Or a willing convert? The mouth of the sea-cave rose up suddenly and Goetz halted, his hand on his sword. Questions were for later. Right now, he had someone he hoped was a friend to save.

THE LONGSHIPS SLID through the mist smoothly. The oars were stowed and the drums were silent, and a spirit-summoned wind filled the sails to bursting. Eyri watched the other ships for a moment, and then turned to Ulfar. The old man sat hunched in the prow, leaning on his staff. It never ceased to amaze Eyri that someone so powerful could look so fragile.

'What are you looking at?' Eyri muttered as he leaned against the rail beside the gudja.

'I'm not looking; I'm concentrating,' Ulfar growled. Eyri blinked and suddenly realised that the sheen on the old man's face was sweat. 'The sea is angry enough as it is.'

'I would be too, with a daemon in my belly.' Eyri grinned at Ulfar's expression. 'I do listen to the legends, old man. I know what we are heading for. The question I have is why? And don't play the concerned father.'

'I am concerned,' Ulfar said.

'But not about her. She's a tool, just like the rest of us,' Eyri said. 'I know the smell of a grudge, old man.'

Ulfar glared at him for a moment. Then the old man sighed and shook his head. 'You know the stories, yes?'

'I said I did.'

'When I was a young man, more than sixty years ago, we – I and my fellow gudjas – bound the Island That Walked to this point on the sea. We broke the power of the creatures that lived there and put a stop to their raids on our villages.'

'Islands don't walk,' Eyri said.

'This one did. It wasn't really an island. It's not an island now.' Ulfar grinned humourlessly. 'It's a corpse.'

'A corpse?' Eyri stared at him incredulously.

'Big corpse,' Ulfar clarified, holding his hands apart. 'Who died?'

'A goddess,' Ulfar said. He looked up and to the north, where the soft ever-present glow of the polar realm lit the horizon with a cursed light. Eyri followed his gaze and made a warding gesture against bad luck.

'One of them?' he said.

'S'vanashi is what our ancestors called her. The Lady of Ten Thousand Cloaks. The Crow-Queen and the Hag-Mother. A daughter of the Great Planner, one of his flock,' Ulfar said slowly. 'Thrown down and buried beneath the sea for some crime we do not know. And beneath the sea, her corpse slept and dreamed, and like roots growing through a barrow, she excreted an island. From the very stuff of this world, she grew herself a body that moved and spoke, and she called her servants to her across the great land bridge and then she taught them all that she knew.'

Eyri turned to the rail and peered into the evening mist. It was growing lighter now, as morning approached. 'Tomorrow night is the Witching Night.'

Ulfar nodded. 'They will kill all they have taken. They will soak the roots of the island in blood and it will break the bonds that bind her in the deep dark.'

Eyri turned. 'You know that for a fact?' he said.

Ulfar shrugged. 'I know what the spirits tell me. What horrors they whisper in my ear as I dream. I know what the hag-girl Myrma thinks. Whether it is true or not, who can say? It is all naught but the laughter of the Dark Gods from where we sit, small and insignificant.'

'Comforting words.'

'They were not meant to be.' Ulfar's head jerked up. 'Look!' He pointed.

Several black shapes wheeled and banked through the misty sky. Eyri's eyes narrowed. 'Crows.'

'Kill them! Now!' Ulfar snarled.

'What–?'

'Now!'

Eyri turned and gave the order. Bowstrings twanged and two of the shapes fell limply into the sea. The others turned and began to glide away. Ulfar made a sound halfway between a whine and a growl and he spun his staff. His veins stood out on his neck as he glared up at the sky. Before the disbelieving eyes of the crew, the mist congealed into a rough shape that pursued the departing crows.

Ulfar hunched forward, stretching out his hand. His fingers curled like hooks as he rotated his wrist with bone-snapping speed. The mist closed around the crows. Eyri heard a distant croak, which cut off abruptly. Black feathers drifted down onto the deck.

'Did you get them?' he asked, turning to look at Ulfar. The old man was on his hands and knees, breathing heavily. Eyri was at his side in an instant. 'What's wrong?'

'I'm old, Goldfinger,' Ulfar said with a wheezy laugh. 'Old and tired.'

'Can you continue on?'

'Going to put me back ashore somewhere? And then where would you be, eh?' Ulfar barked. He stood with a groan. 'No. You'll need what magics I can muster before this day is out.'

'I hope you have some sort of plan, old man. Killing crows is all well and good, but we're going to need a bit more than a mist to get past their harbour defences.' Eyri gestured towards the distant shapes of the pylons which marked the entrance to Svunum's harbour. They would be on them as the day waned, and he knew there was no way they could avoid being spotted.

Ulfar merely shook his head. 'I will handle them. You will handle the landing. You will need to occupy that damnable keep as soon as possible.'

Eyri cut him off with a snort. 'I know my business old man. Besides which, I've wanted to loot that drafty pile for years now. I'll take it, no worries.' He looked back. Behind his vessel, the mist began to clear and more than a dozen longships slid out behind his, sails billowing with Ulfar's wind.

Eyri had built a small fleet of his own, and the other chieftains had brought their swiftest and sturdi- est. Armed men crowded the decks of each, straining for a glimpse of the island that was the source of so many dark childhood tales. He grinned and patted the hatchet on his belt. 'We could sack all the coasts of the Empire with this fleet. I think we can take one island, daemon-possessed or not.'

THE CAVERNOUS GROTTO echoed with the sound of barbarous music. Drums made of stretched human skin were battered with doomful rhythm to the accompaniment of the moans of the beast-things that lurked in the water-logged deep tunnels. These lurked at the edges of the grotto, grunting and excited as the depths of the island trembled with hidden explosions. Strangely hued torches lit the dripping walls as the initiates of the Crow-Queen made the ritual ablutions to the strange, face-like formations scattered about the interior of the cavern.

Raw, ragged waves slapped across the rock as the tide came in with the dull light of the distant morning. They had taken several men and women from the cages and dragged them away over the course of the evening towards a deeper grotto, where the thunder of drums was loudest.

Those drums sounded different from the ones Dalla saw. Their beat was bone-deep and it made her feel as if she had swallowed a stone. At times it overrode the sound of the closer instruments and sometimes seemed to be in rhythm with the occasional tremor that ran through the floor of the cavern. It was an evil sound, and Dalla had a suspicion that the rise in tempo had some connection to the sound of screams cut short that reached her ears, if only rarely.

She was determined not to find out, however. Dalla gestured. The man across from her – Greki, he'd said his name was – nodded and began to pull on a femur that composed part of their cage. With a grunt, he twisted it free of the leather lashings and broke it as quietly as he could.

He tossed the sharper end to her and she caught it and slid it through the back of her belt. Then, face composed, she leaned against the cage and draped her arms above her head, her chest outthrust, legs crossed. She mouthed silently to the closest guard and he stared at her. He licked his lips and looked at his fellows. None of them were paying any attention.

'Come to me, man,' she cooed. She had bedded men before, and knew what sort of look made them stupid enough to trot after her. She pressed herself against the cage and he wrapped an arm around her waist. He popped loose the chains that held the cage shut and pulled her to him, grunting endearments.

She jammed the broken femur into his neck, gouging a hole completely through his windpipe. He staggered against her. His spear clattered to the rocky floor before she could catch it and the other guards turned. One of them said something, and several of the others laughed cruelly.

Acting quickly, she hooked the spear with her foot and flipped it up into the air, catching it even as she allowed the body to tumble. Without missing a beat, she hurled the spear at the closest guard, catching him beneath the arm. He screamed and fell back against the cage. Greki, or perhaps one of the others, wrapped a brawny arm around the man's neck and snapped it.

Snagging the glass dagger from the belt of the body at her feet, she jerked the cage door wide. 'Out! Out! Out! Make for the sea!' Dalla shouted, waving her blade over her head. 'The sea you fools! The sea!' The great mass of slaves didn't listen, being far too panicked to pay attention to a lone voice. Freedom was at hand, and she was forced to press herself back against the cage as they stampeded.

A guard fought his way through the crowd and stabbed at her with a sword. She twisted aside from the blow and drove the dagger up through his chin. His eyes rolled up in his head and he fell away to be trampled into a paste by the escaping slaves, leaving her with his sword.

Greki and the other warriors clustered around her, recognising her presence if not her face. They knew a shieldmaiden when they saw one. 'What now, spear-daughter?' one of them asked, his forked beard streaked with blood. 'Should we go to the shore? See if we can steal a boat?'

'No. We have other prey,' Dalla said with a snap of her teeth. Several muttered, but they all followed as she began to make for the sounds of combat, now echoing from the great stairs that led upwards. Armed Svanii burst out from a side tunnel ahead of them and charged towards her group with eager cries. She killed the first with her stolen blade and picked up his shield. Beating the rim of the shield with her sword, she grinned at the oncoming barbarians. 'Come then, witch-men! Come and die!'

25

GOETZ KILLED THE two guards as quickly as he could. They had watched him warily as he approached the mouth of the sea-caves, but had not otherwise reacted until it was too late. He stared down at the tattooed bodies for a moment, wondering whether it had been the only choice. Then, steeling himself, he stepped inside.

A rush of foul air greeted him, and he raised his free hand to his mouth. He felt a rumble through the soles of his boots that travelled all the way up his spine to his skull. He felt slightly sick, though whether from his wound, the smell, or the situation, he couldn't say.

He stopped, listening to the sound of the sea which echoed through the tunnel before him. He heard something – a sharp rasp of sound. Hand on his sword, he waited. The sound grew louder; with a start, Goetz realised that it was the sound of bare feet slapping on stone. Acting quickly he stepped out of the shadows and the runner smashed into him, falling backwards. Goetz looked down, trying to make out who he had stopped.

His eyes widened. 'Captain Feldmeyer?'

'No! I'm not going back!' the Hochlander snarled, swinging a rusty length of chain at Goetz. Goetz stepped back, letting the links swoosh past him.

'Captain, how did you get here?' Goetz said, holding up his hands. The frenzied seaman didn't reply. Instead he swung his chains again. They scraped sparks off Goetz's cuirass and the knight grabbed them, yanking the other man off balance. 'Calm down,' Goetz said, driving his fist into Feldmeyer's belly. 'What's going on?'

'Escape,' Feldmeyer wheezed. His eyes were unfocused and he looked gaunt and hungry. From somewhere close by, a bell began to ring. Goetz heard voices raised in fear and anger. He smelt smoke on the breeze and he looked up as an orange haze lit up the night. 'She set the slave-pens on fire,' Feldmeyer said, crawling to his feet. 'We have to get away. While there's time!'

'Get away? From what? I thought the Norscans took you?' Goetz said. But the Hochlander was already hobbling away. Goetz watched him disappear into the darkness, and then turned back to the light. 'What's going on?' he muttered, as he started in the direction Feldmeyer had come from.

Balk had mentioned that they'd been buying slaves, hadn't he? But he'd said they were letting them go. Obviously that was a lie. Goetz's face settled into hard lines, the wound on his cheek pulling tight. It was looking more and more like Balk, and by extension his fellow knights, were willing participants in whatever was going on.

The corridor began to fill with people as he drew closer to the scene of the blaze and the stink of it grew stronger. The freed prisoners shied away from him in obvious terror as they caught sight of him. Goetz forced his way through them and they streamed away from him like fish avoiding a shark.

Columns of oily smoke threaded through the tunnel. Somewhere an alarm bell was ringing mindlessly. Goetz loosened his sword in its sheath. A figure stumbled out of the smoke and collapsed, coughing. He recognised the knight as Krauss, a Reiklander.

'Krauss?' Goetz said, rushing forward. He saw a dark stain of blood on the man's scalp and even as he reached him, a burly Norscan charged out of the smoke, lifting a chunk of stone high in both hands. Goetz's sword jumped into his hand and he sent the Norscan spinning away, trailing streamers of blood. More approached, however. They wore chains and carried improvised weapons and they panted like wolves.

'Up, brother,' Goetz said, hooking his arm under Krauss's own and tried to lever the other man to his feet. 'Up or we're dead!'

A length of doubled chain flashed out and nearly battered Goetz's sword from his hand. Awkwardly he spun the injured man out of the way and stabbed out at his attackers. They crowded around him in the close confines of the tunnel with bloodthirsty eagerness. Goetz cursed and tried to back away, while still remaining between them and Krauss.

'Myrmidia! Myrmidia!' An axe split the stalemate, chopping down through the pate of one of the

Norscans. Balk wrenched his weapon free in a spray of gore and nodded grimly to Goetz. 'Well met, brother. It seems we're having a bit of a labour dispute.'

'Is that what you call it?' Goetz said. Faced with two armoured and armed knights, the gang of Norscans hesitated. Then one gave a growl worthy of a bear and they charged forward. Goetz parried a strike with a shovel and spitted the man wielding it. Balk dispatched two more, his axe gleaming crimson as it rose and fell with a precise, smooth rhythm.

'What I call it is an act of sabotage,' Balk said, flicking blood off his weapon. 'Someone set fire to the prisoner pens. They're all loose. All of them.'

'How many is that?'

Balk frowned. 'Hundreds.'

Goetz stared at the hochmeister, the sick feeling coming back. 'Hundreds?' he echoed. 'We didn't take that many prisoners before, did we?'

'Not then, no. But we have been raiding the Norscan coast for several months now,' Balk said. He didn't look at the other knight as he said it, and Goetz's heart sank. 'Mostly under cover of darkness, to preserve our anonymity, but...' He trailed off and glared at Goetz defiantly. 'We needed the labour force!'

'Slavery is against the most sacred tenets of our Order,' Goetz said.

'I didn't say they were slaves, now did I?' Balk said, turning away. 'They're impressed labourers. Prisoners of war. We planned on releasing them once we were finished.'

'But–'

'Do you want to stand here arguing about this, or do you want to help me fix this?' Balk snapped, his eyes gleaming dangerously. Goetz helped Krauss to his feet and gestured with his sword.

'After you, hochmeister.'

Balk snorted and moved into the smoke. Goetz followed and soon they were joined by other knights responding to the alarm. How they had reached the caverns so quickly, Goetz couldn't say, though his suspicion flared bright. Opchek grinned at Goetz, his features stained with soot. 'There's been battle at every turn since you joined us, Hector!'

'You sound almost pleased,' Goetz said.

'We do serve a goddess of battle, brother,' Opchek said teasingly. 'Be a shame if we didn't honour her at every opportunity.'

'Including the slaughter of prisoners?'

Opchek blinked and looked away. He didn't reply. A few minutes later, it didn't matter. A dozen gaunt men, clad in rags and soot, charged towards them in a ragged horde. Goetz parried a shovel and tried to use the flat of his blade. The other knights weren't so forgiving. They cut down the prisoners with brutal efficiency. Goetz held his tongue. It was not an ideal situation, but if he wanted to live long enough to get to the bottom of things, he would have to paddle with the flow.

The Svanii were mobilising as well, and small groups joined up with them in threes and fours, carrying spears and shields. They spoke in their own tongue nervously, casting sidelong glances at the knights. Overhead, the crows flew through the tunnels, their eerie croaks echoing loudly above the din of battle.

'BURN THEM TO the waterline!' Eyri roared to his crew. Men poured over the rails of the longship and onto the black-sailed galley. The knights aboard the galley had been surprised when the fleet of dragonships had ploughed out of the spell-summoned mist and crashed past them, and even more so when Eyri's men had boarded them with eager ferocity. 'Teach them that we are the wolves in these waters, not them!'

Eyri joined his men a few moments later, hurling one of his hatchets into the face of a Svanii sailor. Not pausing to free it, he merely pulled his second axe from his belt and engaged a knight. The brass-skin called out to his goddess as Eyri ducked beneath his sword-stroke and buried the hatchet in his groin.

Ripping his weapon free, Eyri kicked the dying man over the side and turned to meet the next threat. 'Kill them all! No survivors! No prisoners!' he shouted, fighting to catch his breath. His chest and belly still ached from Balk's blow, but he knew what would cure it: the knight's head on a spike. It had been a long time coming.

He had dealt with Balk fairly for far too long, frightened of the manic intensity the man had. Granted, he wouldn't take Balk's head tonight, not unless he was luckier than the old man had predicted. No, tonight was for burning that cursed island to the waterline, and to kill a few hundred of those flesh-eating savages. Maybe, just maybe, to get back the old man's she-wolf of a daughter. He owed them that much, and Eyri Goldfinger always paid his debts.

A wounded knight stumbled towards him, both hands clutching his throat. Eyri allowed him to stumble past and chopped him down. He spit on the body, and turned. The galley was slick with blood stem to stern and he wondered what sound it would make as it sank.

'Burn it!' he shouted, raising his hatchet. 'Burn this cursed boat and let the fires light our path–'

'No!' Ulfar bellowed from back aboard Eyri's own ship. 'Cease, Goldfinger! Or are you as battle-dumb as Thalfi Utergard?'

'What?' Eyri called out as he stepped over bodies and strode to the rail. 'What are you barking about old man?'

'How did you think we were going to get past the harbour guards, you fool?' Ulfar roared, slamming the butt of his staff against the deck. Eyri winced.

'Fine, but–'

'Gather the other chieftains! Now!'

It took far longer than Eyri would have liked to do so, but when the other godi were gathered on the deck of the captured galley, Ulfar explained. He swept his dark gaze across the group. 'There are cannon on those sea-towers,' he growled, motioning towards the distant pylons. 'My mist has concealed us thus far, but once we get too close to the island, the daemon's magics will scatter my own like a flock of scared birds. They will see us and–'

'Sink us,' Kettil said, looking thoughtful. 'Unless we get them first. Clever, old man.'

'There are two galleys. My men took the other. I'll sail it down their gullets,' Grettir Halfhand said, his rune-studded gauntlet creaking. It was a terrible thing, seething with blighted power and when he made a fist, red light crackled between the fingers. 'Who'll take the other?'

'I'll do it,' Eyri said. He looked at Ulfar. 'I've seen what Imperial gunpowder does when you burn a bunch at a time. I'll fire the magazine in the ship's hold

and take the tower on the right while they're busy dealing with the explosion.' He looked at Halfhand, who
growled in anticipation and stroked the Skulltaker's
Mark branded into the flesh between his eyes. 'You
take the left, eh, Halfhand?'

'Aye,' the other chieftain said. 'And the towers?'

'We turn their own devil weapons on them,' Eyri said
with relish. 'Imagine what that oh-so carefully constructed harbour will look like when we do to it what
they did to Eyristaad!'

DALLA TOOK THE hand that grabbed her tangled hair off
at the wrist. The Svanii shrieked beneath his bird mask,
but the yell was cut short as she pinned his head to the
stone with a quick thrust. 'Quiet, hell-hound,' she said,
pulling his sword free. She looked around. The others
had fared equally well. Her companions-in-captivity
had scavenged weapons from the dead guards and now
they were all armed. Shaking blood off her blade she
kept going. They were following the herd of escaping
captives, chivying the stragglers on, arming who they
could.

It was not out of kindness, but desperation that
prompted her to do so. If her father were on the way
with a fleet, she was determined that he would find
the defences of the island as open as a whore's arms
to a customer. That meant causing as much trouble as
possible.

'You know what we must do?' she barked at Greki
and the others.

'We burn this festering pile to the ground, aye,' Greki
said, flashing his broken teeth. 'Do not worry, Ulfarsdottir, if there's one thing we know how to do, it is

burn things to – ack!' He gagged as the crow swept across his face, leaving thin red trails in its wake. He cursed and clutched at his face.

'Myrmidia!' someone shouted and Dalla cursed as the torches her men carried caught the sheen of brass armour charging towards them.

'Take them!' she said, bounding to meet the knights. Her sword whistled out, crashing against a hastily raised blade. She nearly shrieked in frustration as she recognised both the blade and its wielder. 'You!'

'Oh bloody hell, get off me!' Goetz snapped, whirling her around and driving her back towards the wall of the tunnel. The two forces crashed together behind them and he bent towards her, narrowly avoiding the wad of spittle she sent his way. 'Well, this is awkward,' he said.

'I should have gutted you on the boat!' she said.

'It would have simplified things no end if you had,' Goetz said. 'I was coming to free you!' he continued hastily as she tried to kick his legs out from under him.

'Were you so eager to die then, einsark?' she hissed as she forced him around. His back connected with the wall and dust spilled down on him.

'Would you believe that your father sent me?'

'No!'

'Of course you wouldn't! That would be too easy!' Goetz snapped, his voice dripping with frustration. 'Am I going to have to kill you to get you to listen to me?'

'Yes!' she said, shoving him back with a flurry of blows. He stepped back and she broke off, her sword point dipping. Goetz steadied himself against the cavern wall and looked past her. Opchek was behind her, his sword raised.

Goetz hit her with his shoulder, sending her rolling across the floor. He made an apologetic gesture to Opchek who stared at him incredulously and followed after her, his sword drawing sparks off the wall as he made a show of attacking her.

Unencumbered by armour, she bounced to her feet and met him blade to blade, their crosspieces entangling. He was the stronger, but she was as close to berserk as he'd seen anyone not frothing at the mouth. 'I was telling the truth,' he said hoarsely. 'You must believe me!'

'So?' Dalla spat. 'I will burn this daemon-haunted island to ash and bones!'

'Good plan,' Goetz grunted. 'At last we're on the same page. When I drop my sword, run.'

'Run?' Her eyes bulged. 'I do not run!'

'Then make a strategic advance in the opposite direction!' Goetz snarled. 'Just go. Do whatever you were planning on doing, but do it quick!' He shoved her aside and stumbled intentionally into the wall. For all her disbelief, Dalla didn't hesitate. She sprang past him like a she-cat and called out to her companions. Those who could broke off from their combats and followed her, fleeing pell-mell up the tunnel and outside.

They burst past the Svanii guarding the cave mouth, Greki pausing only to behead the one who got in their way and then they were rushing towards the town. 'Some fun, shield-maiden!' he howled. 'Now a fire, hey?'

'A big fire,' Dalla shouted back. Alarms were sounding

everywhere. Most of the prisoners with any sense had likely headed for the harbour or the shore. There would be enough confusion to cover what she needed to do. 'We'll burn it all!'

26

GOETZ GOT TO his feet just in time to meet Balk's fist. The hochmeister's blow sent him sprawling. 'You let her go!' he spat.

'She slipped past me,' Goetz said as Opchek stepped between them.

'We have more escapees to worry about than just that one, Conrad,' Opchek said. 'No reason to strike a brother.'

'I'll strike who I like!' Balk roared, gesticulating with his bloody axe. Opchek paled and stepped back. 'I'll strike anyone the goddess commands!' As if in agreement with Balk's scream, the island gave a bedrock-deep growl that caused the roof of the corridor to rain dust and rock chips.

'Half of them only fled into the depths,' another knight said. 'The Svanii will root them out. We can go after the others if we hurry…'

'Yes. Yes, we'll go after them,' Balk said, spinning and

starting back up the corridor. 'We'll kill them here and now and damn what she says!'

'Wait, what does he mean,' Goetz said, grabbing Opchek's arm. 'What does he mean, "here and now"? In contrast to what?'

'Hector, I–' Opchek pulled his arm free and shook his head. 'You haven't been here long enough. You haven't seen…'

'Seen what?' Goetz said. 'I've seen a man – a prisoner! – carved like a goose and innocents enslaved. I've seen destruction and things that no sane man would countenance in any knightly order, let alone ours! So tell me… What haven't I seen?'

Opchek's mouth opened and shut like a fish's. Before he could reply, Balk swung back around, his youthful features enflamed with rage. 'You haven't seen her!' he said. 'I know you, Hector Goetz. I know you, though I've never seen you before this week! I know what you are!'

'Illuminate me, *hochmeister*,' Goetz said, fighting to stay calm. 'What am I?'

'A false knight!' Balk snapped. 'Maybe you're not a spy, but you're a traitor nonetheless…' He stopped, as if suddenly aware as to what he'd said. The other knights stared at their confrontation with a variety of expressions, ranging from surprise to anger.

'Conrad, let's not say something we'll regret–' Opchek began.

'Quiet,' Balk said and his voice was like the rasp of iron across stone. 'You have no *faith*,' he continued. 'No faith.'

'Better to have no faith, than the wrong kind,' Goetz said, without thinking.

'Hector!' Opchek said. 'Please, just be quiet.'

'Treason! Heresy!' Balk said, hefting his axe. 'And to think, I came to rescue you after – after...' he trailed off, going pale.

'After what?' Goetz said quietly. Part of him already knew the answer. He thought of Oleg's panicked apologies even as he'd tried his best to kill him. *How do you know that they still follow Myrmidia?* Ambrosius had said. 'After what, hochmeister?'

'I–' Balk began and stopped. For a moment, he looked as if he were going to be ill. Then he shook it off and said, 'When this is over, I want you off this island.'

'Are you rescinding your offer of hospitality?' Goetz said, carefully sheathing his sword.

'Yes!' Balk said. 'Go back to Berengar. Tell him that I know what he is. Tell him that Myrmidia is with us, and unless he bends knee and begs her forgiveness, he and the rest of your false order will be ground under our heel.'

'Are you declaring war on your own brothers?' Goetz said, knowing full well that that was exactly what Balk meant. This wasn't rage talking, but cold intent. 'Are you declaring war on your own Order?'

'Not war,' Balk said. 'I'm declaring a death sentence. The goddess is on our side.' His features softened and he licked his lips. 'You're a good man. Everything you've seen... you have to understand... I know that she will welcome you. I know you will join us. Why else would she have spared you?'

'Yes. Why else?' Goetz said hollowly. Balk turned away, shaking his head, and the others followed him back above ground. Goetz watched them go. His fingers found the amulet nestled beneath his armour and he clutched it tight.

Chaos was here, and he was terrified to his very core. He recognised it now, even as he had in the Drakwald. It permeated everything, and he wondered why he hadn't seen it before. Maybe he had wanted to believe.

He looked down the tunnel. He could hear fighting down there, and the screams of the dying. How many of the escaped prisoners had gone the wrong way? What awaited them down there in the dark? He thought of what the old shaman had shown him and repressed a shudder.

'We go where we are needed, we do what must be done,' he said, his voice echoing in the silence of the tunnel. There was nothing he could do here. Not for those down there. But he could possibly save others, such as those who had already fled. Not to mention warning the Marienburg fleet, if such a thing were possible. If there was Chaos here, they had to know. 'We do what must be done,' he said again, though this time it was more in the nature of a curse.

He followed the others up the tunnel, the screams from below following him the entire way.

THE GALLEY EXPLODED in a ball of fire, which swept around the base of the sea-tower. The knight in command gawped as he watched the flames lick upwards and felt the pylon shake. 'What in the name of the goddess…?' he said before ordering his men to see to the guns. It had been one of their galleys, he was certain of that. An accident with the powder magazine perhaps? Surely no one could have been that careless…

The trapdoor that led down to the jetty rattled as

someone pounded on it. Assuming that it was the men he'd sent down to see to the galley, he was taken off guard when the Svanii he ordered to open it fell back, clutching a gashed belly.

'Anyone home?' Eyri said as he climbed into the tower, his hatchet in his hand. With a flick of his wrist he sent it spinning into the knight's unprotected head. The man only had a moment to process the sight of the spinning blade before it sank between his eyes and knocked him head over heels. Eyri had already drawn his second axe when the first of the Svanii on guard duty reacted, diving for a spear that was propped against the wall.

'Ha!' Eyri said, throwing the second hatchet and catching the savage high in the back. As the others moved towards him, he grabbed the hilt of the dead knight's sword and drew it with a flourish. 'Come and show me how you die, eaters of the dead!'

The Svanii came in a silent rush. There were three of them and they died in as many minutes. Eyri kicked a body away from the trapdoor and looked down at the men who'd helped him steer the galley into the tower. 'Up, dogs! We've got guns to aim!'

As the men clambered up, Eyri went to the centre of the room and grabbed hold of the massive wooden crank that occupied a fair amount of space. Pressing his shoulder to one of the dowl-grips, he waited until his men had joined him and they began to turn the crank. The effort set their muscles to wobbling like jelly and sweat streaked their faces in thick sheets. The mechanism gave a squeal as salt-corroded gears bit and the turret began to turn to face the interior of the harbour.

It was a good ploy, as such schemes went. Eyri had

seen it in action in his youth. The clockwork towers could rotate and fire their deadly payload at ships that had breached the outer defences and thought themselves safe within the field of fire. He could still remember what it had been like as those cannons they'd thought facing the other direction had belched and torn through their dragonships and sent men hurtling into the freezing waters. Eyri had only survived that day because one of his father's warriors had thought to hook him aboard the lone surviving ship as it fled back to Norsca.

'Now it's my turn, you brass-skinned bastards,' he growled, straining the final few inches to get the turret in place. He stood and looked at the cannons. Hauling a body out of the way, he checked the gun and saw that it was ready to be loaded. Swiftly he began to explain to his men how it worked. 'Right, powder, ball, pack and light you curs. Let's get this right or I'll use your hides for sails.'

Even as he said it, the cannons in the opposite tower began to fire. A galley in the harbour was ripped asunder as one of the great balls sheared through its mast and crashed across its keel. Eyri howled like a wolf. 'Looks like old Halfhand wasn't just boasting, eh, lads? Hurry up! We can't let the old blood-drinker have all the fun!'

DALLA NEARLY DROPPED the torch as the galley anchored nearby seemed to explode. She shook splinters out of her hair and turned back to the task at hand. Her men moved through the town, setting fires and causing chaos amongst the inhabitants. Alarm bells rang throughout the town, but none of that concerned her.

Swiftly she tossed her torch through an open window and grabbed the thatch drooping over the roof opposite and hauled herself up. Climbing up to the apex of the roof, she looked out to sea and nearly let loose with a cheer as she saw the unmistakable shapes of Norscan ships sailing into the harbour, serenaded on their journey by cannon fire.

'Something interesting, maiden?' Greki said as he pulled himself up after her. Blood oozed from the cuts the crow had left on his face.

'My father comes with the might of Norsca,' she said in satisfaction. 'Now we'll show these creatures who rules here!'

'Will we?' Greki said, his voice sounding odd. 'Will we indeed?'

Dalla turned, her hackles rising. The oozing cuts on the warrior's face spread as she watched, the edges spreading and the unwounded flesh splitting like paper. Greki's eyes bulged in their sockets and turned in opposite directions as if something were forcing its way out of him. His tongue waggled from between slack lips and his skin turned blue in the light of the fire. His mouth suddenly champed spasmodically and his gnashing teeth severed his tongue. It flopped down onto the roof between them and wriggled like a worm.

'Greki?' she said.

His hand shot out, fingers moving independently of one another like the limbs of a squashed spider. They snagged in the amulets around her neck and ripped them free in one frenzied jerk. Greki's bulging eyes rotated until they were both looking at her. 'I seeee you,' he said in a woman's purring tones.

Dalla moved panther-swift, her sword slashing out

to bisect him. His body staggered back, cut nearly in half. Blood spurted, stopped and became something else. Something that tried its best to snag her in its crimson, pulsing coils. Hissing in disgust she cut them free and kicked the shuffling body off the roof. Or tried to at any rate.

One of Greki's hands flailed and caught the edge of the roof. With a horrible ripping noise, the corpse swung itself back up and scuttled towards her on all fours. 'I see you Asgrimdalr's daughter,' it hissed. 'I see you now, and I will have you!'

'Not today, witch-thing!' Dalla said, avoiding the awkward lunge. Her sword looped out, cutting off an arm, and then a leg. The body rolled down the incline of the roof and scrabbled at the thatch in an effort to stay up. Brutally, she chopped down on the clutching fingers. The body rolled down into the street with a distinct thump.

Not waiting around to see whether that was the end of it, she leapt to the next roof. Atop the komturie, the cannons began to fire at the ships entering the harbour.

A sudden weight struck her between the shoulder blades and sent her rolling down the roof. Desperately she clutched at the thatch and dug her fingers in. The crow flapped down, landing above her. It cocked its head and croaked in what might have been amusement. Dalla snarled as more crows joined the first. First two, then three. Four. Five. All watching her with that same expression of amused contempt. As one they croaked, and Dalla felt her grip give way.

27

'To the sea-walls! To the walls!' Balk roared, his voice cracking as he spun his axe over his head. 'Man the wharf defences!'

'How did they even get past the harbour defences?' Taudge snarled as they ran towards the docks.

'That mist, I'll wager,' Opchek said. 'It's devil-summoned or I'm a Reiklander. No offence,' he continued, glancing at Taudge. 'The Norscans weave spells the way a maiden weaves hair!'

'Wizards would be helpful, you should note that along with the crossbows,' Goetz said as he joined them. He looked at the harbour, wondering if he could manage to get one of the boats moving by himself. Realising that it was likely futile he turned to find Taudge glaring at him.

'Why are you still here?' he said.

'I'm a knight of the Order, regardless of how you or any other might feel about me,' Goetz said blithely.

And I need to get off this rock, he thought, matching Taudge glare for glare. Opchek slapped him on the back.

'I knew you'd come around!' he said. 'Glad to have you here! Isn't that right Conrad?'

Balk looked at Goetz warily, but then nodded briskly. 'We must hold them here... we need to give the komturie time to prepare, and to get the Svanii civilians to safety. Are you with us?'

'Yes,' Goetz said.

'And just in time too,' Opchek said. 'Look!'

A burning longship, shredded by cannon-fire, had beached itself near the wharf and men were wading ashore. One of them, a brutal-looking man, larger than the others, raised a blood-red banner and planted it in the shore with a single thrust. He gestured towards them with an evil-looking gauntlet and his men started forward with a throaty cry, echoed by the mutated hounds that kept pace with them.

'Oh pox, that's the Halfhand!' one of the knights said. 'What's he doing this far south?'

'Does it matter? He's here, he dies,' Taudge spat. He raised his sword. 'For Myrmidia! For Svunum!' He charged a moment later, followed by several others. Goetz looked at Balk, whose face had gone the colour of slate.

'Balk?' he said.

'For Myrmidia,' Balk rasped, raising his axe. 'Blood for the goddess!'

The two groups slammed together and confusion ensued. The noise of the battle was drowned out by the roar of the cannons and the screams of dying men. Goetz traded blows with screaming berserkers, their faces scarred up with the eight-pointed mark of the Blood God.

The warrior that had been called Halfhand roared a challenge out to the knights and followed it up by punching his gauntleted hand through one knight's shield. Ripping the shield away, he crushed the unfortunate man's head with his eight-headed flail. Halfhand bellowed laughter as he pushed past the body and lashed out at Taudge, battering him from his feet. Goetz tried to reach him, but the press was too fierce. There were more than thirty warriors following the Halfhand, and only half that number of knights.

Balk, however, managed to hack a path to the chieftain in short order and he met the flail with his axe, shearing through the chains that bound the weighted balls to the bone handle. Halfhand cried out as if he had lost a limb and his armoured fist cracked down on Balk's shoulder, crumpling the ornate armour.

Balk, displaying a strength that Goetz hadn't suspected, shrugged off the blow and chopped off the offending limb. He kicked the hand into the bloody surf and swept his axe around in a figure of eight and drove it up under the warrior's cuirass. Pressing close, Balk snarled in the dying man's face and jerked the axe to the side, gutting him in a gory display. Even then, Halfhand refused to surrender, his remaining hand clawing weakly for Balk's face.

The hochmeister pushed him down and drove his spurred heel into the dying man's throat. Then he raised his axe and roared wordlessly at the Norscans, who began to fall back in disarray. Opchek snagged their banner and tossed it down contemptuously. 'Go back to your pickled fish and ugly women,' he jeered. 'This land is ours!'

'Not unless we can repeat this little victory a hundred or so more times,' Goetz said, pointing. Dozens of vessels were beaching themselves. The guns at the sea-towers were still firing and the Order's fleet had mostly been reduced to kindling. 'We have to fall back,' he said, turning to the others. 'Fall back, regroup. If we can just hold them off until tomorrow—' He stopped himself, hesitating.

'What? What's tomorrow?' Balk said, peering at him vaguely. He appeared to be enraptured by the sight of blood sliding through the sigils carved on the blade of his axe.

'We need to fall back,' Goetz said. 'We need to–'

The distant cannons roared and the wharf disinte-grated beneath their feet. Goetz felt as if he had been picked up by a giant's hand and thrown back. He flew through the cloud of debris and hit the rocky surface of the island skidding into the burning streets. Every muscle screamed in agony as he landed and he found himself unable to move, pinned by burning wreckage. As smoke filled his lungs and burned his sinuses, eve-rything went black.

'Get ashore, you wolves!' Eyri roared. 'Slaughter and fire await! Blood for the Bloody-handed!' He vaulted over the side of the longship and landed in the chill surf. He waded towards shore, holding his shield and his axe up over his head.

A Svanii met him in the surf, stabbing a spear at him with a wild shriek. Eyri swatted the point aside and drove the edge of his shield into the warrior's skull, just above his eyes. The man flopped back, blood leaking from his eyes and nose. Eyri stepped over him, a hundred blood-mad sarls at his heels.

They raged up onto the shore, howling war cries and banging their weapons on their shields, trying to attract the attention of the gods. A foolish notion, in Eyri's opinion, but who was he to gainsay them? So long as they were in the eyes of the gods, he wasn't; that was enough for him.

The town was already aflame when he reached the outskirts, and he smiled, sensing the she-wolf's hand. She did like a good fire, did Dalla. He cut down another savage and waded into the fray. They would burn, loot and pillage as the old man had said they must. To force the einsark's hand in whatever game was being played.

It was a game, Eyri knew that much. A game of gods and daemons, playing dice with the souls of *miklgardrs* like him. Eyri grinned and chopped his axe into a howling warrior, splitting his skull. He had always been good at games. Pulling his axe free, he moved on.

There was little of value in the squalid dwellings of the islanders, but Eyri had his eyes on the fortifications that the knights had built. There were treasures there, to be sure. Treasures only a smart man could appreciate. He led his men towards the burning fortifications at a trot. He had seen the cannonballs split the defences there like a child shattering a toy.

They had left men in both towers, and as long as there was shot, they'd keep firing, even if their aim was altogether poor. Hopefully, having shattered the wharf, they'd raise the barrels as he'd showed them and start firing at the town.

Picking his way through the burning wreckage he

caught sight of Halfhand's body lying half-in, half-out of the surf. The chieftain stared up at the sky blankly and Eyri saluted him. 'May the Blood God accept your skull with honour,' he murmured.

'More than will be said of you,' someone croaked. Debris shifted and a blackened, battered figure lurched upright, an axe dangling from his hand. Eyri grinned.

'Balk. Oh, I was hoping to find you out here, in the thick of things.'

'Were you? How fortuitous,' Balk said, moving unsteadily towards the group. His face was burned and covered in blood and ash. Only his eyes were untouched, and they blazed out at the world with a terrible strength. 'This has been a long time coming, Eyri.'

'You keep saying that,' Eyri said. 'And yet I'm still here.' He circled Balk warily. Even wounded, a man like Balk was dangerous.

'We'll soon fix that.' Balk moved sinuously, his axe looping out and catching Eyri's shield. He yanked it from Eyri's arm, nearly dislocating his shoulder in the process. Eyri stumbled back, surprised. Balk made for him, only stopping as Eyri's men closed in. The first warrior gave a bull-bellow as he charged Balk with a mace gripped in both hands. Balk ducked and spun, and the mace, as well as the hands that held it, flew aside. The axe changed directions and sheared off the screaming man's jaw.

'Quiet,' Balk said. 'I have things to discuss with your chieftain.' He glared at the warriors and they backed off, much to Eyri's astonishment. Balk seemed to swell as the men retreated, and Eyri had a hard time keeping him in focus. It was as if there were two bodies there, and only one of them was Conrad Balk. The other was something else entirely.

'I'll discuss them at leisure, over your body!' Eyri snarled and, mustering his courage, he slammed his hatchet down on Balk's arm. The hochmeister ripped his arm aside, taking Eyri's axe with it, and drove his own axe one-handed into Eyri's chest. The gromril stopped the bite of the blade, but not the force behind it. Eyri fell, the breath punched out of him. Something grated in his chest as he tried to crawl away. Balk was stronger than he remembered… far stronger.

The axe hissed and Eyri screamed as one of his legs spun free. Balk followed him and put a boot between his shoulder blades. 'I told you that the day would come when you would die, Eyri. You should have listened.'

Eyri coughed and tried to snatch the knife from his belt. His hand came off next and was sent sliding to join Halfhand's somewhere in the tide. He didn't even have the strength to scream as Balk rolled him over and raised the axe.

As it fell, Eyri realised that he had lost a game at last.

DALLA RAN AS buildings disintegrated around her. The crows followed, swooping through the smoke and flying timber with supernatural ease. It was all Dalla could do to avoid them and her limbs ached with the strain of it. She had been running for what felt like hours, and she knew that they were herding her somewhere.

But if she could give them the slip… If she could find her father…

She leapt over a contorted body and slid through a sagging door frame. The first crow followed her into the shack, croaking eagerly. She turned on her heel and chopped through the bird's neck. It flopped into the dirt and its body made strange movements, as if it were full of insects. She continued on, but was forced to stop as a blizzard of feathers engulfed her. The feathers were soft but razor-sharp and as they tore at her, the sound they made seemed to be a voice.

It laughed mockingly and she felt strong fingers caress her jaw. Then she was flying backwards. She crashed into a mound of debris and rolled awkwardly to her feet, groping for her sword. Instead of the crude Svanii blade, however, her fingers found the snarling lion-head pommel of a familiar sword. With a victorious cry, she whipped it free and swung it about her head, scattering the feathers.

Breathing softly, she looked about her. The shack was a crippled wreck, torn apart by fire and shot. The birds seemed to have abandoned the chase, though she wondered how long that would last. She looked down at the sword, then around. A burned and scarred gauntlet extruded from the debris, the fingers dangling limply. With a grunt she sank to her haunches and began to clear away the rubble, knowing what she'd find and praying that it wasn't too late.

28

IN THE BRIGHT darkness of the Drakwald, things moved beneath Goetz's skin. The buboes on his side rose black and slick against his sweating flesh as a chorus of crows croaked and laughed in the trees above. Goetz groaned as he clawed at his rotting flesh. He tried to dig out the poison with his numb fingers, but the rubbery flesh resisted his efforts. A white shape faded into view and inhumanly precise fingers gripped his chin, pulling his sweating face up to meet hers.

'Myrmidia?' he rasped, tasting blood. The eyes of the goddess did not meet his as her spear-point caressed the wound on his side. He groaned as pain flared through him and he fell to his hands and knees, black bile bursting through his lips to pool in the dirt. The spear jabbed him again.

'Wake up.'

A familiar length of metal pricked Goetz's throat, snapping him into full wakefulness. He swallowed, looked up and said, 'You need to stop taking things that don't belong to you.'

'I like it,' Dalla said, resting back on her heels as she raised his sword and laid the flat of the blade across her shoulder. 'It is a good sword.'

'I would have thought that you would have been gone by now,' he said as she climbed off him. He sat up and grunted in shock as a wave of agony passed over him. His clothes were sticky and red when he whipped them aside. Though his scars remained as whole as ever, blood stained his side and the ground around him. 'It was just a dream,' he said blankly.

'It looks like blood to me,' Dalla said. 'Get up.'

'Why?'

'You ask too many questions. Get up.'

'Asking questions is the only path to wisdom,' Goetz said. 'Why are you still here?'

'To repay my debt,' she said, as if it were obvious.

'Lot of that going around,' Goetz said, pushing himself to his feet.

'What?' Dalla looked confused.

Goetz shook his head. 'Nothing. I–' He paused. A dim scratching sound reached his ears. A persistent, familiar noise. 'What was that?'

'What was what?'

'That,' Goetz said, as the scratching sound came again.

'Don't move!' Dalla said, grabbing for him. Goetz turned to tell her that he had no intention of doing so when, with a shattering crash, the roof of the ruined shack exploded downwards, showering them both with debris. Something horrible flopped into the room. Goetz recognised it as Myrma's crow… or rather, something that had once been a crow.

The bird croaked as pink flesh bulged hideously beneath black feathers. The croak became a chuckle, then a giggle and the crow hopped forward, shedding feathers and expanding in size with every step. Soon enough, the pink thing stepped out of the bird skin, kicking it aside the way a strumpet might launch a shoe. Massive hands opened and closed in apparent eagerness as it chuckled. It had arms like ropes and its face squatted inside the barrel chest, its tongue lolling between its bandy legs. Beaks opened and closed on its shoulders and its iridescent skin seemed to shift and squirm on whatever passed for its bones.

Goetz felt ill just looking at the horror as it ambled forwards, apparently unconcerned about the sword Dalla held. It giggled and shifted from one foot to the other, sidling around them. 'What does it want?' Goetz said, already knowing the answer.

'Me,' Dalla said, fear reducing her voice to a hoarse whisper. Then, as if to give lie to her assertion, the pink thing lunged, but not for the swordswoman. In a flash of pink, the spade-sized paws crashed down towards Goetz!

Goetz threw himself aside. The ache in his side screamed into full-blown agony and he hit the floor hard, curling into a ball. The creature wheeled around, its chuckles striking his ears like hammer blows.

With a loud cry Dalla chopped her sword down through one of the gangly arms, only to be left staring in shock as the wound knitted itself back together in an instant. The creature turned in a leisurely fashion and swept out a backhand that would certainly have killed her had it connected. Instead, she bent backwards and fell onto her rear.

She crab-crawled backwards, as it ambled after her. Goetz hauled himself to his feet, looking for anything that he might use as a weapon. Desperate, he flipped a chunk of the roof over and wrenched a charred chunk from one of the fallen support beams free in a burst of strength. Then, whirling it over his head, he brought it down solidly on the creature's back. It jerked forward in surprise and twisted, beaks snapping. Goetz stamped forwards, striking out at it again and again, wielding the improvised club like a sword. Splinters and ash flew as he battered the creature.

It flailed at him and he gave ground grudgingly, fending off its blows as best he was able. After another near miss he began to come to the sickening conclusion that the creature was playing with him. It chuckled and grabbed his club, striking him at the same time. He flew backwards. The thing – the daemon, he knew – advanced, its hands clenching and unclenching eagerly.

Pushing himself to his feet, his hands brushed across something hard. He glanced down and saw the amulet of Myrmidia that Abbot Knock had given him. Snatching it up, he stabbed it into one of the daemon's bulbous eyes. It reeled back with a despairing shriek that sent waves of pain radiating through his nerve endings. It clawed at the amulet which sank deeper and deeper into its skull with a bubbling hiss. Its beaks clacked in agony and it hunched over, ignoring the two humans.

'Throw me the sword!' Goetz barked. Dalla hesitated,

but then did as he asked. He caught the blade and whipped it around, driving it through the creature's malformed pink body and into the stone floor below. The shriek became a piercing wail that threatened to puncture their eardrums.

Goetz shut his eyes against the pressure building in his skull, and when it abruptly faded, he was relieved to find that the daemon had vanished, leaving only a sticky residue to mark its passing. He knelt, leaning on the sword for support, and fished the amulet out of the mess. He held it up and thought of what the old shaman had said. 'I wanted a sign,' he murmured. 'I suppose I got one.'

'What are you blathering about?' Dalla said, glaring warily at the patch on the floor.

'Faith renewed,' Goetz said, hanging the amulet from his neck.

'We need to get out of here,' she said, shuffling impatiently. 'The daemon's master will know soon enough that it has been sent back.'

'I'm well aware of that. I–'

The door slammed open and sagged from its blistered hinges. Goetz made to draw his sword, but the figures that faced him convinced him otherwise. 'Hochmeister,' he said.

Balk, flanked by Opchek and Taudge, stepped into the room, his axe in hand. All three men looked as badly used as Goetz felt. 'Brother,' Balk said. 'I see you've caught our runaway. Stand aside.'

'No,' Goetz said, stepping between the trio and Dalla. The latter hissed and tensed. She was ready to spring despite the odds against her. 'No, I think not,' Goetz went on. 'I think, in fact, that we'll be leaving.'

'I told you,' Taudge snapped. 'He's besotted with the wench!'

'Well, she is quite comely,' Opchek said. He frowned. 'Hector, we won't hurt her. Just step aside.'

'I'm sorry my friend, but no,' Goetz said, slowly drawing his blade.

'She has bewitched you,' Balk said. 'Step aside.'

Goetz said nothing. He had a sense of a string being pulled taut and getting ready to snap. When it did, it was Taudge who moved first. Goetz wasn't surprised. He let Taudge's blow glide off his sword and rolled with it, driving his shoulder into the other man's chest. He shoved Taudge back into the others and then jerked his head at Dalla. 'Come on!'

She leapt over the tangle of knights nimbly and she and Goetz fled out into the street. There were men waiting for them – Svanii, armed with spears. Balk had come prepared. Goetz grabbed Dalla and spun her aside even as he threw himself at the feet of the spearmen, sending the group tumbling. Dalla snatched up a fallen spear and pierced the belly of the first man unlucky enough to get back on his feet, shoving him up and back against the far wall. The Svanii shrieked as Dalla left him where he was and made to grab another spear.

The staff came out of nowhere and struck her across the face. The swordmaiden fell and lay still. Goetz got to his feet and Myrma turned to face him, her beautiful features twisted into a furious grimace. She spat strange syllables that crawled down his spine like spiders and a coruscating talon of black-hued lightning clawed for him. Goetz threw himself aside.

'Take him,' the priestess spat. Goetz turned, but not

quickly enough. The haft of Balk's axe connected with the bridge of his nose and he was knocked back into darkness.

'WHAT ABOUT HER?' Taudge said, nudging Dalla's limp form with the toe of his boot. 'Do we take her as well?'

'Why would we do that?' Balk said, directing the Svanii to pick up Goetz. 'Let her lay here and rot with the rest of the Norscan filth.'

'Speaking of Norscan filth…' Opchek gestured towards the komturie, which was seemingly aflame. The sounds of fierce fighting could be heard. 'Even with the defences we built into the inner keep, I'm not sure our brothers can hold out for very long. Not with so many of them engaged in rounding up the escapees.'

'It doesn't matter,' Myrma said, her eyes closed, her face the picture of exhaustion. 'It is too late for them to stop it. The more blood that soaks into these stones, the better.'

'Those are our brothers you are talking about!' Opchek barked. He grabbed Myrma's arm as if to whirl her around, but a blow from Balk sent him reeling. Opchek stared up at his hochmeister in disbelief. 'Conrad?'

'Sacrilege, brother,' Balk said mildly, letting the blade of his axe scrape the stone. With the fire engulfing the village and the harbour behind him, he looked positively daemonic. 'Our brothers gladly give their lives in return for the Order of the Blazing Sun's triumph. Even as you yourself swore you would. As we all would.'

'I so swore,' Opchek began. In his head, he heard the whirring of wings.

'Is your faith wavering brother? Are you losing

heart?' Balk helped Opchek to his feet. 'This close to our sacred goal?' The hochmeister's voice was low and intent and it bit into Opchek's doubts like a sword blade. Opchek frowned. 'I am happy to kill the Order's enemies. But this was one of our own!' he snarled, gesturing to Goetz. 'Just like the other one.'

'I told you… The goddess commanded me!'

'Bollocks!' Opchek spat. It was Balk's turn to flush.

'I am hochmeister! I know what needs to be done!'

'Since when has assassination ever been our remit?' Opchek said.

'Since our Order turned from the path Myrmidia laid out for us!' Balk said. He grabbed Opchek's arms. 'I know you don't want to believe that brother, but it is the truth!'

Opchek shook him off. 'How do you know? Greisen never–'

'Greisen is dead. And all who followed him are dead,' Balk said harshly. He glared at the other knights, as if daring them to disagree. 'Led into a trap and butchered because they thought that they could deal in a civilised manner with the Norscans. And Berengar, damn his hide, encouraged him in that path!' Balk made a fist and shook it. 'Talk, talk , TALK! That is what Berengar wants! He wants the Order of the Blazing Sun to be the thrice-cursed *Reiksguard*–' Balk spat the name of the Emperor's bodyguards, 'Politicking and kowtowing to every petty lordling and bureaucrat! Myrmidia is the patroness of civilisation, yes, but also of war! And Berengar has no stomach for war. Even Greisen knew that!'

'Maybe not, but he is the Grand Master,' Opchek said. 'And now…' He trailed off, looking ill. 'We didn't have to do it. We don't have to do it!'

'But you do,' Myrma said.

'And you know this how?' Opchek said, after a moment of hesitation.

She looked at him. 'I know only what the goddess tells me. If you would but listen, she would tell you the same.' Before he could reply, she held up her arms and spread them like wings. The island gave a groan as the ground shifted and growled. Water splashed over the burning docks and the splintered decks of the wrecked ships and the komturie shuddered in the distance.

'Do you hear her, knight? Do you dare listen?' Myrma said, raising her staff with a flourish. Opchek staggered as a piercing light blazed into being around the priest-ess. In its depths, the Kislevite saw a shape grow from a pinpoint to a rushing shadow. He heard the snap of wings and the face of a goddess looked down on him sadly. He fell to his knees as she reached out with her great spear – or was it a talon? – and touched the tip to his brow. She spoke in a voice at once soft and thun-derous and he clapped his hands to his ears.

Balk grabbed his wrists, forcing his hands away from his head. 'Listen!' the hochmeister said, his eyes blaz-ing with adoration. 'Listen to her!'

Opchek did, as did the others. As one, they sank to their knees, heads bowed.

'It is the Witching Night,' Myrma said in satisfaction. 'The moons have risen and our time draws close. We must begin the ritual!'

Opchek looked at the komturie, and then at the oth-ers. 'But–'

'It is your decision, brother,' Balk said softly. He put his hand on the brawny Kislevite's shoulders and pulled him to his feet. 'Come with us, and see what wonders the future holds, or join our brothers in defending our shores. Either way, you serve the Order.'

'I–' Opchek nodded jerkily. 'I'll go with you.'

'Good!' Balk smiled. The smile faded as he took in the destruction wrought on the island. 'We shall pay them back for this threefold, brothers! Myrmidia will see to it!'

'Can't come soon enough,' Taudge grunted.

As a group, they left the burning shore and descended into the sea-caves. Balk paid little heed to the bodies, though Opchek looked ill and even Taudge made a face as he caught sight of armoured corpses. More knights joined them as they moved down. Kropch, a hardy veteran of the Marienburg Komturie, saluted Balk.

'We've rounded up most of the escapees. But we heard cannon-fire. Should we–?'

'No. The komturie was built for this purpose,' Balk said, making a cutting gesture. 'We can best serve our brothers by seeing to matters here.'

'But the Norscans have invaded,' Kropch said. 'We must toss them back!'

'We will,' Myrma snarled impatiently. She thrust her way into the group and glared at the gathered knights. Her skin sagged alarmingly on her bones and her face was pinched with weariness. 'But the night slips away from us! Myrmidia requires your strength! Will you shirk her?'

'We go where we are needed, brothers,' Balk said.

'We do what must be done,' Kropch and the others echoed. Myrma watched them and nodded in satisfaction. There were eighteen knights gathered here. Two nines, the holy number of the Great Weaver. There was twice that number of seed-pods growing in the deep caverns, enough to match the entirety of the komturie. But for the purposes of the ritual, it would be perfect.

She glanced at the unconscious body of Goetz and a smile spread across her face. She clutched her staff as a wave of weakness spread over her. 'Too late Asgrimdalr. It is too late for you... for all of you.'

THE END OF the staff caught Dalla a blow on the head. 'Up, daughter. There is red work to be done.' Groggily, Dalla looked up. Ulfar looked down at her. 'Up,' he said again.

'What–?' she groaned. Every muscle felt like it was on fire.

'You live, child. I should have thought that would be obvious. Others were not so lucky.' Ulfar turned. Thalfi Utergard, squatting near the water at the edge of the wrecked dock, held up something pale and bloodless.

'I found Goldfinger's hand,' he rumbled.

'I'm pretty sure this was the rest of him,' Kettil Flatnose said, standing over a sodden heap. 'Poor cunning fool.' He looked at Ulfar. 'Halfhand is dead as well, old man. Along with Lok and Hrothgar, that's four godi, dead on this mad venture of yours.'

'Not mine,' Ulfar said, looking down at Eyri's body. Dalla, on her feet, joined him. Still queasy she looked down at the pitiful remains of Eyri Goldfinger and felt a moment of regret. It was washed away a moment later as she realised that someone was missing. 'Goetz!'

'Who?' Ulfar said, looking at her.

'The einsark! They've taken him!'

'You're concerned about one of *them*?' Kettil said incredulously.

'No! But why would they take him?' she said, hesitating.

Ulfar shook his head. 'He is cursed. A poison lurks in him and they will exploit it.' His knuckles turned white as he leaned against his staff. 'I did not foresee this... I had hoped... pah. We must get to those caves.'

'My men and I are ready!' Thalfi bellowed. 'And Halfhand's gauntlet with me!' He held up the grisly trophy and emptied it of its contents before sliding it onto his own hand with a squelch. The gauntlet hissed like a kettle and Thalfi grunted and flexed the brass fingers. 'Yesss.'

'Fool,' Kettil muttered. He looked at Ulfar. 'That thing is cursed.'

'What of it? This island is cursed.'

'All the more reason to leave... My boats are loaded with booty. Their fortress burns, the Svanii are without shelter... We have done this thing and done it well!' Kettil said.

'And what then?' Ulfar spun, his eyes blazing. Even Dalla stepped back, so surprising it was to see the old man actually angry. 'I have done this before, Flatnose! I have burned them to the water's edge and back and like mushrooms in night-soil they grew back and took from me what was mine!' His withered hand clenched like a claw. 'They always come back, fool. That is their nature... but not this time. This time, I will purge this place though it take the life of every sarl and every baersonling, every thane and jarl, every son of Norsca to do it!' Ulfar roared, his staff raised over his head. Both chieftains were reminded of the old man's transformation into a bear and they fell back a step.

'Father,' Dalla said.

Ulfar calmed and took her hand. 'Daughter.' He looked at the chieftains. 'Gather your men. Let the others storm the citadel. We will deliver a dagger-stroke to the beast's heart!

'SOMETHING'S ON FIRE,' Grand Master Ogg said, lowering his spyglass. He tapped it on the rail and looked at Ambrosius. The one-eyed man rubbed the heel of his hand against his eye-patch and grinned.

'I suppose it's too much to hope that they're throwing us a welcoming feast, eh?'

'I'd say not, sir,' Dubnitz said, standing nearby. The big knight looked at his Grand Master. 'Do you think they're preparing for us, sir?'

Ogg said nothing. He swatted the rail with his trident, and looked at the fleet. It was not a large one, as far as fleets went, but it was battle-hardened and armed to the teeth. Weapons straight from the Gunnery School at Nuln lined the decks and men in green armour paced beneath sails bearing Manann's likeness.

He turned. 'No. Something is going on. Those aren't fires of welcome or siege preparation.' He met Ambrosius's eye. The Lord Justicar nodded.

'Norscans,' he said flatly. When they'd heard that the *Nicos* had been taken, they'd feared the worst. Ships being taken weren't an uncommon occurrence by any means, but it was all too perfect. They both assumed that Hector Goetz had met the same fate as Sir Athalhold, victim of some conspiracy none of them could see clearly. 'We may have to fight a two-pronged war, Grand Master.'

'No island is worth that,' Ogg said, frowning.

'Yet we're still heading that way, I notice,' Ambrosius said. 'Would you like to weigh anchor then? Turn the fleet around?'

'No,' Ogg said, unfolding his spyglass again. 'The wisdom of Manann says that when you see a storm, the best thing to do is sail into it and try and find the eye.' He frowned. 'Let's go find the eye of that firestorm, eh?'

29

HE WAS BACK in the Drakwald. The familiarity and frequency of the dream was becoming tedious and in frustration Goetz raised his fists to the ceiling of cruel branches and said, 'What do you want of me?'

'She will not answer,' a hoarse voice intoned. 'We have seen to that.'

Goetz lowered his hands. 'Who are you?'

'A friend.' A shape shuffled out of the close-set trees, leaning heavily on a staff decorated with black feathers. The hood was thrown back, revealing a maggot-pale face that was unpleasantly familiar.

'Myrma,' Goetz said, disgust curling at the edges of his words. If she heard the tone, she gave no sign. She bared rotten teeth in what Goetz supposed was a welcoming smile and nodded. 'I knew there was something wrong with you. Even before the old man told me.'

'Aye.' Her accent was a savage thing, with a rolling

brutal lilt that Goetz had trouble understanding. 'And he should know, being who he is.'

'And who is he?' Goetz said, taking a step back.

'The man who killed me, of course,' Myrma said. She threw off her cloak, revealing a body that was withered and rotting. Black blood streamed down from a cavernous sore in her side. Goetz's own wound tingled in sympathy, and he fought the urge to touch it. She, however, seemed to know what he was thinking.

'Aye. The same we are, sure as sure.' she chuckled wetly. 'Poisoned.'

'That's–' Goetz blinked. Myrma's form seemed to blur, to become slimmer. Goetz felt a rising tide of disgust threaten to overwhelm him. 'How many shapes do you have, witch?'

Myrma laughed and shook her staff. The bones hanging from the tip clattered and the sound was echoed from the trees by the croaking of crows. Goetz twisted in a circle, looking up. Every branch was bent with dark, avian shapes. Hundreds of them. Thousands, even. All of them watching him. He shuddered, his spirit going cold. He put a hand on his side, and his fingers touched wetness.

'Many,' Myrma said. 'Just skins, provided for me by my Mistress, in her benevolence and wisdom. Daughters of daughters' blood, all of them.'

'All of them…' Goetz said. Between the trees, pale, limp shapes moved forward into the light of the witch-fire and the bile in his mouth dried up. Ragged, torn skins stumbling forward on empty feet, their eyes dark blotches on tattooed skin. There were dozens of them, their sagging features all bearing an eerie resemblance to those of Myrma. They drifted towards her and flopped down at her feet in supplication. The rotten teeth clicked together in an exultant grin as her beast-yellow eyes fastened on Goetz.

'Skin of my skin, blood of my blood. My Lady has given me mighty weirdings so that I might aid her in her own,' she said. 'And now... now I will give her you.'

'Me?' Goetz said.

Myrma's lupine smile threatened to split her desiccated face. She tapped his weeping side and flung droplets of oily blood in Goetz's direction. 'You were touched, even as I was, by the stuff of the gods. It has strengthened you. Made you more durable than any other on this island.'

Involuntarily, Goetz's eyes were drawn down to his side. Blood stained his tunic. Frantically, he ripped the cloth aside and saw the black streaks growing across his skin. Pain shot through him as, above, the crows gave voice to what might have been mocking laughter.

'And in the touching, they gained hold of you,' Myrma said, making a fist with her bloody fingers. 'A raw, red door in the meat of you. Just waiting for the right key.' Her gaze dimmed. 'My skins go quickly these past years. They are not fit for my weirdings, let alone the mighty soul that inhabits this place. But you...' she smacked her lips. 'Hollowed out, you will be a fine suit of strong iron for her spirit!'

'No!' Goetz said, staggering. The black streaks grew thicker as they spread across him in a pattern eerily reminiscent of the aura of the sun on his medallion. His wound was a black sun, spreading the cold of oblivion through him. Above, the crows took flight, rising above the trees and spinning into a maelstrom of black feathers. At the eye of the maelstrom, something looked down at Goetz, and his soul shrivelled in horror. 'No,' he said again.

'Yes!' Myrma cackled, spreading her arms and looking up in rapture at the presence above. 'With you as my armour, I shall at last break the stone chains that bind her! I shall rouse her from her mighty dreams! *IA! S'vanashi! IA! Tzeentch!*'

As the hideous syllables smashed through him, Goetz's eyes sprang open and he lurched forward. Strong arms gripped him and hauled him back. 'Too late for that now, brother,' Opchek said sadly. 'Too late for any of it, I'm afraid.'

Goetz shook his head, trying to clear it. He was in a cavern. He could smell the tang of salt water and a number of oddly coloured torches had been stuffed into crevices in the rock and lit. He looked at his captors; they were no longer wearing the dwarfen-wrought armour that was every knight's right. Instead they wore black suits of plate, festooned with odd sigils and features. In place of Myrmidia's sigils were those of some other god entirely, and they hurt Goetz's eyes to look upon them. The armour was the colour of tar and it gleamed with a sickly radiance in the torchlight, looking less like metal than the insides of a nut. Scattered around the cavern were great empty husks that looked like large seed-pods.

'What have you done to yourselves?' he said.

Balk stepped in front of him and used the flat of his axe to lift Goetz's chin. 'We have accepted the blessings of Myrmidia, brother. As you should have done when we gave you the chance,' he said. 'But now, now you will serve her regardless.'

Goetz spat and tried to jerk his head away. Taudge grabbed him by the scalp and forced him to meet the hochmeister's eyes. Balk knelt and leaned on his axe. He indicated his armour with a gesture. 'She grew this armour for us, to replace that which was made by fallible human hands. It is god-forged this stuff, and it will make us Myrmidons in truth… ah, you see? I knew you were no fool,' he said, noting the look on Goetz's face. 'Myrmidon,' Balk said. He tapped his ear. 'She told me all about you, *Sudenlander*. They came from there you know, these folk. Svanii. The children of Myrmidia, driven into the wasteland by the machinations of the Ruinous Powers. But in you is the hope for this Order, for our goddess… I thought at one time, she might bless me in this fashion. But I see now that she has chosen you. It's fitting, in a way. Of course she would choose you. Why disrupt the chain of command when the perfect vessel just drops in your lap, after all?'

'You have no idea what you're doing,' Goetz said. 'This is wrong. All of it.'

'Yes. It is wrong. This world is wrong. It is barbaric and destructive. But we will make it orderly. Tidy, even,' Balk said, rising to his feet. 'And you will lead us, brother. You will be our figurehead. Our living standard, touched by the goddess herself! She will remould your frail flesh into the very stuff of power.' He raised his axe and the other knights gathered in the cavern sent up a cheer that chilled Goetz to the bone.

'Take him to the altar!' Balk said. Goetz was yanked to his feet and propelled forward, towards a gross bubo of rock and dirt that rose blister-like from the stone. Around it had been heaped the discarded armour of the other knights, as well as the lithographs, icons and amulets of Myrmidia. Everything that belonged to the goddess had been tossed here, in the dirt. A web of rusty chains descended from the roof of the cavern, manacles hanging from them at odd points. The cavern walls seemed to tremble in delight as he was dragged forward.

He hadn't truly wanted to believe it. But he couldn't deny the evidence of his own eyes. Opchek and Taudge manacled his hands, the former not looking at him, the latter glaring. 'Don't do this,' Goetz said. 'This is wrong, brothers. You know it.'

'Silence,' Taudge said, backhanding him. Goetz's head rocked back and he tasted blood. He spat it out and looked up. Heaving, flat-bodied shapes clustered across the roof of the cavern, their colourful scales glinting in a hideous rainbow as they squirmed. Every so often, one would emit a screech from an unseen mouth. Goetz shuddered and cast his eyes down.

Myrma looked up at him, leaning tiredly on her staff. Her hair was threaded through with white, and her previously useful face was heavily lined and worn. Nonetheless, she smiled up at him. 'You killed my pet. Not many men could do that. You are everything she promised.'

'Who? Who promised?' Goetz snarled, pulling against his chains. Around them, the cavern trembled as if rocked by titanic laughter.

Myrma raised her arms and gestured to the cavern. 'She who protects us! She who gathered us unto her womb and carried us away from our enemies! She who has planned for this moment from the beginning! *IA! The Queen of Crows! IA! The Maiden of Colours!* Come forth Lady and let him gaze upon your splendour!'

The crows took flight all at once with shrill screams. They spun around and around, faster and faster, as they had in Goetz's dream. Feathered shapes blurred into one another with a sound like snapping bones until what had been a flock was now a pulsing, floating mass. As the mass sank downwards, the island rumbled again, much louder this time. The gathered knights shifted uneasily as the Svanii worshippers threw themselves about in a crooked, flopping dance that reminded him of the movements of a wounded bird. The cavern seemed to contract as the mass of feathers and meat dropped to the ground.

Then, in the silence that followed, the mass unfolded into a horribly tall, slim shape. A hideously familiar face protruded through a mane of sticky black feathers. Slim, talon-tipped fingers reached for Goetz as the thing took a dainty step forward, looming over its followers. The marble-pale face twisted into a smile.

'My lovely boy,' Myrmidia – the thing that wore Myrmidia's face – said. Corpse-black lips peeled back from shiny obsidian teeth as she leaned forward. The sickly-sweet stink of her washed over Goetz, inundating his senses with ever-shifting odours, tastes and images. Her feathers were so black that they seemed to encompass all colours and none, and spots danced in front of his eyes as he tried to focus on them.

Bird talons caressed his face, leaving a sticky residue on the leather-bound edges of the wound on his cheek. The entity leaned close, her glittering eyes boring into his. On his chest, the amulet of Myrmidia seemed to grow warm. 'Your mind is like quicksilver,' the Queen of Crows said, in a pleasant gurgle. 'So much deception. So many thoughts.'

'What – what are you?' Goetz said, trying to twist his face away from its touch. It was a question he already knew the answer to, but something told him that he needed to keep the creature talking if he had any hope of escaping.

'I am the Queen of Crows, the Maiden of Colours, the Hand-Maiden of the Great Mutator, the She-Spider, the Whisperer in Darkness, the Love of Cats, the Sadness of Wolves, the Silence of Tigers…' It recited the names with obvious relish, letting them trip across its lips in a parody of song. 'I am the Lady of the Island, Hector Goetz. I am your goddess.'

'Not mine,' Goetz said, trying for defiance. He was afraid it only registered as petulance. The woman-thing threw back her head and laughed and as she laughed, the island shook. Her face snapped down and talons grabbed his chin. One finger rose and the leather thongs holding his cheek closed snapped and split. Blood spilled down his face and the Queen of Crows leaned forward, extending a feline tongue to lap up the blood with sinister tenderness. As its tongue made contact with him, images invaded his mind, falling across his consciousness like shards of broken glass.

…*a war in heaven, as reality heaved like an angry sea*…

…*falling, she tried to stop her plunge, but HE had taken her wings to punish her and she fell and fell and FELL*…

…*the pain as she forced her blood to mix with the stuff of the sea and grow into an island*…

…*the Knowing that the Game was going on without her was the most exquisite torment*…

Goetz jerked his head back with neck-cracking urgency. He thrashed in his chains, not fully in control of his movements. 'Daemon,' he said.

The hideously beautiful face dipped in acknowledgement, but the mouth said, 'No. Just a ghost.' Goetz shuddered again and tried to pull away. The daemon clucked pityingly and gripped the back of his head. 'Stop. Your plans are all undone, your dreams unfettered and scattered. Give in,' it said softly. 'I will ride you to heights undreamt, and in your skin, in the armour of you, I will retake my place in the Game.'

'Game?' Goetz began. He felt numb, almost pleasantly so. On his chest, the amulet was no longer warm, but hot. The numbness was flushed away by sudden, searing pain and Goetz arched in his chains. The daemon stepped back with a croak as light speared from the amulet.

'Take that off!' it snapped, flailing with one titan paw. Parts of it began to dissolve back into dirt and bird-meat and Goetz realised that this was not its real form, but merely an amalgamation created from the raw stuff of the island. The images showed him the truth… it had no flesh, no physical presence. It was just a phantom, made of decaying matter, the very stuff of its soul rotting the body it had created. 'Take it off!'

Several Svaniis scrambled forward, reaching for Goetz. Muscles straining, shoulder-blades threatening to separate, he hauled himself up and drove a kick into the face of the first to reach him. The man slipped and fell off the altar stone with a howl. Another grabbed Goetz's leg and he swung himself back, pulling the hapless Svanii with him. He shook the man off even as a shout echoed through the cavern.

A spear took the last Svanii on the altar through the chest. Goetz twisted, trying to see what was going on. The knights and their ghoulish retainers were engaged

in battle with a number of shapes; with a start, he recognised them as Norscan!

Dalla darted through the press, Goetz's sword in
her hand. Without looking at the daemon, she sprang
onto the altar and sliced through the chains holding
him aloft. He collapsed onto the stone just as Myrma
scrambled towards them, jabbing her staff at Dalla like
a spear.

'No! He is mine!' the sorceress squealed. Goetz
swung the remnants of his bindings up and across her
face. Her neck snapped with a loud crunch and she fell,
her staff clattering away.

'Die and be damned,' Goetz spat, dropping the
chains. He looked at Dalla. 'You took your time.'

'I was hoping they'd kill you,' she said flatly. 'I got
bored.' She tossed him his sword and drew a hatchet
from her belt. 'Your armour is down there.'

'Yes, but they're up here!' Goetz said, hauling her
aside as one of the flat shapes from the cavern ceiling dropped from its roost and swooped towards them
with a horrible shriek. Goetz's sword flashed up, shearing through the alien flesh and spattering his face and
arms with corrosive droplets. A moment later it was
Dalla's turn to shove him as a second *Screamer* dropped
towards them. Her hatchet buried itself in the thing's
armoured carapace and she was ripped off her feet and
into the air as the thing twisted and bucked.

Goetz dropped from the altar and began shrugging
into what armour he could. Crouched, he buckled on
his cuirass with trembling fingers. There was a scrape
of sound behind him and he managed to turn and
bring his sword up just in time. Opchek's sword met
his for an instant and then they broke apart.

'I'm sorry, Hector,' Opchek said, his voice echoing hollowly from within his grotesque new helm. 'Put the sword down. This can still end well…'

'No. It can't,' Goetz said, lunging forward, aiming the point of his blade for Opchek's gorget. The Kislevite backpedalled and Goetz followed, his blade licking out with startling quickness.

'You're faster than I thought!' Opchek said as Goetz's sword cut a groove in the cheek-guard of his helmet. Goetz didn't reply, merely pressing close. He beat aside Opchek's sword and scored a hit on his chest, knocking the wind out of the other knight. Opchek staggered. 'Much faster,' he wheezed.

'Stop playing with the bastard and kill him!' Taudge roared, charging into Goetz and sending him sprawling. Goetz got to his feet and faced both knights. Taudge's armour was stained with newly-spilled blood and he favoured one leg. 'I told you all this was a bad idea! Let's kill the traitor and put down this thrice-damned Norscan rabble!'

'Feel free to try,' Goetz said. He continued to back away until his foot crashed down on a battered shield. Myrmidia's face gazed serenely up at him from the embossed surface. Goetz stooped and swiftly scooped the shield up, shoving his arm through the loops even as Taudge came for him.

Goetz caught the blow on the shield and swept the other man's sword blade against the altar stone, trapping it. As Taudge gaped in shock, Goetz drove his own blade through a gap in his opponent's armour, scattering mail-links and blood over the ground behind him. Taudge fell back, sinking into a sitting position as blood spilled down his legs and pooled in his lap.

'It was supposed to make us invincible,' he said haltingly. 'She said!'

'She lied,' Goetz said, taking Taudge's head off with a backhanded swipe. Opchek stared at him in shock, but only for a moment. The Kislevite's face hardened and he charged with a roar.

Opchek beat Goetz's shield aside and aimed a chopping blow at his head. Goetz jerked back and twisted, using his momentum to send a blow of his own ringing across Opchek's helmet. The Kislevite staggered and Goetz kicked him in the side of the leg, dropping him to his knees. With brutal desperation he brought his shield down on the top of Opchek's head, driving him face-first into the rocky floor of the cavern. The Kislevite lay still. Goetz kicked his sword away just to be sure and turned, breathing heavily. Every muscle ached and his cheek was a throbbing ball of agony.

'How easily you strike your brothers.' Goetz turned. Balk sat on a nearby rock, his axe across his knees. 'How easily you shed your loyalties. I wish I could be so… fluid,' Balk said, rising to his feet.

'I'm sure Brother Athalhold will feel better knowing that you define murder as loyalty,' Goetz said.

Balk hesitated for a moment, and then continued forward. 'I did what must be done.'

'As do I,' Goetz said.

'Berengar is corrupt!' Balk said. 'He leads the Order into ruin! I will give us back our purpose! Our soul!'

'You sold your soul for a fancy suit of armour and the chance to shed blood,' Goetz snapped. He gestured at the daemon behind them. Its form continued to disintegrate as it watched the battle unfolding at its feet. 'Does that look like a goddess to you? Are you

that blinded by hate that you can mistake *that* for *this*?'
Goetz said, slapping the face of his shield for emphasis. Balk looked at the shield for a moment and then
back up.

'I–'

'How long have you listened to it?' Goetz said. 'How
long has it been filling you with – with poison?' He
pointed at Balk with his sword. 'Because that's all it
is... poison. It's nothing but poison. It eats you away,
from the inside out until all that's left is a hollow suit
of armour for it to wear.' He grabbed the amulet and
thrust it at Balk. 'This! This is our goddess. She does not
take, she does not conquer! She builds! She fights only
to defend what exists!' Even as he said it, a strange sort
of peace filled him. For the first time, in a long time,
he actually believed what he was saying. 'I wanted to
build bridges, Balk. What did you want to do before
she called upon you? Do you even remember?'

Balk shook his head. 'I – I have always served her.'

'Maybe once, but not any longer,' Goetz said.

'No. No, no, no. I serve her! I am the only one who
serves Her!' Balk said, shaking his head furiously. 'Myrmidia!' he snarled.

'Myrmidia!' Goetz roared in reply. Balk's axe licked
out and cut a trench in the face of the shield even as
Goetz's sword did the same in his opponent's buck-
ler. They moved back and forth across the slippery
rock, trading savage blows. After the axe slipped past
his defences and cut a gash in his cuirass, Goetz began
to realise belatedly that the hochmeister was stronger,
and fresh. Also that his armour, unlike Taudge's, didn't
appear to have any weaknesses.

Desperately Goetz parried the axe as it darted for his

face and tried to regain momentum. But Balk was too fast and too experienced. He slammed forward, using his shield like a second blade, jabbing the edge into Goetz's thigh and belly. Breathing heavily, Goetz stumbled back. Balk paced after him with wolf-sure steps. 'The goddess guides my axe,' Balk said. 'Though I wish it was anyone else, brother. You had the potential to be the best of us. Truly blessed of the goddess.' He made a lazy swipe and, tired as he was, it was enough to knock Goetz's feet out from under him and send him crashing to the ground. 'Now you will be just one more nail in the pillar.' Balk stepped on Goetz's wrist, pinning his sword-arm. He raised his axe. 'Forgive me brother.'

'No!' Balk spun as Opchek crashed into him. The two knights reeled for a moment, until Balk shoved the other man away. 'I can't let you do this, Conrad. Not again…' the Kislevite said, his voice slurred and his eyes unfocused.

'Opchek, I grow tired of your obstinacy. Get out of my way!' Balk said.

'No!' Opchek glanced over his shoulder at Goetz. 'Get up, brother. Get out of here. I'll–'

'Die,' Balk said sadly. He whipped his axe out with fierce inevitability, chopping into the Kislevite's neck. Opchek grabbed the handle of the axe and sank to his knees, gagging. Balk tried to rip his weapon free, but to no avail. 'Stubborn until the – ah – end,' Balk grunted.

Goetz lurched up and drove his sword up through Balk's back. He forced the blade up until the tip scraped out from behind Balk's breastplate. 'Forgive me, brother,' Goetz whispered. Then he twisted, jerking the blade free. Balk staggered away, trailing red. Goetz followed him towards the water, pausing only for a glance at Opchek's body. A wave of sadness passed through him, but he let determination replace it. Balk fell onto all fours where the water met the rocks. Wheezing, he ripped his helmet off and tossed it behind him. Goetz kicked it aside as Balk fell into one of the tidal pools and rolled onto his back.

'It's done,' Goetz said.

'No,' Balk coughed. He reached pleadingly towards Goetz. 'D–do what must be done.' The hand fell. Balk closed his eyes. Goetz raised his sword and prepared to grant Balk's final request. Instead, he staggered as trails of fire were carved across his back. Gasping, he fell to his knees. The daemon loomed over him, her human features dissolving into avian hideousness. A massive paw swept him up and Goetz flailed out blindly with his sword, striking sparks off the black-iron feathers.

He found himself tumbling through the air a moment later. His back connected painfully with a stalagmite and he collapsed onto the cavern floor. The daemon stalked towards him, her massive wings unfurling even as they lost cohesion. The island bucked beneath his palms like a dying horse and there was a shrill scream-ing coming from every rock, nook and cranny. The vast shape staggered and seemed to plunge into the limp body of Myrma, filling it like an empty pig's bladder. With a lurch, the dead woman sat up, eyes blazing.

Her mouth opened and it was filled with night-black teeth. 'My Myrmidon…' the daemon hissed and then it laughed. Myrma's flesh blackened as she gestured and a sizzling bolt of energy leapt from her palm and crawled through the air towards Goetz.

'No.' The bolt exploded as it connected with the tip of Ulfar's staff. The old shaman staggered, but did not fall. 'Your story has gone on too long, daemon. It is time for endings.'

Myrma – the daemon – drew itself up and sighed. It plucked a hank of hair from its corrupting scalp and let it drift away. 'The Game does not end, mortal. Win or lose, it keeps going. Win or lose, we persist.'

'Persist elsewhere,' Ulfar said. He roared out a harsh flurry of syllables and frosty lightning struck the dead woman, ripping through her with ease. She staggered, but did not fall. In fact, she seemed to grow stronger and larger. Her body began to balloon, muscle and bone changing into something else entirely.

Her head, still horribly human, shot forward at the end of a serpentine neck, her black teeth snapping together through the middle of Ulfar's staff. For a moment Ulfar stared stupefied at his shattered staff, but he recovered quickly, spitting words of power at the black shape that was doubling in size. Wings made of bloody bone snapped and nearly bowled Ulfar over.

Goetz scrambled to his feet and made to charge towards the creature, but a gesture from Ulfar stopped him. 'No! I will deal with this filth. You must shatter the ley line!'

'The–?' Goetz stared at him.

'The line of power! The root of the daemon, the connection between its corpse and this hell-island! Destroy it!' Ulfar snarled.

'Stop whispering secrets, little bird,' the daemon said, pouncing on the old man and bearing him down with bone-crushing force. It had grown into a grotesque mockery of a bipedal shape, something between reptile, bird and woman, with the lashing tail of a cat and the face of a girl. Goetz narrowly avoided a scaly backhand and backed away as the beast rose and advanced on him, talons scraping the rock. Bits of it bubbled and dropped away and its face was pinched in a mockery of human pain. 'This raiment is not enough,' it purred. 'It is not enough to contain my magnificence. My beauty burns it to cinders.'

'Rot and be damned,' Goetz said, raising his sword. Talons slashed out and he narrowly avoided a blow that would have pulped him. He came to his feet close enough to smell the conflicting sickly sweet stink of the thing and his sword passed through several metallic feathers, sending them rattling to the ground. A wide palm struck him and shoved him back, pinning him to the floor. Myrma's blistered face drew close on its long neck and her cat-like tongue tickled the wound in his cheek.

'I will enter you and wear you to the ball, my Myrmidon. I will remake you and shape you and we will shine like a star in the wa– AHRP!' The human facade burst like a pustule. The creature's head, already reforming, whipped around.

'Up boy,' Ulfar croaked, clutching his chest, the remains of his staff extended, smoke rising from the tip. 'Go where you are needed!'

'Do what must be done,' Goetz said, driving his sword into the creature's paw, freeing himself. A moment later a white-furred bear slammed into the daemon, tearing at its shifting flesh with berserk ferocity. The daemon oozed around the bear, its alien malleability allowing it to reach for Goetz with a cracking of bones and a ripping and re-knitting of warped flesh.

'Einsark! Your hand!'

Goetz looked up as Dalla swept by, her hatchet

buried in the brainpan of one of the Screamers. She
stretched out her hand and he caught it, even as the
daemon lunged. It shrieked in frustration as he was
hauled into the air and onto the broad back of the
daemon-beast. 'Is this thing safe?' he asked, shouting
to be heard.

'No!' Dalla shouted, laughing as she wrenched
the hatchet sideways, sending the Screamer looping
through the air.

'Your father – he said something about a ley line!'
Goetz said, leaning close.

'A what?'

'The root of the daemon! We have to find it!'

Dalla replied by jerking the handle of her axe,
sending their mount hurtling into the upside down
forest of stalactites. As they sped along, more Screamers dropped from the ceiling, falling into pursuit. Their
screams rattled Goetz's teeth in his jaw and he struck
out at them as best as he could whenever they got too
close.

'Look! There!' Dalla said, pointing towards a bulging
stalactite that hung from the upper reaches of the cavern. Tendrils of sickly-hued fibres clung to it and even
as Goetz watched, they flexed slightly. He remembered
what the daemon had shown him and realised all at
once what it was he must do.

'Get me alongside it!' he said, gesturing with his
sword. 'Now!'

Dalla hauled on the hatchet-handle, sending the
Screamer swooping towards the great stone mass. As
they swooped past, Goetz bounded from his seat and
grabbed for one of the thick bundles of matter. His
fingers dug into the spongy mass and somewhere, the

daemon shrilled. The island shook harder than before and a rain of stalactites thudded into the ground and sea. Men, Norscan, Svanii and knight alike screamed and died as the rocks fell.

Goetz hauled himself up towards the root of rock that held the whole mass suspended. His body shuddered with weakness, and he wanted desperately to close his eyes, just for a moment, but he bulled on. Behind him, a sound like a hundred swords being drawn split the air and a great weight landed opposite him. He turned.

The daemon bared a beak full of serrated teeth. Through her feathers, Myrma's screaming face surfaced and sank back. 'You cannot do this,' she hissed, a horribly mellifluous voice emanating from within the sculpted bird-like skull. 'You are my piece, my Myrmidon. It is not allowed,' she continued, bloody fingers crooking. The wound on his side split, and something strained to be free. Goetz howled in agony as black blood slithered up through his armour and sought his throat. More tendrils drifted out through his jerkin and sought to snag his sword-arm and his legs.

'You are almost ready, almost eaten away. You will be scoured clean and I will wear you to war with my faithless flock,' the daemon said, stretching towards him. She reached for him and he slashed at her, ripping his arm free of the black coils of his own blood, now alive and turned against him. She jerked her hand back and his sword connected with the rock. She shrieked and metal feathers drifted loose from her titan frame.

Grinning despite the pain, he said, 'Ha! Struck a nerve?', and pulled himself erect on the bulb of the stalactite. The daemon reared up on the other side, her serpentine neck swaying hypnotically.

'This is not part of the plan,' she said.

'No plan survives contact with the enemy. That's from Litany of Battle... the book of Myrmidia,' Goetz said. 'And she commands that I do what needs doing!' He swung his sword up with what remained of his strength and chopped into the thin stone ligament. The daemon screamed and lunged. But even as the tips of her claws tore his flesh, the stone snapped and she faded like a sea-mist, her stolen flesh going apart like burning paper. The stalactite hurtled downwards, carrying Goetz with it.

Desperately, he thrust his body away from the abominable organ and towards the water. The sea reached up eagerly to meet him...

30

His eyes opened as the sound of massive clockwork gears grinding together filled his head. The temple rotunda glowed with the orange light of eternal dawn and bronze and silver trees rose from beds of dark Tilean clay. A white shape stood among them, letting the delicately engraved shapes of clockwork wrens trip over her fingers.

'This isn't the Drakwald,' he said stupidly.

'How observant, my Myrmidon.'

She turned as Goetz stood. He almost immediately fell to his knees as the warm brass eyes met his own. 'Myrmidia,' he said. She did not reply; instead, the great spear she held rose, its tip pointed unerringly at him. Thick streams of black liquid spilled from his pores and collected on the polished tiles of the temple floor as he watched. The spear dipped, and the pool lengthened into a stream, spilling towards the spear-point. But before it reached it, it grew paler and paler until it was impossible to see.

The spear swung up, the flat of it brushing his chin and lifting him to his feet. The beautiful face examined his own, the eyes lingering on his ruptured cheek and the blistered scars from the troll-bile and the touch of the daemon's claws. 'I–' Goetz began.

The goddess held up a hand and leaned close. 'I trust that you can hear me now?' she said.

'Yes?' Goetz said helplessly.

'Good. We will speak more, soon, I think.' She smiled, and the world seemed to burn brighter than Goetz had ever thought possible. 'For now though… wake up.'

'What?'

'I said… wake up!'

Goetz's eyes sprang open as Dalla shook him hard enough to rattle his teeth. He sat up and groaned, his hand flying immediately to his side. Feeling nothing, not even a trace of scar tissue, let alone a hole, he looked down. His skin was unblemished, save for a dark bruise. His hand flew to his face and his fingers scraped his teeth through the hole in his cheek. He winced and hunched forward.

'Up, einsark!' Dalla said, dragging him to his feet. 'Fret about your looks later. We must go!'

'Go? What? Where?' Goetz looked around, dazed. Bodies lay scattered everywhere across the cavern, and Norscans moved among them, silencing the wounded with grim efficiency. The island gave a groan and its roots shuddered as debris rained from the ceiling. Cracks had appeared in the floor and sea water was lapping at their ankles. 'What happened? I was falling…'

'Yes. Falling and you fell, right enough,' Dalla said, pulling him along. 'And I pulled you out of the water.

No easy feat with your armour weighing us down.'

'That's two I owe you, I expect,' Goetz said.

'Three, but who's counting? We–' Dalla stumbled to a stop, her face collapsing into a mask of pain. Goetz looked past her and saw Ulfar, lying broken and bloody on the ground, the water rushing around him. Goetz hurried forward and knelt by the old man. Ragged wounds covered his thin frame, and his stomach was a gaping mess. Ulfar grinned blearily at him, exposing blood-stained teeth.

'She is gone,' he said.

'Yes,' Goetz said. 'I expect so.'

'And you? Still deaf?'

'My hearing has cleared up some,' Goetz said hoarsely. 'Can you stand?'

'His guts are in the water,' Kettil Flatnose said, coming forward. He was covered in blood and the look he gave Goetz said he wouldn't mind spilling a bit more. 'He won't last the next five minutes, let alone a hike to the beach.'

'That's my father you're talking about,' Dalla snarled, shoving between Kettil and the others. 'He is strong!'

'I am dying,' Ulfar grunted. 'As is this place. It rots, now that the magic keeping it alive has fled. You must go.'

'We can carry you–' Goetz began, knowing even as he said it that it wasn't so. Moving the old man would only mean a more agonising death

'No,' Ulfar said, coughing. His eyes were unfocused and his face was knotted with pain. 'Do what you must, daughter.'

'Father…' Dalla began. She looked at Goetz, her eyes blank. Without speaking, he handed her his sword and turned, moving away to give them what privacy could be had in a crumbling cavern. To distract himself, he searched for Balk's body. It was like trying to find a needle in a pile of needles. He couldn't even recall where he'd seen it last, or whether Balk had actually been dead. He hoped so, for the Order's sake as much as anything else.

Stepping back as a rock splashed down into the water, he wondered what he was going to say. What would he tell Berengar? That his suspicions had been correct? That two entire komturies' worth of brothers had fallen to Chaos? Thinking of that made him wonder about the fate of the men above, those who had been defending the komturie. Were they still alive? Or had the Norscans overwhelmed them? Would it be better if they had? Had they all been corrupted, or simply a few? Almost sixty years on a Chaos-tainted island… could any man be called pure?

He caught sight of Opchek's body, still lying where it had fallen. The black armour had crumbled to dust and rotting meat, and the Kislevite lay bare and shrunken, his pale body looking entirely too fragile. Goetz sank to his haunches and pressed two fingers to the dead man's brow. 'Why did you save me?' he said out loud. There was no answer, for which he was grateful. There was more to the story than he'd seen, more than he'd felt. He looked at the rotting remains of the armour as the current caught it and carried it away.

Beneath his feet, the floor cracked and bucked and he stood abruptly. 'We must go. Now,' Dalla said from behind him. She held his sword down by her side and her face was drawn and tired looking. She turned away, and then turned back just as quickly. 'Thank you,' she said.

Goetz didn't know how to reply. He hurried after her as the cavern began to collapse in earnest. The surviving Norscans joined them in ones and twos, some, he noted, carrying the discarded armour of the knights of the Order. He thought of protesting, but then realised that he had little right to complain about the warriors scavenging what others had so carelessly discarded.

As they moved quickly through the tunnels towards the surface, Goetz saw the fearful movements of what he assumed were the Svanii. They did not try to attack, however. Upon reaching the surface, he saw that the komturie was ablaze and that the besiegers were retreating to their vessels, carrying armfuls of loot. From the smell on the wind, something had happened to the powder-room. Likely one of the brothers had blown it up rather than see it fall into the hands of the Norscans. In that thing, if in no other, the brothers of the Svunum Komturie had been true to the tenets of Myrmidia. Anger and despair flashed through him as he thought of the library, and all that was surely now lost. Had it been worth it? Had it been necessary?

Goetz forced the thought aside. It didn't matter now. The daemon was gone, and the island with it soon enough. The water was slowly creeping up the shoreline, engulfing the remains of the harbour. He stopped and watched a black-sailed galley sink. Something sharp pricked his neck and he turned. A burly Norscan grinned at him. 'One last bit of fun, hey?' he said.

'Step aside, Thalfi,' Dalla said, coming to stand beside Goetz. 'He aided us in the caverns.'

'And so? Nits make lice.' Thalfi stepped back and raised his sword. Goetz tensed, ready to spring aside.

He was suddenly aware of just how isolated he really was now; and he was weaponless to boot.

'Thalfi is right,' Kettil said. 'Kill him, and we're done with the whole sorry lot. That is why we came on this mad venture, eh?'

'You'll have to come through me first,' Dalla said, stepping between the warriors and their prey.

'I think I'd like my sword back now,' Goetz murmured.

'I'm busy now,' Dalla replied.

'Stand aside girl. Your father led us to plunder and I'll not sully his name by killing you,' Thalfi rumbled, making to shove her aside. Dalla twisted around him and tapped the edge of her blade against his hairy throat. Thalfi froze even as his men began to move forward with angry murmurings. Kettil snorted in amusement and stepped around the tableau, his axe swinging loosely.

'You can't fight all of us,' he said to her as he moved towards Goetz.

'We don't have to,' Goetz said, stepping forward quickly and slugging the chieftain across the jaw. Shocked, Kettil stumbled to one knee. Goetz kicked him in the head a moment later and the other man fell, his eyes rolling to the white. Goetz scooped up his axe and pointed it at the converging Norscans. 'I've killed my own brothers today, as well as a daemon. What makes you think I won't butcher the lot of you and make for the mainland on a boat made out of your corpses?' he said in what he hoped was a casual tone of voice. Both Thalfi and Dalla eyed him with respect. Before anyone could reply, however, the crash of a cannon split the air.

One of the Norscan ships gave a groan as it split in two and spilled men into the water. Goetz turned and saw the face of Manann rising above the wreckage. The ships glided into the harbour, armoured men on their decks. Goetz turned back to the stunned Norscans. 'Did I not mention they were coming?' he said.

Thalfi stepped back and gave a roar of laughter. His men were already running for their boats. He saluted Goetz even as he hauled Kettil to his feet. 'Rot in Hel, brass-skin,' the big man said, grinning. He looked at Dalla. 'Coming Ulfarsdottir? We'll need every sword to fight past those yapping sea-curs…'

'I'll be along, Utergard,' Dalla said, not looking at him. She stood in front of Goetz and frowned. 'Good fight, einsark.'

'No such thing,' Goetz said, tossing Kettil's axe aside.

'Shows what you know, hey?' Dalla said. She brought his sword to her temple and saluted him. 'Olric keep you strong.'

'Myrmidia keep you smart,' Goetz said. She grinned and loped off after the others. It was only as the Norscans shoved away from shore that he realised that she still had his sword. Goetz shook his head ruefully and murmured, 'I really need to learn to hold on to things better.' Several ships from the fleet were harrying the Norscans, but not seriously… evidently, the Marien-burg captains, whatever their allegiances, weren't prepared to possibly start a war with a still sizeable Norscan fleet this close to home. He felt some relief at that… after all, if they sunk the ship Dalla was on, how would he ever get his sword back.

Thinking wholly unchivalrous thoughts, he turned back as the landing party reached him. 'Ho! I told you that he was alive!' Dubnitz roared, trotting towards Goetz at the head of a group of his fellow knights. The big man looked as hale and bluff as Goetz had last seen him. 'Saw them off yourself then? Left nothing for us, have you?' The knight of Manann was clad in full plate, one hand on his sword. He took in Goetz's ravaged state and winced at the sight of his face. 'It looks like some-one tried to give you a permanent grin. Does it hurt?'

'No, it feels like the caress of a courtesan,' Goetz said. 'Does it?'

'No. It hurts. Badly,' Goetz said.

'Should we be after them then, Grand Master?' Dub-nitz said, turning back to Ogg as the latter drew close, Lord Justicar Ambrosius by his side and a full contin-gent of marines and knights with them.

'No. Let the barbarians go,' Ogg snarled. He looked around and stumped towards Goetz, his trident extended. The tips of the tines scratched across Goetz's much abused breastplate. 'What have you done to my island?'

'Nothing, though it won't be an island for much longer,' Goetz said as the ground rocked beneath their feet.

'What?'

'It's dying,' Goetz said. 'And we should probably watch it from a safe distance.'

'How can an island die?' Ogg nearly shrieked, turn-ing in place.

'Like this, one imagines,' Ambrosius said. He looked at Goetz. 'The komturie fell to the Norscans, then?' he said carefully.

Goetz hesitated. Then, he nodded. 'They fought valiantly and broke the back of a fleet meant for

Marienburg and the imperial coast,' he said. Ambrosius's good eye narrowed speculatively.

'Valiantly,' he said.

'To the last man,' Goetz said.

'Which is you, I imagine. And thus the final word on what happened here,' Ambrosius said. He nodded. 'Fine. Back to the ship! Let's let this place not collect any more souls, shall we?' An explosion from the komturie punctuated his command, and the group hurried back to its boat.

'I can't believe this! To come all this way and to be denied…' Ogg said, shaking his head. The men pushed the boat off and Goetz watched from the stern as the island trembled. Its contortions were becoming more violent now, and the water released a foul smell.

'Yes,' Goetz said, thinking of the daemon's shrieks as it faded back into whatever darkness awaited one of its kind. 'It's quite a shame.' He turned to find Ambrosius watching him. The Lord Justicar slid towards him and bent his head.

'What will you tell Berengar?' he said, his voice pitched low.

'The truth,' Goetz said. 'The brothers of Svunum met an enemy they could not defeat. And they died.' He looked at Ambrosius. 'Athalhold's death was a result of an unconnected plot, instigated by Chaos cultists. Possibly the same cultists who stirred up the Norscans and set them to invade the coasts…'

'An invasion your Order repelled, at significant cost.' Ambrosius scratched under his eye-patch and smiled thinly. 'A good story. Young men will flock to your Order at the telling, and the loss of a komturie is explained and forgiven.'

'And then the generous donation of an empty house to a penniless order of brother-knights,' Goetz said, nodding towards Ogg's fuming shape. Ambrosius's smile grew feral.

'You're learning to play the Game,' he said.

'No. Merely doing what must be done,' Goetz said.

Svunum trembled and the burning shell of the komturie finally came crashing down. Flames rose high as the island sank low. Goetz turned away, his fingers tight around the amulet of Myrmidia that hung from his neck. As they left Svunum behind, he closed his eyes and said a prayer.

Myrmidia didn't bother to answer, but Goetz knew she was listening all the same.

ABOUT THE AUTHOR

Formerly a roadie for the Hong Kong Cavaliers, **Josh Reynolds** now writes full time and his work has appeared previously in anthologies such as *Specters and Coal Dust, Historical Lovecraft* and *How The West Was Weird* as well as in magazines such as *Innsmouth Free Press* and *Hammer and Bolter*. Feel free to stop by his blog *http://joshuamreynolds.blogspot.com*

DEAD WINTER

The Black Plague

C L WERNER

**The start of a new age in the
Time of Legends range**

Extract from Dead Winter by C.L. Werner

THE PUNGENT SMELL of smouldering warpstone wafted through the blackened chamber, the corrupt fume slithering into every nook and cranny, oozing between the crumbling bricks, burning into beams of oak and ash, discolouring glass and tarnishing bronze. It was the stench of darkest sorcery and this was its night.

The noise of creeping rats inside the walls died out as the fumes incinerated their tiny lungs and liquefied their little brains. Beetles and roaches fell from the rafters, their bodies shrivelled into desiccated husks. Bats took wing, shrieking their fright as they desperately tried to flee the deathly miasma, smashing against walls and ceiling, raining down to the floor in battered, bloodied strips of quivering flesh.

Seerlord Skrittar's whiskers twitched as the smell of blood flickered amidst the searing scent of warpstone. It was an unconscious, instinctive association. Skrittar's mind was far too disciplined to be distracted in this, his hour of terror and triumph.

The Seerlord stood at the head of a ring of creatures dressed in grey robes. Like him, they were ghastly, inhuman things, abominable monstrosities that seemed to blend the most hideous qualities of man and rat. Great horns protruded from their elongated, ratlike heads, terrible symbols were painted or branded into their furry foreheads; the eyes in their verminous faces blazed with malefic energies, glowing green in the omnipresent darkness. Their paws were folded before them, clawed fingers entwined, their fangs clashing together in a low chant of hisses and squeaks.

Seerlord Skrittar felt panic drumming inside his chest, as though any moment his heart might burst from sheer terror. The audacity of what he had thought to achieve! The arrogance! The impudence!

No! The Seerlord forced his nerves to quieten. There was danger, there was always danger when invoking the forces of darkness, when engaging in a conjuration beyond the blackest of the black arts. No other skaven would have dared what he had dared! Yes, the risk was great, but the reward was still greater!

His eyes narrowed as he gazed across the vast chamber. Twelve horned ratmen in grey robes, all of them the most potent of the Order of Grey Seers, with himself, the mighty Seerlord, assuming the sacred role of thirteenth intimate of the cabal. Each of the skaven sorcerers had imbibed in a potent mixture of wormroot and warpstone before the ritual, magnifying their own abilities still further by devouring the still-living brains of their most gifted acolytes. The malign influence of Geheimnisnacht itself increased their powers still further, and whatever extra magic they needed they could draw from the warpstone fumes rising from six caskets arrayed about the edge of their circle.

Protection? Of course, a series of concentric circles composed of sigils and runes drawn in the blood of elf-things mixed with crushed warpstone and the powdered bones of dragons. The greatest protection, though, lay in numbers, playing the chance that if anything went wrong then the aethyric retaliation would claim a different ratman.

Skrittar gazed past his chanting minions, staring above them at the great window of stained glass. It was a relic left behind by the original builders of Skavenblight, the foolish man-things who had reared the Shattered Tower and engineered their vast city, only to have it taken from them by the Horned Rat and bestowed upon his favoured children – the skaven.

There was something of magic about that portal of stained glass set into a spider-web of iron. Only magic could have allowed it alone to survive the tolling of the thirteenth hour, when the Horned Rat's divine malignance had struck down the humans like a mighty earthquake and left their great tower broken and crumbling. Only the most potent of sorcery could have allowed it to endure a million generations of ratkin, staring like a great unclean eye upon the teeming hordes of Skavenblight as they birthed, grew and perished.

Through the window, Skrittar could see the gibbous moon of sorcery, the ghoulish Morrslieb with its erratic orbit and eerie allure. This night, the Chaos Moon was ascendant, perched exactly at the centre of the thirteen constellations. Glancing away from the moon's unsettling glow, Skrittar could see the fangs of the Big Rat and the long tail of the Little Rat, he could see the snarling muzzle of the Cornered Rat and the bloated carcass of the Drowned Rat, there were the feeble nubs of the Pink Rat and the murderous eyes of the Black Rat, and, whining off in the stellar shadows, was that cosmic buffoon, King Mouse, the meat that thought it was skaven.

Rare was such a conjunction. Maybe once in a thousand generations of skaven did moon and stars align in such a way. When such an alignment came to pass, there were certain spells and rituals, handed down from Seerlord to Seerlord, that could be performed. Magic of such awful potency that no other skaven was allowed to even suspect their existence. Yet there was only so much magic a single sorcerer could conjure, and Skrittar wanted far greater things.

The heathen vermin of Clan Pestilens were brewing some new contagion, a great plague they thought might finally bring the surface-dwelling man-things to their knees. Spies from every clan in Skavenblight had reported this to their warlords and now the whole Under-Empire was a seething hotbed of rumour and ambition. Outwardly, Skrittar dismissed the plans of the plague monks as diseased fantasies, delusions brought on by the maggots of madness burrowing through their brains. Inwardly, however, he feared that Arch-Plaguelord Nurglitch really did have such a weapon. If he did, the balance of power in Skavenblight would shift, the other Grey Lords would scurry to curry favour with the plague priests and forget their piety towards the grey seers and the Horned Rat.